Praise for the Sookie

'Delightful . . . Fans will relish these stories, and even those new to Sookie's world will find much to love' Publishers Weekly

'Harris is a master' Tor.com

'*Dead Until Dark* is a hilarious adventure from start to finish' SF Site

'A great mixture of paranormal thriller and laugh-out-loud fun'
Fantasy Book Review on *Dead Until Dark*

'Another excellent book that is hard to put down'
Love Vampires on *Living Dead in Dallas*

'The best in the series yet' Diabolical Plots on *Dead to the World*

'There's never a dull moment in Sookie Stackhouse's hometown of Bon Temps' *LA Times*

THE COMPLETE
SOOKIE
STACKHOUSE
STORIES

Charlaine Harris

This paperback first published in Great Britain in 2020 by Gollancz

First published in Great Britain in 2017 by Gollancz
an imprint of the Orion Publishing Group Ltd
Carmelite House, 50 Victoria Embankment
London EC4Y 0DZ

An Hachette UK Company

1 3 5 7 9 10 8 6 4 2

A CIP catalogue record for this book is
available from the British Library.

ISBN (Mass Market Paperback) 978 1 473 22232 8
ISBN (eBook) 978 1 473 22233 5

Printed in Great Britain by Clays Ltd, Elcograf S.p.A.

MIX
Paper from
responsible sources
FSC® C104740

www.charlaineharris.com
www.gollancz.co.uk

To Toni L. P. Kelner, a.k.a. Leigh Perry,
my dream collaborator on our dream anthologies

CONTENTS

INTRODUCTION

THIS COLLECTION WAS written over a long period, and each new attempt was a learning experience. I had written very few short stories when I began writing these small pieces about Sookie's world; by the time I finished, I had written many.

Another point to note: Most of these stories were written for the anthologies Toni L. P. Kelner (Leigh Perry) and I were producing. The anthologies were a labor of love, and we've always felt we had a part in introducing the mystery world to the urban fantasy world . . . and vice versa. All our anthologies are themed. For example, "If I Had a Hammer" is in Home Improvement: Undead Edition. "Playing Possum" is in An Apple for the Creature, a collection of stories about school. (If you ever see one of the anthologies at a bookstore, give it a try. Selecting the stories and editing them was not only fun but rewarding.)

This is the first time all the stories featuring Sookie Stackhouse have been gathered into one volume. If you'd like to reread the whole series in order, including these stories, the suggested chronology is on my website.

Above all, have fun. Some stories were written to let the

reader know something important about one of the characters or to move the whole story along. But all of them are intended to provide entertainment for the reader.

That's what these are all about.

Charlaine Harris

FAIRY DUST

The triplet fairies—Claudine, Claude, and Claudette—needed a story featuring them and their sleazy (but lucrative) strip club. I felt I had to explain how to kill a fairy, since I had created them as very strong, very powerful, and *very* long-lived. Something had to be their Kryptonite... and I chose something pretty unlikely. Since "Fairy Dust" is also a murder mystery, there was a crime and a solution to be explained—comfortable territory for me.

"Fairy Dust" takes place after *Dead to the World*.

I HATE IT WHEN fairies come into the bar. They don't tip you worth a toot—not because they're stingy, but because they just forget. Take Claudine, the fairy who was walking in the door. Six feet tall, long black hair, gorgeous; Claudine seemed to have no shortage of cash or clothing (and she entranced men the way a watermelon draws flies). But Claudine hardly ever remembered to leave you even a dollar. And if it's lunchtime, you have to take the bowl of lemon slices off the table. Fairies are allergic to lemons and limes, like vamps are allergic to silver and garlic.

That spring night when Claudine came in I was in a bad mood already. I was angry with my ex-boyfriend, Bill Compton, a.k.a. Vampire Bill; my brother, Jason, had again postponed helping me shift an armoire; and I'd gotten my property tax notice in the mail.

So when Claudine sat at one of my tables, I stalked over to her with no very happy feelings.

"No vamps around?" she asked straightaway. "Even Bill?"

Vamps like fairies the way dogs like bones: great toys, good food. "Not tonight," I said. "Bill's down in New Orleans. I'm picking up his mail for him." Just call me sucker.

Claudine relaxed. "Dearest Sookie," she said.

"You want what?"

"Oh, one of those nasty beers, I guess," she said, making a face. Claudine didn't really like to drink, though she did like bars. Like most fairies, she loved attention and admiration: my boss, Sam, said that was a fairy characteristic.

I brought her the beer. "You got a minute?" she asked. I frowned. Claudine didn't look as cheerful as usual.

"Just." The table by the door was hooting and hollering at me.

"I have a job for you."

Though it called for dealing with Claudine, whom I liked but didn't trust, I was interested. I sure needed some cash. "What do you need me to do?"

"I need you to come listen to some humans."

"Are these humans willing?"

Claudine gave me innocent eyes. "What do you mean, Precious?"

I hated this song and dance. "Do they want to be, ah, listened to?"

"They're guests of my brother, Claude."

I hadn't known Claudine had a brother. I don't know much about fairies; Claudine was the only one I'd met. If she was typical, I wasn't sure how the race had survived eradication. I wouldn't have thought northern Louisiana was very hospitable toward beings of the fairy persuasion, anyway. This part of the state is largely rural, very Bible Belt. My small town of Bon Temps, barely big enough to have its own Wal-Mart, didn't even see a vampire for two years after they'd announced their existence and their intention to live peaceably amongst us. Maybe that delay was good, since local folks had had a chance to get used to the idea by the time Bill showed up.

But I had a feeling that this PC vamp tolerance would vanish if my fellow townsfolk knew about Weres, and shifters, and fairies. And who knows what all else.

"Okay, Claudine. When?"

The rowdy table was hooting, "Crazy Sookie! Crazy Sookie!" People only did that when they'd had too much to drink. I was used to it, but it still hurt.

"When do you get off tonight?"

We fixed it that Claudine would pick me up at my house fifteen minutes after I got off work. She left without finishing her beer. Or tipping.

My boss, Sam Merlotte, nodded a head toward the door through which she'd just exited. "What'd the fairy want?" Sam's a shifter himself.

"She needs me to do a job for her."

"Where?"

"Wherever she lives, I guess. She has a brother, did you know?"

"Want me to come with you?" Sam is a friend, the kind of friend you sometimes have fantasies about.

X-rated.

"Thanks, but I think I can handle Claudine."

"You haven't met the brother."

"I'll be okay."

I'm used to being up at night, not only because I'm a barmaid, but also because I had dated Bill for a long time. When Claudine picked me up at my old house in the woods, I'd had time to change from my Merlotte's outfit into some black jeans and a sage green twinset (JCPenney on sale), since the night was chilly. I'd let my hair down from its ponytail.

"You should wear blue instead of green," Claudine said, "to go with your eyes."

"Thanks for the fashion tip."

"You're welcome." Claudine sounded happy to share her
style sense with me. But her smile, usually so radiant, seemed
tinged with sadness.

"What do you want me to find out from these people?" I
asked.

"We'll talk about it when we get there," she said, and after
that she wouldn't tell me anything else as we drove east. Ordinarily Claudine babbles. I was beginning to feel it wasn't
smart of me to have accepted this job.

Claudine and her brother lived in a big ranch-style house
in suburban Monroe, a town that not only had a Wal-Mart,
but a whole mall. She knocked on the front door in a pattern.
After a minute, the door opened. My eyes widened. Claudine
hadn't mentioned that her brother was her twin.

If Claude had put on his sister's clothes, he could have
passed for her; it was eerie. His hair was shorter, but not by a
lot; he had it pulled back to the nape of his neck, but his ears
were covered. His shoulders were broader, but I couldn't see a
trace of a beard, even this late at night. Maybe male fairies
don't have body hair? Claude looked like a Calvin Klein underwear model; in fact, if the designer had been there, he'd have
signed the twins on the spot, and there'd have been drool all
over the contract.

Claude stepped back to let us enter. "This is the one?" he
said to Claudine.

She nodded. "Sookie, my brother, Claude."

"A pleasure," I said. I extended my hand. With some surprise, he took it and shook. He looked at his sister. "She's a
trusting one."

"Humans," Claudine said, and shrugged.

Claude led me through a very conventional living room,
down a paneled hall to the family room. A man was sitting in

a chair, because he had no choice. He was tied to it with what looked like nylon cord. He was a small man, buff, blond, and brown-eyed. He looked about my age, twenty-six.

"Hey," I said, not liking the squeak in my voice. "Why is that man tied?"

"Otherwise, he'd run away," Claude said, surprised.

I covered my face with my hands for a second. "Listen, you two, I don't mind looking at this guy if he's done something wrong, or if you want to eliminate him as a suspect in a crime committed against you. But if you just want to find out if he really loves you, or something silly like that . . . What's your purpose?"

"We think he killed our triplet, Claudette."

I almost said, "There were three of you?" then realized that wasn't the most important part of the sentence.

"You think he murdered your sister."

Claudine and Claude nodded in unison. "Tonight," Claude said.

"Okeydokey," I muttered, and bent over the blond. "I'm taking the gag off."

They looked unhappy, but I slid the handkerchief down to his neck. The young man said, "I didn't do it."

"Good. Do you know what I am?"

"No. You're not a thing like them, are you?"

I don't know what he thought Claude and Claudine were, what little otherworldly attribute they'd sprung on him. I lifted my hair to show him that my ears were round, not pointed, but he still looked dissatisfied.

"Not a vamp?" he asked.

Showed him my teeth. The canines only extend when vamps are excited by blood, battle, or sex, but they're noticeably sharp even when they're retracted. My canines are quite normal.

"I'm just a regular human," I said. "Well, that's not quite true. I can read your thoughts."

He looked terrified.

"What are you scared for? If you didn't kill anybody, you have nothing to fear." I made my voice warm, like butter melting on corn on the cob.

"What will they do to me? What if you make a mistake and tell them I did it? What are they gonna do?"

Good question. I looked up at the two.

"We'll kill him and eat him," Claudine said, with a ravishing smile. When the blond man looked from her to Claude, his eyes wide with terror, she winked at me.

For all I knew, Claudine might be serious. I couldn't remember if I'd ever seen her eat or not. We were treading on dangerous ground. I try to support my own race when I can. Or at least get 'em out of situations alive.

I should have accepted Sam's offer.

"Is this man the only suspect?" I asked the twins. (Should I call them twins? I wondered. It was more accurate to think of them as two-thirds of triplets. Nah. Too complicated.)

"No, we have another man in the kitchen," Claude said.

"And a woman in the pantry."

Under other circumstances, I would've smiled. "Why are you sure Claudette is dead?"

"She came to us in spirit form and told us so." Claude looked surprised. "This is a death ritual for our race."

I sat back on my heels, trying to think of intelligent questions. "When this happens, does the spirit let you know any of the circumstances of the death?"

"No," Claudine said, shaking her head so her long black hair switched. "It's more like a final farewell."

"Have you found the body?"

They looked disgusted. "We fade," Claude explained, in a haughty way.

So much for examining the corpse.

"Can you tell me where Claudette was when she, ah, faded?" I asked. "The more I know, the better questions I can ask." Mind reading is not so simple. Asking the right questions is the key to eliciting the correct thought. The mouth can say anything. The head never lies. But if you don't ask the right question, the right thought won't pop up.

"Claudette and Claude are exotic dancers at Hooligans," Claudine said proudly, as if she was announcing they were on an Olympic team.

I'd never met strippers before, male or female. I found myself more than a little interested in seeing Claude strip, but I made myself focus on the deceased Claudette.

"So, Claudette worked last night?"

"She was scheduled to take the money at the door. It was ladies' night at Hooligans."

"Oh. Okay. So you were, ah, performing," I said to Claude.

"Yes. We do two shows on ladies' night. I was the Pirate."

I tried to suppress that mental image.

"And this man?" I tilted my head toward the blond, who was being very good about not pleading and begging.

"I'm a stripper, too," he said. "I was the Cop."

Okay. Just stuff that imagination in a box and sit on it.

"Your name is?"

"Barry Barber is my stage name. My real name is Ben Simpson."

"Barry Barber?" I was puzzled.

"I like to shave people."

I had a blank moment, then felt a red flush creep across my cheeks as I realized he didn't mean whiskery cheeks. Well, not facial cheeks. "And the other two people are?" I asked the twins.

"The woman in the pantry is Rita Child. She owns Hooligans," Claudine said. "And the man in the kitchen is Jeff Puckett. He's the bouncer."

"Why did you pick these three out of all the employees at Hooligans?"

"Because they had arguments with Claudette. She was a dynamic woman," Claude said seriously.

"Dynamic my ass," said Barry the Barber, proving that tact isn't a prerequisite for a stripping job. "That woman was hell on wheels."

"Her character isn't really important in determining who killed her," I pointed out, which shut him right up. "It just indicates why. Please go on," I said to Claude. "Where were the three of you? And where were the people you've held here?"

"Claudine was here, cooking supper for us. She works at Dillard's in customer service." She'd be great at that; her unrelenting cheer could pacify anyone. "As I said, Claudette was scheduled to take the cover charge at the door," Claude continued. "Barry and I were in both shows. Rita always puts the first show's take in the safe, so Claudette won't be sitting up there with a lot of cash. We've been robbed a couple of times. Jeff was mostly sitting behind Claudette, in a little booth right inside the main door."

"When did Claudette vanish?"

"Soon after the second show started. Rita says she got the first show's take from Claudette and took it back to her safe, and that Claudette was still sitting there when she left. But Rita hates Claudette, because Claudette was about to leave Hooligans for Foxes, and I was going with her."

"Foxes is another club?" Claude nodded. "Why were you leaving?"

"Better pay, larger dressing rooms."

"Okay, that would be Rita's motivation. What about Jeff's?"

"Jeff and I had a thing," Claude said. (My pirate-ship fantasy sank.) "Claudette told me I had to break up with him, that I could do better."

"And you listened to her advice about your love life?"

"She was the oldest, by several minutes," he said simply. "But I lo— I am very fond of him."

"What about you, Barry?"

"She ruined my act," Barry said sullenly.

"How'd she do that?"

"She yelled, 'Too bad your nightstick's not bigger!' as I was finishing up."

It seemed that Claudette had been determined to die.

"Okay," I said, marshaling my plan of action. I knelt before Barry. I laid my hand on his arm, and he twitched. "How old are you?"

"Twenty-five," he said, but his mind provided me with a different answer.

"That's not right, is it?" I asked, keeping my voice gentle.

He had a gorgeous tan, almost as good as mine, but he paled underneath it. "No," he said in a strangled voice. "I'm thirty."

"I had no idea," Claude said, and Claudine told him to hush.

"And why didn't you like Claudette?"

"She insulted me in front of an audience," he said. "I told you."

The image from his mind was quite different. "In private? Did she say something to you in private?" After all, reading minds isn't like watching television. People don't relate things in their own brains the way they would if they were telling a story to another person.

Barry looked embarrassed and even angrier. "Yes, in private. We'd been having sex for a while, and then one day she just wasn't interested anymore."

"Did she tell you why?"

"She told me I was . . . inadequate."

That hadn't been the phrase she used. I felt embarrassed for him when I heard the actual words in his head.

"What did you do between shows tonight, Barry?"

"We had an hour. So I could get two shaves in."

"You get paid for that?"

"Oh, yeah." He grinned, but not as though something was funny. "You think I'd shave a stranger's crotch if I didn't get paid for it? But I make a big ritual out of it; act like it turns me on. I get a hundred bucks a pop."

"When did you see Claudette?"

"When I went out to meet my first appointment, right as the first show was ending. She and her boyfriend were standing by the booth. I'd told them that was where I'd meet them."

"Did you talk to Claudette?"

"No, I just looked at her." He sounded sad. "I saw Rita, she was on her way to the booth with the money pouch, and I saw Jeff, he was on the stool at the back of the booth, where he usually stays."

"And then you went back to do this shaving?"

He nodded.

"How long does it take you?"

"Usually about thirty, forty minutes. So scheduling two was kind of chancy, but it worked out. I do it in the dressing room, and the other guys are good about staying out."

He was getting more relaxed, the thoughts in his head calming and flowing more easily. The first person he'd done tonight had been a woman so bone-thin he'd wondered if she'd die while he did the shaving routine. She'd thought she was beautiful, and she'd obviously enjoyed showing him her body. Her boyfriend had gotten a kick out of the whole thing.

I could hear Claudine buzzing in the background, but I kept my eyes closed and my hands on Barry's, seeing the second "client," a guy, and then I saw his face. Oh, boy. It was someone I knew, a vampire named Maxwell Lee.

"There was a vamp in the bar," I said, out loud, not opening my eyes. "Barry, what did he do when you finished shaving him?"

"He left," Barry said. "I watched him go out the back door. I'm always careful to make sure my clients are out of the backstage area. That's the only way Rita will let me do the shaving at the club."

Of course, Barry didn't know about the problem fairies have with vamps. Some vamps had less self-control when it came to fairies than others did. Fairies were strong, stronger than people, but vamps were stronger than anything else on earth.

"And you didn't go back out to the booth and talk to Claudette again?"

"I didn't see her again."

"He's telling the truth," I said to Claudine and Claude. "As far as he knows it." There were always other questions I could ask, but at first "hearing," Barry didn't know anything about Claudette's disappearance.

Claude ushered me into the pantry, where Rita Child was waiting. It was a walk-in pantry, very neat, but not intended for two people, one of them duct-taped to a rolling office chair. Rita Child was a substantial woman, too. She looked exactly like I'd expect the owner of a strip club to look—painted, dyed brunette, packed into a challenging dress with high-tech underwear that pinched and pushed her into a provocative shape.

She was also steaming mad. She kicked out at me with a high heel that would have taken my eye out if I hadn't jerked back in the middle of kneeling in front of her. I fell on my fundament in an ungraceful sprawl.

"None of that, Rita," Claude said calmly. "You're not the boss here. This is our place." He helped me stand up and dusted off my bottom in an impersonal way.

"We just want to know what happened to our sister," Claudine said.

Rita made sounds behind her gag, sounds that didn't seem to be conciliatory. I got the impression that she didn't give a damn about the twins' motivation in kidnapping her and tying her up in their pantry. They'd taped her mouth, rather than using a cloth gag, and after the kicking incident, I kind of enjoyed ripping the tape off.

Rita called me some names reflecting on my heritage and moral character.

"I guess that's just the pot calling the kettle black," I said, when she paused to breathe. "Now you listen here! I'm not taking that kind of talk off of you, and I want you to shut up and answer my questions. You don't seem to have a good picture of the situation you're in."

The club owner calmed down a little bit after that. She was still glaring at me with her narrow brown eyes and straining at her ropes, but she seemed to understand a little better.

"I'm going to touch you," I said. I was afraid she might bite if I touched her bare shoulder, so I put my hand on her forearm just above where her wrist was tied to the arm of the rolling chair.

Her head was a maze of fury. She wasn't thinking clearly because she was so angry, and all her mental energy was directed into cursing at the twins and now at me. She suspected me of being some kind of supernatural assassin, and I decided it wouldn't hurt if she was scared of me for a while.

"When did you see Claudette tonight?" I asked.

"When I went to get the money from the first show," she growled, and sure enough, I saw Rita's hand reaching out, a long white hand placing a zippered vinyl pouch in it. "I was in my office working during the first show. But I get the money in between, so if we get stuck up, we won't lose so much."

"She gave you the money bag, and you left?"

"Yeah. I went to put the cash in the safe until the second show was over. I didn't see her again."

And that seemed to be the truth to me. I couldn't see another vision of Claudette in Rita's head. But I saw a lot of satisfaction that Claudette was dead, and a grim determination to keep Claude at her club.

"Will you still go to Foxes, now that Claudette's gone?" I asked him, to spark a response that might reveal something from Rita.

Claude looked down at me, surprised and disgusted. "I haven't had time to think of what will come tomorrow," he snapped. "I just lost my sister."

Rita's mind sort of leaped with joy. She had it bad for Claude. And on the practical side, he was a big draw at Hooligans, since even on an off night he could engender some magic to make the crowd spend big. Claudette hadn't been so willing to use her power for Rita's profit, but Claude didn't think about it twice. Using his inbred fairy skills to draw people to admire him was an ego thing with Claude, which had little to do with economics.

I got all this from Rita in a flash.

"Okay," I said, standing up. "I'm through with her."

She was happy.

We stepped out of the pantry into the kitchen, where the

final candidate for murderer was waiting. He'd been pushed under the table, and he had a glass in front of him with a straw stuck in it, so he could lean over to drink. Being a former lover had paid off for Jeff Puckett. His mouth wasn't even taped.

I looked from Claude to Jeff, trying to figure it out. Jeff had a light brown mustache that needed trimming, and a two-day growth of whiskers on his cheeks. His eyes were narrow and hazel. As much as I could tell, Jeff seemed to be in better shape than some of the bouncers I'd known, and he was even taller than Claude. But I was not impressed, and I reflected for maybe the millionth time that love was strange.

Claude braced himself visibly when he faced his former lover.

"I'm here to find out what you know about Claudette's death," I said, since we'd been around a corner when we'd questioned Rita. "I'm a telepath, and I'm going to touch you while I ask you some questions."

Jeff nodded. He was very tense. He fixed his eyes on Claude. I stood behind him, since he was pushed up under the table, and put my hands on his thick shoulders. I pulled his T-shirt to one side, just a little, so my thumb could touch his neck.

"Jeff, you tell me what you saw tonight," I said.

"Claudette came to take the money for the first set," he said. His voice was higher than I'd expected, and he was not from these parts. Florida, I thought. "I couldn't stand her because she messed with my personal life, and I didn't want to be with her. But that's what Rita told me to do, so I did. I sat on the stool and watched her take the money and put it into the money bag. She kept some in a money drawer to make change."

"Did she have trouble with any of the customers?"

"No. It was ladies' night, and the women don't give any trouble coming in. They did during the second set. I had to go haul a gal offstage who got a little too enthusiastic about our Construction Worker, but mostly I just sat on the stool and watched."

"When did Claudette vanish?"

"When I come back from getting that gal back to her table, Claudette was gone. I looked around for her, went and asked Rita if Claudette had said anything to her about having to take a break. I even checked the ladies' room. Wasn't till I went back in the booth that I seen the glittery stuff."

"What glittery stuff?"

"What we leave when we fade," Claude murmured. "Fairy dust."

Did they sweep it up and keep it? It would probably be tacky to ask.

"And next thing I knew, the second set was over and the club was closing, and I was checking backstage and everywhere for traces of Claudette, then I was here with Claude and Claudine."

He didn't seem too angry.

"Do you know anything about Claudette's death?"

"No. I wish I did. I know this is hard on Claude." His eyes were as fixed on Claude as Claude's were on him. "She separated us, but she's not in the picture anymore."

"I have to know," Claude said, through clenched teeth.

For the first time, I wondered what the twins would do if I couldn't discover the culprit. And that scary thought spurred my brain to greater activity.

"Claudine," I called. Claudine came in, with an apple in her hand. She was hungry, and she looked tired. I wasn't surprised. Presumably, she'd worked all day, and here she was, staying up all night, and grieving, to boot.

"Can you wheel Rita in here?" I asked. "Claude, can you go get Barry?"

When everyone was assembled in the kitchen, I said,

"Everything I've seen and heard seems to indicate that Claudette vanished during the second show." After a second's consideration, they all nodded. Barry's and Rita's mouths had been gagged again, and I thought that was a good thing.

"During the first show," I said, going slow to be sure I got it right, "Claudette took up the money. Claude was onstage. Barry was onstage. Even when he wasn't onstage, he didn't come up to the booth. Rita was in her office."

There were nods all around.

"During the interval between shows, the club cleared out."

"Yeah," Jeff said. "Barry came up to meet his clients, and I checked to make sure everyone else was gone."

"So you were away from the booth a little."

"Oh, well, yeah, I guess. I do it so often, I didn't even think of that."

"And also during the interval, Rita came up to get the money pouch from Claudette."

Rita nodded emphatically.

"So, at the end of the interval, Barry's clients have left." Barry nodded. "Claude, what about you?"

"I went out to get some food during the interval," he said. "I can't eat a lot before I dance, but I had to eat something. I got back, and Barry was by himself and getting ready for the second show. I got ready, too."

"And I got back on the stool," Jeff said. "Claudette was back at the cash window. She was all ready, with the cash drawer and the stamp and the pouch. She still wasn't speaking to me."

"But you're sure it was Claudette?" I asked, out of the blue.

"Wasn't Claudine, if that's what you mean," he said. "Claudine's as sweet as Claudette was sour, and they even sit different."

Claudine looked pleased and threw her apple core in the

garbage can. She smiled at me, already forgiving me for asking questions about her.

The apple.

Claude, looking impatient, began to speak. I held up my hand. He stopped.

"I'm going to ask Claudine to take your gags off," I said to Rita and Barry. "But I don't want you to talk unless I ask you a question, okay?" They both nodded.

Claudine took the gags off, while Claude glared at me.

Thoughts were pounding through my head like a mental stampede.

"What did Rita do with the money pouch?"

"After the first show?" Jeff seemed puzzled. "Uh, I told you. She took it with her."

Alarm bells were going off mentally. Now I knew I was on the right track.

"You said that when you saw Claudette waiting to take the money for the second show, she had everything ready."

"Yeah. So? She had the hand stamp, she had the money drawer, and she had the pouch," Jeff said.

"Right. She had to have a second pouch for the second show. Rita had taken the first pouch. So when Rita came to get the first show's take, she had the second pouch in her hand, right?"

Jeff tried to remember. "Uh, I guess so."

"What about it, Rita?" I asked. "Did you bring the second pouch?"

"No," she said. "There were two in the booth at the beginning of the evening. I just took the one she'd used, then she had an empty one there for the take from the second show."

"Barry, did you see Rita walking to the booth?"

The blond stripper thought frantically. I could feel every idea beating at the inside of my head.

"She had something in her hand," he said finally. "I'm sure of it."

"No," Rita shrieked. "It was there already!"

"What's so important about the pouch, anyway?" Jeff asked. "It's just a vinyl pouch with a zipper like banks give you. How could that hurt Claudette?"

"What if the inside were rubbed with lemon juice?"

Both the fairies flinched, horror on their faces.

"Would that kill Claudette?" I asked them.

Claude said, "Oh, yes. She was especially susceptible. Even lemon scent made her vomit. She had a terrible time on wash-day until we found out the fabric sheets were lemon scented. Claudine has to go to the store since so many things are scented with the foul smell."

Rita began screaming, a high-pitched car-alarm shriek that just seemed to go on and on. "I swear I didn't do it!" she said. "I didn't! I didn't!" But her mind was saying, "Caught, caught, caught, caught."

"Yeah, you did it," I said.

The surviving brother and sister stood in front of the roll-ing chair. "Sign over the bar to us," Claude said.

"What?"

"Sign over the club to us. We'll even pay you a dollar for it."

"Why would I do that? You got no body! You can't go to the cops! What are you gonna say? 'I'm a fairy. I'm allergic to lem-ons.'" She laughed. "Who's gonna believe that?"

Barry said weakly, "Fairies?"

Jeff didn't say anything. He hadn't known the triplets were allergic to lemons. He didn't realize his lover was a fairy. I worry about the human race.

"Barry should go," I suggested.

Claude seemed to rouse himself. He'd been looking at Rita

the way a cat eyes a canary. "Good-bye, Barry," he said politely, as he untied the stripper. "I'll see you at the club tomorrow night. Our turn to take up the money."

"Uh, right," Barry said, getting to his feet.

Claudine's mouth had been moving all the while, and Barry's face went blank and relaxed. "See you later, nice party," he said genially.

"Good to meet you, Barry," I said.

"Come see the show sometime." He waved at me and walked out of the house, Claudine shepherding him to the front door. She was back in a flash.

Claude had been freeing Jeff. He kissed him, said, "I'll call you soon," and gently pushed him toward the back door. Claudine did the same spell, and Jeff's face, too, relaxed utterly from its tense expression. "'Bye," the bouncer called as he shut the door behind him.

"Are you gonna mojo me, too?" I asked, in a kind of squeaky voice.

"Here's your money," Claudine said. She took my hand. "Thank you, Sookie. I think you can remember this, huh, Claude? She's been so good!" I felt like a puppy that'd remembered its potty-training lesson.

Claude considered me for a minute, then nodded. He turned his attention back to Rita, who'd been taking the time to climb out of her panic.

Claude produced a contract out of thin air. "Sign," he told Rita, and I handed him a pen that had been on the counter beneath the phone.

"You're taking the bar in return for your sister's life," she said, expressing her incredulity at what I considered a very bad moment.

"Sure."

She gave the two fairies a look of contempt. With a flash of her rings, she took up the pen and signed the contract. She pushed up to her feet, smoothed the skirt of her dress across her round hips, and tossed her head. "I'll be going now," she said. "I own another place in Baton Rouge. I'll just live there."

"You'll start running," Claude said.

"What?"

"You better run. You owe us money and a hunt for the death of our sister. We have the money, or at least the means to make it." He pointed at the contract. "Now we need the hunt."

"That's not fair."

Okay, that disgusted even me.

"'Fair' is only part of 'fairy' as letters of the alphabet." Claudine looked formidable: not sweet, not dotty. "If you can dodge us for a year, you can live."

"A year!" Rita's situation seemed to be feeling more and more real to her by then. She was beginning to look desperate.

"Starting . . . now." Claude looked up from his watch. "Better go. We'll give ourselves a four-hour handicap."

"Just for fun," Claudine said.

"And, Rita?" Claude said, as Rita made for the door. She paused, looked back at him.

Claude smiled at her. "We won't use lemons."

DRACULA NIGHT

❦

"Dracula Night" was intended to spotlight a more credulous side of Eric. Whom would a vampire (even a very old and powerful one) revere? Who would be Eric's "Great Pumpkin"? It's the one area where Eric might lose his pragmatism and become positively fanboy-ish, and it was fun to see him that way. Pam and Sookie are the voices of cold reason, in an enjoyable turnaround.

"Dracula Night" takes place in the time following *Dead to the World*, like "Fairy Dust."

FOUND THE INVITATION in the mailbox at the end of my driveway. I had to lean out of my car window to open it, because I'd paused on my way to work after remembering I hadn't checked my mail in a couple of days. My mail was never interesting. I might get a flyer for Dollar General or Wal-Mart, or one of those ominous mass mailings about pre-need burial plots.

Today, after I'd sighed at my Entergy bill and my cable bill, I had a little treat: a handsome, heavy, buff-colored envelope that clearly contained some kind of invitation. It had been addressed by someone who'd not only taken a calligraphy class but passed the final with flying colors.

I got a little pocketknife out of my glove compartment and slit open the envelope with the care it deserved. I don't get a lot of invitations, and when I do, they're usually more Hallmark than watermark. This was something to be savored. I carefully pulled out the stiff, folded paper and opened it. Something fluttered into my lap: an enclosed sheet of tissue. Without absorbing the revealed words, I ran my finger over the embossing. Wow.

I'd strung out the preliminaries as long as I could. I bent to actually read the italic typeface.

Eric Northman
and the Staff of Fangtasia

Request the honor of your presence
at Fangtasia's annual party
to celebrate the birthday of
the Lord of Darkness

Prince Dracula

On January 13, 10:00 p.m.
music provided by the Duke of Death
Dress Formal   RSVP

I read it twice. Then I read it again.

I drove to work in such a thoughtful mood that I'm glad there wasn't any other traffic on Hummingbird Road. I took the left to get to Merlotte's, but then I almost sailed right past the parking lot. At the last moment, I braked and turned in to navigate my way to the parking area behind the bar that was reserved for employees.

Sam Merlotte, my boss, was sitting behind his desk when I peeked in to put my purse in the deep drawer in his desk that he let the servers use. He had been running his hands over his hair again, because the tangled red gold halo was even wilder than usual. He looked up from his tax form and smiled at me.

"Sookie," he said, "how are you doing?"

"Good. Tax season, huh?" I made sure my white T-shirt was tucked in evenly so that the MERLOTTE'S embroidered over my left breast would be level. I flicked one of my long blond hairs off my black pants. I always bent over to brush my hair out so my ponytail would look smooth. "You not taking them to the CPA this year?"

"I figure if I start this early, I can do them myself."

He said that every year, and he always ended up making an appointment with the CPA, who always had to file for an extension.

"Listen, did you get one of these?" I asked, extending the invitation.

He dropped his pen with some relief and took the sheet from my hand. After scanning the script, he said, "No. They wouldn't invite many shifters, anyway. Maybe the local packmaster, or some supe who'd done them a significant service . . . like you."

"I'm not supernatural," I said, surprised. "I just have a . . . problem."

"Telepathy is a lot more than a problem," Sam said. "Acne is a problem. Shyness is a problem. Reading other people's minds is a gift."

"Or a curse," I said. I went around the desk to toss my purse in the drawer, and Sam stood up. I'm around five foot six, and Sam tops me by maybe three inches. He's not a big guy, but he's much stronger than a plain human his size, since Sam's a shapeshifter.

"Are you going to go?" he asked. "Halloween and Dracula's birthday are the only holidays vampires observe, and I understand they can throw quite a party."

"I haven't made up my mind," I said. "When I'm on my break later, I might call Pam." Pam, Eric's second-in-command, was as close to a friend as I had among the vampires.

I reached her at Fangtasia pretty soon after the sun went down. "There really was a Count Dracula? I thought he was made up," I said after telling her I'd gotten the invitation.

"There really was," Pam said. "Vlad Tepes. He was a Wallachian king whose capital city was Târgovişte, I think." Pam was quite matter-of-fact about the existence of a creature I'd thought was a joint creation of Bram Stoker and Hollywood. "Vlad III was more ferocious and bloodthirsty than any vampire, and this was when he was a live human. He enjoyed executing people by impaling them on huge wooden stakes. They might last for hours."

I shuddered. Ick.

"His own people regarded him with fear, of course. But the local vamps admired Vlad so much they actually brought him over when he was dying, thus ushering in the new era of the vampire. After monks buried him on an island called Snagov, he rose on the third night to become the first modern vampire. Up until then, the vampires were like . . . well, disgusting. Completely secret. Ragged, filthy, living in holes in cemeteries, like animals. But Vlad Dracula had been a ruler, and he wasn't going to dress in rags and live in a hole for any reason." Pam sounded proud.

I tried to imagine Eric wearing rags and living in a hole, but it was almost impossible. "So Stoker didn't just dream the whole thing up based on folktales?"

"Just parts of it. Obviously, he didn't know a lot about what Dracula, as he called him, really could or couldn't do, but he was so excited at meeting the prince that he made up a lot of details he thought would give the story zing. It was just like Anne Rice meeting Louis: an early *Interview with the Vampire*. Dracula really wasn't too happy afterward that Stoker caught him at a weak moment, but he did enjoy the name recognition."

"But he won't actually be there, right? I mean, vampires'll be celebrating this all over the world."

Pam said, very cautiously, "Some believe he shows up

somewhere every year, makes a surprise appearance. That chance is so remote, his appearance at our party would be like winning the lottery. Though some believe it could happen."

I heard Eric's voice in the background saying, "Pam, who are you talking to?"

"Okay," Pam said, the word sounding very American with her slight British accent. "Got to go, Sookie. See you then."

As I hung up the office phone, Sam said, "Sookie, if you go to the party, please keep alert and on the watch. Sometimes vamps get carried away with the excitement on Dracula Night."

"Thanks, Sam," I said. "I'll sure be careful." No matter how many vamps you claimed as friends, you had to be alert. A few years ago the Japanese had invented a synthetic blood that satisfies the vampires' nutritional requirements, which has enabled the undead to come out of the shadows and take their place at the American table. British vampires had it pretty good, too, and most of the Western European vamps had fared pretty well after the Great Revelation (the day they'd announced their existence, through carefully chosen representatives). However, many South American vamps regretted stepping forward, and the bloodsuckers in the Muslim countries—well, there were mighty few left. Vampires in the inhospitable parts of the world were making efforts to immigrate to countries that tolerated them, with the result that our Congress was considering various bills to limit undead citizens from claiming political asylum. In consequence, we were experiencing an influx of vampires with all kinds of accents as they tried to enter America under the wire. Most of them came in through Louisiana, since it was notably friendly to the Cold Ones, as *Fangbanger Xtreme* called them.

It was more fun thinking about vampires than hearing the thoughts of my fellow citizens. Naturally, as I went from table to table, I was doing my job with a big smile, because I like good tips, but I wasn't able to put my heart into it tonight. It had been a warm day for January, way into the fifties, and people's thoughts had turned to spring.

I try not to listen in, but I'm like a radio that picks up a lot of signals. Some days I can control my reception a lot better than other days. Today I kept picking up snippets. Hoyt Fortenberry, my brother's best friend, was thinking about his mom's plan for Hoyt to put in about ten new rosebushes in her already extensive garden. Gloomy but obedient, he was trying to figure out how much time the task would take. Arlene, my longtime friend and another waitress, was wondering if she could get her latest boyfriend to pop the question, but that was pretty much a perennial thought for Arlene. Like the roses, it bloomed every season.

As I mopped up spills and hustled to get chicken strip baskets on the tables (the supper crowd was heavy that night), my own thoughts were centered on how to get a formal gown to wear to the party. Though I did have one ancient prom dress, handmade by my aunt Linda, it was hopelessly outdated. I'm twenty-six, but I didn't have any bridesmaid dresses that might serve. None of my few friends had gotten married except Arlene, who'd been wed so many times that she never even thought of bridesmaids. The few nice clothes I'd bought for vampire events always seemed to get ruined . . . some in very unpleasant ways.

Usually, I shopped at my friend Tara's store, but she wasn't open after six. So after I got off work, I drove to Monroe to Pecanland Mall. At Dillard's, I got lucky. To tell the truth, I was so pleased with the dress I might have gotten it even if it hadn't been on sale, but it had been marked down to twenty-five dollars from a hundred and fifty, surely a shopping triumph. It was rose pink, with a sequin top and a chiffon bottom, and it was strapless and simple. I'd wear my hair down, and my gran's pearl earrings, and some silver heels that were also on major sale.

That important item taken care of, I wrote a polite acceptance note and popped it in the mail. I was good to go.

Three nights later, I was knocking on the back door of Fangtasia, my garment bag held high.

"You're looking a bit informal," Pam said as she let me in.

"Didn't want to wrinkle the dress." I came in, making sure the bag didn't trail, and hightailed it for the bathroom.

There wasn't a lock on the bathroom door. Pam stood outside so I wouldn't be interrupted, and Eric's second-in-command smiled when I came out, a bundle of my more mundane clothes rolled under my arm.

"You look good, Sookie," Pam said. Pam herself had elected to wear a tuxedo made out of silver lamé. She was a sight. My hair has some curl to it, but Pam's is a paler blond and very straight. We both have blue eyes, but hers are a lighter shade and rounder, and she doesn't blink much. "Eric will be very pleased."

I flushed. Eric and I have a History. But since he had amnesia when we created that history, he doesn't remember it. Pam does. "Like I care what he thinks," I said.

Pam smiled at me sideways. "Right," she said. "You are totally indifferent. So is he."

I tried to look like I was accepting her words on their surface level and not seeing through to the sarcasm. To my surprise, Pam gave me a light kiss on the cheek. "Thanks for coming," she said. "You may perk him up. He's been very hard to work for these past few days."

"Why?" I asked, though I wasn't real sure I wanted to know.

"Have you ever seen *It's the Great Pumpkin, Charlie Brown?*"

I stopped in my tracks. "Sure," I said. "Have you?"

"Oh, yes," Pam said calmly. "Many times." She gave me a minute to absorb that. "Eric is like that on Dracula Night. He thinks, every year, that this time Dracula will pick his party to attend. Eric fusses and plans; he frets and stews. He sent the invitations back to the printer twice so they were late going out. Now that the night is actually here, he's worked himself into a state."

"So this is a case of hero worship gone crazy?"

"You have such a way with words," Pam said admiringly. We were outside Eric's office, and we could both hear him bellowing inside.

"He's not happy with the new bartender. He thinks there are not enough bottles of the blood the count is said to prefer, according to an interview in *American Vampire*."

I tried to imagine Vlad Tepes, impaler of so many of his own countrymen, chatting with a reporter. I sure wouldn't want to be the one holding the pad and pencil. "What brand would that be?" I scrambled to catch up with the conversation.

"The Prince of Darkness is said to prefer Royalty."

"Ew." Why was I not surprised?

Royalty was a very, very rare bottled blood. I'd thought the brand was only a rumor until now. Royalty consisted of part synthetic blood and part real blood—the blood of, you guessed it, people of title. Before you go thinking of enterprising vamps ambushing that cute Prince William, let me reassure you. There were plenty of minor royals in Europe who were glad to give blood for an astronomical sum.

"After a month's worth of phone calls, we managed to get two bottles." Pam was looking quite grim. "They cost more than we could afford. I've never known my maker to be other than business-wise, but this year Eric seems to be going over-board. Royalty doesn't keep forever, you know, with the real blood in it . . . and now he's worried that two bottles might not be enough. There is so much legend attached to Dracula, who can say what is true? He has heard that Dracula will only drink Royalty or . . . the real thing."

"Real blood? But that's illegal, unless you've got a willing donor."

Any vampire who took a human's blood—against the human's will—was liable to execution by stake or sunlight, according to the vamp's choice. The execution was usually carried out by another vamp, kept on retainer by the state. I personally thought any vampire who took an unwilling person's blood deserved the execution, because there were enough fang-bangers around who were more than willing to donate.

"And no vampire is allowed to kill Dracula, or even strike him," Pam said, chiming right in on my thoughts. "Not that we'd want to strike our prince, of course," she added hastily.

Right, I thought.

"He is held in such reverence that any vampire who assaults him must meet the sun. And we're also expected to offer our prince financial assistance."

I wondered if the other vampires were supposed to floss his fangs for him, too.

The door to Eric's office flew open with such vehemence that it bounced right back. It opened again more gently, and Eric emerged.

I had to gape. He looked positively edible. Eric is very tall, very broad, very blond, and tonight he was dressed in a tuxedo that had not come off any rack. This tux had been made for Eric, and he looked as good as any James Bond in it. Black cloth without a speck of lint, a snowy white shirt, and a hand-tied bow at his throat, with his beautiful hair rippling down his back . . .

"James Blond," I muttered. Eric's eyes were blazing with excitement. Without a word, he dipped me as though we were dancing and planted a hell of a kiss on me: lips, tongue, the entire osculant assemblage. Oh boy, oh boy, oh boy. When I was quivering, he assisted me to rise. His brilliant smile revealed glistening fangs. Eric had enjoyed himself.

"Hello to you, too," I said tartly, once I was sure I was breathing again.

"My delicious friend," Eric said, and bowed.

I wasn't sure I could be correctly called a friend, and I'd have to take his word for it that I was delicious. "What's the program for the evening?" I asked, hoping that my host would calm down very soon.

"We'll dance, listen to music, drink blood, watch the entertainment, and wait for the count to come," Eric said. "I'm so glad you'll be here tonight. We have a wide array of special guests, but you're the only telepath."

"Okay," I said faintly.

"You look especially lovely tonight," said Lyle. He'd been standing right behind Eric, and I hadn't even noticed him. Slight and narrow-faced, with spiked black hair, Lyle didn't have the presence Eric had acquired in a thousand years of life. Lyle was a visiting vamp from Alexandria, interning at the very successful Fangtasia because he wanted to open his own vampire bar. Lyle was carrying a small cooler, taking great care to keep it level.

"The Royalty," Pam explained in a neutral voice.

"Can I see?" I asked.

Eric lifted the lid and showed me the contents: two blue bottles (for the blue blood, I presumed), with labels that bore the logo of a tiara and the single word "Royalty" in gothic script.

"Very nice," I said, underwhelmed.

"He'll be so pleased," Eric said, sounding as happy as I'd ever heard him.

"You sound oddly sure that the—that Dracula will be coming," I said. The hall was crowded, and we began moving to the public part of the club.

"I was able to have a business discussion with the Master's handler," he said. "I was able to express how much having the Master's presence would honor me and my establishment."

Pam rolled her eyes at me.

"You bribed him," I translated. Hence Eric's extra excitement this year, and his purchase of the Royalty.

I had never suspected Eric harbored this depth of hero worship for anyone except himself. I would never have believed he would spend good money for such a reason, either. Eric was charming and enterprising, and he took good care of his employees; but the first person on Eric's admiration list was Eric, and his own well-being was Eric's number one priority.

"Dear Sookie, you're looking less than excited," Pam said, grinning at me. Pam loved to make trouble, and she was finding fertile ground tonight. Eric swung his head back to give me a look, and Pam's face relaxed into its usual bland smoothness.

"Don't you believe it will happen, Sookie?" he asked. From behind his back, Lyle rolled his eyes. He was clearly fed up with Eric's fantasy.

I'd just wanted to come to a party in a pretty dress and have a good time, and here I was, up a conversational creek.

"We'll all find out, won't we?" I said brightly, and Eric seemed satisfied. "The club looks beautiful." Normally, Fangtasia was the plainest place you could imagine, besides the lively gray and red paint scheme and the neon. The floors were concrete, the tables and chairs basic metal restaurant furnishings, the booths not much better. I could not believe that Fangtasia had been so transformed. Banners had been hung from the club's ceiling. Each banner was white with a red bear on it: a sort of stylized bear on its hind legs, one paw raised to strike.

"That's a replica of the Master's personal flag," Pam said in answer to my pointed finger. "Eric paid an historian at LSU to research it." Her expression made it clear she thought Eric had been gypped, big-time.

In the center of Fangtasia's small dance floor stood an actual throne on a small dais. As I neared the throne, I decided Eric had rented it from a theater company. It looked good from thirty feet away, but up close . . . not so much. However, it had been freshened up with a plump red cushion for the Dark Prince's derriere, and the dais was placed in the exact middle of a square of dark red carpet. All the tables had been covered with white or dark red cloths, and elaborate flower arrangements were in the middle of each table. I had to laugh when I examined one of the arrangements: in the explosion of red carnations and greenery were miniature coffins and full-size stakes. Eric's sense of humor had surfaced, finally.

Instead of WDED, the all-vampire radio station, the sound system was playing some very emotional violin music that was both scratchy and bouncy. "Transylvanian music," said Lyle, his face carefully expressionless. "Later, the DJ Duke of Death will take us for a musical journey." Lyle looked as though he would rather eat snails.

Against one wall by the bar, I spied a small buffet for beings who ate food, and a large blood fountain for those who didn't.

The red fountain, flowing gently down several tiers of gleaming milky glass bowls, was surrounded by crystal goblets. Just a wee bit over the top.

"Golly," I said weakly as Eric and Lyle went over to the bar.

Pam shook her head in despair. "The money we spent," she said.

Not too surprisingly, the room was full of vampires. I recognized a few of the bloodsuckers present: Indira, Thalia, Clancy, Maxwell Lee, and Bill Compton, my ex. There were at least twenty more I had only seen once or twice, vamps who lived in Area Five under Eric's authority. There were a few bloodsuckers I didn't know at all, including a guy behind the bar who must be the new bartender. Fangtasia ran through bartenders pretty quickly.

There were also some creatures in the bar who were not vamps and not human, members of Louisiana's supernatural community. The head of Shreveport's werewolf pack, Colonel Flood, was sitting at a table with Calvin Norris, the leader of the small community of werepanthers who lived in and around Hot Shot, outside of Bon Temps. Colonel Flood, now retired from the air force, was sitting stiffly erect in a good suit, while Calvin was wearing his own idea of party clothes—a western shirt, new jeans, cowboy boots, and a black cowboy hat. He tipped it to me when he caught my eye, and he gave me a nod that expressed admiration. Colonel Flood's nod was less personal but still friendly.

Eric had also invited a short, broad man who strongly reminded me of a goblin I'd met once. I was sure this male was a member of the same race. Goblins are testy and ferociously strong, and when they are angry, their touch can burn, so I decided to stay a good distance away from this one. He was deep in conversation with a very thin woman with mad eyes.

She was wearing an assemblage of leaves and vines. I wasn't
going to ask.

Of course, there weren't any fairies. Fairies are as intoxicating to vampires as sugar water is to hummingbirds.

Behind the bar was the newest member of the Fangtasia
staff, a short, burly man with long, wavy dark hair. He had a
prominent nose and large eyes, and he was taking everything
in with an air of amusement while he moved around prepar-
ing drink orders.

"Who's that?" I asked, nodding toward the bar. "And who
are the strange vamps? Is Eric expanding?"

Pam said, "If you're in transit on Dracula Night, the proto-
col is to check in at the nearest sheriff's headquarters and
share in the celebration there. That's why there are vampires
here you haven't met. The new bartender is Milos Griesniki,
a recent immigrant from the Old Countries. He is disgusting."

I stared at Pam. "How so?" I asked.

"A sneaker. A pryer."

I'd never heard Pam express such a strong opinion, and I
looked at the vampire with some curiosity.

"He tries to discover how much money Eric has, and how
much the bar makes, and how much our little human bar-
maids get paid."

"Speaking of whom, where are they?" The waitresses and
the rest of the everyday staff, all vampire groupies (known in
some circles as fangbangers), were usually much in evidence,
dressed in filmy black and powdered almost as pale as the real
vampires.

"Too dangerous for them on this night," Pam said simply.
"You will see that Indira and Clancy are serving the guests."
Indira was wearing a beautiful sari; she usually wore jeans and
T-shirts, so I knew she had made an effort to dress up for the

occasion. Clancy, who had rough red hair and bright green eyes, was in a suit. That was also a first. Instead of a regular tie, he wore a scarf tied into a floppy bow, and when I caught his eye, he swept his hand from his head to his pants to demand my admiration. I smiled and nodded, though truthfully I liked Clancy better in his usual tough-guy clothes and heavy boots.

Eric was buzzing from table to table. He hugged and bowed and talked like a demented thing, and I didn't know if I found this endearing or alarming. I decided it was both. I'd definitely discovered Eric's weak side.

I talked to Colonel Flood and Calvin for a few minutes. Colonel Flood was as polite and distant as he always was; he didn't care much for non-Weres, and now that he had retired, he only dealt with regular people when he had to. Calvin told me that he'd put a new roof on his house himself, and invited me to go fishing with him when the weather was warmer. I smiled but didn't commit to anything. My grandmother had loved fishing, but I was only good for two hours, tops, and then I was ready to do something else. I watched Pam doing her second-in-command job, making sure all the visiting vampires were happy, sharply admonishing the new bartender when he made a mistake with a drink order. Milos Griesniki gave her back a scowl that made me shiver. But if anyone could take care of herself, it was Pam.

Clancy, who'd been managing the club for a month, was checking every table to make sure there were clean ashtrays (some of the vampires smoked) and that all dirty glasses and other discarded items were removed promptly. When DJ Duke of Death took over, the music changed to something with a beat. Some of the vampires turned out onto the dance floor, flinging themselves around with the extreme abandon only the undead show.

Calvin and I danced a couple of times, but we were no-where in the vampire league. Eric claimed me for a slow dance, and though he was clearly distracted by thoughts of what the night might hold—Dracula-wise—he made my toe-nails quiver.

"Some night," he whispered, "there's going to be nothing else but you and me."

When the song was over, I had to go back to the table and have a long, cold drink. Lots of ice.

As the time drew closer to midnight, the vampires gath-ered around the blood fountain and filled the crystal goblets. The non-vamp guests also rose to their feet. I was standing beside the table where I'd been chatting with Calvin and Col-onel Flood when Eric brought out a tabletop hand gong and began to strike it. If he'd been human, he'd have been flushed with excitement; as it was, his eyes were blazing. Eric looked both beautiful and scary, because he was so intent.

When the last reverberation had shivered into silence, Eric raised his own glass high and said, "On this most memorable of days, we stand together in awe and hope that the Lord of Darkness will honor us with his presence. O Prince, appear to us!"

We actually all stood in hushed silence, waiting for the Great Pumpkin—oh, wait, the Dark Prince. Just when Eric's face began to look downcast, a harsh voice broke the tension.

"My loyal son, I shall reveal myself!"

Milos Griesniki leaped from behind the bar, pulling off his tux jacket and pants and shirt to reveal . . . an incredible jumpsuit made from black, glittery stretchy stuff. I would have expected to see it on a girl going to her prom, a girl with-out much money who was trying to look unconventional and sexy. With his blocky body and dark hair and mustache, the one-piece made Milos look more like an acrobat in a third-rate circus.

There was an excited babble of low-voiced reaction. Calvin said, "Well . . . shit." Colonel Flood gave a sharp nod, to say he agreed completely.

The bartender posed regally before Eric, who after a startled instant bowed before the much shorter vampire. "My lord," Eric said, "I am humbled. That you should honor us . . . that you should actually be here . . . on this day, of all days . . . I am overcome."

"Fucking poser," Pam muttered in my ear. She'd glided up behind me in the hubbub following the bartender's announcement.

"You think?" I was watching the spectacle of the confident and regal Eric babbling away, actually sinking down on one knee.

Dracula made a hushing gesture, and Eric's mouth snapped shut in midsentence. So did the mouths of every vamp in the place. "Since I have been here incognito for a week," Dracula said grandly, his accent harsh but not unattractive, "I have become so fond of this place that I propose to stay for a year. I will take your tribute while I am here, to live in the style I enjoyed during life. Though the bottled Royalty is acceptable as a stopgap, I, Dracula, do not care for this modern habit of drinking artificial blood, so I will require one woman a day. This one will do to start with." He pointed at me, and Colonel Flood and Calvin moved instantly to flank me, a gesture I appreciated. The vampires looked confused, an expression that didn't sit well on undead faces; except Bill. His face went completely blank.

Eric followed Vlad Tepes's stubby finger, identifying me as the future Happy Meal. Then he stared at Dracula, looking up from his kneeling position. I couldn't read his face at all, and I felt a stirring of fear. What would Charlie Brown have done if the Great Pumpkin wanted to eat the little red-haired girl?

"And as for my financial maintenance, a tithe from your club's income and a house will be sufficient for my needs, with some servants thrown in: your second-in-command, or your club manager, one of them should do. . . ." Pam actually growled, a low-level sound that made my hair stand up on my neck. Clancy looked as though someone had kicked his dog.

Pam was fumbling with the centerpiece of the table, hidden by my body. After a second, I felt something pressed into my hand. I glanced down. "You're the human," she whispered.

"Come, girl," Dracula said, beckoning with a curving of his fingers. "I hunger. Come to me and be honored before all these assembled."

Though Colonel Flood and Calvin both grabbed my arms, I said very softly, "This isn't worth your lives. They'll kill you if you try to fight. Don't worry," and I pulled away from them, meeting their eyes, in turn, as I spoke. I was trying to project confidence. I didn't know what they were getting, but they understood there was a plan.

I tried to glide toward the spangled bartender as if I were entranced. Since that's something vamps can't do to me, and Dracula obviously never doubted his own powers, I got away with it.

"Master, how did you escape from your tomb at Târgovişte?" I asked, doing my best to sound admiring and dreamy. I kept my hands down by my sides so the folds of rosy chiffon would conceal them.

"Many have asked me that," the Dark Prince said, inclining his head graciously as Eric's own head jerked up, his brows drawn together. "But that story must wait. My beautiful one,

I am so glad you left your neck bare tonight. Come closer to me . . . *ERRRK!*"

"That's for the bad dialogue!" I said, my voice trembling as I tried to shove the stake in even harder.

"And that's for the embarrassment," Eric said, giving the end a tap with his fist, just to help, as the "Prince" stared at us in horror. The stake obligingly disappeared into his chest.

"You dare . . . you dare," the short vampire croaked. "You shall be executed."

"I don't think so," I said. His face went blank, and his eyes were empty. Flakes began to drift from his skin as he crumpled.

But as the self-proclaimed Dracula sank to the floor and I looked around me, I wasn't so sure. Only the presence of Eric at my side kept the assemblage from falling on me and taking care of business. The vampires from out of town were the most dangerous; the vampires that knew me would hesitate.

"He wasn't Dracula," I said as clearly and loudly as I could. "He was an impostor."

"Kill her!" said a thin female vamp with short brown hair. "Kill the murderess!" She had a heavy accent, I thought Russian. I was about tired of the new wave of vamps.

Pot calling the kettle black, I thought briefly. I said, "You-all really think this goober was the Prince of Darkness? I pointed to the flaking mess on the floor, held together by the spangled jumpsuit.

"He is dead. Anyone who kills Dracula must die," said Indira quietly, but not like she was going to rush over and rip my throat out.

"Any *vampire* who kills Dracula must die," Pam corrected. "But Sookie is not a vampire, and this was not Dracula."

"She killed one impersonating our founder," Eric said,

making sure he could be heard throughout the club. "Milos was not the real Dracula. I would have staked him myself if I had had my wits about me." But I was standing right by Eric, my hand on his arm, and I knew he was shaking.

"How do you know that? How could she tell, a human who had only a few moments in his presence? He looked just like the woodcuts!" This from a tall, heavy man with a French accent.

"Vlad Tepes was buried at the monastery on Snagov," Pam said calmly, and everyone turned to her. "Sookie asked him how he'd escaped from his tomb at Târgoviște."

Well, that hushed them up, at least temporarily. I began to think I might live through this night.

"Recompense must be made to his maker," pointed out the tall, heavy vampire. He'd calmed down quite a bit in the last few minutes.

"If we can determine his maker," Eric said, "certainly."

"I'll search my database," Bill offered. He was standing in the shadows, where he'd lurked all evening. Now he took a step forward, and his dark eyes sought me out like a police helicopter searchlight catches the fleeing felon on *Cops*. "I'll find out his real name, if no one here has met him before."

All the vamps present glanced around. No one stepped forward to claim Milos/Dracula's acquaintance.

"In the meantime," Eric said smoothly, "let's not forget that this event should be a secret amongst us until we can find out more details." He smiled with a great show of fang, making his point quite nicely. "What happens in Shreveport, stays in Shreveport."

There was a murmur of assent.

"What do you say, guests?" Eric asked the non-vamp attendees.

Colonel Flood said, "Vampire business is not pack business. We don't care if you kill each other. We won't meddle in your affairs."

Calvin shrugged. "Panthers don't mind what you do."

The goblin said, "I've already forgotten the whole thing," and the madwoman beside him nodded and laughed. The few other non-vamps hastily agreed.

No one solicited my answer. I guess they were taking my silence for a given, and they were right.

Pam drew me aside. She made an annoyed sound, like "tchk," and brushed at my dress. I looked down to see a fine spray of blood had misted across the chiffon skirt. I knew immediately that I'd never wear my beloved bargain dress again.

"Too bad, you look good in pink," Pam said.

I started to offer the dress to her, then thought again. I would wear it home and burn it. Vampire blood on my dress? Not a good piece of evidence to leave hanging around someone's closet. If experience has taught me anything, it's to dispose of bloodstained clothing instantly.

"That was a brave thing you did," Pam said.

"Well, he was going to bite me," I said. "To death."

"Still," she said.

I didn't like the calculating look in her eyes.

"Thank you for helping Eric when I couldn't," Pam said. "My maker is a big idiot about the prince."

"I did it because he was going to suck my blood," I told her.

"You did some research on Vlad Tepes."

"Yes, I went to the library after you told me about the original Dracula, and I Googled him."

Pam's eyes gleamed. "Legend has it that the original Vlad III was beheaded before he was buried."

"That's just one of the stories surrounding his death," I said.

"True. But you know that not even a vampire can survive a beheading."

"I would think not."

"So you know the whole thing may be a crock of shit."

"Pam," I said, mildly shocked. "Well, it might be. And it might not. After all, Eric talked to someone who said he was the real Dracula's gofer."

"You knew that Milos wasn't the real Dracula the minute he stepped forth."

I shrugged.

Pam shook her head at me. "You're too soft, Sookie Stackhouse. It'll be the death of you some day."

"Nah, I don't think so," I said. I was watching Eric, his golden hair falling forward as he looked down at the rapidly disintegrating remains of the self-styled Prince of Darkness. The thousand years of his life sat on him heavily, and for a second I saw every one of them. Then, by degrees, his face lightened, and when he looked up at me, it was with the expectancy of a child on Christmas Eve.

"Maybe next year," he said.

ONE WORD ANSWER

"One Word Answer" is one of the first short stories I ever wrote. The idea was born when I pictured a car sweeping up to our favorite barmaid's humble house back in the woods of Louisiana—at night, of course. It took some serious thinking for me to imagine who might be in the car and what we could learn about Sookie and her world from this encounter. Since Hadley is essential to the narrative of the books, I afterward discovered it was a mistake to introduce her in a short story. Ever since, readers have asked me, "Did I miss something?" All around, this story was a learning experience. But I was aiming for creepy and mysterious, and I hope I got there.

"One Word Answer" is set after *Dead as a Doornail*.

BUBBA THE VAMPIRE and I were raking up clippings from my newly trimmed bushes about midnight when the long black car pulled up. I'd been enjoying the gentle scent of the cut bushes and the songs of the crickets and frogs celebrating spring. Everything hushed with the arrival of the black limousine. Bubba vanished immediately, because he didn't recognize the car. Since he changed over to the vampire persuasion, Bubba's been on the shy side.

I leaned against my rake, trying to look nonchalant. In reality, I was far from relaxed. I live pretty far out in the country, and you have to want to be at my house to find the way. There's not a sign out at the parish road that points down my driveway reading "Stackhouse home." My home is not visible from the road, because the driveway meanders through some woods to arrive in the clearing where the core of the house has stood for a hundred and sixty years.

Visitors are not real frequent, and I didn't remember ever seeing a limousine before. No one got out of the long black car for a couple of minutes. I began to wonder if maybe I should have hidden myself, like Bubba. I had the outside lights on, of course, since I couldn't see in the dark like Bubba, but the limousine windows were heavily smoked. I was real tempted to whack the shiny bumper with my rake to find out what would happen. Fortunately, the door opened while I was still thinking about it.

A large gentleman emerged from the rear of the limousine. He was six feet tall, and he was made up of circles. The largest circle was his belly. The round head above it was almost bald, but a fringe of black hair circled it right above his ears. His little eyes were round, too, and black as his hair and his suit. His shirt was gleaming white, but his tie was black without a pattern. He looked like the director of a funeral home for the criminally insane.

"Not too many people do their yard work at midnight," he commented, in a surprisingly melodious voice. The true answer—that I liked to rake when I had someone to talk to, and I had company that night with Bubba, who couldn't come out in the sunlight—was better left unsaid. I just nodded. You couldn't argue with his statement.

"Would you be the woman known as Sookie Stackhouse?" asked the large gentleman. He said it as if he often addressed creatures that weren't men or women, but something else entirely.

"Yes, sir, I am," I said politely. My grandmother, God rest her soul, had raised me well. But she hadn't raised a fool; I wasn't about to invite him in. I wondered why the driver didn't get out.

"Then I have a legacy for you."

"Legacy" meant someone had died. I didn't have anyone left except for my brother, Jason, and he was sitting down at Merlotte's Bar with his girlfriend, Crystal. At least that's where he'd been when I'd gotten off my barmaid's job a couple of hours before.

The little night creatures were beginning to make their

sounds again, having decided the big night creatures weren't going to attack.

"A legacy from who?" I said. What makes me different from other people is that I'm telepathic. Vampires, whose minds are simply silent holes in a world made noisy to me by the cacophony of human brains, make restful companions for me, so I'd been enjoying Bubba's chatter. Now I needed to rev up my gift. This wasn't a casual drop-in. I opened my mind to my visitor. While the large, circular gentleman was wincing at my ungrammatical question, I attempted to look inside his head. Instead of a stream of ideas and images (the usual human broadcast), his thoughts came to me in bursts of static. He was a supernatural creature of some sort.

"Whom," I corrected myself, and he smiled at me. His teeth were very sharp.

"Do you remember your cousin Hadley?"

Nothing could have surprised me more than this question. I leaned the rake against the mimosa tree and shook the plastic garbage bag that we'd already filled. I put the plastic band around the top before I spoke. I could only hope my voice wouldn't choke when I answered him. "Yes, I do." Though I sounded hoarse, my words were clear.

Hadley Delahoussaye, my only cousin, had vanished into the underworld of drugs and prostitution years before. I had her high school junior picture in my photo album. That was the last picture she'd had taken, because that year she'd run off to New Orleans to make her living by her wits and her body. My aunt Linda, her mother, had died of cancer during the second year after Hadley's departure.

"Is Hadley still alive?" I said, hardly able to get the words out.

"Alas, no," said the big man, absently polishing his black-framed glasses on a clean white handkerchief. His black shoes gleamed like mirrors. "Your cousin Hadley is dead, I'm afraid." He seemed to relish saying it. He was a man—or whatever—who enjoyed the sound of his own voice.

Underneath the distrust and confusion I was feeling about this whole weird episode, I was aware of a sharp pang of grief. Hadley had been fun as a child, and we'd been together a lot, naturally. Since I'd been a weird kid, Hadley and my brother, Jason, had been the only children I'd had to play with for the most part. When Hadley hit puberty, the picture changed; but I had some good memories of my cousin.

"What happened to her?" I tried to keep my voice even, but I knew it wasn't.

"She was involved in an Unfortunate Incident," he said.

That was the euphemism for a vampire killing. When it appeared in newspaper reports, it usually meant that some vampire had been unable to restrain his bloodlust and had attacked a human. "A vampire killed her?" I was horrified.

"Ah, not exactly. Your cousin Hadley was the vampire. She got staked."

This was so much bad and startling news that I couldn't take it in. I held up a hand to indicate he shouldn't talk for a minute, while I absorbed what he'd said, bit by bit.

"What is your name, please?" I asked.

"Mr. Cataliades," he said. I repeated that to myself several times since it was a name I'd never encountered. Emphasis on the *tal*, I told myself. And a long *e*.

"Where might you hail from?"

"For many years, my home has been New Orleans."

New Orleans was at the other end of Louisiana from my little town, Bon Temps. Northern Louisiana is pretty darn different from southern Louisiana in several fundamental ways: it's the Bible Belt without the pizzazz of New Orleans;

it's the older sister who stayed home and tended the farm while the younger sister went out partying. But it shares other things with the southern part of the state, too: bad roads, corrupt politics, and a lot of people, both black and white, who live right on the poverty line.

"Who drove you?" I asked pointedly, looking at the front of the car.

"Waldo," called Mr. Cataliades, "the lady wants to see you."

I was sorry I'd expressed an interest after Waldo got out of the driver's seat of the limo and I'd had a look at him. Waldo was a vampire, as I'd already established in my own mind by identifying a typical vampire brain signature, which to me is like a photographic negative, one I "see" with my brain. Most vampires are good-looking or extremely talented in some way or another. Naturally, when a vamp brings a human over, the vamp is likely to pick a human who attracted him or her by beauty or some necessary skill. I didn't know who the heck had brought over Waldo, but I figured it was somebody crazy. Waldo had long, wispy white hair that was almost the same color as his skin. He was maybe five foot eight, but he looked taller because he was very thin. Waldo's eyes looked red under the light I'd had mounted on the electric pole. The vampire's face looked corpse white with a faint greenish tinge, and his skin was wrinkled. I'd never seen a vampire who hadn't been taken in the prime of life.

"Waldo," I said, nodding. I felt lucky to have had such long training in keeping my face agreeable. "Can I get you anything? I think I have some bottled blood. And you, Mr. Cataliades? A beer? Some soda?"

The big man shuddered and tried to cover it with a graceful half bow. "Much too hot for coffee or alcohol for me, but perhaps we'll take refreshments later." It was maybe sixty-two degrees, but Mr. Cataliades was indeed sweating, I noticed. "May we come in?" he asked.

"I'm sorry," I said, without a bit of apology in my voice. "I think not." I was hoping that Bubba had had the sense to rush across the little valley between our properties to fetch my nearest neighbor, my former lover Bill Compton, known to the residents of Bon Temps as Vampire Bill.

"Then we'll conduct our business out here in your yard," Mr. Cataliades said coldly. He and Waldo came around the body of the limousine. I felt uneasy when it wasn't between us anymore, but they kept their distance. "Miss Stackhouse, you are your cousin's sole heir."

I understood what he said, but I was incredulous. "Not my brother, Jason?" Jason and Hadley, both three years older than I, had been great buddies.

"No. In this document, Hadley says she called Jason Stackhouse once for help when she was very low on funds. He ignored her request, so she's ignoring him."

"When did Hadley get staked?" I was concentrating very hard on not getting any visuals. Since she was older than I by three years, Hadley had been a mere twenty-nine when she'd died. She'd been my physical opposite in most ways. I was robust and blond, she was thin and dark. I was strong, she was frail. She'd had big, thickly lashed brown eyes, mine were blue; and now, this strange man was telling me, she had closed those eyes for good.

"A month ago." Mr. Cataliades had to think about it. "She died about a month ago."

"And you're just now letting me know?"

"Circumstances prevented."

I considered that.

"She died in New Orleans?"

"Yes. She was a handmaiden to the queen," he said, as though he were telling me she'd gotten her partnership at a big law firm or managed to buy her own business.

"The Queen of Louisiana," I said cautiously.

"I knew you would understand," he said, beaming at me. "'This is a woman who knows her vampires,' I said to myself when I met you."

"She knows this vampire," Bill said, appearing at my side in that disconcerting way he had.

A flash of displeasure went across Mr. Cataliades's face like quick lightning across the sky.

"And you would be?" he asked with cold courtesy.

"I would be Bill Compton, resident of this parish and friend to Miss Stackhouse," Bill said ominously. "I'm also an employee of the queen, like you."

The queen had hired Bill so the computer database about vampires he was working on would be her property. Somehow, I thought Mr. Cataliades performed more personal services. He looked like he knew where all the bodies were buried, and Waldo looked like he had put them there.

Bubba was right behind Bill, and when he stepped out of Bill's shadow, for the first time I saw the vampire Waldo show an emotion. He was in awe.

"Oh, my gracious! Is this El " Mr. Cataliades blurted.

"Yes," said Bill. He shot the two strangers a significant glance. "This is Bubba. The past upsets him very much." He waited until the two had nodded in understanding. Then he looked down at me. His dark brown eyes looked black in the stark shadows cast by the overhead lights. His skin had the pale gleam that said "vampire." "Sookie, what's happened?"

I gave him a condensed version of Mr. Cataliades's message. Since Bill and I had broken up when he was unfaithful to me, we'd been trying to establish some other workable relationship. He was proving to be a reliable friend, and I was grateful for his presence.

"Did the queen order Hadley's death?" Bill asked my visitors.

Mr. Cataliades gave a good impression of being shocked. "Oh, no!" he exclaimed. "Her Highness would never cause the death of someone she held so dear."

Okay, here came another shock. "Ah, what kind of dear . . . ? How dear did the queen hold my cousin?" I asked. I wanted to be sure I was interpreting the implication correctly.

Mr. Cataliades gave me an old-fashioned look. "She held Hadley dearly," he said.

Okay, I got it.

Every vampire territory had a king or queen, and with that title came power. But the Queen of Louisiana had extra status, since she was seated in New Orleans, which was the most popular city in the United States if you were one of the undead. Since vampire tourism now accounted for so much of the city's revenue, even the humans of New Orleans listened to the queen's wants and wishes, in an unofficial way. "If Hadley was such a big favorite of the queen's, who'd be fool enough to stake her?" I asked.

"The Fellowship of the Sun," said Waldo, and I jumped. The vampire had been silent so long, I'd assumed he wasn't ever going to speak. The vampire's voice was as creaky and peculiar as his appearance. "Do you know the city well?"

I shook my head. I'd only been to the Big Easy once, on a school field trip.

"You are familiar, perhaps, with the cemeteries that are called the Cities of the Dead?"

I nodded. Bill said, "Yes," and Bubba muttered, "Uh-huh."

Several cemeteries in New Orleans had aboveground crypts because the water table in southern Louisiana was too high to allow ordinary belowground burials. The crypts look like small white houses, and they're decorated and carved in some cases, so these very old burial grounds are called the Cities of the Dead. The historic cemeteries are fascinating and sometimes dangerous. There are living predators to be feared in the Cities of the Dead, and tourists are cautioned to visit them in large, guided parties and to leave at the end of the day.

"Hadley and I had gone to St. Louis Number One that night, right after we rose, to conduct a ritual." Waldo's face looked quite expressionless. The thought that this man had been the chosen companion of my cousin, even if just for an evening's excursion, was simply astounding. "They leaped from behind the tombs around us. The Fellowship fanatics were armed with holy items, stakes, and garlic—the usual paraphernalia. They were stupid enough to have gold crosses."

The Fellowship refused to believe that all vampires could not be restrained by holy items, despite all the evidence. Holy items worked on the very old vampires, the ones who had been brought up to be devout believers. The newer vampires only suffered from crosses if they were silver. Silver would burn any vampire. Oh, a wooden cross might have an effect on a vamp—if it was driven through his heart.

"We fought valiantly, Hadley and I, but in the end, there were too many for us, and they killed Hadley. I escaped with some severe knife wounds." His paper white face looked more regretful than tragic.

I tried not to think about Aunt Linda and what she would have had to say about her daughter becoming a vampire. Aunt Linda would have been even more shocked by the circumstances of Hadley's death: by assassination, in a famous cemetery reeking of Gothic atmosphere, in the company of this grotesque creature. Of course, all these exotic trappings wouldn't have devastated Aunt Linda as much as the stark fact of Hadley's murder.

I was more detached. I'd written Hadley off long ago. I'd never thought I would see her again, so I had a little spare emotional room to think of other things. I still wondered, painfully, why Hadley hadn't come home to see us. She might have been afraid, being a young vampire, that her bloodlust would rise at an embarrassing time and she'd find herself yearning to suck on someone inappropriate. She might have been shocked by the change in her own nature; Bill had told me over and over that vampires were human no longer, that they were emotional about different things than humans. Their appetites and their need for secrecy had shaped the older vampires irrevocably.

But Hadley had never had to operate under those laws; she'd been made vampire after the Great Revelation, when vampires had revealed their presence to the world.

And the post-puberty Hadley, the one I was less fond of, wouldn't have been caught dead or alive with someone like Waldo. Hadley had been popular in high school, and she'd certainly been human enough then to fall prey to all the teenage stereotypes. She'd been mean to kids who weren't popular, or she'd just ignored them. Her life had been completely taken up by her clothes and her makeup and her own cute self.

She'd been a cheerleader, until she'd started adopting the Goth image.

"You said you two were in the cemetery to perform a ritual. What ritual?" I asked Waldo, just to gain some time to think. "Surely Hadley wasn't a witch as well." I'd run across a werewolf witch before, but never a vampire spell caster.

"There are traditions among the vampires of New Orleans," Mr. Cataliades said carefully. "One of these traditions is that the blood of the dead can raise the dead, at least temporarily. For conversational purposes, you understand."

Mr. Cataliades certainly didn't have any throwaway lines. I had to think about every sentence that came out of his mouth. "Hadley wanted to talk to a dead person?" I asked, once I'd digested his latest bombshell.

"Yes," said Waldo, chipping in again. "She wanted to talk to Marie Laveau."

"The voodoo queen? Why?" You couldn't live in Louisiana and not know the legend of Marie Laveau, a woman whose magical power had fascinated both black and white people, at a time when black women had no power at all.

"Hadley thought she was related to her." Waldo seemed to be sneering.

Okay, now I knew he was making it up. "Duh! Marie Laveau was African-American, and my family is white," I pointed out.

"This would be through her father's side," Waldo said calmly.

Aunt Linda's husband, Carey Delahoussaye, had come from New Orleans, and he'd been of French descent. His family had been there for several generations. He'd bragged about it until my whole family had gotten sick of his pride. I wondered if Uncle Carey had realized that his Creole bloodline had been enriched by a little African-American DNA somewhere back in the day. I had only a child's memory of Uncle Carey, but I figured that piece of knowledge would have been his most closely guarded secret.

Hadley, on the other hand, would have thought being descended from the notorious Marie Laveau was really cool. I found myself giving Waldo a little more credence. Where Hadley would've gotten such information, I couldn't imagine. Of course, I also couldn't imagine her as a lover of women, but evidently that had been her choice. My cousin Hadley, the cheerleader, had become a vampire lesbian voodooienne. Who knew?

I felt glutted with information I hadn't had time to absorb, but I was anxious to hear the whole story. I gestured to the emaciated vampire to continue.

"We put the three X's on the tomb," Waldo said. "As people do. Voodoo devotees believe this ensures their wish will be granted. And then Hadley cut herself, and let the blood drip on the stone, and she called out the magic words."

"Abracadabra, please, and thank you," I said automatically, and Waldo glared at me.

"You ought not to make fun," he said. With some notable exceptions, vampires are not known for their senses of humor, and Waldo was definitely a serious guy. His red-rimmed eyes glared at me.

"Is this really a tradition, Bill?" I asked. I no longer cared if the two men from New Orleans knew I didn't trust them.

"Yes," Bill said. "I haven't ever tried it myself, because I think the dead should be left alone. But I've seen it done."

"Does it work?" I was startled.

"Yes. Sometimes."

"Did it work for Hadley?" I asked Waldo.

The vampire glared at me. "No," he hissed. "Her intent was not pure enough."

"And these fanatics, they were just hiding among the tombs, waiting to jump out at you?"

"Yes," Waldo said. "I told you."

"And you, with your vampire hearing and smell, you didn't know there were people in the cemetery around you?" To my left, Bubba stirred. Even a vamp as dim as the too hastily recruited Bubba could see the sense of my question.

"Perhaps I knew there were people," Waldo said haughtily, "but those cemeteries are popular at night with criminals and whores. I didn't distinguish which people were making the noises."

"Waldo and Hadley were both favorites of the queen," Mr. Cataliades said admonishingly. His tone suggested that any favorite of the queen's was above reproach. But that wasn't what his words were saying. I looked at him thoughtfully. At the same moment, I felt Bill shift beside me. We hadn't been soul mates, I guess, since our relationship hadn't worked out, but at odd moments we seemed to think alike, and this was one of those moments. I wished I could read Bill's mind for once—though the great recommendation of Bill as a lover had been that I couldn't. Telepaths don't have an easy time of it when it comes to love affairs. In fact, Mr. Cataliades was the only one on the scene who had a brain I could scan, and he was none too human.

I thought about asking him what he was, but that seemed kind of tacky. Instead, I asked Bubba if he'd round up some folding yard chairs so we could all sit down, and while that was being arranged, I went in the house and heated up some TrueBlood for the three vampires and iced some Mountain Dew for Mr. Cataliades, who professed himself to be delighted with the offer.

While I was in the house, standing in front of the microwave and staring at it like it was some kind of oracle, I thought of just locking the door and letting them all do what they would. I had an ominous sense of the way the night was going, and I was tempted to let it take its course without me. But Hadley had been my cousin. On a whim, I took her picture down from the wall to give it a closer look.

All the pictures my grandmother had hung were still up;

despite her death, I continued to think of the house as hers. The first picture was of Hadley at age six, with one front tooth. She was holding a big drawing of a dragon. I hung it back beside the picture of Hadley at ten, skinny and pigtailed, her arms around Jason and me. Next to it was the picture taken by the reporter for the parish paper, when Hadley had been crowned Miss Teen Bon Temps. At fifteen, she'd been radiantly happy in her rented white sequined gown, glittering crown on her head, flowers in her arms. The last picture had been taken during Hadley's junior year. By then, Hadley had begun using drugs, and she was all Goth: heavy eye makeup, black hair, crimson lips. Uncle Carey had left Aunt Linda some years before this incarnation, moved back to his proud New Orleans family; and by the time Hadley left, too, Aunt Linda had begun feeling bad. A few months after Hadley ran away, we'd finally gotten my father's sister to go to a doctor, and he'd found the cancer.

In the years since then, I'd often wondered if Hadley had ever found out her mother was sick. It made a difference to me. If she'd known but hadn't come home, that was a horse of one color. If she'd never known, that was a horse of a different one. Now that I knew she had crossed over and become the living dead, I had a new option. Maybe Hadley had known, but she just hadn't cared.

I wondered who had told Hadley she might be descended from Marie Laveau. It must have been someone who'd done enough research to sound convincing, someone who'd studied Hadley enough to know how much she'd enjoy the piquancy of being related to such a notorious woman.

I carried the drinks outside on a tray, and we all sat in a circle on my old lawn furniture. It was a bizarre gathering: the strange Mr. Cataliades, a telepath, and three vampires—

though one of those was as addled as a vampire can be and still call himself undead.

When I was seated, Mr. Cataliades passed me a sheaf of papers, and I peered at them. The outside light was good enough for raking but not really good for reading. Bill's eyes were twenty times stronger than mine, so I passed the papers over to him.

"Your cousin left you some money and the contents of her apartment," Bill said. "You're her executor, too."

I shrugged. "Okay," I said. I knew Hadley couldn't have had much. Vampires are pretty good at amassing nest eggs, but Hadley could only have been a vampire for a very few years.

Mr. Cataliades raised his nearly invisible brows. "You don't seem excited."

"I'm a little more interested in how Hadley met her death."

Waldo looked offended. "I've described the circumstances to you. Do you want a blow-by-blow account of the fight? It was unpleasant, I assure you."

I looked at him for a few moments. "What happened to you?" I asked. This was very rude, to ask someone what on earth had made him so weird-looking, but common sense told me that there was more to learn. I had an obligation to my cousin, an obligation unaffected by any legacy she'd left me. Maybe this was why Hadley had left me something in her will. She knew I'd ask questions, and God love my brother, he wouldn't.

Rage flashed across Waldo's features, and then it was like he'd wiped his face with some kind of emotion eraser. The paper white skin relaxed into calm lines and his eyes were calm. "When I was human, I was an albino," Waldo said stiffly, and I felt the knee-jerk horror of someone who's been unpardonably curious about a disability. Just as I was about to apologize, Mr. Cataliades intervened again.

"And, of course," the big man said smoothly, "he's been punished by the queen."

This time, Waldo didn't restrain his glare. "Yes," he said finally. "The queen immersed me in a tank for a few years."

"A tank of what?" I was all at sea.

"Saline solution," Bill said, very quietly. "I've heard of this punishment. That's why he's wrinkled, as you see."

Waldo pretended not to hear Bill's aside, but Bubba opened his mouth. "You're sure 'nuff wrinkled, man, but don't you worry. The chicks like a man who's different."

Bubba was a kind vampire and well-intentioned.

I tried to imagine being in a tank of seawater for years and years. Then I tried not to imagine it. I could only wonder what Waldo had done to merit such a punishment. "And you were a favorite?" I asked.

Waldo nodded, with a certain dignity. "I had that honor."

I hoped I'd never receive such an honor. "And Hadley was, too?"

Waldo's face remained placid, though a muscle twitched in his jaw. "For a time."

Mr. Cataliades said, "The queen was pleased with Hadley's enthusiasm and childlike ways. Hadley was only one of a series of favorites. Eventually, the queen's favor would have fallen on someone else, and Hadley would have had to carve out another place in the queen's entourage."

Waldo looked quite pleased at that and nodded. "That's the pattern."

I couldn't get why I was supposed to care, and Bill made a small movement that he instantly stilled. I caught it out of the corner of my eye, and I realized Bill didn't want me to speak. Pooh on him; I hadn't been going to, anyway.

Mr. Cataliades said, "Of course, your cousin was a little different from her predecessors. Wouldn't you say, Waldo?"

"No," Waldo said. "In time, it would have been just like before." He seemed to bite his lip to stop himself from talking; not a smart move for a vampire. A red drop of blood formed, sluggishly. "The queen would have tired of her. I know it. It was the girl's youth; it was the fact that she was one of the new vampires who has never known the shadows. Tell our queen that, Cataliades, when you return to New Orleans. If you hadn't kept the privacy glass up the whole trip, I could have discussed this with you as I drove. You don't have to shun me, as though I were a leper."

Mr. Cataliades shrugged. "I didn't want your company," he said. "Now we'll never know how long Hadley would have reigned as favorite, will we, Waldo?"

We were on to something here, and we were being goaded and prodded in that direction by Waldo's companion, Mr. Cataliades. I wondered why. For the moment, I'd follow his lead. "Hadley was real pretty," I said. "Maybe the queen would've given her a permanent position."

"Pretty girls glut the market," Waldo said. "Stupid humans. They don't know what our queen can do to them."

"If she wants to," Bill murmured. "If this Hadley had a knack for delighting the queen, if she had Sookie's charm, then she might have been happy and favored for many years."

"And I guess you'd be out on your ass, Waldo," I said prosaically. "So tell me, were there really fanatics in the cemetery? Or just one skinny, white, wrinkled fanatic, jealous and desperate?"

Then, suddenly, we were all standing, all but Mr. Cataliades, who was reaching into the briefcase.

Before my eyes, Waldo turned into something even less human. His fangs ran out, and his eyes glowed red. He became even thinner, his body folding in on itself. Beside me, Bill and Bubba changed, too. I didn't want to look at them when they were angry. Seeing my friends change like that was even worse than seeing my enemies do it. Full fighting mode is just scary.

"You can't accuse a servant of the queen," Waldo said, and he actually hissed.

Then Mr. Cataliades proved himself capable of some surprises of his own, as if I'd doubted it. Moving quickly and lightly, he rose from his lawn chair and tossed a silver lariat around the vampire's head, large enough in circumference to circle Waldo's shoulders. With a grace that startled me, he drew it tight at the critical moment, pinning Waldo's arms to his sides.

I thought Waldo would go berserk, but the vampire surprised me by holding still. "You'll die for this," Waldo said to the big round man, and Mr. Cataliades smiled at him.

"I think not," he said. "Here, Miss Stackhouse."

He tossed something in my direction, and quicker than I could watch, Bill's hand shot out to intercept it. We both stared at what Bill was holding in his hand. It was polished, sharp, and wooden; a hardwood stake.

"What's up with this?" I asked Mr. Cataliades, moving closer to the long black limo.

"My dear Miss Stackhouse, the queen wanted you to have the pleasure."

Waldo, who had been glaring with considerable defiance at everyone in the clearing, seemed to deflate when he heard what Mr. Cataliades had to say.

"She knows," the albino vampire said, and the only way I can describe his voice is "heartbroken." I shivered. He loved his queen, really loved her.

"Yes," the big man said, almost gently. "She sent Valentine and Charity to the cemetery immediately, when you rushed in with your news. They found no traces of human attack on what was left of Hadley. Only your smell, Waldo."

"She sent me here with you," Waldo said, almost whispering.

"Our queen wanted Hadley's kin to have the right of execution," Mr. Cataliades said.

I came closer to Waldo, until I was as close as I could get. The silver had weakened the vampire, though I had a feeling that he wouldn't have struggled even if the chain hadn't been made of the metal that vampires can't tolerate. Some of the fire had gone out of Waldo, though his upper lip drew back from his fangs as I put the tip of the stake over his heart. I thought of Hadley, and I wondered, if she were in my shoes, could she do this?

"Can you drive the limo, Mr. Cataliades?" I asked.

"Yes, ma'am, I can."

"Could you drive yourself back to New Orleans?"

"That was always my plan."

I pressed down on the wood, until I could tell it was hurting him. His eyes were closed. I had staked a vampire before, but it had been to save my life and Bill's. Waldo was a pitiful thing. There was nothing romantic or dramatic about this vampire. He was simply vicious. I was sure he could do extreme damage when the situation called for it, and I was sure he had killed my cousin Hadley.

Bill said, "I'll do it for you, Sookie." His voice was smooth and cold, as always, and his hand on my arm was cool.

"I can help," Bubba offered. "You'd do it for me, Miss Sookie."

"Your cousin was a bitch and a whore," Waldo said, unexpectedly. I met his red eyes.

"I expect she was," I said. "I guess I just can't kill you." My hand, the one holding the stake, dropped to my side.

"You have to kill me," Waldo said, with the arrogance of surety. "The queen has sent me here to be killed."

"I'm just gonna have to ship you right back to the queen," I said. "I can't do it."

"Get your whoremonger to do it; he's more than willing."

Bill was looking more vampiric by the second, and he tugged the stake from my fingers.

"He's trying to commit suicide by cop, Bill," I said.

Bill looked puzzled, and so did Bubba. Mr. Cataliades's round face was unreadable.

"He's trying to make us mad enough, or scared enough, to kill him, because he can't kill himself," I said. "He's sure the queen will do something much, much worse to him than I would. And he's right."

"The queen was trying to give you the gift of vengeance," Mr. Cataliades said. "Won't you take it? She may not be happy with you if you send him back."

"That's really her problem," I said. "Isn't it?"

"I think it might be very much your problem," Bill said quietly.

"Well, that just bites," I said. "You . . ." I paused, and told myself not to be a fool. "You were very kind to bring Waldo down here, Mr. Cataliades, and you were very clever in steering me around to the truth." I took a deep breath and considered. "I appreciate your bringing down the legal papers, which I'll look over at a calmer moment." I thought I'd covered everything. "Now, if you'd be so good as to pop the trunk open, I'll ask Bill and Bubba to put him in there." I jerked my head toward the silver-bound vampire, standing in silence not a yard away.

At that moment, when we were all thinking of something else, Waldo threw himself at me, jaws open wide like a snake's, fangs fully extended. I threw myself backward, but I knew it wouldn't be enough. Those fangs would rip open my throat, and I would bleed out here in my own yard. But Bubba and Bill were not bound with silver, and with a speed that was terrifying in itself, they gripped the old vampire and knocked him to the ground. Quicker than any human could wink, Bill's arm rose and fell, and Waldo's red eyes looked down at the stake in his chest with profound satisfaction. In the next second, those eyes caved in and his long, thin body began the instant process of disintegration. You never have to bury a really dead vampire.

For a few long moments, we stayed frozen in the tableau; Mr. Cataliades was standing, I was on the ground on my butt, and Bubba and Bill were on their knees beside the thing that had been Waldo.

Then the limo door opened, and before Mr. Cataliades could scramble to help her out, the Queen of Louisiana stepped out of the vehicle.

She was beautiful, of course, but not in a fairy-tale princess sort of way. I don't know what I expected, but she wasn't it. While Bill and Bubba scrambled to their feet and then bowed deeply, I gave her a good once-over. She was wearing a very expensive midnight blue suit and high heels. Her hair was a rich reddish brown. Of course, she was pale as milk, but her eyes were large, tilted, and almost the same brown as her hair. Her fingernails were polished red, and somehow that seemed very weird. She wore no jewelry.

Now I knew why Mr. Cataliades had kept the privacy glass up during the trip north. And I was sure that the queen had ways of masking her presence from Waldo's senses, as well as his sight.

"Hello," I said uncertainly. "I'm . . ."

"I know who you are," she said. She had a faint accent; I thought it might be French. "Bill. Bubba."

Oooh-kay. So much for polite chitchat. I huffed out a breath and shut my mouth. No point in talking until she explained her presence. Bill and Bubba stood upright. Bubba was smiling. Bill wasn't.

The queen examined me head to toe, in a way I thought was downright rude. Since she was a queen, she was an old vampire, and the oldest ones, the ones who sought power in the vampire infrastructure, were among the scariest. It had been so long since she'd been human that there might not be much remembrance of humanity left in her.

"I don't see what all the fuss is about," she said, shrugging.

My lips twitched. I just couldn't help it. My grin spread across my face, and I tried to hide it with my hand. The queen eyed me quizzically.

"She smiles when she's nervous," Bill said.

I did, but that's not why I was smiling now.

"You were going to send Waldo back to me, for me to torture and kill," the queen said to me. Her face was quite blank. I couldn't tell if she approved or disapproved, thought I was clever or thought I was a fool.

"Yes," I said. The shortest answer was definitely the best.

"He forced your hand."

"Uh-huh."

"He was too frightened of me to risk returning to New Orleans with my friend Mr. Cataliades."

"Yes." I was getting good at one-word answers.

"I wonder if you engineered this whole thing."

"Yes" would not be the right answer here. I maintained silence.

"I'll find out," she said, with absolute certainty. "We'll meet again, Sookie Stackhouse. I was fond of your cousin, but even she was foolish enough to go to a cemetery alone with her bitterest enemy. She counted too much on the power of my name alone to protect her."

"Did Waldo ever tell you if Marie Laveau actually rose?" I asked, too overwhelmed with curiosity to let the question go unanswered.

She was getting back in the car as I spoke, and she paused with one foot inside the limo and one foot in the yard. Anyone else would have looked awkward, but not the Queen of Louisiana.

"Interesting," she said. "No, actually, he didn't. When you come to New Orleans, you and Bill can repeat the experiment."

I started to point out that unlike Hadley, I wasn't dead, but I had the sense to shut my mouth. She might have ordered me to become a vampire, and I was afraid, very afraid, that then Bill and Bubba would have held me down and made me so. That was too awful to think about, so I smiled at her.

After the queen was all settled in the limo, Mr. Cataliades bowed to me. "It's been a pleasure, Miss Stackhouse. If you have any questions about your cousin's estate, call me at the number on my business card. It's clipped to the papers."

"Thanks," I said, not trusting myself to say more. Besides, one-word answers never hurt. Waldo was almost disintegrated. Bits of him would be in my yard for a while. Yuck. "Where's Waldo? All over my yard," I could say to anyone who asked.

The night had clearly been too much for me. The limo purred out of my yard. Bill put his hand to my cheek, but I didn't lean into it. I was grateful to him for coming, and I told him so.

"You shouldn't be in danger," he said. Bill had a habit of using a word that changed the meaning of his statements, made them something ambiguous and unsettling. His dark eyes were fathomless pools. I didn't think I would ever understand him.

"Did I do good, Miss Sookie?" Bubba asked.

"You did great, Bubba," I said. "You did the right thing without me even having to tell you."

"You knew all along she was in the limo," Bubba said. "Didn't you, Miss Sookie?"

Bill looked at me, startled. I didn't meet his eyes. "Yes, Bubba," I said gently. "I knew. Before Waldo got out, I listened with my other sense, and I found two blank spots in the limo." That could only mean two vampires. So I'd known Cataliades had had a companion in the back of the limousine.

"But you played it all out like she wasn't there." Bill couldn't seem to grasp this. Maybe he didn't think I'd learned anything since I'd met him. "Did you know ahead of time that Waldo would make a try for you?"

"I suspected he might. He didn't want to go back to her mercies."

"So." Bill caught my arms and looked down at me. "Were you trying to make sure he died all along, or were you trying to send him back to the queen?"

"Yes," I said.

One-word answers never hurt.

LUCKY

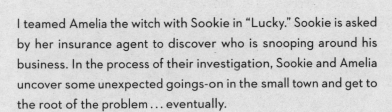

I teamed Amelia the witch with Sookie in "Lucky." Sookie is asked by her insurance agent to discover who is snooping around his business. In the process of their investigation, Sookie and Amelia uncover some unexpected goings-on in the small town and get to the root of the problem... eventually.

"Lucky" should be read right after *All Together Dead*.

AMELIA BROADWAY AND I were painting each other's toe-nails when my insurance agent knocked at the front door. I'd picked Roses on Ice. Amelia had opted for Mad Burgundy Cherry Glacé. She'd finished my feet, and I had about three toes to go on her left foot when Greg Aubert interrupted us.

Amelia had been living with me for months, and it had been kind of nice to have someone else sharing my old house. Amelia is a witch from New Orleans, and she had been stay-ing with me because she'd had a magical misfortune she didn't want any of her witch buddies in the Big Easy to know about. Also, since Katrina, she really didn't have anything to go home to, at least for a while. My little hometown of Bon Temps was swollen with refugees.

Greg Aubert had been to my house after I'd had a fire that caused a lot of damage. As far as I knew, I didn't have any in-surance needs at the moment. I was pretty curious about his purpose, I confess.

Amelia had glanced up at Greg, found his sandy hair and rimless glasses uninteresting, and completed painting her lit-tle toe while I ushered him to the wingback chair.

"Greg, this is my friend Amelia Broadway," I said. "Amelia, this is Greg Aubert."

Amelia looked at Greg with more interest. I'd told her Greg was a colleague of hers, in some respects. Greg's mom had been a witch, and he'd found using the craft very helpful in protecting his clients. Not a car got insured with Greg's agency without having a spell cast on it. I was the only one in Bon Temps who knew about Greg's little talent. Witchcraft wouldn't be popular in our devout little town. Greg always handed his clients a lucky rabbit's foot to keep in their new vehicles or homes.

After he turned down the obligatory offer of iced tea or water or Coke, Greg sat on the edge of the chair while I resumed my seat on one end of the couch. Amelia had the other end.

"I felt the wards when I drove up," Greg told Amelia. "Very impressive." He was trying real hard to keep his eyes off my tank top. I would have put on a bra if I'd known we were going to have company.

Amelia tried to look indifferent, and she might have shrugged if she hadn't been holding a bottle of nail polish. Amelia, tan and athletic, with short glossy brown hair, is not only pleased with her looks but really proud of her witchcraft abilities. "Nothing special," she said, with unconvincing modesty. She smiled at Greg, though.

"What can I do for you today, Greg?" I asked. I was due to go to work in an hour, and I had to change and pull my long hair up in a ponytail.

"I need your help," he said, yanking his gaze up to my face.

No beating around the bush with Greg.

"Okay, how?" If he could be direct, so could I.

"Someone's sabotaging my agency," he said. His voice was suddenly passionate, and I realized Greg was really close to a major breakdown. He wasn't quite the broadcaster Amelia was—I could read most thoughts Amelia had as clearly as if she'd spoken them—but I could certainly read his inner workings.

"Tell us about it," I said, because Amelia could not read Greg's mind.

"Oh, thanks," he said, as if I'd agreed to do something. I opened my mouth to correct this idea, but he plowed ahead.

"Last week I came into the office to find that someone had been through the files."

"You still have Marge Barker working for you?"

He nodded. A stray beam of sunlight winked off his glasses. It was October, and still warm in northern Louisiana. Greg got out a snowy handkerchief and patted his forehead. "I've got my wife, Christy; she comes in three days a week for half a day. And I've got Marge full-time." Christy, Greg's wife, was as sweet as Marge was sour.

"How'd you know someone had been through the files?" Amelia asked. She screwed on the top of the polish bottle and put it on the coffee table.

Greg took a deep breath. "I'd been thinking for a couple of weeks that someone had been in the office at night. But nothing was missing. Nothing was changed. My wards were okay. But two days ago, I got into the office to find that one of the drawers on our main filing cabinet was open. Of course, we lock them at night," he said. "We've got one of those filing systems that locks up when you turn a key in the top drawer. Almost all of the client files were at risk. But every day, last thing in the afternoon, Marge goes around and locks all the cabinets. What if someone suspects . . . what I do?"

I could see how that would shiver Greg down to his liver. "Did you ask Marge if she remembered locking the cabinet?"

"Sure I asked her. She got mad—you know Marge—and said she definitely did. My wife had worked that afternoon, but she couldn't remember if she watched Marge lock the cabinets or not. And Terry Bellefleur had dropped by at the last minute, wanting to check again on the insurance for his damn dog. He might have seen Marge lock up."

Greg sounded so irritated that I found myself defending Terry. "Greg, Terry doesn't like being the way he is, you know," I said, trying to gentle my voice. "He got messed up fighting for our country, and we got to cut him some slack."

Greg looked grumpy for a minute. Then he relaxed. "I know, Sookie," he said. "He's just been so hyped up about this dog."

"What's the story?" Amelia asked. If I have moments of curiosity, Amelia has an imperative urge. She wants to know everything about everybody. The telepathy should have gone to her, not me. She might actually have enjoyed it, instead of considering it a disability.

"Terry Bellefleur is Andy's cousin," I said. I knew Amelia had met Andy, a police detective, at Merlotte's. "He comes in after closing and cleans the bar. Sometimes he substitutes for Sam. Maybe not the few evenings you were working." Amelia filled in at the bar from time to time.

"Terry fought in Vietnam, got captured, and had a pretty bad time of it. He's got scars inside and out. The story about the dogs is this: Terry loves hunting dogs, and he keeps buying himself these expensive Catahoulas, and things keep happening to them. His current bitch has had puppies. He's just on pins and needles lest something happen to her and the babies."

"You're saying Terry is a little unstable?"

"He has bad times," I said. "Sometimes he's just fine."

"Oh," Amelia said, and a lightbulb might as well have popped on above her head. "He's the guy with the long gray

ing auburn hair, going bald at the front? Scars on his cheek?
Big truck?"

"That's him," I said.

Amelia turned to Greg. "You said for at least a couple of
weeks you'd felt someone had been in the building after it
closed. That couldn't be your wife, or this Marge?"

"My wife is with me all evening unless we have to take the
kids to different events. And I don't know why Marge would
feel she had to come back at night. She's there during the day,
every day, and often by herself. Well, the spells that protect
the building seem okay to me. But I keep recasting them."

"Tell me about your spells," Amelia said, getting down to
her favorite part.

She and Greg talked spells for a few minutes, while I listened but didn't comprehend. I couldn't even understand
their thoughts.

Then Amelia said, "What do you want, Greg? I mean, why
did you come to us?"

He'd actually come to me, but it was kind of nice to be an
"us."

Greg looked from Amelia to me, and said, "I want Sookie to
find out who opened my files, and why. I worked hard to become the best-selling Pelican State agent in northern Louisiana, and I don't want my business fouled up now. My son's
about to go to Rhodes in Memphis, and it ain't cheap."

"Why are you coming to me instead of the police?"

"I don't want anyone else finding out what I am," he said,
embarrassed but determined. "And it might come up if the
police start looking into things at my office. Plus, you know,
Sookie, I got you a real good payout on your kitchen."

My kitchen had been burned down by an arsonist months

before. I'd just finished getting it all rebuilt. "Greg, that's your job," I said. "I don't see where the gratitude comes in."

"Well, I have a certain amount of discretion in arson cases," he said. "I could have told the home office that I thought you did it yourself."

"You wouldn't have done that," I said calmly, though I was seeing a side of Greg I didn't like. Amelia practically had flames coming out of her nose, she was so incensed. But I could tell that Greg was already ashamed of bringing up the possibility.

"No," he said, looking down at his hands. "I guess I wouldn't. I'm sorry I said that, Sookie. I'm scared someone'll tell the whole town what I do, why people I insure are so . . . lucky. Can you see what you can find out?"

"Bring your family into the bar for supper tonight, give me a chance to look them over," I said. "That's the real reason you want me to find out, right? You suspect your family might be involved. Or your staff."

He nodded, and he looked wretched.

"I'll try to get in there tomorrow to talk to Marge. I'll say you wanted me to drop by."

"Yeah, I make calls from my cell phone sometimes, ask people to come in," he said. "Marge would believe it."

Amelia said, "What can I do?"

"Well, can you be with her?" Greg said. "Sookie can do things you can't, and vice versa. Maybe between the two of you . . ."

"Okay," Amelia said, giving Greg the benefit of her broad and dazzling smile. Her dad must have paid dearly for the perfect white smile of Amelia Broadway, witch and waitress.

Bob the cat padded in just at that moment, as if belatedly

realizing we had a guest. Bob jumped on the chair right beside Greg and examined him with care.

Greg looked down at Bob just as intently. "Have you been doing something you shouldn't, Amelia?"

"There's nothing strange about Bob," Amelia said, which was not true. She scooped up the black-and-white cat in her arms and nuzzled his soft fur. "He's just a big ole cat. Aren't you, Bob?" She was relieved when Greg dropped the subject. He got up to leave.

"I'll be grateful for anything you can do to help me," he said. With an abrupt switch to his professional persona, he said, "Here, have an extra lucky rabbit's foot," and reached in his pocket to hand me a lump of fake fur.

"Thanks," I said, and decided to put it in my bedroom. I could use some luck in that direction.

After Greg left, I scrambled into my work clothes (black pants and white boatneck T-shirt with MERLOTTE'S embroidered over the left breast), brushed my long blond hair and secured it in a ponytail, and left for the bar, wearing Teva sandals to show off my beautiful toenails. Amelia, who wasn't scheduled to work that night, said she might go have a good look around the insurance agency.

"Be careful," I said. "If someone really is prowling around there, you don't want to run into a bad situation."

"I'll zap 'em with my wonderful witch powers," she said, only half joking. Amelia had a fine opinion of her own abilities, which led to mistakes like Bob. He had actually been a thin young witch, handsome in a nerdy way. While spending the night with Amelia, Bob had been the victim of one of her less successful attempts at major magic. "Besides, who'd want to break into an insurance agency?" she said quickly, having read the doubt on my face. "This whole thing is ridiculous. I do want to check out Greg's magic, though, and see if it's been tampered with."

"You can do that?"

"Hey, standard stuff."

To MY RELIEF, the bar was quiet that night. It was Wednesday, which is never a very big day at supper time, since lots of Bon Temps citizens go to church on Wednesday night. Sam Merlotte, my boss, was busy counting cases of beer in the storeroom when I got there; that was how light the crowd was. The waitresses on duty were mixing their own drinks.

I stowed my purse in the drawer in Sam's desk that he keeps empty for them, then went out front to take over my tables. The woman I was relieving, a Katrina evacuee I hardly knew, gave me a wave and departed.

After an hour, Greg Aubert came in with his family as he'd promised. You seated yourself at Merlotte's, and I surreptitiously nodded to a table in my section. Dad, Mom, and two teenagers, the nuclear family. Greg's wife, Christy, had medium-light hair like Greg, and like Greg she wore glasses. She had a comfortable middle-aged body, and she'd never seemed exceptional in any way. Little Greg (and that's what they called him) was about three inches taller than his father, about thirty pounds heavier, and about ten IQ points smarter. That is, book smart. Like most nineteen-year-olds, he was pretty dumb about the world. Lindsay, the daughter, had lightened her hair five shades and squeezed herself into an outfit at least a size too small, and could hardly wait to get away from her folks so she could meet the Forbidden Boyfriend.

While I took their drink and food orders, I discovered that (a) Lindsay had the mistaken idea that she looked like Christina Aguilera, (b) Little Greg thought he would never go into insurance because it was so boring, and (c) Christy thought Greg might be interested in another woman because he'd been so distracted lately. As you can imagine, it takes a lot of mental doing to separate what I'm getting from people's minds from what I'm hearing directly from their mouths, which accounts for the strained smile I often wear—the smile that's led some people to think I'm just crazy.

After I'd brought them their drinks and turned in their food order, I puttered around studying the Aubert family. They seemed so typical it just hurt. Little Greg thought about his girlfriend mostly, and I learned more than I wanted to know.

Greg was just worried.

Christy was thinking about the dryer in their laundry room, wondering if it was time to get a new one.

See? Most people's thoughts are like that. Christy was also weighing Marge Barker's virtues (efficiency, loyalty) against the fact that she seriously disliked the woman.

Lindsay was thinking about her secret boyfriend. Like teenage girls everywhere, she was convinced her parents were the most boring people in the universe and had pokers up their asses besides. They didn't understand anything. Lindsay herself didn't understand why Dustin wouldn't take her to meet his folks, why he wouldn't let her see where he lived. No one but Dustin knew how poetic her soul was, how fascinating she truly could be, how misunderstood she was.

If I had a dime for every time I'd heard that from a teenager's brain, I'd be as rich as John Edward, the psychic.

I heard the bell ding in the service window, and I trotted over to get the Auberts' order from our current cook. I loaded my arms with the plates and hustled them over to the table. I had to endure a full-body scan from Little Greg, but that was par for the course, too. Guys can't help it. Lindsay didn't register me at all. She was wondering why Dustin was so secretive about his daytime activities. Shouldn't he be in school?

Okay, now. We were getting somewhere.

But then Lindsay began thinking about her D in algebra and how she was going to get grounded when her parents found out and then she wouldn't get to see Dustin for a while unless she climbed out of her bedroom window at two in the morning. She was seriously considering going all the way.

Lindsay made me feel sad and old. And very smart.

By the time the Aubert family paid their bill and left, I was tired of all of them, and my head was exhausted (a weird feeling, and one I simply can't describe).

I plodded through work the rest of the night, glad to the very ends of my Roses on Ice toenails when I headed out the back door.

"Psst," said a voice from behind me while I was unlocking my car door.

With a stifled shriek, I swung around with my keys in my hand, ready to attack.

"It's me," Amelia said gleefully.

"Dammit, Amelia, don't sneak up on me like that!" I sagged against the car.

"Sorry," she said, but she didn't sound very sorry. "Hey," she continued, "I've been over by the insurance agency. Guess what!"

"What?" My lack of enthusiasm seemed to register with Amelia.

"You tired or something?" she asked.

"I just had an evening of listening in on the world's most

typical family," I said. "Greg's worried, Christy's worried, Little Greg is horny, and Lindsay has a secret love."

"I know," Amelia said. "And guess what?"

"He might be a vamp."

"Oh." She sagged. "You already knew?"

"Not for sure. I know other fascinating stuff, though. I know he understands Lindsay as she's never been understood before in her whole underappreciated life, that he just might be The One, and that she's thinking of having sex with this goober."

"Well, I know where he lives. Let's go by there. You drive; I need to get some stuff ready." We got into Amelia's car. I took the driver's seat. Amelia began fumbling in her purse through the many little Ziplocs that filled it. They were all full of magic ready to go: herbs and other ingredients. Bat wings, for all I knew.

"He lives by himself in a big house with a FOR SALE sign in the front yard. No furniture. Yet he looks like he's eighteen." Amelia pointed at the house, which was dark and isolated.

"Hmmm." Our eyes met.

"What do you think?" Amelia asked.

"Vampire, almost surely."

"Could be. But why would a strange vampire be in Bon Temps? Why don't any of the other vamps know about him?" It was all right to be a vampire in today's America, but the vamps were still trying to keep a low profile. They regulated themselves rigorously.

"How do you know they don't? Know about him, that is."

Good question. Would the area vampires be obliged to tell me? It wasn't like I was an official vampire greeter or anything.

"Amelia, you went looking around after a vampire? Not smart."

"It wasn't like I knew he might be fangy when I started. I just followed him after I saw him cruising around the Auberts' house."

"I think he's in the middle of seducing Lindsay," I said. "I better make a call."

"But does this have anything to do with Greg's business?"

"I don't know. Where is this boy now?"

"He's at Lindsay's house. He finally just parked outside. I guess he's waiting for her to come out."

"Crap." I pulled in a little way down the street from the Auberts' ranch-style home. I flipped open my cell phone to call Fangtasia. Maybe it's not a good sign when the area vampire bar is on your speed dial.

"Fangtasia, the bar with a bite," said an unfamiliar voice. Just as Bon Temps and our whole area was saturated with human evacuees, the vampire community in Shreveport was, too.

"This is Sookie Stackhouse. I need to speak with Eric, please," I said.

"Oh, the telepath. Sorry, Miss Stackhouse. Eric and Pam are out tonight."

"Maybe you can tell me if any of the new vampires are staying in my town, Bon Temps?"

"Let me inquire."

The voice was back after a few minutes. "Clancy says no." Clancy was like Eric's third-in-command, and I was not his favorite person. You'll notice Clancy didn't even ask the phone guy to find out why I needed to know. I thanked the unknown vampire for his trouble and hung up.

I was stumped. Pam, Eric's second-in-command, was sort of a buddy of mine, and Eric was, occasionally, something more than that. Since they weren't there, I'd have to call our local vampire, Bill Compton.

I sighed. "I'm going to have to call Bill," I said, and Amelia knew enough of my history to understand why the idea was so traumatic. And then I braced myself and dialed.

"Yes?" said a cool voice.

Thank goodness. I'd been scared the new girlfriend, Selah, would answer.

"Bill, this is Sookie. Eric and Pam are out of touch, and I have a problem."

"What?"

Bill has always been a man of few words.

"There's a young man in town we think is a vampire. Have you met him?"

"Here in Bon Temps?" Bill was clearly surprised and displeased.

That answered my question. "Yes, and Clancy told me they hadn't farmed out any new vamps to Bon Temps. So I thought maybe you'd encountered this individual?"

"No, which means he's probably taking care not to cross my path. Where are you?"

"We're parked near the Auberts' house. He's interested in the daughter, a teenager. We've pulled into the driveway of a house for sale across the street, middle of the block on Hargrove."

"I'll be there very soon. Don't approach him."

As if I would. "He thinks I'm stupid enough—" I began, and Amelia already had her "Indignant for You" face on when the driver's door was yanked open and a white hand latched onto my shoulder. I squawked until the other hand clamped over my mouth.

"Shut up, breather," said a voice that was even colder than

Bill's. "Are you the one that's been following me around all night?"

Then I realized that he didn't know Amelia was in the passenger's seat. That was good.

Since I couldn't speak, I nodded slightly.

"Why?" he growled. "What do you want with me?" He shook me like I was a dustcloth, and I thought all my bones would come disjointed.

Then Amelia leaped from the other side of the car and darted over to us, tossing the contents of a Ziploc on his head. Of course, I had no idea what she was saying, but the effect was dramatic. After a jolt of astonishment, the vampire froze. The problem was, he froze with me clasped with my back to his chest in an unbreakable hold. I was mashed against him, and his left hand was still hard over my mouth, his right hand around my waist. So far, the investigative team of Sookie Stackhouse, telepath, and Amelia Broadway, witch, was not doing a top-flight job.

"Pretty good, huh?" Amelia said.

I managed to move my head a fraction. "Yes, if I could breathe," I said. I wished I hadn't wasted breath speaking.

Then Bill was there, surveying the situation.

"You stupid woman, Sookie's trapped," Bill said. "Undo the spell."

Under the streetlight, Amelia looked sullen. Undoing was not her best thing, I realized with some anxiety. I couldn't do anything else, so I waited while she worked on the counter-spell.

"If this doesn't work, it'll only take me a second to break his arm," Bill told me. I nodded . . . well, I moved my head a fraction of an inch . . . because that was all I could do. I was getting pretty breathless.

Suddenly there was a little *pop!* in the air, and the younger vampire let go of me to launch himself at Bill—who wasn't there. Bill was behind him, and he grabbed one of the boy's arms and twisted it up and back. The boy screamed, and down they went to the ground. I wondered if anyone was going to call the police. This was a lot of noise and activity for a residential neighborhood after one o'clock. But no lights came on.

"Now, talk." Bill was absolutely determined, and I guess the boy knew it.

"What's your problem?" the boy demanded. He had spiked brown hair and a lean build and a couple of diamond studs in his nose. "This woman's been following me around. I need to know who she is."

Bill looked up at me questioningly. I jerked my head toward Amelia.

"You didn't even grab the right woman," Bill said. He sounded kind of disappointed in the youngster. "Why are you here in Bon Temps?"

"Getting away from Katrina," the boy said. "My sire was staked by a human when we ran out of bottled blood substitute after the flood. I stole a car outside of New Orleans, changed the license plates, and got out of town. I reached here at daylight. I found an empty house with a FOR SALE sign and a windowless bathroom, so I moved in. I've been going out with a local girl. I take a sip every night. She's none the wiser," he sneered.

"What's your interest?" Bill asked me.

"Have you two been going into her dad's office at night?" I asked.

"Yeah, once or twice." He smirked. "Her dad's office has a couch in it." I wanted to slap the shit out of him, maybe smacking the jewelry in his nose just by accident.

"How long have you been a vampire?" Bill asked.

"Ah . . . maybe two months."

Okay, that explained a lot. "So that's why he didn't know to check in with Eric. That's why he doesn't realize what he's doing is foolish and liable to get him staked."

"There's only so much excuse for stupidity," Bill said.

"Have you gone through the files in there?" I asked the boy, who was looking a little dazed.

"What?"

"Did you go through the files in the insurance office?"

"Uh, no. Why would I do that? I was just loving up the girl, to get a little sip, you know? I was real careful not to take too much. I don't have any money to buy artificial stuff."

"Oh, you are *so dumb*." Amelia was fed up with this kid. "For goodness' sake, learn something about your condition. Stranded vampires can get help just like stranded people. You just ask the Red Cross for some synthetic blood, and they dole it out free."

"Or you could have found out who the sheriff of the area is," Bill said. "Eric would never turn away a vampire in need. What if someone had found you biting this girl? She's under the age of consent, I gather?" For blood "donation" to a vampire.

"Yeah," I said, when Dustin looked blank. "It's Lindsay, daughter of Greg Aubert, my insurance agent. He wanted us to find out who'd been going into his building at night. Called in a favor to get me and Amelia to investigate."

"He should do his own dirty work," Bill said quite calmly. But his hands were clenched. "Listen, boy, what's your name?"

"Dustin." He'd even given Lindsay his real name.

"Well, Dustin, tonight we go to Fangtasia, the bar in Shreveport that Eric Northman uses as his headquarters. He will talk to you there, decide what to do with you."

"I'm a free vampire. I go where I want."

"Not within Area Five, you don't. You go to Eric, the area sheriff."

Bill marched the young vampire off into the night, probably to load him into his car and get him to Shreveport.

Amelia said, "I'm sorry, Sookie."

"At least you stopped him from breaking my neck," I said, trying to sound philosophical about it. "We still have our original problem. It wasn't Dustin who went through the files, though I'm guessing it was Dustin and Lindsay going into the office at night that disturbed the magic. How could they get past it?"

"After Greg told me his spell, I realized he wasn't much of a witch. Lindsay's a member of the family. With Greg's spell to ward against outsiders, that made a difference," Amelia said. "And sometimes vampires register as a void on spells created for humans. After all, they're not alive. I made my 'freeze' spell vampire specific."

"Who else can get through magic spells and work mischief?"

"Magical nulls," she said.

"Huh?"

"There are people who can't be affected by magic," Amelia said. "They're rare, but they exist. I've only met one before."

"How can you detect nulls? Do they give off a special vibration or something?"

"Only very experienced witches can detect nulls without casting a spell on them that fails," Amelia admitted. "Greg probably has never encountered one."

"Let's go see Terry," I suggested. "He stays up all night."

The baying of a dog announced our arrival at Terry's cabin. Terry lived in the middle of three acres of woods. Terry liked being by himself most of the time, and any social needs he might feel were satisfied by an occasional stint of working as a bartender.

"That'll be Annie," I said, as the barking rose in intensity. "She's his fourth."

"Wife? Or dog?"

"Dog. Specifically, a Catahoula. The first one got hit by a truck, I think, and one got poisoned, and one got bit by a snake."

"Gosh, that is bad luck."

"Yeah, unless it's not chance at all. Maybe someone's making it happen."

"What are Catahoulas for?"

"Hunting. Herding. Don't get Terry started on the history of the breed, I'm begging you."

Terry's trailer door opened, and Annie launched herself off the steps to find out if we were friends or foes. She gave us a good bark, and when we stayed still, she eventually remembered she knew me. Annie weighed about fifty pounds, I guess, a good-sized dog. Catahoulas are not beautiful unless you love the breed. Annie was several shades of brown and red, and one shoulder was a solid color while her legs were another, though her rear half was covered with spots.

"Sookie, did you come to pick out a puppy?" Terry called. "Annie, let them by." Annie obediently backed up, keeping her eyes on us as we began approaching the trailer.

"I came to look," I said. "I brought my friend Amelia. She loves dogs."

Amelia was thinking she'd like to slap me upside the head because she was definitely a cat person.

Annie's puppies and Annie had made the small trailer quite doggy, though the odor wasn't really unpleasant. Annie herself maintained a vigilant stance while we looked at the three pups Terry still had. Terry's scarred hands were gentle as he handled the dogs. Annie had encountered several gentleman dogs on her unplanned excursion, and the puppies were diverse. They were adorable. Puppies just are. But they were sure distinctive. I picked up a bundle of short reddish fur with a white muzzle, and felt the puppy wiggle against me and snuffle my fingers. Gee, it was cute.

"Terry," I said, "have you been worried about Annie?"

"Yeah," he said. Since he was off base himself, Terry was very tolerant of other people's quirks. "I got to thinking about the things that have happened to my dogs, and I began to wonder if someone was causing them all."

"Do you insure all your dogs with Greg Aubert?"

"Naw, Diane at Liberty South insured the others. And see what happened to them? I decided to switch agents, and everyone says Greg is the luckiest son of a bitch in Renard Parish."

The puppy began chewing on my fingers. Ouch. Amelia was looking around her at the dingy trailer. It was clean enough, but the furniture arrangement was strictly utilitarian, like the furniture itself.

"So, did you go through the files at Greg Aubert's office?"

"No, why would I do that?"

Truthfully, I couldn't think of a reason. Fortunately, Terry didn't seem interested in why I wanted to know. "Sookie," he said, "if anyone in the bar thinks about my dogs, knows anything about 'em, will you tell me?"

Terry knew about me. It was one of those community secrets that everyone knows but no one ever discusses. Until they need me.

"Yes, Terry, I will." It was a promise, and I shook his hand. Reluctantly, I set the puppy back in its improvised pen, and Annie checked it over anxiously to make sure it was in good order.

We left soon after, none the wiser.

"So, who've we got left?" Amelia said. "You don't think the family did it, the vampire boyfriend is cleared, and Terry, the only other person on the scene, didn't do it. Where do we look next?"

"Don't you have some magic that would give us a clue?" I asked. I pictured us throwing magic dust on the files to reveal fingerprints.

"Uh. No."

"Then let's just reason our way through it. Like they do in crime novels. They just talk about it."

"I'm game. Saves gas."

We got back to the house and sat across from each other at the kitchen table. Amelia brewed a cup of tea for herself, while I got a caffeine-free Coke.

I said, "Greg is scared that someone is going through his files at work. We solved the part about someone being in his office. That was the daughter and her boyfriend. So we're left with the files. Now, who would be interested in Greg's clients?"

"There's always the chance that some client doesn't think Greg paid out enough on a claim, or maybe thinks Greg is cheating his clients." Amelia took a sip of her tea.

"But why go through the files? Why not just bring a complaint to the national insurance agents' board, or whatever?"

"Okay. Then there's . . . the only other answer is another insurance agent. Someone who wonders why Greg has such phenomenal luck in what he insures. Someone who doesn't believe it's chance or those cheesy synthetic rabbits' feet."

It was so simple when you thought about it, when you cleared away the mental debris. I was sure the culprit had to be someone in the same business.

I was pretty sure I knew the other three insurance agents in Bon Temps, but I checked the phone book to be sure.

"I suggest we go from agent to agent, starting with the local ones," Amelia said. "I'm relatively new in town, so I can tell them I want to take out some more insurance."

"I'll come with you, and I'll scan them."

"During the conversation, I'll bring up the Aubert Agency, so they'll be thinking about the right thing." Amelia had asked enough questions to understand how my telepathy worked.

I nodded. "First thing tomorrow morning."

We went to sleep that night with a pleasant tingle of anticipation. A plan was a beautiful thing. Stackhouse and Broadway swing into action.

The next day didn't start exactly like we'd planned. For one thing, the weather had decided to be fall. It was cool. It was pouring rain. I put my shorts and tank tops away sadly, knowing I probably wouldn't wear them again for several months.

The first agent, Diane Porchia, was guarded by a meek clerk. Alma Dean crumpled like a fender when we insisted on seeing the actual agent. Amelia, with her bright smile and gorgeous teeth, simply beamed at Ms. Dean until she called Diane out of her office. The middle-aged agent, a stocky woman in a green pantsuit, came out to shake our hands. I said, "I've been taking my friend Amelia around to all the agents in town, starting with Greg Aubert." I was listening as hard as I could to the result, and all I got was professional pride . . . and a hint of desperation. Diane Porchia was scared by the number of claims she had processed lately. It was abnormally high. All she was thinking of was selling. Amelia gave me a little hand wave. Diane Porchia was not a magical null.

"Greg Aubert thought he'd had someone break into his office at night," Amelia said.

"Us, too," Diane said, seeming genuinely astonished. "But nothing was taken." She rallied and got back to her purpose. "Our rates are very competitive with anything Greg can offer you. Take a look at the coverage we provide, and I think you'll agree."

Shortly after that, our heads filled with figures, we were on our way to Bailey Smith. Bailey was a high school classmate of my brother Jason's, and we had to spend a little longer there playing "What's he/she doing now?" But the result was the same. Bailey's only concern was getting Amelia's business, and maybe getting her to go out for a drink with him if he could think of a place to take her that his wife wouldn't hear about.

He had had a break-in at his office, too. In his case, the window had been shattered. But nothing had been taken. And I heard directly from his brain that business was down. Way down.

At John Robert Briscoe's we had a different problem. He didn't want to see us. His clerk, Sally Lundy, was like an angel with a flaming sword guarding the entrance to his private office. We got our chance when a client came in, a little withered woman who'd had a collision the month before. She said, "I don't know how this could be, but the minute I signed with John Robert, I had an accident. Then a month goes by, and I have another one."

"Come on back, Mrs. Hanson." Sally gave us a mistrustful look as she took the little woman to the inner sanctum. The minute they were gone, Amelia went through the stack of paperwork in the in-box, to my surprise and dismay.

Sally came back to her desk, and Amelia and I took our

departure. I said, "We'll come back later. We've got another appointment right now."

"They were all claims," Amelia said, when we were out of the door. "Every one of them." She pushed back the hood on her slicker since the rain had finally stopped.

"There's something wrong with that. John Robert has been hit even harder than Diane or Bailey."

We stared at each other. Finally, I said what we were both thinking. "Did Greg upset some balance by claiming more than his fair share of good luck?"

"I never heard of such a thing," Amelia said. But we both believed that Greg had unwittingly tipped over a cosmic applecart.

"There weren't any nulls at any of the other agencies," Amelia said. "It's got to be John Robert or his clerk. I didn't get to check either of them."

"He'll be going to lunch any minute," I said, glancing down at my watch. "Probably Sally will be, too. I'll go to the back where they park and stall them. Do you just have to be close?"

"If I have one of my spells, it'll be better," she said. She darted over to the car and unlocked it, pulling out her purse. I hurried around to the back of the building, just a block off the main street but surrounded by crepe myrtles.

I managed to catch John Robert as he left his office to go to lunch. His car was dirty. His clothes were disheveled. He slumped. I knew him by sight, but we'd never had a conversation.

"Mr. Briscoe," I said, and his head swung up. He seemed confused. Then his face cleared, and he tried to smile.

"Sookie Stackhouse, right? Girl, it's been an age since I saw you."

"I guess you don't come in Merlotte's much."

"No, I pretty much go home to the wife and kids in the evening," he said. "They've got a lot of activities."

"Do you ever go over to Greg Aubert's office?" I asked, trying to sound gentle.

He stared at me for a long moment. "No, why would I do that?"

And I could tell, hear from his head directly, that he absolutely didn't know what I was talking about. But there came Sally Lundy, steam practically coming out of her ears at the sight of me talking to her boss when she'd done her best to shield him.

"Sally," John Robert said, relieved to see his right-hand woman, "this young woman wants to know if I've been to Greg's office lately."

"I'll just bet she does," Sally said, and even John Robert blinked at the venom in her voice.

And I got it then, the name I'd been waiting for.

"It's you," I said. "You're the one, Ms. Lundy. What are you doing that for?" If I hadn't known I had backup, I would've been scared. Speaking of backup . . .

"What am I doing it for?" she screeched. "You have the gall, the nerve, the . . . the *balls* to ask me that?"

John Robert couldn't have looked more horrified if she'd sprouted horns.

"Sally," he said, very anxiously. "Sally, maybe you need to sit down."

"You can't see it!" she shrieked. "You can't see it. That Greg Aubert, he's dealing with the devil! Diane and Bailey are in the same boat we are, and it's sinking! Do you know how many claims he had to handle last week? Three! Do you know how many new policies he wrote? Thirty!"

John Robert literally staggered when he heard the numbers. He recovered enough to say, "Sally, we can't make wild accusations against Greg. He's a fine man. He'd never . . ."

But Greg had, however blindly.

Sally decided it would be a good time to kick me in the shins, and I was really glad I was wearing jeans instead of shorts that day. *Okay, anytime now, Amelia*, I thought. John Robert was windmilling his arms and yelling at Sally—though not moving to restrain her, I noticed—and Sally was yelling back at the top of her lungs and venting her feelings about Greg Aubert and that bitch Marge who worked for him. She had a lot to say about Marge. No love lost there.

By that time I was holding Sally off at arm's length, and I was sure my legs would be black-and-blue the next day.

Finally, finally, Amelia appeared, breathless and disarranged. "Sorry," she panted, "you're not going to believe this, but my foot got stuck between the car seat and the doorsill, then I fell, and my keys went under the car. . . . Anyway, *Congelo!*"

Sally's foot stopped in midswing, so she was balancing on one skinny leg. John Robert had both hands in the air in a gesture of despair. I touched his arm, and he felt as hard as the frozen vampire had the other night. At least he wasn't holding me.

"Now what?" I asked.

"I thought you knew!" she said. "We've got to get them off thinking about Greg and his luck!"

"The problem is, I think Greg's used up all the luck going around," I said. "Look at the problems you had just getting out of the car here."

She looked intensely thoughtful. "Yeah, we have to have a chat with Greg," she said. "But first, we've got to get out of this situation." Holding out her right hand toward the two frozen people, she said, "Ah—*amicus cum Greg Aubert.*"

They didn't look any more amiable, but maybe the change

was taking place in their hearts. "*Regelo*," Amelia said, and Sally's foot came down to the ground hard. The older woman lurched a bit, and I caught her. "Watch out, Miss Sally," I said, hoping she wouldn't kick me again. "You were a little off balance there."

She looked at me in surprise. "What are you doing back here?"

Good question. "Amelia and I were just cutting through the parking lot on our way to McDonald's," I said, gesturing toward the golden arches that stuck up one street over. "We didn't realize that you had so many high bushes around the back here. We'll just return to the front parking lot and get our car and drive around."

"That would be better," John Robert said. "That way we wouldn't have to worry about something happening to your car while it was parked in our parking lot." He looked gloomy again. "Something's sure to hit it, or fall on top of it. Maybe I'll just call that nice Greg Aubert and ask him if he's got any ideas about breaking my streak of bad luck."

"You do that," I said. "Greg would be glad to talk to you. He'll give you lots of his lucky rabbits' feet, I bet."

"Yep, that Greg sure is nice," Sally Lundy agreed. She turned to go back into the office, a little dazed but none the worse for wear.

Amelia and I went over to the Pelican State office. We were both feeling pretty thoughtful about the whole thing.

Greg was in, and we plopped down on the client side of his desk.

"Greg, you've got to stop using the spells so much," I said, and I explained why.

Greg looked frightened and angry. "But I'm the best agent in Louisiana. I have an incredible record."

"I can't make you change anything, but you're sucking up all the luck in Renard Parish," I said. "You gotta let loose of some of it for the other guys. Diane and Bailey are hurting so much they're thinking about changing professions. John Robert Briscoe is almost suicidal." To do Greg credit, once we explained the situation, he was horrified.

"I'll modify my spells," he said. "I'll accept some of the bad luck. I just can't believe I was using up everyone else's share." He still didn't look happy, but he was resigned. "And the people in the office at night?" Greg asked meekly.

"Don't worry about it," I said. "Taken care of." At least, I hoped so. Just because Bill had taken the young vampire to Shreveport to see Eric didn't mean that he wouldn't come back again. But maybe the couple would find somewhere else to conduct their mutual exploration.

"Thank you," Greg said, shaking our hands. In fact, Greg cut us a check, which was also nice, though we assured him it wasn't necessary. Amelia looked proud and happy. I felt pretty cheerful myself. We'd cleaned up a couple of the world's problems, and things were better because of us.

"We were fine investigators," I said, as we drove home.

"Of course," said Amelia. "We weren't just good. We were lucky."

GIFT WRAP

～◦～

"Gift Wrap" is about Niall and his love for Sookie, which manifests itself in an unexpected (and morally questionable) gift. Sookie is alone and lonely on Christmas Eve when a noise in the woods causes her to go to the aid of a stranded traveler. Sookie cannot resist helping someone who needs her assistance. In the end, she isn't alone on Christmas Eve any longer . . . but she'll never really know who stayed with her, either. Pretty creepy.

The events in "Gift Wrap" occur following *From Dead to Worse*.

IT WAS CHRISTMAS Eve. I was all by myself.

Does that sound sad and pathetic enough to make you say, "Poor Sookie Stackhouse!"? You don't need to. I was feeling plenty sorry for myself, and the more I thought about my solitude at this time of the year, the more my eyes welled and my chin quivered.

Most people hang with their family and friends at the holiday season. I actually do have a brother, but we aren't speaking. I'd recently discovered I have a living great-grandfather, though I didn't believe he would even realize it was Christmas. (Not because he's senile—far from it—but because he's not a Christian.) Those two are it for me, as far as close family goes.

I actually do have friends, too, but they all seemed to have their own plans this year. Amelia Broadway, the witch who lives on the top floor of my house, had driven down to New Orleans to spend the holiday with her father. My friend and employer, Sam Merlotte, had gone home to Texas to see his mom, stepfather, and siblings. My childhood friends Tara and JB would be spending Christmas Eve with JB's family; plus, it was their first Christmas as a married couple. Who could horn in on that? I had other friends . . . friends close enough that if I'd made puppy-dog eyes when they were talking about their holiday plans, they would have included me on their guest list in a heartbeat. In a fit of perversity, I hadn't wanted to be pitied for being alone. I guess I wanted to manage that all by myself.

Sam had gotten a substitute bartender, but Merlotte's Bar closes at two o'clock in the afternoon on Christmas Eve and remains closed until two o'clock the day after Christmas, so I didn't even have work to break up a lovely uninterrupted stretch of misery.

My laundry was done. The house was clean. The week before, I'd put up my grandmother's Christmas decorations, which I'd inherited along with the house. Opening the boxes of ornaments made me miss my grandmother with a sharp ache. She'd been gone almost two years, and I still wished I could talk to her. Not only had Gran been a lot of fun, she'd been really shrewd and she'd given good advice—if she decided you really needed some. She'd raised me from the age of seven, and she'd been the most important figure in my life.

She'd been so pleased when I'd started dating the vampire Bill Compton. That was how desperate Gran had been for me to get a beau; even Vampire Bill was welcome. When you're telepathic like I am, it's hard to date a regular guy; I'm sure you can see why. Humans think all kinds of things they don't want their nearest and dearest to know about, much less a woman they're taking out to dinner and a movie. In sharp contrast, vampires' brains are lovely silent blanks to me, and werewolf brains are nearly as good as vampires', though I get a big waft of emotions and the odd snatch of thought from my occasionally furred acquaintances.

Naturally, after I'd thought about Gran welcoming Bill, I began wondering what Bill was doing. Then I rolled my eyes at my own idiocy. It was midafternoon, daytime. Bill was sleeping somewhere in his house, which lay in the woods to the south of my place, across the cemetery. I'd broken up with Bill, but I was sure he'd be over like a shot if I called him—once darkness fell, of course.

Damned if I would call him. Or anyone else.

But I caught myself staring longingly at the telephone every time I passed by. I needed to get out of the house or I'd be phoning someone, anyone.

I needed a mission. A project. A task. A diversion.

I remembered having awakened for about thirty seconds in the wee hours of the morning. Since I'd worked the late shift at Merlotte's, I'd only just sunk into a deep sleep. I'd stayed awake only long enough to wonder what had jarred me out of that sleep. I'd heard something out in the woods, I thought. The sound hadn't been repeated, and I'd dropped back into slumber like a stone into water.

Now I peered out the kitchen window at the woods. Not too surprisingly, there was nothing unusual about the view. "The woods are snowy, dark, and deep," I said, trying to recall the Frost poem we'd all had to memorize in high school. Or was it "lovely, dark, and deep"?

Of course, my woods weren't lovely or snowy—they never are in Louisiana at Christmas, even northern Louisiana. But it was cold (here, that meant the temperature was about thirty-eight degrees Fahrenheit). And the woods were definitely dark and deep—and damp. So I put on my lace-up work boots that I'd bought years before when my brother, Jason, and I had gone hunting together, and I shrugged into my heaviest "I don't care what happens to it" coat, really more of a puffy quilted jacket. It was pale pink. Since a heavy coat takes a long time to wear out down here, the coat was several years old, too; I'm twenty-seven, definitely past the pale pink stage. I bundled all my hair up under a knit cap, and I pulled on the gloves I'd found stuffed into one pocket. I hadn't worn this coat for a long, long time, and I was surprised to find a couple of dollars and some ticket stubs in the pockets, plus a receipt for a little Christmas gift I'd given Alcide Herveaux, a werewolf I'd dated briefly.

Pockets are like little time capsules. Since I'd bought Alcide the sudoku book, his father had died in a struggle for the job of packmaster, and after a series of violent events, Alcide himself had ascended to the leadership. I wondered how pack affairs were going in Shreveport. I hadn't talked to any of the Weres in two months. In fact, I'd lost track of when the last full moon had been. Last night?

Now I'd thought about Bill and Alcide. Unless I took action, I'd begin brooding over my most recent lost boyfriend, Quinn. It was time to get on the move.

My family has lived in this humble house for over a hundred and fifty years. My much-adapted home lies in a clearing in the middle of some woods off Hummingbird Road, outside of the small town of Bon Temps, in Renard Parish. The trees are deeper and denser to the east at the rear of the house, since they haven't been logged in a good fifty years. They're thinner on the south side, where the cemetery lies. The land is gently rolling, and far back on the property there's a little stream, but I hadn't walked all the way back to the stream in ages. My life had been very busy, what with hustling drinks at the bar, telepathing (is that a verb?) for the vampires, unwillingly participating in vampire and Were power struggles, and other magical and mundane stuff like that.

It felt good to be out in the woods, though the air was raw and damp, and it felt good to be using my muscles.

I made my way through the brush for at least thirty minutes, alert for any indication of what had caused the ruckus the night before. There are lots of animals indigenous to northern Louisiana, but most of them are quiet and shy: possums, raccoons, deer. Then there are the slightly less quiet but still shy mammals, like coyotes and foxes. We have a few more formidable creatures. In the bar, I hear hunters' stories all the time. A couple of the more enthusiastic sportsmen had glimpsed a black bear on a private hunting preserve about two miles from my house. And Terry Bellefleur had sworn to me he'd seen a panther less than two years ago. Most of the avid hunters had spotted feral hogs, razorbacks.

Of course, I wasn't expecting to encounter anything like that. I had popped my cell phone into my pocket, just in case, though I wasn't sure I could get a signal out in the woods.

By the time I'd worked my way through the thick woods to the stream, I was warm inside the puffy coat. I was ready to crouch down for a minute or two to examine the soft ground by the water. The stream, never big to begin with, was level with its banks after the recent rainfall. Though I'm not Nature Girl, I could tell that deer had been here; raccoons, too; and maybe a dog. Or two. Or three. *That's not good*, I thought with a hint of unease. A pack of dogs always had the potential to become dangerous. I wasn't anywhere near savvy enough to tell how old the tracks were, but I would have expected them to look drier if they'd been made over a day ago.

There was a sound from the bushes to my left. I froze, scared to raise my face and turn in toward the right direction. I slipped my cell phone out of my pocket, looked at the bars. OUTSIDE OF AREA, read the legend on the little screen. *Crap*, I thought. That hardly began to cover it.

The sound was repeated. I decided it was a moan. Whether

it had issued from man or beast, I didn't know. I bit my lip, hard, and then I made myself stand up, very slowly and carefully. Nothing happened. No more sounds. I got a grip on myself and edged cautiously to my left. I pushed aside a big stand of laurel.

There was a man lying on the ground, in the cold wet mud. He was naked as a jaybird, but patterned in dried blood.

I approached him cautiously, because even naked, bleeding, muddy men could be mighty dangerous; maybe *especially* dangerous.

"Ah," I said. As an opening statement, that left a lot to be desired. "Ah, do you need help?" Okay, that ranked right up there with "How do you feel?" as a stupid opening statement.

His eyes opened—tawny eyes, wild and round like an owl's. "Get away," he said urgently. "They may be coming back."

"Then we'd better hurry," I said. I had no intention of leaving an injured man in the path of whatever had injured him in the first place. "How bad are you hurt?"

"No, run," he said. "It's not long until dark." Painfully, he stretched out a hand to grip my ankle. He definitely wanted me to pay attention.

It was really hard to listen to his words since there was a lot of bareness that kept my eyes busy. I resolutely focused my gaze above his chest. Which was covered, not too thickly, with dark brown hair. Across a broad expanse. Not that I was looking!

"Come on," I said, kneeling beside the stranger. A mélange of prints indented the mud, indicating a lot of activity right around him. "How long have you been here?"

"A few hours," he said, gasping as he tried to prop himself up on one elbow.

"In this cold?" Geez Louise. No wonder his skin was bluish.

"We got to get you indoors," I said. "Now." I looked from the blood on his left shoulder to the rest of him, trying to spot other injuries.

That was a mistake. The rest of him—though visibly muddy, bloody, and cold—was really, really . . .

What was wrong with me? Here I was, looking at a complete (naked and handsome) stranger with lust, while he was scared and wounded. "Here," I said, trying to sound resolute and determined and neutered. "Put your good arm around my neck, and we'll get you to your knees. Then you can get up, and we can start moving."

There were bruises all over him, but not another injury that had broken the skin, I thought. He protested several more times, but the sky was getting darker as the night drew in, and I cut him off sharply. "Get a move on," I advised him. "We don't want to be out here any longer than we have to be. It's going to take the better part of an hour to get you to the house."

The man fell silent. He finally nodded. With a lot of work, we got him to his feet. I winced when I saw how scratched and filthy they were.

"Here we go," I said encouragingly. He took a step, did a little wincing of his own. "What's your name?" I said, trying to distract him from the pain of walking.

"Preston," he said. "Preston Pardloe."

"Where you from, Preston?" We were moving a little faster now, which was good. The woods were getting darker and darker.

"I'm from Baton Rouge," he said. He sounded a little surprised.

"And how'd you come to be in my woods?"

"Well . . ."

I realized what his problem was. "Are you a Were, Preston?" I asked. I felt his body relax against my own. I'd known it already from his brain pattern, but I didn't want to scare him by telling him about my little disability. Preston had a—how can I describe it?—a smoother, thicker pattern than other Weres I'd encountered, but each mind has its own texture.

"Yes," he said. "You know, then."

"Yeah," I said. "I know." I knew way more than I'd ever wanted to. Vampires had come out in the open with the advent of the Japanese-marketed synthetic blood that could sustain them, but other creatures of the night and shadows hadn't yet taken the same giant step.

"What pack?" I asked, as we stumbled over a fallen branch and recovered. He was leaning on me heavily. I feared we'd actually tumble to the ground. We needed to pick up the pace. He did seem to be moving more easily now that his muscles had warmed up a little.

"The Deer Killer pack, from south of Baton Rouge."

"What are you doing up here in my woods?" I asked again.

"This land is yours? I'm sorry we trespassed," he said. His breath caught as I helped him around a devil's walking stick. One of the thorns caught in my pink coat, and I pulled it out with difficulty.

"That's the least of my worries," I said. "Who attacked you?"

"The Sharp Claw pack from Monroe."

I didn't know any Monroe Weres.

"Why were you here?" I asked, thinking sooner or later he'd have to answer me if I kept asking.

"We were supposed to meet on neutral ground," he said, his face tense with pain. "A werepanther from out in the country somewhere offered the land to us as a midway point, a neutral zone. Our packs have been . . . feuding. He said this would be a good place to resolve our differences."

My brother had offered my land as a Were parley ground? The stranger and I struggled along in silence while I tried to think that through. My brother, Jason, was indeed a werepanther, though he'd become one by being bitten; his estranged wife was a born werepanther, a genetic panther. What was Jason thinking, sending such a dangerous gathering my way? Not of my welfare, that's for sure.

Granted, we weren't on good terms, but it was painful to think he'd actually want to do me harm. Any more than he'd already done me, that is.

A hiss of pain brought my attention back to my companion. Trying to help him more efficiently, I put my arm around his waist, and he draped his arm across my shoulder. We were able to make better time that way, to my relief. Five minutes later, I saw the light I'd left on above the back porch.

"Thank God," I said. We began moving faster, and we reached the house just as dark fell. For a second, my companion arched and tensed, but he didn't change. That was a relief.

Getting up the steps turned into an ordeal, but finally I got Preston into the house and seated at the kitchen table. I looked him over anxiously. This wasn't the first time I'd brought a bleeding and naked man into my kitchen, oddly enough. I'd found a vampire named Eric under similar circumstances. Was that not incredibly weird, even for my life? Of course, I didn't have time to mull that over, because this man needed some attention.

I tried to look at the shoulder wound in the improved light of the kitchen, but he was so grimy it was hard to examine in detail. "Do you think you could stand to take a shower?" I asked, hoping I didn't sound like I thought he smelled or any-thing. Actually, he did smell a little unusual, but his scent wasn't unpleasant.

"I think I can stay upright that long," he said briefly.

"Okay, stay put for a second," I said. I brought the old af-ghan from the back of the living room couch and arranged it around him carefully. Now it was easier to concentrate.

I hurried to the hall bathroom to turn on the shower con-trols, added long after the claw-footed bathtub had been in-stalled. I leaned over to turn on the water, waited until it was hot, and got out two fresh towels. Amelia had left shampoo and crème rinse in the rack hanging from the showerhead, and there was plenty of soap. I put my hand under the water. Nice and hot.

"Okay!" I called. "I'm coming to get you!"

My unexpected visitor was looking startled when I got back to the kitchen. "For what?" he asked, and I wondered if he'd hit his head in the woods.

"For the shower. Hear the water running?" I said, trying to sound matter-of-fact. "I can't see the extent of your wounds until I get you clean."

We were up and moving again, and I thought he was walk-ing better, as if the warmth of the house and the smoothness of the floor helped his muscles relax. He'd just left the afghan on the chair. No problem with nudity, like most Weres, I no-ticed. Okay, that was good, right? His thoughts were opaque to me, as Were thoughts sometimes were, but I caught flashes of anxiety.

Suddenly he leaned against me much more heavily, and I staggered into the wall. "Sorry," he said, gasping. "Just had a twinge in my leg."

"No problem," I said. "It's probably your muscles stretching." We made it into the small bathroom, which was very old-fashioned. My own bathroom off my bedroom was more modern, but this was less personal.

But Preston didn't seem to note the black-and-white-checkered tile. With unmistakable eagerness, he was eyeing the hot water spraying down into the tub.

"Ah, do you need me to leave you alone for a second before I help you into the shower?" I asked, indicating the toilet with a tip of my head.

He looked at me blankly. "Oh," he said, finally understanding. "No, that's all right." So we made it to the side of the tub, which was a high one. With a lot of awkward maneuvering, Preston swung a leg over the side, and I shoved, and he was able to raise the second leg enough to climb completely in. After making sure he could stand by himself, I began to pull the shower curtain closed.

"Lady," he said, and I stopped. He was under the stream of hot water, his hair plastered to his head, water beating on his chest and running down to drip off his . . . Okay, he'd gotten warmer everywhere.

"Yes?" I was trying not to sound like I was choking.

"What's your name?"

"Oh! Excuse me." I swallowed hard. "My name is Sookie. Sookie Stackhouse." I swallowed again. "There's the soap; there's the shampoo. I'm going to leave the bathroom door open, okay? You just call me when you're through, and I'll help you out of the tub."

"Thanks," he said. "I'll yell if I need you."

I pulled the shower curtain, not without regret. After checking that the clean towels were where Preston could easily reach them, I returned to the kitchen. I wondered if he would like coffee or hot chocolate or tea? Or maybe alcohol?

I had some bourbon, and there were a couple of beers in the refrigerator. I'd ask him. Soup, he'd need some soup. I didn't have any homemade, but I had Campbell's Chicken Tortilla. I put the soup into a pan on the stove, got coffee ready to go, and boiled some water in case he opted for the chocolate or tea. I was practically vibrating with purpose.

When Preston emerged from the bathroom, his bottom half was wrapped in a large blue bath towel of Amelia's. Believe me, it had never looked so good. Preston had draped a towel around his neck to catch the drips from his hair, and it covered his shoulder wound. He winced a little as he walked, and I knew his feet must be sore. I'd gotten some men's socks by mistake on my last trip to Wal-Mart, so I got them from my drawer and handed them to Preston, who'd resumed his seat at the table. He looked at them very carefully, to my puzzlement.

"You need to put on some socks," I said, wondering if he paused because he thought he was wearing some other man's garments. "They're mine," I said reassuringly. "Your feet must be tender."

"Yes," said Preston, and rather slowly, he bent to put them on.

"You need help?" I was pouring the soup in a bowl.

"No, thank you," he said, his face hidden by his thick dark hair as he bent to the task. "What smells so good?"

"I heated some soup for you," I said. "You want coffee or tea or . . ."

"Tea, please," he said.

I never drank tea myself, but Amelia had some. I looked through her selection, hoping none of these blends would turn him into a frog or anything. Amelia's magic had had unexpected results in the past. Surely anything marked LIPTON was okay? I dunked the tea bag into the scalding water and hoped for the best.

Preston ate the soup carefully. Maybe I'd gotten it too hot. He spooned it into his mouth like he'd never had soup before. Maybe his mama had always served homemade. I felt a little embarrassed. I was staring at him, because I sure didn't have anything better to look at. He looked up and met my eyes.

Whoa. Things were moving too fast here. "So, how'd you get hurt?" I asked. "Was there a skirmish? How come your pack left you?"

"There was a fight," he said. "Negotiations didn't work." He looked a little doubtful and distressed. "Somehow, in the dark, they left me."

"Do you think they're coming back to get you?"

He finished his soup, and I put his tea down by his hand. "Either my own pack or the Monroe one," he said grimly.

That didn't sound good. "Okay, you better let me see your wounds now," I said. The sooner I knew his fitness level, the sooner I could decide what to do. Preston removed the towel from around his neck, and I bent to look at the wound. It was almost healed.

"When were you hurt?" I asked.

"Toward dawn." His huge tawny eyes met mine. "I lay there for hours."

"But . . ." Suddenly I wondered if I'd been entirely intelligent, bringing a stranger into my home. I knew it wasn't wise to let Preston know I had doubts about his story. The wound had looked jagged and ugly when I'd found him in the woods. Yet now that he came into the house, it healed in a matter of minutes? What was up? Weres healed fast, but not instantly.

"What's wrong, Sookie?" he asked. It was pretty hard to

think about anything else when his long wet hair was trailing across his chest and the blue towel was riding pretty low.

"Are you really a Were?" I blurted, and backed up a couple of steps. His brain waves dipped into the classic Were rhythm, the jagged, dark cadence I found familiar.

Preston Pardloe looked absolutely horrified. "What else would I be?" he said, extending an arm. Obligingly, fur rippled down from his shoulder and his fingers clawed. It was the most effortless change I'd ever seen, and there was very little of the noise I associated with the transformation, which I'd witnessed several times.

"You must be some kind of super werewolf," I said.

"My family is gifted," he said proudly.

He stood, and his towel slipped off.

"No kidding," I said in a strangled voice. I could feel my cheeks turning red.

There was a howl outside. There's no eerier sound, especially on a dark, cold night; and when that eerie sound comes from the line where your yard meets the woods, well, that'll make the hairs on your arm stand up. I glanced at Preston's wolfy arm to see if the howl had had the same effect on him, and saw that his arm had reverted to human shape.

"They've returned to find me," he said.

"Your pack?" I said, hoping that his kin had returned to retrieve him.

"No." His face was bleak. "The Sharp Claws."

"Call your people. Get them here."

"They left me for a reason." He looked humiliated. "I didn't want to talk about it. But you've been so kind."

I was not liking this more and more. "And that reason would be?"

"I was payment for an offense."

"Explain in twenty words or less."

He stared down at the floor, and I realized he was counting in his head. This guy was one of a kind. "Packleader's sister wanted me, I didn't want her, she said I'd insulted her, my torture was the price."

"Why would your packleader agree to any such thing?"

"Am I still supposed to number my words?"

I shook my head. He'd sounded dead serious. Maybe he just had a really deep sense of humor.

"I'm not my packleader's favorite person, and he was willing to believe I was guilty. He himself wants the sister of the Sharp Claw packmaster, and it would be a good match from the point of view of our packs. So, I was hung out to dry."

I could sure believe that the packmaster's sister had lusted after him. The rest of the story was not outrageous, if you've had many dealings with the Weres. Sure, they're all human and reasonable on the outside, but when they're in their Were mode, they're different.

"So, they're here to get you and keep on beating you up?"

He nodded somberly. I didn't have the heart to tell him to rewind the towel. I took a deep breath, looked away, and decided I'd better go get the shotgun.

Howls were echoing, one after another, through the night by the time I fetched the shotgun from the closet in the living room. The Sharp Claws had tracked Preston to my house, clearly. There was no way I could hide him and say that he'd gone. Or was there? If they didn't come in . . .

"You need to get in the vampire hole," I said. Preston turned from staring at the back door, his eyes widening as he took in the shotgun. "It's in the guest bedroom." The vampire hole dated from when Bill Compton had been my boyfriend, and we'd thought it was prudent to have a light-tight place at my house in case he got caught by day.

When the big Were didn't move, I grabbed his arm and hustled him down the hall, showed him the trick bottom of the bedroom closet. Preston started to protest—all Weres would rather fight than flee—but I shoved him in, lowered the "floor," and threw the shoes and junk back in there to make the closet look realistic.

There was a loud knock at the front door. I checked the shotgun to make sure it was loaded and ready to fire, and then I went into the living room. My heart was pounding about a hundred miles a minute.

Werewolves tend to take blue-collar jobs in their human lives, though some of them parlay those jobs into business empires. I looked through my peephole to see that the werewolf at my front door must be a semipro wrestler. He was huge. His hair hung in tight gelled waves to his shoulders, and he had a trimmed beard and mustache, too. He was wearing a leather vest and leather pants and motorcycle boots. He actually had leather strips tied around his upper arms, and leather braces on his wrists. He looked like someone from a fetish magazine.

"What do you want?" I called through the door.

"Let me come in," he said, in a surprisingly high voice. *Little pig, little pig, let me come in!*

"Why would I do that?" *Not by the hair of my chinny-chin-chin.*

"Because we can break in if we have to. We got no quarrel with you. We know this is your land, and your brother told us you know all about us. But we're tracking a guy, and we gotta know if he's in there."

"There was a guy here; he came up to my back door," I

called. "But he made a phone call and someone came and picked him up."

"Not out here," the mountainous Were said.

"No, the back door." That was where Preston's scent would lead.

"Hmmmm." By pressing my ear to the door, I could hear the Were mutter, "Check it out," to a large dark form, which loped away. "I still gotta come in and check," my unwanted visitor said. "If he's in there, you might be in danger."

He should have said that first, to convince me he was trying to save me.

"Okay, but only you," I said. "And you know I'm a friend of the Shreveport pack, and if anything happens to me, you'll have to answer to them. Call Alcide Herveaux if you don't believe me."

"Oooo, I'm scared," said Man Mountain in an assumed falsetto. But as I swung open the front door and he got a look at the shotgun, I could see that he truly did look as if he was having second thoughts. Good.

I stood aside, keeping the Benelli pointed in his direction to show I meant business. He strode through the house, his nose working all the time. His sense of smell wouldn't be nearly as accurate in his human form, and if he started to change, I intended to tell him I'd shoot if he did.

Man Mountain went upstairs, and I could hear him opening closets and looking under beds. He even stepped into the attic. I heard the creak its old door makes when it swings open.

Then he clomped downstairs in his big old boots. He was dissatisfied with his search, I could tell, because he was practically snorting. I kept the shotgun level.

Suddenly he threw back his head and roared. I flinched,

and it was all I could do to hold my ground. My arms were exhausted.

He was glaring at me from his great height. "You're pulling something on us, woman. If I find out what it is, I'll be back."

"You've checked, and he's not here. Time to go. It's Christmas Eve, for goodness' sake. Go home and wrap some presents."

With a final look around the living room, out he went. I couldn't believe it. The bluff had worked. I lowered the gun and set it carefully back in the closet. My arms were trembling from holding it at the ready. I shut and locked the door behind him.

Preston was padding down the hall in the socks and nothing else, his face anxious.

"Stop!" I said, before he could step into the living room. The curtains were open. I walked around shutting all the curtains in the house, just to be on the safe side. I took the time to send out my special sort of search, and there were no live brains in the area around the house. I'd never been sure how far this ability could reach, but at least I knew the Sharp Claws were gone.

When I turned around after drawing the last drape, Preston was behind me, and then he had his arms around me, and then he was kissing me. I swam to the surface to say, "I don't really . . ."

"Pretend you found me gift-wrapped under the tree," he whispered. "Pretend you have mistletoe."

It was pretty easy to pretend both those things. Several times. Over hours.

When I woke up Christmas morning, I was as relaxed as a girl can be. It took me a while to figure out that Preston was gone; and while I felt a pang, I also felt just a bit of relief. I didn't know the guy, after all, and even after we'd been up close and personal, I had to wonder how a day alone with him would have gone. He'd left me a note in the kitchen.

"Sookie, you're incredible. You saved my life and gave me the best Christmas Eve I've ever had. I don't want to get you in any more trouble. I'll never forget how great you were in every way." He'd signed it.

I felt let down, but oddly enough I also felt happy. It was Christmas Day. I went in and plugged in the lights on the tree and sat on the old couch with my grandmother's afghan wrapped around me, which still smelled faintly of my visitor. I had a big mug of coffee and some homemade banana nut bread to have for breakfast. I had presents to unwrap. And about noon, the phone began to ring. Sam called, and Amelia; and even Jason called just to say "Merry Christmas, Sis." He hung up before I could charge him with loaning my land out to two packs of Weres. Considering the satisfying outcome, I decided to forgive and forget—at least that one transgression. I put my turkey breast in the oven, and fixed a sweet potato casserole, and opened a can of cranberry sauce, and made some cornbread dressing and some broccoli and cheese.

About thirty minutes before the somewhat simplified feast was ready, the doorbell rang. I was wearing a new pale blue pants and top outfit in velour, a gift from Amelia. I was feeling self-sufficient as hell.

I was astonished how happy I was to see my great-grandfather at the door. His name's Niall Brigant, and he's a fairy prince. Okay, long story, but that's what he is. I'd only met him a few weeks before, and I couldn't say we really knew each other well, but he was family. He's about six feet tall, he almost always wears a black suit with a white shirt and a black tie, and he has pale golden hair as fine as cornsilk; it's longer than my hair, and it seems to float around his head if there's the slightest breeze.

Oh, yeah, my great-grandfather is over a thousand years old. Or thereabouts. I guess it's hard to keep track after all those years.

Niall smiled at me. All the tiny wrinkles that fissured his fine skin moved when he smiled, and somehow that just added to his charm. He had a load of wrapped boxes, to add to my general level of amazement.

"Please come in, Great-grandfather," I said. "I'm so happy to see you! Can you have Christmas dinner with me?"

"Yes," he said. "That's why I've come. Though," he added, "I was not invited."

"Oh," I said, feeling ridiculously ill-mannered. "I just never thought you'd be interested in coming. I mean, after all, you're not . . ." I hesitated, not wanting to be tacky.

"Not Christian," he said gently. "No, dear one, but you love Christmas, and I thought I would share it with you."

"Yay," I said.

I'd actually wrapped a present for him, intending to give it to him when I next encountered him (for seeing Niall was not a regular event), so I was able to bask in complete happiness. He gave me an opal necklace; I gave him some new ties (that black one had to go) and a Shreveport Mudbugs pennant (local color).

When the food was ready, we ate dinner, and he thought it was all very good.

It was a great Christmas.

THE CREATURE SOOKIE Stackhouse knew as Preston was standing in the woods. He could see Sookie and her great-grandfather moving around in the living room.

"She really is lovely, and sweet as nectar," he said to his companion, the hulking Were who'd searched Sookie's house.

"I only had to use a touch of magic to get the attraction started."

"How'd Niall get you to do it?" asked the Were. He really was a werewolf, unlike Preston, who was a fairy with a gift for transforming himself.

"Oh, he helped me out of a jam once," Preston said. "Let's just say it involved an elf and a warlock, and leave it at that. Niall said he wanted to make this human's Christmas very happy, that she had no family and was deserving." He watched rather wistfully as Sookie's figure crossed the window. "Niall set up the whole story tailored to her needs. She's not speaking to her brother, so he was the one who 'loaned out' her woods. She loves to help people, so I was 'hurt'; she loves to protect people, so I was 'hunted.' She hadn't had sex in a long time, so I seduced her." Preston sighed. "I'd love to do it all over again. It was wonderful, if you like humans. But Niall said no further contact, and his word is law."

"Why do you think he did all this for her?"

"I've no idea. How'd he rope you and Curt into this?"

"Oh, we work for one of his businesses as couriers. He knew we do a little community theater, that kind of thing." The Were looked unconvincingly modest. "So I got the part of Big Threatening Brute, and Curt was Other Brute."

"And a good job you did, Preston the fairy said bracingly. "Well, back to my own neck of the woods. See you later, Ralph."

"'Bye now," Ralph said, and Preston popped out of sight.

"How the hell do they do that?" Ralph said, and stomped off through the woods to his waiting motorcycle and his buddy Curt. He had a pocketful of cash and a story he was charged to keep secret.

Inside the old house, Niall Brigant, fairy prince and loving great-grandfather, pricked his ears at the faint sound of Preston's and Ralph's departures. He knew it was audible to only his ears. He smiled down at his great-granddaughter. He didn't understand Christmas, but he understood that it was a time humans received and gave gifts, and drew together as families. As he looked at Sookie's happy face, he knew he had given her a unique yuletide memory.

"Merry Christmas, Sookie," he said, and kissed her on the cheek.

TWO BLONDES

❧

"Two Blondes" is my favorite Sookie story, hands down. I grew up in Tunica, Mississippi, and the concept of featuring the nearby casinos was simply irresistible. Pam has always been one of my favorite characters in the Sookieverse, and her and Sookie's curious friendship is something I felt I could explore. I also wanted to point out that Eric figured the two of them could take care of themselves... and, as it turns out, he is absolutely right.

The road trip in "Two Blondes" was taken after *Dead and Gone*.

"**S**O WHY ARE we going to Tunica?" I asked Pam. "And what are we supposed to do when we get there?"

"We're going to see the sights and gamble," Pam said. The headlights of a passing car glinted on Pam's pale, straight hair. Pam was paler than her hair and approximately a hundred and sixty years old, give or take a decade. She'd become a vampire when Victoria was still a young queen.

"It's hard to believe you'd want to go to Mississippi. For that matter, it's hard to believe you'd want to take me along."

"Are we not friends, Sookie?"

"Yes," I said, after a little hesitation. Though it didn't seem polite to say so, I was closer to being a friend of Pam's than I was of any other vampire. "Somehow, I got the feeling you really didn't think enough of humans to want to claim one as a friend."

"You're not as intolerable as most," Pam said lightly.

"Thanks for the glowing testimony."

"Oh, you're quite welcome." She grinned, flashing just a bit of fang.

"I hope this is fun, considering I'm using my two days off to make this little trip." I sounded a little grumpy, with good reason.

"It's a vacation! A chance to get out of your rut. Don't you get tired of Bon Temps? Don't you get tired of hustling drinks at Sam's bar?"

Truthfully, no. I love my little Louisiana town. I feel as comfortable as a telepath can be among the people I know so well (better than most of them will ever understand). And I love working for Sam at Merlotte's. I'm a very good waitress and barmaid. My life brings me enough excitement without me having to leave town to get more.

"Something always goes wrong when I go out of town," I said, trying not to sound whiny.

"Such as?"

"Remember when I went to Dallas? All those people got shot? When I went to Jackson, I got staked." Which was pretty ironic, since I'm human. "And when I flew up to Rhodes with you-all, the hotel got blown up."

"And you saved my life," Pam said, suddenly serious.

"Well," I said, and then could think of nothing more to add. I started to say, *You would have done the same for me*, but I was by no means sure that was true. Then I started to say, *You would have been okay, anyway*, but that wasn't true, either. I shrugged, at a loss. Even in the darkness, Pam saw me.

"I won't forget," she said.

"So, we're really just going to see the casinos and gamble? Can we go see a show?" I wanted to change the subject.

"Of course we'll do all those things. Oh, we do have one tiny errand to perform for Eric."

Eric and I are—I'm not sure what we are. We're lovers, and in an unofficial vampire way, we're married. Not that I had anything to do with that; Eric maneuvered me into it. He had good intentions. I think. Anyway, it's not a straight-forward situation, me and Eric. Pam is gung ho Eric, because she's his right hand. "So what do we have to do? And why do I need to come along?"

"A human is involved," Pam said. "You can let me know if he's sincere or not."

"All right," I said, not caring one little bit that I sounded reluctant. "As long as I get to see all the casinos and a good show that I pick."

"It's a promise," Pam said.

As we went up Highway 61, we started to see casino bill-boards flashing by in the night. Pam had been driving since darkness had fallen. . . . That had been at five thirty, since it was February. Though I remembered February as being the coldest month when I was a child, now it was an eerie sixty degrees. Pam had picked me up in Bon Temps, then we'd gone through Vicksburg to turn north on Highway 61. There were a few casinos in Vicksburg and a few more in Greenville, but we kept driving up the western side of Mississippi. It was flat, flat, flat. Even in the dark, I could tell that.

"Nowhere to hide, here," I said brightly.

"Even for a vampire," Pam said. "Unless one found a bayou and crouched down to bury oneself in the mud."

"With the crawdaddies." I was full of cheerful thoughts.

"What do people do here?" Pam asked.

"Farm," I said. "Cotton, soybeans."

Pam's upper lip curled. Pam was a city girl. She'd grown up in London. England. See? We couldn't be more different. City girl, country girl. Experienced and well traveled, inexperienced and stay-at-home. Bisexual, heterosexual. She's dead, I'm alive.

Then she turned on the CD player in her Nissan Murano, and the Dixie Chicks began singing.

We did have something in common, after all.

We saw the first turnoff to the casinos at two in the morning.

"There's a second turnoff, and that's where we're staying," Pam said. "At Harrah's."

"Okay," I said, peering at the signs. To find these street lights, this traffic, and all the neon in the distance in the middle of the Mississippi Delta was like finding out Mrs. Butterworth had pierced her navel. "There!" I said. "We turn there."

Pam put on her blinker (she was an excellent driver), and following the signs, we pulled up in front of the casino/hotel where we had a reservation. It was large and new, as everything in the casino complex seemed to be. Since there wasn't a whole lot going on at that hour, several jacketed young men made a beeline for the Murano.

Pam said, "What are they doing?" Her fangs popped out.

"Chill. They're just going to valet-park the car," I said, proud that I knew something Pam didn't.

"Oh." She relaxed. "All right. They take the keys, park the car, and bring it back when I require it?"

"Right." A high school classmate of mine had had that job at a casino in Shreveport. "You tip 'em," I prompted, and Pam opened her purse, a Prada. Pam was a purse snob.

She laughed when one of the young men wanted to carry her luggage. We both entered the hotel with our weekend bags slung over our shoulders. Eric had given me my bag as a Christmas gift, and I really, really liked it. My initials were embroidered on it, and it was red with blue and gold flowers. In fact, it coordinated with the coat he'd given me the year before, the coat I didn't need this unseasonably warm night.

Pam had reserved one of the designated vampire rooms, a no-window space with two sets of doors. Our rooms were on the same floor at the back of the hotel. Of course, I'd gotten one of the much cheaper regular human rooms. I was glad we were here on a weekday, because one glimpse of the weekend rates had almost rendered me speechless. I *really* didn't travel much.

Very few people turned to look as we made our way to the elevator. Not only were vampires seen pretty frequently at casinos—after all, they were open all night—but everyone was absorbed in the gambling. The slot machines were in rows across the huge floor, and it was always night in here. Sunlight didn't have a hope of penetrating. The noise was incredible. The chiming and ringing and humming never came to a stop. I don't know how the people working there managed to stay sane.

In fact, one of the servers wending her way through the chaos in a slacks-shirt-vest uniform was a vampire. She was a thin strawberry blonde with such large boobs that I suspected she'd had a little augmentation before she was brought over. She was carrying a heavy tray of drinks and managing it with ease. She caught Pam's eyes and gave her a nod. Pam nodded back, giving her own head exactly the same degree of inclination.

On the third floor, Pam peeled off to find her room, and I followed the numbers to mine. Once I'd tossed my bag on my bed, I didn't know what to do with myself. Pam knocked, and when I let her in, she said, "My room is adequate. I'm going to go down and look around. Are you going to bed?"

"I think I will. What are our plans for tomorrow?"

"Do whatever you like during the day. There's a shuttle that runs between the casinos, so you can go to whichever one you like. There are shops, and there are restaurants. If you notice a show you'd like to see, book us for the first one after dark. After that, we'll run our errand."

"Okay. I think I'll turn in, then." You notice I didn't ask

about the errand? That was because I wanted to enjoy myself the next day. I'd find out soon enough what Eric wanted us to do. It couldn't be too bad, right? He was my lover and Pam's boss. On the other hand, he was frighteningly practical about taking care of himself. *No,* I told myself. *He wouldn't risk both of us. At the same time.*

"Good night, Sookie." She gave me a cold kiss on the cheek.

"Have a good time," I said faintly.

She smiled, happy at having startled me. "I plan on it. There are plenty of us here. I'll go . . . network."

Pam would always rather hang with her own kind than grub around with "breathers."

It took me all of ten minutes to unpack and get ready for bed. I crawled in. It was a king, and I felt lost in the middle of it. It would be more fun if Eric were here. I pushed the thought away and turned on the television. I could watch a movie on pay-per-view, I discovered. But if I paid specially for a movie, I'd feel obliged to stay up. Instead, I found an old Western that I followed for maybe half an hour until my eyes wouldn't stay open anymore.

About ten the next day, I was eating a wonderful breakfast at a buffet that was as long as the Merlotte's building. I had sausage and biscuits and gravy, and some chopped fruit so I could say I'd eaten something healthy. I also drank three cups of excellent coffee. This was a great way to start the day, and no dishes to do afterward. That was the kind of vacation I could appreciate.

I retreated to my room to brush my teeth, and then I went outside to catch the bus. The sky was overcast, and the temperature was as unnaturally warm as it had been the day before. One of the valet-parking attendants told me where the shuttle bus would pick me up to take me to the other casinos, and I waited for it with a stout couple from Dyersburg, Tennessee, who had cornered the market on chattiness. They'd won some money the night before; their son was going to the University of Memphis; they were Baptists but their pastor liked to visit the boats (all the casinos were theoretically boats, since casinos couldn't be built on solid land) so that made a little gambling okay. Since I was young and alone, these two decided I was applying for a job at the casinos. They assured me someone as young and perky and pretty as me would have no trouble.

"Now, don't you go to that bad place north of here!" the woman said, with mock admonishment.

"What place would that be?"

"Henry, close your ears," she told her husband. Henry good-naturedly pretended to hold his hands over his ears. "There's what's called a *gentleman's club* up there," she said in a stage whisper. "Though what someone calling himself a gentleman would be doing there, I don't know."

I didn't say that I was pretty sure real gentlemen had sex urges, too, because I understood what she meant. "So it's a strip club?"

Mrs. Dyersburg said, "My Lord, I don't know what all goes on in a place like that. I won't ever see the inside of one, you can bet. Listen, our oldest son is twenty-four, and he's single, got a good job. You dating anyone?"

Then, thank God, the bus came. Whatever casino the Dyersburgs chose, I'd pick another one. Luckily, they got off pretty quickly, so I waited to disembark at Bally's. I went in, to be assaulted by the newly familiar chiming and clicking of slot machines. I saw a sign for a huge buffet. I got a discount coupon immediately from a smiling older woman with elaborate brown hair and lots of gold jewelry. There were three restaurants in Bally's, and I could eat till I popped at any one of them, according to the material on the coupon. I wondered how much of an appetite I could work up playing a slot machine.

Out of sheer curiosity I walked over to an empty machine, looked at it carefully while I worked out what to do, fed it one of my hard-earned dollars, and pulled the lever. There, I felt it—a distinct frisson of excitement. Then my dollar was lost for good. Was I willing to spend my money on that thrill? No.

I wandered around for a while, looking at the people who were so intent on what they were doing that they never glanced at me, or smiled. The casino employees, on the other hand, were full of good cheer.

Over the course of the day, thanks to the shuttle, I discovered that all the casinos were basically the same. The "décor" changed, the staff uniforms were different colors, the layout might vary a bit, but the noise level and the gambling facilities . . . those were constant.

I had lunch at yet another casino in the middle of the afternoon. Each casino seemed to have two or three places to eat. I decided I couldn't face another buffet. I made my way to the lower-priced restaurant that offered menus. When I tired of people-watching, I pulled out the paperback I carried in my purse.

At the casino after that, I had to fend off a persistent admirer, a man missing an important front tooth. He wore his hair pulled back in a long, graying ponytail. He was sure we could have some fun together, and I was just as sure we could not. I got back on the shuttle.

I returned to Harrah's with a feeling of relief. I'd seen lots of new things, including a riverboat and a golf course, but all in all the casinos seemed kind of sad to me. The gamblers weren't people like you see in James Bond movies, rich people dressed to the nines who could afford losing. Some of the people I'd seen today didn't look like they could afford to waste even ten dollars. But I had to admit, they'd seemed to be having a good time, and after all, that was the point of a vacation.

It was lovely to shut the door of my room and enjoy the silence. I threw myself down on the bed and closed my eyes. It wouldn't be long until Pam rose.

Sure enough, she knocked on the door thirty minutes later. "Did you get some tickets?" she asked.

"Hi, Pam, good to see you. Yes, I had an interesting day," I said. "I got us tickets to the Mucho Macho contest."

"*What?*"

"It's a strongman competition. I wasn't sure you'd like any of the music acts. The groups I actually knew, they were all sold out for tonight. So I got tickets to see big strong guys. I thought you'd like that? You like guys, too, right?"

"I like men," Pam agreed guardedly.

"Well, we have an hour before the show," I said. "You want to go get some warm blood?"

"Yes," she said, and followed me to the elevator, still looking dubious.

While Pam drank a couple of bottles of TrueBlood Type A, I had a bowl of ice cream. (Calories don't count while you're on vacation.) Then we went to the casino next door to watch the Mucho Macho contestants do their manly thing. I got to say, I really enjoyed it: muscular guys lifting heavy weights, swinging big hammers, pulling farm equipment with their teeth. No, I'm just kidding about the teeth. They used a rope harness.

It was like monster trucks, but with men. Even Pam got into the spirit, yelling encouragement to Billy Bob the Brawler from Yazoo City as he harnessed up for his second attempt to move the tractor a yard across the floor.

Of course, Pam herself could have done it easily.

She got a call on her cell phone as we were leaving the show.

"Yes, Eric. Oh, we've just finished watching big, muscular, sweaty men move large things around. Sookie's idea."

Her eyes went sideways to meet mine. She grinned at me. "I'm sure you could, Eric. You could probably do it without your hands!" She laughed. Whatever Eric said next got her serious attention. "All right, then. We'll go now." She handed the phone to me. I didn't like the compressed lips and narrowed eyes. Something was up.

"Hey," I said. I felt a surge of lust down to my toenails just knowing that Eric was on the other end of the connection.

"I miss you," he said.

I pictured him in his office at Fangtasia, the nightclub he and Pam owned. He'd be sitting in his leather office chair, his thick golden hair falling in a waving curtain past his shoulders, and he'd be wearing a T-shirt and jeans. Eric had been a Viking, and he looked like it.

"I miss you, too," I whispered. I knew he could hear me. He could hear a cricket fart at twenty paces.

"When you return, I'll show you how much."

"I look forward to that," I said, trying to sound brisk and businesslike, since Pam could hear the conversation.

"You're not in any danger tonight," he said, sounding more businesslike himself. "Victor insisted you go with Pam. The vampire you're meeting has a human companion. You will know if Michael is dealing with us in good faith or not."

"Can you tell me what this is about?"

"Pam will brief you on the way. I wish I'd had time to discuss it with you myself, but this opportunity came up very quickly." He sounded, just for a second, like he was wondering why it had come up so quickly.

"Is something funny about that?" I asked. "Funny strange, I mean?"

"No," he said. "I was considering that . . . but no. Let me talk to Pam again."

I handed the phone back. A glimmer of surprise crossed Pam's face. "Sir?" she said.

Whatever transpired in the rest of the conversation was lost to me, because the Ittabena Hulk plowed through the crowd in his street clothes, looking neither to the right nor the left. He was intent on the stacked brunette who was waiting for him by the WAIT TO BE SEATED sign at the entrance to yet another buffet. She curved in all the right places. She was wearing a tight leopard-print stretch top, and a black leather miniskirt grazed the tops of her tan legs. Four-inch black heels completed the ensemble.

"Wow," I said, in genuine tribute. "I wish I had the guts to wear something that bold." The cumulative effect was literally stunning.

"I would look excellent in that," Pam said, a simple statement of fact.

"But would you want to?"

"I see what you mean." Pam looked down at her own silk blouse and well-cut pants, her low heels and conservative jewelry.

"So where are we going?" I asked, after the valet had retrieved Pam's car. We turned north on 61. The traffic was heavy. Though it was a weekday, everyone seemed to be in a great hurry to lose their hard-earned cash and experience something a little different from their everyday lives.

"We're going to a club that's just west of this highway, about ten miles north of here," Pam said. "It's called Blonde, and it's owned by a vampire named Michael."

I remembered my conversation with the couple on the bus. "This would be a 'gentleman's club'?"

Pam looked massively sardonic. "Yes, that's what they call it."

"Why are we going there? Eric said a vampire runs it. We're across the state line in Russell Edgington's territory." Russell Edgington was the vampire king of Mississippi. Though most humans didn't know it, there were other systems of government in the USA besides the one in Washington, D.C.

Not every state has its own vampire ruler; some states are populous enough to have two or even more. (New York City has its own king, I understand.) Visiting vamps were supposed to check in when they had to cross into another vamp's territory. I'd met Russell, and he was no joke.

"This must go no further, you understand?" Pam gave me a very meaningful look before turning her attention back to the road. The oncoming traffic heading south from Memphis was moving easily, but it was also nonstop.

"I understand," I said. I didn't sound enthusiastic. Vampire secrets are unpleasant and dangerous.

"Our new masters have been chipping away at Edgington's control of Mississippi," Pam said.

This was very bad news. Louisiana, where Bon Temps lay, had been taken over from its previous management by the vampires of Nevada. Since Arkansas had previously allied with Louisiana (long story), the king of Nevada (Felipe de Castro) had gotten two states for the price of one. His ambitious lieutenant, Victor Madden, had apparently decided to go for the trifecta.

"Why would they want to do that?" Felipe owned two poor states. If he added Mississippi, he'd have the equivalent of one prosperous state, but his people would be spread thin.

"The casinos," Pam said.

Of course. The big business in Nevada was casinos, and there were lots of casinos in Mississippi. Felipe had already acquired casinos in Louisiana, and had the state of Arkansas thrown in for free.

"Vampires can't own casinos," I said. "It's against the law." A powerful human lobby had pushed that legislation.

"Do you imagine that Felipe *doesn't* control what happens at the casinos in Las Vegas? At least in large part?"

"No," I admitted. I'd met Felipe.

"In fact, our king is bringing a lawsuit to challenge that legislation through the human courts, and I'm confident he'll win," Pam said. "In the meantime, Victor told Eric to use us as an advance team."

I had seen Victor much more often than the king himself. Victor Madden was Felipe de Castro's man on the ground in Louisiana, while Felipe stayed at his castle in Las Vegas. "Ah, Pam, do you think this is all on the up and up?"

"What do you mean?"

I thought she knew perfectly well what I meant. "Victor specified us. Why do *we* have this top secret mission, instead of someone better at negotiation? Not that you're not a great fighter," I added quickly. "But you'd think if we're trying to pinch off parts of Mississippi, Victor would send Eric himself." Eric was the only remaining sheriff that the previous ruler had put in place. All the others were dead. I remembered

Victor's adorable, smiling face, and I got worried. "You *sure* this Michael is willing to ditch Russell?"

"Victor says so."

"And Michael has a human companion."

"Yes, a man named Rudy."

"This is dangerous, no matter what Victor told Eric. We're in foreign territory. This isn't a real vacation. We're *poaching*."

"Russell doesn't know why we're here."

"How can you be sure?"

"I told his headquarters that I was having a weekend here, so they wouldn't think my presence was caused by business of any kind."

"And?"

"Russell himself came on the phone to extend his hospitality. He told me to feel free to enjoy myself in the area, that Eric's second-in-command was always welcome."

"And you don't think that's fishy?"

"If Russell had any idea what Felipe was considering, he would have counterattacked by now."

Vampires pretty much wrote the book on chicanery, double-dealing, and what you might call drastic politics. If Pam wasn't worried, should I be?

Sure. Pam could take a lot more damage than I could.

Blonde was not an attractive edifice. No matter how much female beauty might be on the inside (and the billboards promised plenty), on the outside it was a metal building in the middle of nowhere. It had a huge parking lot, and there were at least forty vehicles there. The ground had risen as we approached Memphis and its bluffs, and the club stood on top of a hill with a deep ravine behind. The whole area outside the parking lot was covered with kudzu, like it had been carpeted in the plant. The trees were covered, too.

"We go to the back," Pam said, and she drove around the building.

The back was even less appealing than the front. The parking lot was poorly lit. Michael was not too concerned for the safety of his workers. Of course, I told myself, *maybe he walks each of the girls to her car every night.* But I doubted it. "Pam, I have a bad feeling about this," I said. "I want to be on record as letting you know that."

"Thanks for the pep talk," Pam muttered, and I realized that she had more misgivings than she'd revealed. "But I have my orders and I have to do this."

"Who issued those orders—Felipe, Victor, or Eric?"

"Victor called me into Eric's office and told me what to do and to take you. Eric was present."

"How do you think he feels about this?"

"He isn't happy," Pam said. "But he's under new management, and he has to obey direct orders."

"So we have to do this."

"I have to. I am Eric's to command." Eric had made Pam a vampire. "You aren't, though Eric pretends to Victor that you obey him in all things. You can leave. Or you can stay in the car and wait for me. There's a pistol under the backseat."

"What?"

"A pistol, a gun, you know? Eric thought you'd feel more comfortable with one, since we're so much stronger than you."

I hate guns. Having said that, I also have to admit that a firearm has saved my life in the past. "You're not going in by yourself, armed or unarmed," I said. I hesitated, because I was afraid. "Give it to me," I said. We were parked at the very back of the lot, right by the kudzu. I hoped it wouldn't take Pam's car while we were inside.

Pam reached under the seat and drew out a revolver. "Point

and shoot," she said, shrugging. "Eric got it for you specially. He says it is called a Ruger LCP. It fires six shots, and there's one in the chamber."

It was about as big as a cell phone. Good God Almighty. "What if I need to reload?"

"If you have to shoot that much, we are dead."

I got that feeling that had become familiar since I'd started hanging with vampires; the feeling that says, *How the hell did I get into this?* If you examined the process step-by-step, you could see how it had happened; but when you looked at where you'd ended up, you just had to shake your head. I was walking into a very dubious situation, and Eric thought I needed a gun. "Hey, at least we'll match the décor," I said at last.

Pam looked blank.

"Blondes," I said helpfully. "Us."

She almost smiled.

We got out of the car. I tucked the gun in at the small of my back, and Pam checked to make sure it was covered by my fitted black jacket. I never looked as put-together as Pam, but since we'd been going to a show and then out, I'd worn my good black pants and a blue and black knit top with long sleeves. The jacket didn't look ridiculous, since the temperature had fallen into the forties. Pam pulled on her white trench coat and belted it tightly around her waist, and then off she went.

I trotted along behind her, second-guessing myself every step of the way. Pam knocked once on the employee entrance. After a pause, the door opened, and I saw that the male holding it was a vampire. Not Michael, though, if I was any judge at all. This male had only been a vampire for a few years. He had a Mohawk, colored green and gelled to a high crest on his otherwise bald head. I tried to imagine going through the centuries like that, and I thought I might throw up.

"We're here to see Michael," Pam said, her voice especially cool and regal. "We're expected."

"You the ladies from Shreveport?"

"We are."

"There's a lot going on here tonight," he said. "You going to try out after you talk to Michael? I'm in charge of the try-outs." He was proud of that. "Just come right to this door when you're ready." He pointed at a door to the right that had a hand-lettered sheet of typing paper taped to it. Straggly letters spelled DANCERS IN HERE.

We didn't say anything to that, and he cast a glance back at us that I couldn't read.

"Let me see if the boss is ready," Mohawk said.

When he'd knocked and been admitted through a door on the left, Pam said, "I can't believe they let someone so deficient answer the door. In fact, I can't believe anyone bothered to turn him. I think he's slow."

Mohawk popped back out of the door as quickly as he'd popped in.

"He's ready for you," he said, which I found an ominous way to put it.

Pam and I followed his sweeping gesture, which led into an unexpectedly luxurious office. Michael believed in treating himself well. The room was carpeted in dark blue and topped with a lovely Persian-style rug in cream, blue, and red. The furniture was dark and polished. The contrast with the bare corridor was almost painful.

Michael himself was a short, broad blond with a distinct Slavic look. Russian, maybe. A dull throb underlay all the polish of his office, and I realized the throb, which I'd been aware of since I entered the building, was the sound of the music playing in the club. The bass was turned up all the way.

It was impossible to tell what the song was, not that the lyrics were the point.

"Ladies, be seated, please," Michael said. He gestured toward the two very impressive guest chairs in front of his desk. He had a heavy accent and a bad suit. He was smoking. It smelled just as bad when a vampire did it. Of course, he wouldn't suffer any consequences. An open bottle of Royalty Blended was on the desk by the ashtray. "This is my associate, Rudy," Michael told us.

Rudy was standing behind Michael. He was the human I'd come to read. He was slim and black-haired, with an extensively scarred face. He looked as if he was eighteen, but I figured he was at least ten years older than that. He gave off a very strange mental signature. Maybe he wasn't completely human. Everyone I know has a brain pattern: Humans have one kind, weres of all sorts have another, fairies are opaque but identifiable, and vampires leave a sort of void. Rudy didn't fall into any of those categories.

"You can leave," Michael said to Mohawk, his voice contemptuous. "Go back to organize the tryouts. We'll be there soon." Mohawk backed out of the room, pulling the door closed behind him. The noise level abruptly dropped, thank God. The boss's office was soundproofed. But the drumbeat was pulsing in my head, and I swore I could feel it through my feet even if I couldn't hear it any longer.

"Please let me offer you a drink," Michael said, smiling at both of us. Rudy decided to smile, too. His teeth were very sharp; in fact, they were pointed. Okay, half human at most. I was suddenly and deeply frightened. The last time I'd seen teeth like that, they'd bitten bits out of me.

"You've never met anyone like Rudy?" Michael asked. He was looking directly at me.

I'm good at schooling my face. Telepaths learn that lesson

early in life, or they don't survive, is my guess. How had he known?

"I sense your pulse speeding up," Michael said charmingly, and I knew I didn't like him at all. "Rudy is a rarity, aren't you, my darling one?"

Rudy smiled again. It was just as bad the second time.

"Half human and half what?" Pam said. "Elf, I suppose. The teeth are a giveaway."

"I've seen teeth like that before," I said, "on fairies who'd filed them to look that way."

"Mine are natural," said Rudy. His voice was surprisingly deep and smooth. "What can I get you to drink?"

"Some blood, please," Pam said. She loosened her coat and leaned back in the chair.

"Nothing for me, thank you." I didn't want to drink anything Rudy had touched. I hoped the human-elf hybrid would leave the room to get Pam's drink, but instead he turned and bent down to a little refrigerator to extricate a bottle of Royalty Blended, a premium drink that mixed synthetic blood with a large dash of the real blood of certified royalty. He popped the top off the bottle and put it in a microwave sitting atop a low filing cabinet. There were odds and ends on top of the microwave: a bottle opener, a corkscrew, a few straws in paper wrappers, a small paring knife, a folded towel. Quite the home away from home.

"So, you come from Eric? How is the Northman?" Michael asked. "We were together in St. Petersburg at one time."

"Eric is flourishing under our new ruler. He wishes you well. He's heard good things about your club," Pam said, which was outrageous flattery and almost certainly untrue. Unless there was a lot below the surface, this was a sleazy little club catering to sleazy little people.

The microwave dinged. Rudy, who'd been fiddling with the items on top of the microwave, took the drink out, putting one of his thumbs over the open top of the bottle so he could shake it gently. Not the most hygienic way of doing the job, but since vampires almost never get ill, that wouldn't make any difference to Pam. He came around the desk to hand the bottle to her, and she accepted it with a nod of her head.

Michael picked up his own bottle and raised it. "To our mutual venture," he said, and they both drank.

"Are you truly interested in having a further discussion with our new masters?" she asked. She took another sip, a longer one.

"I am considering it," Michael said slowly, his accent even heavier. "I am tired of Russell, though we share a liking of men." Russell liked men as fish like water. I'd been in his mansion, and it was full of guys who ranked from cute to cuter. "However, unlike Russell, I also like women, and women like me." Michael gave us an unmistakable leer.

This woman didn't like him. I glanced at Pam, who also enjoyed sex with either gender, to see her reaction. To my dismay, her cheeks were red—really red. I was so used to her milky pallor I found the effect shocking.

She looked down at the bottle in her hand. "This was poisoned," she said slowly, almost slurring her words. "What did you put in it, elf?"

Rudy's smile became even more disagreeable. He held his hand up so we could see the cut in his thumb. He'd put his own blood into the Royalty Blended. The human blood had disguised the taste.

"Pam, what's this going to do to you?" I asked, as if the men weren't there.

"Elf blood isn't intoxicating like fairy blood, but . . . it's like taking a huge tranquilizer or having lots of alcohol." Her speech was even slower.

"Why have you done this?" I asked Michael. "Don't you know what will happen to you?"

"I know how much Eric will pay me to get you two back," Michael said. He was leaning forward over the desk, his expression one of sheer greed. "And while he's getting the ransom together, Rudy will be drawing up a paper about your mission in coming here, which you and the vampire will sign. That way, when we return you to Eric, he can't retaliate. If anything happens to us, Russell will have the ammunition to start a war. Your new masters will be quick to dispose of Eric if he causes a war."

Michael was as deep a thinker as he was charming. That was to say, not at all. "Do you have something personal against Eric, or are you always this double-dealing?" Keep 'em talking while Pam got in a little recovery time.

"Oh, always," he said, and he and Rudy laughed. They were certainly two peas in the same pod; they were relishing my anxiety and Pam's intoxication.

"Stand up, Pam," I said, and she laboriously worked her way to her feet.

Rudy laughed again. My insides were burning with a huge brushfire of hate.

My friend's face was mottled, her movements sluggish, and her eyes were frightened. I had never seen Pam scared of anything. She was a revered fighter, even among the vampires, who were known for savagery and ruthlessness. "Let's try walking it off."

"That won't help you," Rudy said with a sneer. He was lounging against the wall. "She won't be feeling herself again for a couple of hours. In the meantime, we'll have fun with you first, Michael and me. Then we'll have her."

"Pam, look at me," I said sharply, trying not to picture their idea of fun. She did look. "You have to help me," I said intently, trying to get a message into her addled brain. "These men are going to hurt us." Her eyes finally focused on mine, and she nodded slowly. I moved my head slightly to the right, pointed a thumb at my own chest. Then I inclined my head oh-so-slightly toward Michael, pointing the same thumb at her.

"I understand," Pam said clearly, but only with great effort.

Michael was still seated, but Rudy had pulled away from the wall the moment I drew the gun. They smelled it as I was drawing (and they might have sooner if Michael hadn't been smoking) and reacted with the quickness of their races. I fired into Rudy's face as he grabbed for me, and Pam threw herself across the desk to grip Michael's ears. He clawed at her arms and slammed her down onto the desk. Ordinarily she would have tossed him over her shoulder or something equally spectacular. But in her drugged state, she could only hold on to what she had. He was hitting her repeatedly, too angry to pry her hands away when he could be doing damage to her body. She'd have to loosen her grip, eventually.

While Rudy gurgled and grabbed at the hole in his face under his left cheekbone, I said, "Pull, Pam!" and she obeyed.

She pulled Michael's ears off.

When he flinched back, his mouth open with the pain, she lunged again and stuck her thumbs in his eyes. Instead of throwing up, I shot Rudy again, this time in the chest.

Michael wasn't dead, of course, but he was rocking in silent agony. While he was distracted, Pam pulled out his tongue. I averted my eyes as quickly as I could and swallowed down the bile that rose in my throat. This was Pam on a *bad* night.

I checked on my target. Rudy was down, though he wouldn't stay that way. If elves were as tough as fairies, he'd be up within a half hour. I grabbed the towel from the top of the microwave and wiped off the gun, then tossed it on the desk. I don't really know why—I just had to get rid of it.

"We have to get out of here," I said to Pam, and she dropped the bloody ears. Slowly and deliberately, she wiped her hands on the chair cushion. The ears lying on the desk looked like discarded Play-Doh shells with red paint sprinkled on them. I wondered briefly if Michael could stick the ears back on, if the eyes and tongue would regenerate.

Whoops! Rudy was already up on his elbows, trying to drag himself toward us. I kicked him under the chin as hard as I possibly could, and he collapsed. Pam had started to waver, but I put my arm around her again and she steadied.

"I took care of him," Pam said, enunciating with care. She smiled at me. Speckles of blood had landed on her pink silk blouse, so I told her to button her coat up again. I tied it shut. "That was fun," she said guilelessly.

"I'm glad you had a good time," I muttered, "since I planned all this for your benefit." We stepped out of the office into the corridor and let the door shut behind us. If we could just make it to the car . . . Mohawk was staring at us from his place on the stool by the back door.

Then that door opened, and two cops walked in.

And we'd been doing so well.

The pulsing noise of the stripper music and the office soundproofing had drowned out the shots. I knew this, because no employees had come to check on the gunfire. So no one had summoned these guys; therefore, they must be friends of the management, since they'd entered through the rear.

I was trying to think, and think fast, and my brain was a little too crowded (what with shooting an elf, seeing a guy lose his facial features, and whatnot). One thing I was clear about was wanting to stay out of jail. These cops might not even be within their own jurisdiction, but we had to avoid coming to their attention.

After giving Mohawk a casual wave, they'd stopped to talk to a short, curvy stripper in a platinum wig, which meant they were blocking the rear exit. If we reversed direction and tried to walk out through the front, we'd attract even more attention, I figured.

"Whoops," said Pam cheerfully. "What now, my perky friend?"

"You girls ready to try out?" Mohawk called, and the cops glanced at us before resuming their conversation. Mohawk pointed to the DANCERS IN HERE sign.

I said, "We sure are, sugar! We go in there to put on our costumes?"

He nodded, and his Mohawk swayed. Pam giggled. I'd never heard Pam giggle like that. "Course, most girls don't even bother with a costume," Mohawk said, grinning.

"I think you'll find we're not most girls," I said, arch as all hell.

He was interested. "How're you two different?"

"We're always together," I said. "Get what I mean?"

"Uh, yeah," he said. His eyes darted from the clearly sloshed Pam to me. "So, go change. It's audience night. They vote after you take your turn. You could end up on permanent staff."

Oh . . . yay. I knew there were speckles of blood on Pam. Vampires could always smell blood. As we passed him in the narrow hall, I didn't dare to meet Mohawk's eyes.

I steered my drunken vampire friend into the designated room. It was a huge nothing. There were about twenty folding chairs set around at random, and about six of those were occupied by women waiting their turn. The others had already had their stage time and left, I assumed. No screen to change behind, no makeup table, no hangers—no clothes hooks, even. There was a full-length mirror propped against the wall, and that was it. The glamour just overwhelmed me.

The aspiring strippers were all blondes: At least, they'd achieved blonde-dom by some means. They glanced at us and looked away. One face looked vaguely familiar.

I helped Pam to a chair. She sat heavily. Her complexion was still hectic, but at least the red patches were fading and she looked more like a regular vampire and less like cherry vanilla ice cream. Speaking of red dots, I hastily spat on a tissue and dabbed at the specks of blood on Pam's blouse. I'd been very fortunate; a quick glance into the full-length mirror confirmed that I was unbloodied. "All right, genius, what do we do now?" I asked myself, aloud.

Pam said, "I'll, I'll . . . appeal to her. She has two extra costumes." She nodded toward the woman I sort of recognized.

Pam was oddly sure about what the wannabe dancer—who I realized was a vamp—had in her huge tote bag.

"Pam, you did great in there," I whispered.

"So did you. You're so cute," she said. "No wonder Eric likes you."

I glanced out into the hall. The cops were still there, still having a lively conversation with the curvaceous stripper. Crap.

Pam rose cautiously and went over to the vamp, who was sitting by herself, looking bored. She had the requisite blond hair (so did the only African-American applicant, by the way) and enormous boobs, and she was a few decades old, I figured. She was thin, with the sulky expression of someone who's used to being spoiled. She wore a yellow bikini top with a tiny pleated gray and yellow skirt, a take on the "naughty schoolgirl" image. Where had I seen her before?

As soon as Pam acknowledged her, the vamp straightened in her chair, inclined her head, and dropped the sulkiness. When Pam murmured in her ear, she began rummaging around in the big bag. She handed Pam a handful of material and two pairs of shoes. I was amazed until I realized that she could have carried twenty costumes in there, if the size of the one she was wearing was any gauge.

Pam cocked her head at me, and I hurried to help.

"What you got?" I asked. She dropped the garments into my hands. She'd snagged a glittery gold spandex bandeau to go around the chest and a matching—well, it was flattering it to call it a thong. There was a pair of translucent heels to wear with it. Then there was a sort of sky blue leotard with black trim: a former leotard, since most of it had been snipped away. A little swath of blue for boob coverage, descending in a tiny strip to the bottom part, which was like an abbreviated bikini. Black heels and thigh-high black hose completed the look.

Pam sat down on a chair, hard. She giggled again. "Get ready, buttercup! I'll take the gold; you take the blue. It'll look great with your tan." She shrugged off her coat, and when the speckled blouse came into view, she read the alarm on my face correctly. She turned her back to the room to unbutton it, then turned it inside out and tossed it on the floor, close to the vamp. To my amazement, the vamp waited for a moment, then in one quick movement picked up the blouse and stuffed it into her huge bag.

Pam was out of her clothes and into the costume as if it were her daily routine.

I turned my back on the room, though no one seemed in the least bit interested in my goodies. In the course of wriggling into the thing, I found out the descending strip Velcroed to the bottom of the costume. Convenient.

I looked at us together. "Wow," I said. "Pam, we look *great*."

"We do," Pam agreed, with no attempt at modesty. We gave each other a high five. "I'm coming down," Pam said. "Really, I'm feeling almost like myself."

Mohawk called from the door. "Okay, the doubles act!"

I had no idea how we were going to get out of this, so we started toward the door. Even drugged, Pam managed walking in her platform shoes without a wobble in her step, but I had to concentrate ferociously to master the spike heels.

"What's the names?" Mohawk asked.

"Sugar and Butterscotch," I said, and Pam turned her head to give me a look that clearly said she thought I was an idiot.

"'Cause she's white and you're brown," Mohawk said. "Cute."

I hadn't spent all that time tanning for nothing.

"Okay, you're on," Mohawk said, opening the door at the end of the corridor to reveal a short flight of steps leading up into darkness. The noise surged out at us. A Latina blonde stomped down the steps, topless, followed by the sound of whistles and catcalls. She looked sweaty and bored.

The cops were still in the hall.

"Shepherd of Judea," I muttered, and Pam and I looked at each other and shrugged.

"New skills," she said. "Eric told me you are quite the dancer. You just have to try doing it naked."

So we went up the steps, teetering in our high, high heels, to begin our careers as strippers. Suddenly we were on the stage, which was simply wood painted black, punctuated with three stripper poles.

The emcee was a brunette guy with a big white smile. He was saying, "Remember, gentlemen! The applause each girl gets is measured with our applause-o-meter, and out of all our dancers tonight, the three girls getting the most audience response will be hired to appear right here at Blonde!"

So we were supplying the audience with free entertainment in the faint hope that we might get a job out of it. Michael was an even bigger asshole than I'd thought, which was saying something.

"Here, straight from their record-breaking engagement in Vegas, I give you Sugar and Butterscotch!" the emcee said, with considerable drama. I figured he took drugs.

I put on my biggest and emptiest smile, and managed to make it to the front of the stage without falling down, thanks to Pam's sudden grip on my hand. Together, we looked out at the men hidden in the darkness, catching a glint of beard here, shine reflecting off a belt buckle there. The hoots and whistles were deafening.

We hadn't specified a song, of course. Justin Timberlake's "SexyBack" came blaring over the sound system, and that was all right with me. "Move it," yelled a rough voice.

We had to *dance*. NOW. And then we had to get the hell out of here before Michael and Rudy recovered enough to come after us.

I half turned to look at Pam flirtatiously, and she stared blankly back at me until she got my drift. "The pole," I muttered, and she gave the audience a saucy smile and wound herself around the nearest pole. The cheering started. I felt the lust begin to dominate the men's minds as I hugged Pam from behind. Pam got with the program, and we swung around the pole together as if we'd been glued. I caught a glimpse of Pam's face. She was licking her lips in a lascivious way.

"You go, Pam!" I said.

"They want a show, we'll give them a show," she said. She bent me over her knee and pretended to spank me in perfect time to the music. In fact, Pam got a little carried away. But the guys loved it; oh boy, did they. I got spanked, licked in the ear, had Pam's hands running over my barely covered chest, and more stuff I just won't mention. We both ended up doing things the stripper pole had probably endured many times.

You know, it was kind of fun after I got the hang of it.

I wouldn't go close enough to the side of the stage to get grabbed. And since I already felt naked, I wouldn't take off my top. Since that was something the audience clearly expected us to do, it was lucky that at that moment the police pulled the plug on the music and switched on the house lights.

They weren't the cops who'd been in the hall. "All right, everyone!" called a tall detective in a blue Windbreaker. "There's been a murder here, and we need to talk with all of you."

"Murder," I said to Pam. "Murder?"

As our eyes met, I could see she was just as bewildered as I was. And I have to say here: With the lights up, we could see our audience, and they looked even worse than I'd expected.

OFFICER WASHINGTON, NEAT and shiny in his brown uniform, tried to look anywhere but at my chest. He'd been on the force long enough to have a kind of worn-out face, but he hadn't become so world-weary as to be able to completely ignore the abundance of Pam and me that was on display. I learned that the idea of being with a white woman didn't do a thing for Officer Washington, which helped him do his job.

"You ladies talked to the manager of this club earlier, I understand?" he asked. He had a pad and pencil out. By now we knew that the victims were Michael and Rudy.

"Yes, we had an appointment," I said.

"What for? None of the other strippers had to talk to the manager."

"We used to work at another vamp-owned club," I said, improvising. I could give Fangtasia's phone number. "We hoped if we told him that, we'd get the job. He said he'd take it into account."

Pam and I shrugged, at very nearly the same moment. Pam seemed to be a little high even now, but there was more control in her movements and she was keeping her mouth resolutely shut. She was still holding my hand, though.

We'd waited our turn in the bigger room where we'd left our clothes. We'd been allowed to change, thank goodness. Pam was still wearing her gold bandeau top. In sympathy, I'd only pulled on my slacks.

Our friend the stripper vamp had passed by the door on her way out. She was escorted by a cop. She glanced our way, her face composed and indifferent. I finally remembered where I'd seen her: working at Harrah's, carrying drinks, when we'd checked in. Huh. She had a sizable purse hanging from her shoulder; I wondered where the big bag was? Pam's bloodstained blouse was in it. . . .

As the other strippers had been questioned, they'd been released. We were the last ones to be brought to this room, which I figured had been Rudy's office. Officer Washington had been waiting for us there.

"What else happened while you were in there? They want you two to give them a free sample?" Washington was young enough to look faintly self-conscious.

"They seemed more interested in each other," I said carefully.

The policeman glanced at our linked hands and didn't comment. "So they were both alive and well when you left the room?"

"Yes, sir," I said. "In fact, they wanted us to hustle out of there because they were about to talk to someone else, had a guy coming in from out of town, they said."

"That right? Did they say anything else about this man? Vampire or human?"

"No," Pam said, opening her mouth for the first time. "They were just anxious for us to leave so they could get ready."

"Get ready? How?"

We shrugged simultaneously. "They wouldn't hardly tell us," I said.

"Okay, okay." Officer Washington snapped his notepad shut and stowed away his pencil. "Ladies, good night to you. You can go pick up your personal items."

But we didn't have any. Pam only had the car keys in her pants pocket and her white trench coat. We had nothing we could have brought costumes in. Would Officer Washington or Windbreaker Guy wonder about that?

Now that the big room was empty, it looked even more depressing. Only a litter of tissues and cigarette butts showed that the women had been here at all. That, and the big bag the vamp stripper had carried, sitting on the chair that was draped with Pam's white coat and my jacket. Windbreaker Guy was staring at the bag. Without hesitation, Pam strode across the floor in those incredible shoes and scooped it up by the shoulder strap.

"Come on, Butterscotch," she told me, "We need to hit the road." Her voice had no trace of the faint English accent I was used to.

And just like that, we left Blonde, doing our stripper walks all the way out to Pam's car.

Mohawk was leaning against the driver's door.

He smiled at us as we approached. His smile was not dim or goofy or naïve.

"Thanks for giving me the opening, ladies," he said, and there was nothing slow in his speech, either. "I've been waiting a year to have them down long enough for me to finish them off."

If Pam was as shocked as I was, she didn't show it. "You're welcome," she said. "I take it you're not going to tell the police anything about us?"

"What's to tell?" He looked up at the night sky. "Two strippers wanted to tell the boss and his buddy something before they tried out. I'm sure you explained that. When you went onstage, that asshole Michael and his buddy Rudy were alive and kicking. I made sure the cops knew that. I'm betting you also told them something about Michael mentioning he was expecting someone else or expecting trouble."

Pam nodded.

"And stupid, slow me, I was cleaning the toilet, like my boss Michael had told me to do. No one was more surprised than me when I went in the office later and found Rudy dead and Michael flaking away." Mohawk rolled his eyes theatrically. "I must have just missed the killer." He grinned. "By the way, I threw the gun in the ravine back there, right down into the kudzu, before I called the local law. The skinny blond vamp did the same thing with your blouse—Sugar."

"Right," Pam said.

"So off you go, ladies! Have a nice night!"

After a moment of silence, we got in the car. Mohawk watched us as we drove away.

"How long do you think he'll last?" I asked Pam.

"Russell has a reputation for acuity. If Mohawk is a good club manager, he'll get away with killing Michael, for a while. If he doesn't earn money, Russell will make sure he doesn't last. And Russell won't forget that Mohawk is patient and wily, and willing to wait for someone else to do the dirty work."

We drove for a few minutes. I was anxious to get back to my room and wash away the atmosphere of the Blonde.

"What did you promise the vamp that helped us?" I asked.

"A job at Fangtasia. I had a conversation with Sara—that's her name—after you went to bed last night. She hates her job in Tunica. And she used to be a stripper, which gave me the idea of planting her here in case we needed some help. Besides extra costumes, she brought a number of handy items in her bag."

I didn't inquire as to their nature. "And she did all that for us."

"She did all that because she wants a better job. She doesn't seem to have much . . . planning ability."

"In the end, the trip was for nothing. It was a trap."

"It was a bad trap," Pam said briskly. "But it's true that because of Victor's greed, we were almost in serious trouble." She glanced over at me. "Eric and I never thought Victor was exactly sincere about his motives in sending us here."

"You think he was trying to hamstring Eric by getting rid of both you and me? That he knew Michael really wasn't going to defect?"

"I think we're going to keep a very sharp eye on our new master's deputy."

We rode in silence for a couple of minutes.

"You think Sara would mind if we kept the costumes?" I asked, now that Eric was on my mind.

"Oh," said Pam, "I'm planning on it. Without some souvenirs, it's not a real vacation."

SMALL-TOWN WEDDING

"Small-Town Wedding" is the only Sookie novella, and I had a great time imagining it and writing it. Sookie, masquerading as Sam's girlfriend, accompanies her boss and friend to a family wedding in Sam's hometown in Texas. Sookie meets Sam's family, including his brother, the groom; and she likes them all. But there's a black cloud on the horizon. Everyone in Sam's family has shifter blood, and prejudice is at an all-time high against the two-natured and the Weres. The bride is completely human. The wedding becomes a test case as the anti-were groups arrive to protest the union. The situation escalates almost beyond saving, when the were community steps up to protect the shifters. This was a great pleasure to write, since I had the chance to introduce some important themes and to establish the groundwork for the ending of the series.

The upheaval of American society that forms the basis of "Small-Town Wedding" takes place after *Dead in the Family*.

ONE

IT WAS MAY, I had a great tan, and I was going on a road trip, leaving vampire politics behind. I felt better than I had in a long time. Wearing only my underwear, I stood in my sunny bedroom and went down my checklist.

1. *Give Eric and Jason address and dates*

I'd done that. My boyfriend, Eric Northman, vampire sheriff of Area Five of Louisiana, had all the information he needed. So did my brother, Jason.

2. *Ask Bill to watch house*

Okay. I'd left a letter pushed under my neighbor Bill Compton's door. He'd find it when he rose for the night. His "sister" Judith (sired by the same vampire) was still staying at his place. If Bill could tear himself away from her company, he would walk across the cemetery separating our properties to have a look at my house, and he'd get my mail and my newspaper and put them on my front porch.

3. *Call Tara*

I'd done that; my pregnant friend Tara reported all was well with the twins she was carrying, and she'd call or get her husband to call if there was any news. She wasn't due for three more months. But twins, right? You never knew.

4. *Bank*

I'd deposited my last paycheck and gotten more cash than I usually carried.

5. *Claude and Dermot*

My cousin and my great-uncle had decided to stay at Claude's house in Monroe while I was gone. Claude had been living with me for about a month, and Dermot had joined him only two weeks ago, so Dermot said he still felt funny being in my house without me there. Claude, of course, had no such qualms, since he's about as sensitive as a sheet of sandpaper, but Dermot had carried the day.

All my clothes were clean, and I thought I was packed. Though it would be a good idea to review my packing list, which was completely separate from my "things to do" list. Since my friend and boss, Sam Merlotte, had invited me to go with him to his brother's wedding, I'd been in a nervous tizzy about forgetting something essential and somehow making Sam look bad in front of his family.

I had borrowed a pretty dress, sleeveless and blue, like my eyes, to wear to the wedding, and I had some black pumps with three-inch heels that were in great condition. For everything else, I packed the best and newest of my casual clothes: two pairs of good shorts, an extra pair of jeans. I threw in a yellow and gray skirt outfit, just in case.

I counted my underwear, made sure I had the right bras, and checked the little jewelry pouch to be sure my gran's pearls were there. I shut the bag, triumphant. I'd done my best to cover every contingency, and I'd fit everything into a hanging bag and a weekender bag.

Just as I reopened the bag to make sure I'd included my

blow-dryer, I heard Sam's truck coming up the driveway that wound through the woods. In thirty seconds I pulled on my khaki shorts and a very thin white tank top with a teal tank layered over it. I had a little gold chain on, and I slid my feet into my new sandals. My toenails were a happy pink (Run Run Rosy). I felt great. I hurried to the front door and opened it just as Sam was about to knock.

He was wearing his usual jeans and Merlotte's Bar and Grill T-shirt, but he was sporting ancient cowboy boots. Yep, we were going to Texas, all right. His red gold hair was shorter these days, and I could tell he'd taken special care shaving.

"Sorry I'm a little late," he said. "I had to give Kennedy and Terry some extra instructions." The two substitute bartenders were going to be in charge while Sam was gone, and Sam was pretty nervous about it.

"No problem. I'm ready." He picked up my overnighter while I got my hanging bag and locked the door behind me. Luckily, Sam's pickup had an extended cab, and we were able to put our clothes on the backseat.

"You looking forward to this?" I asked him, when we were on the interstate. We were going across the state line from Louisiana into Texas to a small town called Wright, south of the interstate past Dallas, where Sam's folks had settled after his dad got out of the service.

"This is the first nice thing that's happened in my family in months, and for a while I didn't think this wedding would ever come off," he said. "I really appreciate your going with me."

"Are they putting pressure on you to get married?" I should have realized before that there might be another reason Sam wanted me to accompany him, something beyond the pleasure of my company. Some women have long careers as bridesmaids; I had a long career of being a pretend girlfriend. I hoped that wasn't going to be a perpetual pattern.

"That might be overstating it," Sam said. He grinned at me. "But my mom and my sister sure are ready for me to show them I'm thinking about the subject. Of course, the shifters going public and my mom's troubles kind of put my own marital status on the back burner."

The Weres had revealed their existence on television a few months before, following the vampire model. Many of the other two-natured (or "twoeys," as the pop-culture magazines had immediately started calling them) had shown themselves at the same time. Oddly, the American public seemed to be more upset about the werewolves and werepanthers living among them than they'd been when they found out vampires were real.

"Does your mom try to set you up with nice shifter girls all the time?"

"So far she hasn't been able to find another pure shifter like me, though my sister, Mindy, told me Mom had gone online trying to track one down." Sam could turn into anything: lion, dog, raccoon. His kind was pretty rare.

"Gosh. Are you sure you shouldn't have brought Jannalynn? She may not be exactly who your family wants you to bring home—at least, that's what you said—but she's a werewolf, and that's better than a human like me, right? At least to your mom. If your mom's looking for a woman for you online, that's kind of . . . desperate, huh?"

Sam laughed. "Definitely. But Mom means well. She was really happy with my dad, and their first date was a setup. If she can find an unattached female shifter the right age, she's hoping lightning will strike twice in the Merlotte family."

"You told me that you'd almost gotten married once."

"Yeah, when I was in the army. She was a good ol' girl, regular human. My dad would have liked her. But it just didn't work out."

I wanted to ask why, but I knew it was none of my business.

He asked, "You think you and Eric might get married now that it's legal?"

I started to tell him we were married already, according to my big blond vampire boyfriend, but decided it would be better to skip that discussion entirely.

"He hasn't asked me," I said, which was the truth. He hadn't asked me about the vampire marriage rite, either. I'd handed him a ceremonial knife in front of a witness without asking a single question, which proves how little sense I could have when I was around Eric.

As the miles carried me away from Eric, the bond between us stretched but did not break. Eric was a silent presence. Miles of Texas interstate rolled by, and though I knew Eric was in his bed, dead to the world, I couldn't help thinking about him. It wasn't nearly as bad as it would have been if he'd been awake, though.

"A penny for your thoughts," Sam said.

I jumped because my thoughts weren't family-rated at that moment.

"I was hoping Bill recovers from the silver poisoning. I found a vampire sibling of his, and I got her to come visit. He'd told me if he got some blood from a sib, it would really help him heal."

Sam looked a little nonplussed. "How'd you do that?" he asked.

When I told him how I'd tracked Judith down, he shook his head. "How'd you know he wouldn't get mad at you?"

"I was doing it for him," I said, not understanding Sam's point. "Why would he get mad?"

Sam said gently, "Sook, Bill obviously knew where this Judith was, and he didn't call her on his own. He must have had a reason."

I knew that. But I'd gone ahead and contacted her anyway. I'd only thought about how worried I was about Bill. I could feel myself tearing up. I didn't want to admit to Sam that he was right.

I looked out the window so Sam wouldn't have to watch my eyes brim over.

"Sook?" he said, and from his voice I could tell he had leaned forward to try to see my face. "Sook? Hey, I'm sorry. Listen, I was just blowing hot air. You were watching out for him, and I'm probably just jealous."

I could read his mind enough to know he wasn't being entirely truthful—but he did sincerely want me to feel better, and he was truly sorry I was upset. "You're right," I said, though my voice wobbled in a pathetic way. "Sam, you're absolutely right. I've made so many mistakes."

"Don't we all? I've made more than a few, and I don't seem to stop making them," Sam said, and there was bitterness in his voice.

"Okay. We're both human; we got that settled," I said, making myself smile. "Or, at least, we're mostly human."

He laughed, and I felt better. I rummaged around in my purse for a Kleenex and patted my eyes carefully to keep my makeup intact. I got a Coca-Cola out of the ice chest behind Sam's seat and popped it open for him, and got myself one, too. We talked about the sorry season the Bon Temps Hawks baseball team was having, and I told Sam about watching the softball team practice the week before. I felt good when I was confident everything was back to normal between us.

When we stopped to get gas outside Dallas, I watched a

black Ford Focus shoot by. "That's funny," I said to Sam, who was punching his PIN into the pump. "That's the same car I saw when we pulled over to find out what that noise was." A branch had caught under the truck and had been making an alarming *whap-whap-whap*.

Sam glanced up. "Huh," he said. "Well, the interstate is always busy, and the Focus is a popular model."

"This is the same one," I said. "There's a place on the driver's side of the windshield where a rock hit."

Then I went inside the station to visit the ladies' room, because I could tell Sam didn't want to be worrying about a Ford Focus. I didn't, either, but there it was.

I kept a sharp eye out for the car after that, but I didn't bring up the subject again. As a result, we made pleasant conversation past Dallas and Fort Worth, all the way to the turn off the interstate that would lead us south to Wright.

I'd offered to drive, but Sam said he was so familiar with the route that he didn't mind being at the wheel. "I'm just glad to have company making the drive, for once," he said. "I've had to go over to Wright so often since the announcement." Sam's mom had had a huge crisis the evening of the big two-natured reveal, broadcast worldwide; her second husband had been so startled by the fact that his wife could turn into an animal that he'd shot her.

"But you've got the one sister and the one brother," I said.

"Yeah, Mindy and Craig. Mindy's twenty-six. She's married to Doke Ballinger. She went to high school with him. They have two kids, Mason and Bonnie. They live about thirty miles away in Mooney."

"What's the name of the woman Craig's marrying? Daisy? Denise?"

"Deidra. She's from Wright, too. She and Craig have both

been going to UT Dallas. She's a real pretty girl, only nineteen, and Craig's twenty-four. He went into the army before he started college."

"Lots of military service in your family." Sam and Craig's dad had been retired army.

Sam shrugged. "Because of Dad, we're all used to the service as an option. It's not a huge leap like it is for some families. Craig always liked Deidra, but when he was in high school, she was way too young for him to think about as a date. He did call her when he found out another kid from Wright was going to UT Dallas, and he says they were gone on each other after the first date."

"Aw. That's so sweet. I guess all this trouble has been really hard on them."

"Yeah. Craig was pretty mad at me and Mom for a while, and then he accepted it, but Deidra's folks freaked out. The wedding got postponed a couple of times."

I nodded. Sam had told me how his brother's fiancée's family had reacted to the news that her about-to-be mother-in-law sometimes ran on four feet.

"So instead of sending out new invitations, the Lisles just put a notice in the Wright paper."

"How big is Wright?"

Sam laughed. "About as big as Bon Temps. Except in the tourist season. There's a river that runs a little west of Wright, and there's a lot of rafting and camping. At night, those rafters and campers are looking for something to do, so there're a couple of big bars that have live bands. And there's a western-wear store and a riding stable for beginners on up, for when people want to take a break from the water. Stuff like that. Wright's a pretty conservative place, though. Everyone's glad when the tourists leave in the fall."

"Has your mom had any trouble with the rest of the town since the shooting?" Sam had been the target of one protest in the Merlotte's parking lot, but since then things had died down—for good, I hoped.

"I'm reading between the lines, but yes, I think people haven't been as friendly as they used to be. Don's a local guy. He's got cousins and stuff all around Wright."

"He's in jail now, right?"

"Yeah, he couldn't make bail. He never denied he shot Mom. I don't understand why there's any sympathy for him."

I didn't say anything, but I could sort of understand feeling sympathy for someone who'd suddenly discovered his wife changed into a different creature. Of course, shooting that wife was a gross overreaction, but watching your wife transform into a dog . . . That would shake any man. However, that was not my problem to solve, and I was certainly sorry the whole incident had happened.

I was not walking into a normal, happy family wedding. I already knew some of what Sam was saying, but maybe I should have asked more questions before I got in the truck. I thought of the shotgun my brother had given me, sitting uselessly in the closet in my house.

"You look kinda worried, Sookie," Sam said, and I could read the dismay in his brain. "I wouldn't have brought you if I thought there was a way in the world something bad would happen to you."

"Sam, I hope you have the whole picture of what's going on in Wright," I said. "I know you asked me to go with you before you started dating Jannalynn, but I really wouldn't have minded if you'd wanted to take her." He understood the subtext. Though he'd told me Jannalynn's habits and manners weren't family-pleasing, she had excellent natural defenses. In fact, she was the enforcer for the Shreveport pack. What was I going to do if we were attacked? Mind-read someone to death?

"This isn't any mob situation," Sam said, and he laughed. "I finished high school there when my dad retired from the military, and Mindy and Craig did even more of their growing up in Wright than I did. People will get used to the new things in their world, even the people in a conservative little place like Wright. These are just regular folks. They've known us for years."

Pardon me if I felt a tad skeptical.

I saw the black Focus one more time, and then I didn't spot it again. I told myself that there were hundreds of cars on this section of interstate, and a hell of a lot of them were going west like we were.

The landscape got less and less green, more and more arid. Trees were smaller, rocks were more plentiful, and there were cacti in the scrubby brush. After the turnoff south, towns were fewer and farther between. They were small, and the stretches of road were lined by fences of all kinds. This was ranching country.

Wright looked very normal when we rolled in. The highway ran through Wright going north–south, and it was the main drag. In its stretch through Wright, it was called Main Street, which made me smile. It was a one-story town. Everything was low and long and dusty. I looked at the people we passed, the gas stations, the Sonic, the Dairy Queen, the McDonald's. There were three motels, which seemed excessive until I remembered that Sam had told me about the river west of the town. The trailer park was full, and I saw a few people walking west, flip-flops on their feet and towels over their shoulders. Early vacationers. We passed a rental place for canoes, tubes, rafts, grills, and tents.

"People can grill on the sandbars in the river," Sam said.

"It's fun. You take your ice chest out there, a tube of sunblock, drink your beer, and grill your meat. Get in the water whenever you want."

"I wish we had time to do that," I said. Then, thinking that might sound like a complaint or a hint, I said brightly, "But I know we're here to get this wedding done! Maybe you can bring Jannalynn over here sometime later in the summer."

Sam didn't respond. I'd seen Jannalynn be aggressive, physical, even savage. But surely she had a softer side? I mean, it couldn't be all skull-cracking, bustiers, spike heels, and kill-my-enemies. Right?

It was a warm feeling, seeing the town where Sam had done a lot of his growing up. "Where's your school?" I asked, trying to picture the young Sam. He turned east to take me by the little high school where he'd played sports and been named Mr. Yellowjacket. Yellowjacket Stadium was about the same size as Bon Temps's Hawks Stadium and in much better repair, though the old high school had seen better days. The town library was brand-new, and the post office was proudly flying the flag. It whipped in the warm wind.

"Why'd your dad decide to retire here after he left the service?" I asked. "What do people do here besides cater to tourists?"

"They ranch, mostly," he said. "A few of them farm, but mostly the land's too rocky, and we don't get much rain. A lot of people make the bulk of their income during the tourist season, and they just coast along on odd jobs the rest of the year. We get a big influx of hunters when the tourists run out, so that's a major source of income, too. My dad commuted to Mooney, where Doke and Mindy live now. He had a job doing security for a big plant over there. It manufactures wind turbines for wind energy. Doke works there now."

"And you-all moved here instead of Mooney because . . . ?"

"My dad wanted us to have the whole small-town experience. He thought it would be the best way to finish out my teen years and to bring up Mindy and Craig. Some of my mom's family was still living in Wright then, too. And he loved the river."

I looked at the people coming in and out of the businesses we passed. There were lots more brown faces than I was used to seeing, though even Bon Temps had experienced an upsurge in its Spanish-speaking population in the past decade. Some were identifiably Native American. There were very few black faces. I'd really traveled somewhere different. In addition to the differences in skin color, there were more people in western-style clothes, which made sense. We'd passed a rodeo ground on our way into town.

We took a left when we were within sight of the south boundary of the city limits, turning onto a narrow street that could be anywhere in the United States. The houses were small ranch styles, one or two had a trailer in the backyard where maybe a mother-in-law or a newlywed child lived, and most had a prefab toolshed tucked into a corner of the yard. There were lots of open windows. People in Wright didn't turn on their air conditioners as early as we did in Bon Temps. Instead of garages, there were carports attached to almost every house, some to the side, some added on in front.

At Sam's mom's home, the awning extended over half of the front of the house, covering enough area to park two vehicles. Unattractive, but efficient. "This is the house you lived in after you-all moved to Wright?" I asked.

"Yeah, this is the house Mom and Dad bought after Dad got out of the army. Don moved in here when he and Mom got married. By the way, she's still Bernadette Merlotte. She never took Don's name."

Bernadette Merlotte's home was a modest house, maybe

twelve hundred square feet, with white siding and ornamental dark green shutters. The little yard space had barely any grass because it was almost entirely given over to beds containing flowers, smooth river rocks, and concrete statues, which were various in the extreme. One was a little girl with a dog, one was a large frog, and one was a creature that was supposed to be a fairy. (Any fairy I knew would want to kill Sam's mom after a good look at that statue.) From the dry state of the patches of grass and dirt, it was evident that Sam's mom cared for her flowers lovingly.

There was a little sidewalk winding to the front porch from the covered driveway, and the "porch" was flush with the ground. This was a slab house.

After an almost imperceptible sigh and a moment of bracing himself, Sam jumped out. I didn't stand on ceremony. I slid out, too. I wanted to stretch my legs and back after sitting in the truck for so long, and I was almost as nervous about meeting Sam's family as if I were his real girlfriend.

A screen door slammed, and Sam's mother hurried down the sidewalk to hug her son. She was about my height, five-six, and very slim. She'd had his hair color, but the red gold had faded now. She'd obviously spent a lot of time out in the sun, so at least we'd have that in common. Then she was in Sam's arms and laughing.

"It's so good to see you!" she cried. After giving Sam a final, hard hug, she pulled away and turned to me. "You must be Sookie. Sam's told me a lot about you!" The words were warm and welcoming, but I could tell how she really felt . . . which was more like cautious.

Shaking hands seemed a little too distant somehow, so I half hugged her. "It's good to meet you, Mrs. Merlotte. I'm glad you're doing so well."

"Now, you just call me Bernie. Everybody does." She hesitated. "I thank you for taking care of the bar while Sam came down when I was shot." It was an effort for her to so casually mention what had happened.

"Are you going to let them come in, Mama?" said a young woman standing in the doorway.

"You just hold your horses," Bernie said. "We're coming!"

There were a few moments of confusion as we got out our hanging and overnight bags. Finally we went into the house. Bernie Merlotte's right-hand neighbor, a man in his sixties, came out into his yard—ostensibly to check his mailbox—while all this was going on. I happened to catch his eye, and I gave him a friendly nod. To my amazement, he looked right through me, though I knew from his thoughts that he could see me plainly.

That had never happened to me in my life. If I'd been reading a Regency romance, I would have termed it "the cut direct." No one else had noticed, and he wasn't my neighbor, so I didn't say anything.

Then we were inside, and I had to stuff my bafflement into a corner of my mind because there were more people to meet. The small house was crowded. First there was Sam's sister, Mindy, a young mother of two. Her husband, Doke Ballinger, was as thin and laconic as Mindy was plump and chatty. Their children, five-year-old Mason and three-year-old Bonnie, eyed me from behind their mother. And finally I met the groom, Craig, who was like a more carefree clone of Sam. The brothers were the same in coloring, height, and build. His fiancée, Deidra Lisle, was so pretty it hurt to look at her. She was lightly tanned, with big hazel eyes and reddish brown hair that fell to her waist. She couldn't have stood five foot two, and she was all compact curves and femininity.

She shook my hand shyly, and her smile showed that her teeth were as perfect as her complexion. Wow.

She was pregnant. She was hoping she wasn't showing, that no one could tell. Now that I knew, I could sort of sense that other mind floating around inside her, but it was a weird read—no language, no thoughts.

Well, another thing that was none of my business. More power to them. I was the only one who could sense that other presence in her womb.

By that time Bernie was showing me to a very small room that contained a pullout couch, a sewing machine, a computer desk, and a card table that was cluttered with scrapbooking materials. "We're not fancy here," Bernie said. "I hope you don't mind sleeping in what the magazines call the all-purpose room. Course, I just call it the room-Mindy-finally-left-out-of-so-I-could-have-it-back." There was a hint of challenge in her voice.

"No, ma'am, I don't mind at all." I set my bag down by the end of the couch. "I'll just hang these up in the closet, if that's okay," I said, taking my hanging bag over to the closet door in the corner and waiting for her permission.

"Go right ahead," Bernie said, and she relaxed a bit.

The closet had just enough spare room right in the middle.

"Oh, I'm sorry," Bernie said. "I meant to get in there and make you some more space. It's taken me longer to get over this injury than I'd figured."

"No problem," I said. There was a hook on the outside of the closet door, so I hung my bag there rather than cram it in and wrinkle my dress.

"What's the matter with your neighbor?" I said, my mind suddenly leaping back to my previous source of misgiving.

"Jim Collins? Oh, he's such a grouch," she said with a half

smile. "Why do you ask? Was he giving you a mean look when you came in?"

"Yes."

"Don't pay any attention," she said. "He's just a lonely man since his wife died, and he was a big friend of Don's. Don helped him out in the yard all the time, and they went fishing together. He's blaming me for all Don's problems."

That seemed a strange way to refer to Don's being in jail for shooting her. "Jim Collins hates you," I said.

She gave me a very strange look. "That's a lot to read into a look across the yard," Bernie said. "Don't worry about Jim, Sookie. Let's go get you some ice tea."

So Sam hadn't told his mom that I could read minds. Interesting.

I followed Bernie down the short hall and into the kitchen. The kitchen was quite a bit larger than I'd expected, since it also encompassed an eating area set in a bay window. Deidra was sitting at the big round table with Mindy's little girl, Bonnie, in her lap. The child was holding a soggy cookie and looked quite happy. Through the bay window, I saw Mason and his dad in the backyard playing catch with Craig and Sam. I went to the door and looked out at the family scene. When he saw me, Sam darted an inquiring look my way, to ask if I was okay. He was willing to come in if I needed support.

I smiled at him, genuinely pleased. I nodded reassuringly before I turned to the table. There was a pitcher of tea and a glass filled with ice ready for me. I poured my tea and sat down beside Deidra. Mindy had put a laundry basket full of clean clothes on the kitchen counter, and she was busy folding them. Bernie was drying dishes. I'd thought I might feel like an intruder, but I didn't.

"Sookie, you're the first girl Sam's brought home in years," Mindy said. "We're dying to know all about you."

Nothing like cutting to the chase; I appreciated the direct approach. I didn't want to lie to them about our relationship, but Sam had brought me here to deflect the wedding fever. I would have felt worse if Sam and I hadn't been genuinely fond of each other. After all, I told myself, I was literally Sam's "girl friend," if not his "girlfriend," so we were more bending the truth than breaking it.

"I've worked for Sam for several years," I said, picking my words carefully. "My mom and dad passed away when I was seven, and after that my grandmother brought me and my brother up. Gran died a couple of years ago, and I inherited her house. My brother lives in my parents' house," I added, so they'd know that was fair. "I graduated from high school in Bon Temps, but I never got to carry my education any further than that."

This Sookie-in-a-capsule got a mixed reception.

"Is your brother married?" Mindy asked. She was thinking of her own brother who was getting married, and the possibility of another grandchild to make her mother happy. Bernie was going to get one sooner than Mindy imagined.

"He's a widower," I said.

"Gosh," Deidra blurted, "people in your family don't have a long life expectancy, huh?"

Ouch. "My parents died in a flash flood," I said, because that was the public story. "My grandmother was murdered. My sister-in-law was murdered. So we never got to find out how long they would live." Actually, they'd *all* been murdered. I'd never put it to myself like that before. People in my family really, truly had a short life expectancy. If I followed the family trend, I could expect to meet my end through violence in the not-too-distant future.

I glanced at the appalled faces of Sam's womenfolk, who'd gotten more than they'd expected. Guess they wouldn't be asking me any more personal questions, huh? "But my brother's still alive," I said brightly. "His name is Jason."

They all looked relieved. Deidra grabbed a napkin and began dabbing at Bonnie's smeared face. "Bonnie, you have a chocolate mouth," Deidra said, and Mindy and Bernie laughed while Bonnie stretched her mouth into a wide grin, enjoying the attention.

"How big is your family, Deidra?" I said, to get off the topic of my life.

"I got two sisters," Deidra said. "I'm the oldest. They're seventeen and fifteen, still in high school. And I've got two brothers, both older. One brother works here in Wright, and one brother's in the army."

"How about you, Bernie? Do you have any younger brothers or sisters?" I asked Sam's mother, to keep the conversational ball rolling.

"Oh, they have to be younger? I must be showing my age." Bernie turned a wry face to me. She was stirring something on the stove.

"You have to be the oldest, if you're the shifter."

Then they were all looking at me, this time in surprise. "Sam did tell you a lot," Mindy said. "Humph. He doesn't usually talk much about his heritage."

"I'm not sure if I heard it from Sam or from a werewolf," I said.

"Unusual," Bernie said. "Have you dated other shifters?"

"Yes," I said simply. "And my brother's a bitten panther."

There was another round-robin of exchanged glances among

the women, broken by Bonnie demanding to go potty. Mindy stopped matching socks to sweep her up and carry her off to the hall bathroom.

"So you have no problem with wereanimals at all," Bernie said.

"No," I replied, and I'm sure I sounded as surprised as I felt.

"We just figured . . ."

"What?"

"We just figured," Deidra said, "that your family wouldn't like the idea of you marrying into a shifter family, like my family didn't. I mean, they've come around now, but when they saw the woman change on television, they freaked out." The two-natured, following the vampire pattern, had sent their most personable representatives to local television stations to change on the air.

Don hadn't been the only one who'd reacted with panic.

"If I had a big family, there might be more of a problem. But my brother wouldn't mind me marrying into a family with the shifter gene," I said. "He's all I've got to worry about." And I wasn't any too worried about his opinion. "Not that I have any plans to get married," I added hastily. I hadn't even planned on getting married in the vampire way, for that matter. "Are you going to wear the traditional white dress, Deidra?" I had a doomed feeling that no matter how I tried to keep the conversation on the actual wedding about to take place, the women of the family were going to continue to steer it toward a possible future match between Sam and me.

The bride nodded, smiling. Gosh, Deidra was a dentist's dream. "Yeah, it's pure white and strapless," she said. "I got it on sale at a bridal shop in Waco. It was worth the drive."

"How many bridesmaids?"

A cloud crossed her face. "Well," she began. After a perceptible pause, she tried again. "Two," she said, smiling for all she was worth. "My sisters."

"Two of her friends backed out after the shooting," Bernie said, her back to us. Her voice was flat.

Mindy had come back into the kitchen with a scrubbed daughter, and she let Bonnie out into the backyard with the men. "Incoming," she yelled, and shut the door. "Bitches," Mindy said abruptly, and I knew she was referring to the bridesmaids who'd reneged on their obligations.

Deidra flinched.

"I'm sorry, sweetie, but that behavior was low," Mindy said. "Any true friend would be thinking more about you and your feelings than about their disapproval of our family."

Mindy had good sense.

"Well, you still got the two best ones," Bernie said, and Deidra smiled at her mother-in-law-to-be. "Sookie, I hope you like baked chicken."

"I sure do," I said. "Is there anything I can be doing to help?"

Bernie said no, and I could see that the cooking area would be easier for one person to manage without a newcomer getting in her way. To keep the conversation going, I told them about having to step in at the Bellefleur double wedding when one of the bridesmaids had had a sudden attack of appendicitis. They all laughed when I described trying not to breathe in the too-tight dress or move too quickly in the too-small high heels, and I began to feel a little more at ease. Mindy finished folding clothes, Bonnie came in crying with a skinned knee, and Craig accidentally threw the ball over Doke's shoulder and into Mr. Collins's backyard.

In the background, I'd heard the men's voices as they called to one another and to Mason, and I was alerted when they all fell silent. I listened.

Then I was out the door and looking to my right. Jim Collins was standing there at a gap in the overgrown hedge, his balding head shining under the sun, the baseball in his age-spotted hands. I knew what he was going to do before he did it; I knew it as his intent formed. Collins was in his sixties, but hale and fit, and the ball went right toward Sam with impressive force. My hand shot out to intercept it. It stung like hell, but I would not have winced for all the cotton in the Delta. I caught Collins's gaze and held it. I didn't let myself speak. I was afraid of what I'd say.

There was a long moment of silence. Mindy's husband, Doke, took two steps forward. He told Collins, "Don't think about acting out in front of my son." Doke was so angry he had to exercise all his restraint.

At that moment, I wished I were a witch so I could throw Bernie's neighbor's malevolence back at him. But I didn't have any superpowers or any supernatural powers, or any kind of power at all. All that I had that was mine was my unpredictable ability to read minds and my unexpected strength and quickness, which came from taking the occasional sip of Eric. My arm dropped to my side, the ball clenched in my fist, and Sam came over to put his hand on my shoulder. We watched Jim Collins, still expressionless, turn to go back into his house.

"Was he trying to hit me?" Sam asked quietly.

I was too angry to speak. I turned my head to look into Sam's eyes. I nodded.

"Thanks, Sookie," he said. "That would have been bad. Maybe I could have caught it in time. Maybe not." Sam was very, very quick, like all twoeys—but he'd been caught off guard.

"I only moved quicker because I knew about it ahead of time," I said, leaving Eric and his blood out of the conversation. "That creep wants to provoke you. I hope none of the rest of your neighbors are like him."

"They never used to be," he said, his voice bleak. "Now it's hard to tell."

"To hell with them," I said. "You-all are good people, Sam. There's nothing wrong with you and your mother, except maybe your mom didn't pick her second husband too well."

I could hear the other men going into the house, Mason's piping voice exclaiming over my good catch.

"Mom understands that now," Sam said. "I think it never occurred to her that Don would be so angry about her other nature, because she was so sure he loved her."

Time to change the subject. "Your mom's fixing chicken," I said. "Oven baked, with Parmesan cheese and bread crumbs."

"Yeah? She's a pretty good cook." Sam's eyes brightened.

"I don't know how we're all going to squeeze in around that table."

"I'll get the other card table out of the closet. We'll all make it."

And we did. No one mentioned Jim Collins again, and no one asked me any questions about what I'd done. The Merlottes (extended version) seemed to be a clan that accepted the odd without a blink . . . at least, they did now.

It was a long evening after a long day, and I was ready to retire when the dishes were done and Deidra had departed to her parents' house. Mindy and Doke had left for home soon after supper was eaten so they could bathe the kids and get them to bed. The next day, Saturday, would hold both the wedding rehearsal (in the morning) and the wedding itself at four in the afternoon, followed by a reception. All three events would be at Deidra's church.

Craig made a point of having a conversation with me while

I was washing dishes and he was drying them. He told me that the reception would be only a punch and cake affair, which is often the case in the South. "We made up our minds too quick to do anything else," he said with a smile. "After Deidra's folks—the Lisles—kicked up a fuss and postponed the first date and made us go to counseling, we didn't want anything to get in the way of this one. We don't care about having a sit-down dinner. Punch and cake is fine with us, and a lot cheaper."

"Where will you live?" I asked. "In Dallas? Sam said you-all went to college there."

"I took an apartment in Houston after I graduated," Craig said. "I got a job doing tech support for a big firm of CPAs. Deidra's got to finish training as an EMT."

I assumed she'd have to put that off because of the pregnancy, but it was none of my business to say anything.

"She'd really like to become a physician's assistant, after we get on our feet," he said.

"I hope she can do that," I said. Deidra would have a hard row to hoe, with a new husband and a new baby.

"What about you?" Craig asked.

"And my future?" I actually had to think about it. Craig and I were alone in the kitchen. Sam had gone outside to move his truck because it had been blocking Deidra's car. Bernie was in the bathroom.

"I've got a good job working for this really nice guy," I said, and Craig laughed. I hesitated. "Maybe I'll take some online courses. I don't do well in classroom situations."

Craig was silent for a few moments. He was thinking he could tell I wasn't dumb, so what could my problem be? Maybe I had ADD, or just a total lack of ambition? Why hadn't I advanced further in life?

Though I felt a flash of resentment, I realized that Craig naturally wanted his brother to be dating a girl who had some goals and aspirations. It was hard to resist showing off, trying to impress Craig with my one unique ability.

For example, I could have told him that I knew he'd recently quit smoking at Deidra's request and that right now he was craving a cigarette. Or I could have told him that I knew he and Deidra were going to be parents. Or I could have told him that my boobs were real, which would have answered another unspoken question.

When you opened yourself up and stayed in a person's head for more than a second, you could really pick up on a lot of stuff.

Analyze what you've thought of in the last few minutes. Would you want anyone else to know about it? No. Sam had asked me once if I thought I could do a good job for Homeland Security. I tried to imagine how. Standing in an airport by the search line? Would any bomber or terrorist be going over his plan mentally, in detail, in an airport chosen at random? No, I thought not. I'd have to have a little more direction than that.

I wanted to discuss this with Craig, as I'd wanted to say it to so many people in the past. I'd often wished that other people understood my daily path, understood what I lived with. Not that I wanted to act all whiny and put-upon—"Poor Pitiful Pearl," as my grandmother used to call me when she thought I was in danger of being sorry for myself.

I sighed. It wasn't Be Kind to Telepaths week, and I had better tighten up my suspenders and get on with my life. I told Craig good night and took my turn in the bathroom when it was empty. It felt good to shower away the long day, and I belted my robe around my waist and emerged with the bundle of clothes I'd removed.

Sam was waiting by the door to my assigned bedroom. He looked tired but relaxed, and I could tell he was happy to be at home. He stood aside to let me enter first, and I put my clothes down on top of my tote bag and straightened up to find him looking at me with affection. Not lust, not frustration . . . affection. My heart went all gooey. We hugged, and it felt wonderful to breathe him in. He didn't mind the damp hair, the bare face, the worn bathrobe. He was happy I was here. He stood off a little, though he didn't entirely let go. "Thanks for coming with me, Sookie," he whispered. "And thanks for defusing that situation with Mr. Collins." Sam thought Jannalynn would have sprung over into the old man's yard and given him a shellacking. He seemed to believe that the problem with his mom's neighbor was over. I didn't know what to say to him. I decided, *I should let him sleep well and be happy. Tomorrow is the wedding.*

"No problem," I said. "I'm glad my softball training came in handy."

Sam went to the doorway. "I'm down there, in my old room," he said, jerking his head toward a door on the other side of the hall and down a bit. "Craig's in there with me. Mom's at the end of the hall."

I started to ask him why he'd told me, but then I realized I did indeed feel better knowing where he d be in the night.

"You going to call Eric?" he said, almost inaudibly.

"I may try," I said. "He'd probably appreciate it."

"Tell him . . . Nah, don't tell him anything." Sam was not a big fan of the Northman. "I was going to say, 'Tell him thanks for letting you come,' but you can go where you damn well want to."

I smiled at Sam. "Yes, I can, and I'm glad you know that." Over his shoulder, I saw the door at the end of the hall open just a crack, and I could see Bernie's eyes peering at us. Sam gave me a little grin, and I knew he could tell we were being observed. I winked at Sam with the eye away from Bernie, and I kissed him. It wasn't long, but it was warm. There was a look in Sam's eyes when we let go of each other, a look that let me know he might've enjoyed putting on a much longer show for his mom, but I laughed and stepped back.

"Night," I said, and shut the door. I heard Sam's steps move away, and I fished my cell phone out of my purse. "Hey, you," I said quietly when Eric answered. Bernie would surely have the sharp shifter hearing.

"Are you well?" he asked. I could hear some noise in the background. It didn't sound like the familiar bar noises.

"I'm fine," I said. "There seems to be a lot of hostility here in this town against Sam and his mom, and I'm a little bit worried about that. Maybe the hater is just their cranky old neighbor, but I got a feeling there's more to worry about." This was what I hadn't discussed with Sam, so I was glad to pour it out to Eric.

"That's worrisome," he said, but he didn't sound too worried. "Can you handle it, or do you need help? What's the name of the town?"

"I'm in Wright, Texas," I said, and I may have said it a little sharply. After all, you expect your boyfriend to listen when you tell him stuff, and I knew I'd told him about the wedding. "It's west and a little south of Dallas."

"How far?"

I described the route we'd taken to Wright, and Eric said, "That would still be in Joseph Velasquez's territory. When Stan became king, he gave Joseph the sheriffdom."

"Your point?"

"I'd have to ask Joseph for permission to send someone to help you."

"Well, I appreciate the thought." Though I noticed that Eric hadn't actually said he'd do it. "But the wedding will be tomorrow afternoon in the daytime, so I don't think a vampire would be a big help."

"If you're really worried, you could call Alcide," Eric said reluctantly. "Maybe he knows the leader of the nearest pack down there, and it's possible the packleader would be willing to come to make sure things go well. Though surely Sam and his mother know the other two-natured in the area."

I didn't know how seriously to take one man's malice, but I did know from the shadow of his thoughts that there were more people in the town who believed the way he did. Maybe sending out a request for help would be a good idea. On the other hand, that was hardly my call to make.

"What's going on with you?" I asked, trying to sound completely focused. Eric had his own political problems, and the representative of the Bureau of Vampire Affairs was breathing down his neck about a violation of one of the rules for operating a vampire-owned business. A barmaid had promised a female customer that she (the barmaid, Cyndee) could bribe one of Eric's vamps to bite the woman. Cyndee'd been blowing smoke, but the BVA had to investigate the allegation. Plus, there was a tense situation with Eric's boss, Victor Madden.

"I think the BVA investigation is going to exonerate us," he said, "but Victor was here today with his own accountant, going through my books. This is well-nigh intolerable. I can fire Cyndee, and I have. I understand that's all I can do to her."

"Don't worry about things down here, then," I said. "You've got your hands full."

We talked a little longer, but Eric was preoccupied, and so was I. It wasn't a very satisfactory conversation.

I'd unfolded the couch to find it was already made up, and I discovered a folded bedspread and a pillow lying on the sewing machine. The evening was warm and the windows open, so I didn't exactly need the bedspread, but the pillow was nice and fluffy. I turned off the overhead light and stretched out on the lumpy mattress. As I adjusted my spine, I wondered if there was any foldout couch in the world that was as comfortable as a bed. I reminded myself to be glad I wasn't sleeping on the floor.

I could hear a muffled conversation coming from the room Sam was sharing with Craig. The brothers laughed. Their voices died away gradually. Through the open window, I heard a small animal outside, and the hoot of an owl. The breeze coming in didn't even smell like the wind at home.

I considered the possibility of calling Alcide Herveaux, the Were packleader in Shreveport. He was the werewolf I knew the best, and he might have some insight for me about the situation in neighboring Texas. But not only was I harboring a great resentment toward Alcide since he'd pressured me into taking hallucinogenic drugs so I could solve a pack dispute; I knew he was feeling resultant guilt himself. People who felt guilty lashed out, in my experience. It would be just my luck if he sent Jannalynn to provide backup.

Awkward.

Geez Louise, I'd be on the chopping block in no time flat. I wondered what kind of conversation Sam had had with her before we'd left. ("Yes, I'm going to my brother's wedding, but I'm taking Sookie because she's more presentable." I thought not.) And truly, it was another thing that was none of my business.

Then I fell to wondering if there were any other two-natured in Wright or its environs. If there were, maybe Sam could ask them to help when—if—trouble arose. The two-natured didn't always stick together. Of course, neither did any other minority group I'd ever heard of. . . . The owl hooted again.

I woke the next morning to the welcome smell of coffee and pancakes with a side of bacon. Oh, *yeah*. I could hear a couple of voices in the kitchen, and the water was running in the bathroom. The household was up early. This was the day of the rehearsal and the wedding. I smiled up at the ceiling in anticipation. My room looked over the front yard, and I got up and padded over to the window to see what kind of day it was.

It was a bad day.

TWO

PULLED ON SHORTS and a T-shirt, and hurried out into the kitchen. Sam and his mother looked up as I appeared in the doorway. They'd been smiling, and Sam was raising his coffee cup to his lips while Bernie was flipping the bacon in the frying pan. Sam put down his cup hastily and jumped to his feet.

"What?" he said.

"Go look in the front yard," I said, and stood aside while they hurried from the kitchen.

Someone had stuck a big sign in the yard, facing the house. The message was definitely for Bernie. DOGS BELONG IN THE POUND, it said. I'd already jumped to a conclusion about its meaning.

"Where is it?" I asked Sam. "The pound? I hope I'm wrong, but I have to check."

"If you go back to the highway, head south," he said. There was a ring of white around his mouth. "It's on Hall Road, to the right. I'm coming."

"No. Give me your keys. This is your brother's wedding day. You have to take care of your mother."

"It's not safe."

"Whatever's happened there, if anything has . . . it's already done."

He handed me his keys without another word. I hurried out to the truck, noticing along the way that not a soul was outside in any of the yards, though Saturday mornings are good for washing cars, yard work, garage sales, shooting hoops. Maybe Bernie's neighbors had already seen that trouble was brewing and wanted no part of it.

In fact, not that many people were out and about in the entire town of Wright. I saw a stout man about Sam's age putting gas in his car at the filling station. I caught his eye as I drove by, and he turned away pointedly. Perhaps he'd recognized the truck. I saw an elderly woman walking her dog, an equally elderly dachshund. She nodded civilly. I nodded back.

I found Hall Road without any trouble and took a right. It was a dusty stretch of asphalt with a few straggling businesses, places in little faux-adobe structures spaced far apart. I began looking at signs, and it didn't take long to spot the one that read LOS COLMILLOS COUNTY ANIMAL SHELTER. It stood in front of a very small cement block building. Roofed pens extended in a long line on either side of a concrete run behind the building.

I turned off the motor and jumped out of the truck. I was

struck by how quiet it was. Outside any animal shelter, I would expect to hear yapping and barking.

The pens out back were silent.

The front door was unlocked. I took a deep breath, let it out. I steeled myself and pushed it open, left it that way.

I stepped into a little room containing a desk topped with a battered and grimy old computer. There was a phone with an answering machine, half-buried under a pile of folders. A dilapidated file cabinet stood in a corner. In the opposite corner were two huge bags of dog food and some plastic containers of chemicals that I supposed were used to clean the pens. And that was all.

A door in the center of the rear wall stood open. I could see that it allowed access to the runway between the pens where the ownerless dogs were kept.

Had been kept.

They were all dead. I'd stepped through the door with dread in my heart, and that dread was justified. Bundles of bloody fur were in every cage.

I squatted simply because my knees gave way. My face was wet without my even realizing I'd started crying.

I'd seen dead human beings plenty of times, and the sight hadn't made me feel this awful. I guess, in the back of my mind, I believed most people could defend themselves to some extent, if only by running away. And I also believed people sometimes—sometimes—shared responsibility in the situation that brought about their deaths, if only by making unwise choices. But animals . . . not animals.

I heard another car pull into the parking area. I looked out through the open doors to see the black Ford Focus with the cracked windshield. If I could have felt more frightened, I would have. Its doors opened, and three ill-assorted people got out and approached the animal shelter slowly, their heads swinging from side to side as they sniffed the air. They came through the little room very carefully, the tallest man in the lead.

"What's happened here, babe?" he said. He was tall and muscular, with a shaved head and purple eyes. I knew him fairly well. His name was Quinn, and he was a weretiger.

"Someone shot all the dogs," I said, stating the obvious because I was trying desperately to pull myself together. I hadn't seen Quinn in weeks, not since he'd tried to visit me at my home. That hadn't worked out too well.

Quinn knew they were dead already. His sense of smell had told him that. He squatted down by me. "I came to Wright to make a chance to talk to you," he said. "I didn't want it to be here, with all this death around us."

One of Quinn's companions came to stand by him. The two of them were like a pair of amazing bookends. Quinn's friend was a huge man, a coal black man, with his hair in short dreads. He looked like some exotic animal, and, of course, he was. He stared down at me in an incurious assessment, and then his eyes moved to the sad corpses in the pens, the streaks of blood running everywhere. The blood was beginning to dry at the edges.

Quinn extended his hand to me, and together we stood up.

"I don't understand why anyone would do this to our brothers," the black man said, his English clear and crisp but heavily accented.

"It's because of the wedding today," I said. "Bernie Merlotte's younger son is getting married."

"But a younger son will never change into anything. Only the oldest son." His accent was sort of French, which made the whole conversation more surrealistic.

"People here don't seem to know that," I said. "Or maybe they just don't care."

The third wereanimal was pacing outside the pens, circling the area. She would pick up the scents of the shooter. Or shooters. Tears were streaming down her face, and that wouldn't help her sense of smell. She was also furious. The set of her shoulders was eloquent.

"Babe, I don't know that this wedding is going to go off without more trouble," Quinn said. His big hand took mine. "I have a lot to say to you, but it's going to have to wait until later."

I nodded. The wedding day of Craig Merlotte and Deidra Lisle had definitely gotten off to a sad start. "Anything that upsets the Merlotte family upsets me. How did you come to be here?" I tried to keep my gaze away from the pitiful, limp forms.

"I was checking the twoey message board for information about the Shreveport area," Quinn said. "Sam posts on there from time to time, or sometimes I talk to the members of the Long Tooth pack." The Long Tooth pack was Alcide Herveaux's. "Someone posted that you were coming to Wright with Sam, and I already knew Trish and Togo here. Texas is part of my territory, you know." Quinn worked for Special Events, a branch of the national event-planning company E(E)E. Special Events staged important rites of passage for the supernatural community, like vampire weddings and first changes for the two-natured. "I knew Trish has a ranch outside Wright. I decided to take the chance to see you without the deader around." That would be Eric. "I flew into Dallas, and they picked me up. We were able to track you. I didn't want anything to happen to you on the way. I should have worried about what would happen when you got to Wright."

"This town is full of hate," the man called Togo said.

"I'm afraid so." I looked up at the broad nose, the high cheekbones, the gleaming skin. He was quite extraordinary. He stood out in these surroundings like a bird of paradise in a wren flock . . . not that there was anything avian about him.

The third wereanimal had finished her prowling, and now she appeared beside us. "I'm Trish Pulaski," she said. "You must be Sookie. Oh my God and his angels! Who would ever conceive of hurting poor dumb dogs to make a point?" She was lovely, and she was also clearly in her fifties. Her hair was solid gray, thick and curly. She didn't wear glasses, and her eyes were bright chips of blue in a tan face. Her jeans left no doubt she was in excellent shape. She wasn't thinking about herself or her companions. She was beside herself with rage and pain. I understood at that moment that the pound was her special project, that she'd raised the money to build it, she came every day to feed the animals, and she'd loved them all.

I said, "They left a sign in Bernie's yard."

"Bernie? They're targeting *Bernie?* Those fools!" she said, and her anger blazed like a flame within her. She turned to Quinn. "When we agreed to come out like the vampires did, this is the last thing I imagined would happen." She looked around at the dead dogs and the pools of blood, her gray curls dancing gaily and incongruously in the morning wind. She sighed, and her shoulders straightened. She said to me, "I'm sorry we had to meet here. This big guy is Togo Olympio. Quinn tells me you two are old friends. What was on the sign?"

I wanted to ask a lot of questions, but now was clearly not the time. I explained the little I knew. I also told them about Jim Collins.

"On Craig's wedding day," Trish said. She was angry and tearful and hurt. "Assholes!" Togo put a huge hand on Trish's thin shoulder. She laid her cheek on it for just a moment. "I'm not surprised to hear Jim Collins is involved," she continued. "Ever since we came out, he's been posting hate messages on his website."

"He has a website?" I said stupidly.

"Yeah, he's Mr. Right Wing. One of my jobs is monitoring websites like his. They've sprung up everywhere since the vamps came out, and they sprouted like mushrooms when we did. I watch Jim's especially closely since we're in the same area. He's even had postings from the Newlins." Steve and Sarah Newlin were the leaders of the radical religious underground in America. "Jim's website backs every extreme conservative position you can think of. Some of his principles I actually agree with, though it chokes me to say so. But most of his beliefs are so radical they scare me, and he doesn't seem to care how people will be hurt as a consequence of acting on those beliefs. Obviously, he doesn't care about animals," she added quietly.

Togo Olympio had entered one of the pens and bent over to touch the side of one of the fallen dogs. Flies were swarming now, and though I hadn't noticed their buzzing before, it droned in my ears. His dark eyes met mine, and I shivered. I was glad we were on the same side.

"I have to go back to the house and tell them," I said. "What will happen at the wedding if people are this determined to do them harm?"

"That's the big question, isn't it?" Trish said. She was pulling herself together. "Quinn says you're a friend of the shifters and the vampires though you're human."

I saw Quinn twitch out of the corner of my eye.

"But you're not completely human, right?" Trish persisted.

"No, ma'am." My bloodline wasn't exactly her concern, I figured, so I stopped at that.

"If you're Sam's friend, you're special already," she said, nodding to indicate she'd made a quick decision. I felt absurdly pleased. "Well, Sookie, Togo roams through every few weeks, and he and I are the scandal of the county. I've known Quinn, here, for years. Together, maybe we can hold back this hatred long enough for the young people to get married. After the wedding's over, I'm hoping like hell that feeling dies down and things go back to normal."

"Did you come out?" I asked. "With the other wereanimals?"

"This town's always thought I was a wild card, and no one was that surprised." Trish smiled broadly. "Bernie—she shocked everyone because she always seemed like Hannah Housewife; she and her first husband had such a great marriage, such good kids. Then, after she married Don . . . That was the trouble, Don's going nuts like that. His reaction was so violent and public, though I don't think he was in his right mind. Look, let's get out of here. All of this is making me sick."

I glanced at Quinn, and he nodded. "Togo and I'll come back later and dig a pit," he said, answering a question I hadn't wanted to ask.

To my surprise, Togo brought out a digital camera and began taking pictures. "My brothers and sisters need to know," he told me when he saw me watching. "This is to post on our own websites."

This just got more and more interesting.

"I've got to get back. I'm sorry I can't help you clean up," I said, which was a total lie. I was hugely relieved to have good reason to avoid burying the poor dogs. "Where are the cats?" I asked, struck by the fact that all the corpses were canine.

"I keep the cats at my place, thank God," Trish said, and I could only say *Amen* to that.

I walked back through the little building. When I got to the parking lot, I leaned against Sam's truck. The awfulness of the morning rolled over me again like a heavy wave. It was abominable that someone had slaughtered innocent dogs in a vicious attempt to ruin a day that should be happy. I felt the swell of a huge anger. I'd always had a slow temper. I didn't get really angry very often. But when I did, I did it right and proper. Since my time in the hands of the fae, my control over that anger seemed to have slipped. The second wave, the weight of my rage, threatened to pull me under. I'm not myself, I thought distantly.

It took a moment for the feeling to pass. When I was sure I was in control, I opened the door of the truck, dreading my return to the Merlotte house with the burden of my bad news.

What a lousy, rotten way to start the day.

"Sookie," Quinn said, and I turned to show him my face. I paused with one foot on the running board.

"All right," he said carefully. "I get it that you're way upset now, and so am I. But I've got to talk to you sometime."

"I understand," I said with equal care. "And we'll try to make the chance. Putting all personal issues aside, I'm glad you're here. Sam's family is up against more than we know. You're willing to help?" My eyes were telling him I'd think less of him if he wasn't.

"Yes," he said, surprised. "Of course I'll help. Trish will put out a bulletin on the Web. It's probably too late for much of anyone to come, since Wright's out in the middle of nowhere, but we'll all help. And I'm putting personal problems aside. For now." I looked up into his eyes, and I read in his head that he was serious, determined, and unswerving.

"I'd better go," I said. "You know where Bernie lives?"

"Yeah, we followed you at a distance. You spotted us, right? I hope you didn't call Eric."

I was a little shocked. "I wouldn't do that, Quinn."

"You didn't protest too much when Bill showed up at your house and beat the hell out of me the last time I tried to talk to you."

Eric had ordered Bill to intervene, since he'd banned Quinn from his area. "Excuse me," I said sharply. "You'll remember I was knocked unconscious! What happened to putting personal issues aside? You got Sam's number? You got the same cell as you did?"

We swapped phone numbers before Quinn returned to the building. I had to face the fact that there was nothing to keep me from driving back to Bernie's house. As I negotiated the streets of Wright, I found myself looking at each person I passed. Who was our friend? Who was our enemy?

A lightning bolt of a thought hit me. I was almost all human. I could legitimately claim this wasn't my fight.

No, I couldn't. I'd be as bad as Deidra's bridesmaids.

I'd been Sam's friend for years, and his family was human, too. I'd already taken a side, and there was no point in reviewing it.

I pondered Quinn's appearance. His story had amazed me. He'd gone to a huge amount of trouble and inconvenience to rendezvous with me here in Texas, and he'd only been acting on a tip.

I'd had a brief but ardent relationship with Quinn before I'd broken up with him—awkwardly and painfully—over family issues . . . his family issues. I'd been feeling guilty ever since, though I still thought I'd made the wise decision. Quinn seemed to think we had more to discuss, and possibly he was right, but I wanted to get through one crisis at a time.

I looked at the dashboard clock when I parked in front of the house. I'd been gone only forty-five minutes. I sure felt a lot more than forty-five minutes older. I got out and crossed the yard to the front door.

As I came close to the damn sign, I ripped it out of the ground. Moving with a lot more velocity, I strode over to the neighbor's house. Jim Collins was looking out of his open front window when I jabbed the stake into his dirt. Well, yee-haw. "You damn murderer," I said, and then I made myself walk away before I climbed through the window to choke Collins.

His creased face had been shocked and almost frightened, and for a blinding second I'd felt sorry that he didn't have a weak heart. After seeing the pathetic heaps of blood and fur, I would have enjoyed the sensation of scaring him to death.

I didn't knock on Bernie's door since I was staying there, and once I was inside, I went right to the kitchen at the back of the house. Sam, Bernie, and Craig were all there. They looked eerily alike as I appeared in the kitchen: apprehensive, upset, unhappy.

"All the dogs at the shelter are dead," I said. "They were shot."

Sam rose to take a tentative step toward me, and I could tell he wanted to offer me comfort. But I was too angry to accept it, and I held the palm of my hand toward him to let him know that.

"I moved the sign into Jim Collins's yard, I said. That man's a murderer." My rage deflated just a little.

"Oh, Sookie," Bernie began, sounding both alarmed and a little reproachful, and I held up the same palm to her.

"It was him," I said. "He was not the only one, but it was him."

She sat back and looked at me with more objective attention than she'd given me since I'd met her. "And you know this how?" she said.

"He's condemned by his own words, from his own brain."

"Sookie can read minds, Mom," Sam said, and after a second's thought, Bernie flushed a dull red. She had thought a few unflattering things about me. I'm a big girl; I can live with that. It wasn't like I hadn't heard plenty of similar things before.

"Shapeshifters are hard to read, if that makes you feel any better," I offered, and I sat down at the table with a thud. As the rage oozed out of me, it left an empty space, an aching hole. I looked down at my leg as if I could see it through my clothes, see the thickened, whiter flesh of the scarring. I made myself sit straighter. This family had enough on their plate without having to bolster me up.

"My friend Quinn showed up," I said, and from the corner of my eye I saw Sam start. "He came with a couple you know, Bernie," I said, looking at Sam's mother. "A woman named Trish Pulaski and a man named Togo Olympio."

"Trish and I have been friends since we moved to Wright," Bernie said. "You probably remember her as Trish Graham, Sam. She divorced a while ago, took back her maiden name, and started up with Togo. I'll never understand that relationship, but I tell myself it's none of my business." Bernie's face suddenly reflected much more of the woman behind it and less of the mom, as if she'd switched hats internally.

"The point is, they're very concerned about Craig and Deidra's wedding going off without a hitch." I watched Bernie's face pass from incomprehension to reluctant horror.

"You think there may be *more*?" she said.

I found myself understanding why Bernie had been stunned when her husband had reacted so drastically to her revelation. As well as being unimaginative, Bernie was a wee bit on the unrealistic side.

"Mom," Sam said, "if they're starting off by killing all the dogs in the pound, I think you can assume there's going to be something else happening. Maybe we should think about postponing the wedding? Move it somewhere else?" He looked at his brother.

Craig said, "No." His face hardened as I watched. "We put it off once because Deidra's family wanted to understand more about what she'd be getting into, being married to me. We got the couples counseling. We got the totally unnecessary genetics counseling. Deidra's ready to marry me. Her family is used to the idea, if not exactly thrilled. We set another date, and then we had to move it up." He cast a quick glance at me. He was wondering if I knew exactly why. "Because of Deidra's brother going overseas."

"Next month," I said helpfully.

"Right. Well, we didn't want to wait till the last minute. In fact, we don't want to wait another day."

Sam was looking from me to Craig.

"But everyone has been pitching in to help," Bernie said, still stuck on the hate. She'd lived here for years, and I could tell she was having a very hard time believing that people she'd known for more than a decade could turn on her. "I mean, the ladies in the church, the pastor . . . they've all been so happy that Craig and Deidra were going to get married. They threw Deidra a wedding shower in the fellowship hall."

"See, most people aren't bad," I said, as if I were reassuring a child. "I'm sure it's a minority here in Wright, a handful of people, but we don't want anything bad to happen that would ruin the wedding. Craig and Deidra need happy memories of this day, not . . ." My voice trailed off as I thought of what I'd seen at the shelter.

"Yes, I understand," Bernie said. She sat up a little straighter. "Craig, honey, I think you need to call Deidra right now. I hope nothing has happened over at her place."

Nothing could have gotten Craig moving as fast as that idea, and he had speed-dialed his fiancée almost before his mother had finished speaking. He stepped into the living room while he spoke to her, and he snapped his phone shut and came back into the kitchen with an air of relief.

"They're fine," he said. "I didn't tell them about the animal shelter. I hope they won't find out until after the wedding. Deidra's at the Clip N Curl, getting her hair done."

It was all of eight thirty in the morning. Despite the important issues we were facing, I shuddered at the idea of how long a day it was going to be for Deidra.

"When are Mindy and Doke and their kids coming?" I asked.

"They're supposed to be here in an hour," Bernie said. "Should I call their cell, tell them to turn back?"

"No," Sam said. "No, this wedding is going to take place. We are not going to let a few crackpots make us back down. That is," he said more quietly, "if that's what Craig and Deidra want to do."

Craig smiled at Sam briefly. "I'm getting married today," he said. "I don't want to put anyone in danger, but we're having this wedding." He shook his head from side to side. I could see the unhappiness, the bewilderment, the determination. "They all know us. Why do we seem like we're any different from the way we've always been? And it's not like Deidra or I turn into anything."

Sam stared at his brother, and Bernie winced.

To his credit, Craig noticed. He said, "Sam, we talked this all out a couple of months ago. You're my brother, and you and

Mom are like God made you. If they've got a problem with that, they can take it up with him."

Sam laughed, though unwillingly, and I nodded at Craig. That was a good little speech. I hoped the next time Sam felt down about being different, he would remember his brother's words. I wouldn't forget them myself.

I went to the guest room to put on my makeup. I'd dashed out of the house in such a hurry that morning, I'd left out several important steps in my daily routine. I wasn't an essential part of the rehearsal (or the wedding), but the family clearly expected me to go with them.

I tried to think of some tangible help I could provide—besides looking at dead animals and/or threatening a neighbor who already hated the family. (In retrospect, that hadn't been a smart thing.) When Sam knocked on the door thirty minutes later, I let him in. I'd pulled on the yellow and gray skirt outfit with matching yellow sandals. The top zipped up the back, and I turned around so Sam could finish zipping for me. I didn't have the flexibility in my arms that I'd had before . . . Oh, the hell with it. Not today.

Sam zipped me up as though this were our routine. He was wearing a dress shirt and khakis, and his loafers were shined. He'd brushed his hair neatly back. I admired the new look, but I found myself missing the long tangle of hair he'd had before.

"Listen, I did something I shouldn't have done," I said when I was zipped. I picked up my brush and began untangling my hair, which was very long now.

"If you're about to tell me what you said to Collins, I heard. So did Mom. Shifters have real sharp hearing, you know . . . and the windows were open."

I could feel my cheeks turn red. "Sorry," I said.

"I would have gone in and hit him," Sam said, and that was so close to what I'd been thinking that I jumped.

"I almost did," I confessed.

"Sook," he said seriously, "I appreciate your caring about my family so much."

"But it's not my family or my business, and I should back off and let you handle it? I know," I said, turning away and brushing my hair forcefully.

"I was going to say I'm glad I brought you." Pause. "Jannalynn's got her good points, or I wouldn't be going out with her—but she has no restraint, and she'd have gone batshit crazy this morning. The good thing about Jannalynn is that she's fully into her animal nature, and the bad thing is, it seems like she likes it more."

Without revealing how close I had come to going batshit crazy myself, I turned to face him, brush in hand. "I get what you're saying. Eric loves being a vampire. He loves it more than anything." *Maybe more than he loves me*, I thought, surprising myself. "You remember that black Focus we thought might be following us? Well, it was Quinn. Trish and Togo are his local contacts. He came here to talk to me."

Sam said, "Didn't you tell me that Eric had banned Quinn from Area Five?"

"Yeah, but he found out I was coming here from some kind of website. Isn't that crazy? Quinn flew from wherever he was working, and he got Togo and Trish to pick him up at the airport and bring him here."

"You and he . . ."

"Yeah, we had a thing, but I kind of told him to take a hike—I didn't put it that mean—because his family is . . . well, complicated. His mom's not really sane, and his little sister is a real piece of work, though I guess I never really had a chance to get to know her. I didn't break up with him well," I admitted. "He wants to have some kind of conversation about it. I sure don't need that, though I guess I owe him. I just don't understand how my being here got on the Internet."

Sam looked embarrassed. "That might be my fault," he said. "We keep track of each other now, all of us who change. Since the announcement, we never know what people are going to do. Humans don't always react in predictable ways. You know that better than anyone."

"So you put it on the Web that you and I were coming here to this wedding?"

"No! No! But I did mention it when I was talking to Travis." Travis, a trucker who was a Were not affiliated with a pack, stopped in at Merlotte's about once every two weeks.

"But why would you have mentioned me?"

Sam closed his eyes briefly. "You're kind of famous in the supe community, Sookie."

"What?" This made no sense at all.

"You're unique. Weres like something different as much as anyone else. You're a friend of the Shreveport pack. You've done a lot for twoeys."

"Okay, several thoughts. I haven't seen a computer around here, or I'd ask you to check Jim Collins's website. I want to know what he's saying about what's happening in Wright. And here's my second thought—I've been assuming that Jannalynn knows I came with you . . . right?"

"Sookie, of course Jannalynn knows I brought you to this wedding. I explained that I'd asked you before we'd started dating." Sam looked even more embarrassed, which I didn't think was possible. He'd already more or less admitted that that wasn't the only reason he'd left Jannalynn at home.

Plus, Jannalynn would realize that anyone who saw on the

Web that I was going with Sam to his family home would know that she was not the only woman in Sam's life. Even though Sam and I had a platonic relationship, I knew I would have been pretty jealous if I'd been in her shoes. Or on her paws.

"Jannalynn's going to want to kill you," I said flatly. "Or me. And I guess I wouldn't really blame her."

Sam flushed, but his gaze was unwavering. "She's a big girl. She knows better than anyone else that . . ."

"That you've lost your frickin' mind? Well, it's done now." I sighed and regrouped, realizing that worrying about Sam's indiscretion would have to wait until later. We needed to focus on getting Craig and Deidra married without any violence disrupting the ceremony.

"Have you thought about how Quinn and Togo and Trish can be useful? I've got Quinn's cell phone number. They're probably at the pound . . . cleaning up. Of course, I'll help however I can." I handed Sam the scrap of paper with Quinn's number.

"What I'm going to ask them to do," Sam said, "is stand guard. When we get to the church for the rehearsal, I hope you four will set up a perimeter outside. That way we'll have plenty of warning if Collins and his buddies try something. The time of the rehearsal isn't public knowledge, not like the wedding time. That was in the paper because the whole community was invited."

That was a common practice in Bon Temps, too, so I wasn't surprised. Many engagement announcements included the particulars of the marriage ceremony with the invitation, "All friends of the couple are welcome."

"Sure," I said. "I'll be a lookout." I'd feel better standing watch with a shotgun in my hands, but I figured that if I had the Benelli, (a) I might actually shoot someone, and (b) I might get arrested. I didn't know Texas gun laws, and there was no telling how stringently they'd be enforced on a local level.

"You look too pretty to be standing out in the churchyard. I'm sorry," Sam said, shaking his head. "This isn't how I thought we'd be spending this time."

"Sam, it's not your fault. I'm glad I can help out. I only regret it's necessary." There was a chance that planting the sign and killing the dogs was the end of the protest against the marriage. But that was a remote possibility.

"I'm sorry you had to see the dogs; I guess . . . Well, that's just sad. No one should have to see something like that." Sam stared down at his feet.

"I agree," I said, my voice as steady as I could manage.

From the flurry of voices in the living room, I could tell that Doke and Mindy and the kids had arrived. Sam and I went out to join them. We told them all the news. After some quiet discussion, they decided they'd stay at the house with the kids until it was time for the wedding. Mindy said, "All we'd do at the rehearsal is find out when to come down the aisle and sit in a pew, and I think Doke and I can manage that, right?" They were worried about Mason and Bonnie, and I didn't blame them.

When it was time to leave the house, I walked out with the others to find that a car was parked in front that didn't belong to anyone in the family.

"Hey," called a short brunette who was leaning on the hood of the Saturn. She straightened and came forward to hug Sam.

"Hey, yourself," he said, and hugged her back.

"That's Sister Mendoza," Craig explained. "They've been friends a long time." Craig was afraid I'd get mad at Sam touching another woman.

"She's a nun?"

"What?" Craig stared for a second. "Oh. Oh, no! Sister is her name." He laughed. "She and Sam have been friends ever since we moved here. She's a deputy at the sheriff's department."

"Why is she here?"

"I have no idea. Hey, Sister! Did you come because of that parking ticket I forgot to pay?"

"Hell, no," Sister Mendoza said, letting go of Sam. "I came here to be a watchman. Me and Rafe." A short, thick-bodied man got out of the car. He was as pale-haired as Sister was brunette.

"Rafe played football with Sam," Craig told me, but I think I would have figured it out by the way they were thumping each other.

Sam beckoned me over. "Sookie, these are some old friends of mine, Sister and Rafe," he said. "You two, you be nice to this woman." Sam was in no doubt that they would be. His brain was practically rolling with pleasure at seeing his old buddies.

The two friends gave me a quick once-over, seemed okay with what they saw. Rafe gave Sam a fist to the shoulder. "She's way too pretty for you, you old dog," Rafe said, and they laughed together.

"I'm taking the backyard," Sister said, and she left.

Rafe gave Sam a sharp nod. "You-all go to the church and don't worry about things here," he said. "We got your back. You got someone coming to the church?"

Sam said, "We got the church covered." He paused. "You two aren't in uniform," he said carefully.

"Well, we're off duty," Rafe said. He shrugged. "You know how it is, Sam."

Sam looked pretty grim. "I'm getting the picture," he said.

I felt much better about the safety of both the kids and the house itself as Sam and I got into his truck to drive behind Craig and his mom to the church.

It wasn't a long drive. Wright was no bigger than Bon Temps. Drier, dustier, browner—but I didn't imagine it was essentially different. We'd had trouble with demonstrators in front of the bar, but they'd gotten tired of getting hustled out of the parking lot, and they'd gone back to writing letters. Could my fellow townspeople do what someone had done here at the dog pound?

But there wasn't time to worry about that because we were two blocks west of Main Street at the corner of Mesquite (the north–south street) and St. Francis (the east–west). Gethsemane Baptist Church was a faux-adobe structure with a red-tiled roof and a squat bell tower. I could hear the organist practicing inside. The sound was strangely peaceful.

There was parking at the front and at the left side, between the church and the parsonage. The fellowship hall was directly behind the church, connected by the umbilical cord of a covered walkway. The yard was full of thin grass, though what grew there was neatly mown.

A man who could only be the pastor was walking over from the parsonage, which looked like a smaller version of the church. He was middle-aged with a big belly and graying black hair. From my first dip into his head, I concluded that Bart Arrowsmith was a genial man who was not equipped to handle a situation this volatile. I knew that by now word must have spread all over Wright about what had happened, and I knew this situation had spooked Brother Arrowsmith.

This was a day when I had to know the capabilities and weaknesses of the people around me, no matter how invasive it felt to enter their thoughts. What I saw in Brother Arrowsmith's head gave me the sad suspicion that he was not going to be the tower of strength we needed today. He was a conflicted man who couldn't decide what God wanted him to do when he was faced with a situation he couldn't interpret scripturally.

He was troubled on this day that should be so happy. And that made him feel even worse. He liked Craig and Deidra. He had always liked Bernie. For that matter, he liked Sam, but when he looked at Sam, he now saw something subhuman.

I took a deep breath and got out of Bart Arrowsmith's head. It wasn't a healthy, happy place to be.

A light breeze had been stirring the leaves on the short trees. Now it gained power. It hadn't rained in Wright for a while, and my cheeks felt the sting of the sandy particles picked up by the wind. I didn't know who'd appointed me Grim Nemesis, but I was in a weird state of apprehension.

I intercepted the minister as he reached the steps. I introduced myself. After Bart Arrowsmith shook my hand and asked me if Craig was already inside, I told him, "You need to take a stand on this."

"What?" he said. He peered through his wire rims at me.

"You know what's happening here is wrong. You know this is hate, and you know God doesn't want hatred to happen here."

See? Like I was the voice of God. But I felt *compelled*.

Something shifted around behind Bart Arrowsmith's eyes. "Yes, I hear you," he said. He sighed. "Yes." He turned to go into the church.

Next I'd be nailing a list of demands to the door.

Trish, Quinn, and Togo drifted across the dry yard. Their feet hardly made a sound on the crisp grass. I hadn't seen them approach, but they all looked the worse for the wear. Quinn and Togo had been digging.

"Quinn will take the front," Trish said, sounding calm and authoritative though her eyes were red from weeping. "Togo, honey, you take the rear. Sookie and I will take the right side." I hoped we could take it for granted that no one was going to attack from the parsonage on the left.

I nodded, then exchanged a glance with Quinn as I started moving east into position.

Deidra and her parents arrived in one car, her sisters and her brothers in another. Mrs. Lisle was almost as pretty as Deidra, but with shorter hair and a few more pounds. Mr. Lisle looked exactly like a man who worked in a hardware store: capable, skilled, and unimaginative. The whole family was obviously very anxious.

Mr. Lisle wanted to ask us what we were doing standing around the churchyard, but his nerve failed him. So he and Mrs. Lisle, Deidra and her sisters, and Deidra's oldest brother scurried across the yard to the open doors of the church. Deidra's other brother, the one in the service, took up a stand beside me. Since I was sure he was armed, I was glad to see him. He nodded at my companion. "Miss Trish," he said politely. She patted him on the shoulder. "Jared Lisle," he said to me.

"Sookie Stackhouse. I came with Sam."

And then we watched.

A pair of girls arrived and scooted up the sidewalk and into the church, casting a glance at Jared as they hurried by. He smiled and raised his hand in greeting.

"They're singing," he explained. "I'm kind of surprised they showed up." Sam and Deidra's oldest brother were Craig's groomsmen, so the wedding party was complete.

Through the open church windows, I listened to "Jesu, Joy of Man's Desiring" as the organist ran through some opening music. I could faintly hear Brother Arrowsmith giving instructions to the wedding party.

A car or two drove by, with nothing more than a curious glance from the drivers. I fidgeted, unable to find a casual way to be just hanging around the side of the church. I felt both conspicuous and awkward.

Jared didn't have that problem. Since he was in the army, he was used to spending time being on alert. He didn't talk to me or Trish for a long time, but I figured that was okay because he had something more important to think about.

As for me, I was wondering what on earth I would do if there was some kind of attack. Read their thoughts really, really quickly? That wouldn't be much help. I missed my shotgun more than ever. Could I shoot another human being if he attacked the church or tried to disrupt Sam's brother's wedding?

Yes, I thought I could. Hell, yes. My back stiffened.

It's both interesting and unpleasant to get a big revelation about your own character, especially at a moment when you can't do a damn thing about it. I couldn't abandon my post, run to the nearest gun store to make a purchase, don some black leather and high-heeled boots, and reinvent myself as a kick-ass heroine. A gun would make me *feel* tough, but it wouldn't make me *be* tough. The desire to shoot someone wouldn't make me an accurate shot with a handgun. Though if I had my shotgun, it would be hard to miss.

I had a hundred scattered ideas in the space of a few seconds. And those few seconds multiplied as the assorted band I'd joined kept watch over nothing. Only Jared and Trish showed no signs of impatience or restlessness, but they did relax enough to exchange a few comments. I gathered that Trish had taught Jared in high school—English and composition. She was enjoying her early retirement. She'd been doing a lot of volunteer work and selling her handmade jewelry. Jared told her about his posting in Afghanistan. He was ready to go.

Then we heard the sounds of several engines approaching the turnoff to the church from the main drag. We all stiffened, and our eyes went to the stop sign at the end of the street.

Three motorcycles turned onto the street, motors rumbling. And there was a Suburban right behind them, full of people.

We formed a line across the sidewalk without saying a word.

The engines were turned off, and there was silence. The only sound in the neighborhood was the wind through the branches of the live oak in the front yard and the organ music wafting from the church windows.

I tried to develop a plan, and finally I decided the only way I could stop someone from entering the church was by tackling him. The three people astride cycles swung off and removed their helmets. They were all women. Ha! That was unexpected. And I realized after just a moment that they were all shifters, something Togo and Trish had picked up on in a fraction of a second.

"What are you doing here, sisters?" Togo said, his wonderful accent and deep voice fascinating.

The people in the Suburban began to climb out. Two of them were male; two were women. They were also two-natured.

"Hey, buddy," called the man who'd been driving. "We heard about the problem here, from the Web. We've come to be of service."

There was a long moment of thoughtful silence. Then Trish stepped forward. She was holding back her wind-tossed gray curls with both hands. She introduced herself. "I'm a friend of the groom's family. We're here to keep strangers out of the church. You know there've already been a couple of incidents today. All the dogs in the pound were killed to protest this wedding."

I was a little unnerved to hear the newcomers growl. Most two-natured didn't let themselves express their animal sides when they were in public. Then I realized that Deidra's brother and I were the only humans around. We were in the minority.

The newly arrived Weres, both the Suburban wolves and the Biker Babes—I didn't make that up; that's what their jackets said—reinforced our picket around the church. A couple of trucks drove by, but if the men in them had pictured themselves stopping, they changed their minds when they saw the assortment of people waiting.

I introduced myself to a Biker Babe named Brenda Sue, who told me she was a trauma nurse at a hospital about fifty miles away. This was her afternoon off. I told her about the four o'clock wedding, and she looked as if she was working something out in her head. "We'll be here," she said.

At the moment, I thought that Trish, when she'd posted that call to arms on the twoey website, had done us a good deed. And maybe Jim Collins had actually given us a present by killing those poor animals. He might as well have shot a flaming arrow into the sky.

I heard the traditional music a couple more times, and I could hear the voice of an older woman giving some quick instructions. The rehearsal was over much more quickly than I'd anticipated. I didn't know if that was because Brother Arrowsmith was hurrying it up or if forty-five minutes was normal for the rehearsal for a small family ceremony.

The wedding party came out of the church. They were obviously shocked to see the increased number of watchmen in the yard. Sam and Bernie grinned, and though the regular humans held back a little, all the two-natured had a great meet and greet. After some conversation all the way around, Jared Lisle shook my hand and got in a car with his brother and his sisters. No one wanted to linger in this exposed space. Trish and Togo had volunteered to feed the out-of-town visitors an impromptu lunch out at Trish's ranch, and they led the little procession south out of town. Sam's mom and Craig got into their car to go home, leaving Sam and me in front of the church.

"You and I are going to the police department," he said briefly, and I scrambled up into the truck. Sam was silent on the short drive—everything in Wright was a short drive— and by the time we parked in front of the small brick structure labeled LOS COLMILLOS POLICE DEPT, I understood that Sam was angry, stressed, and feeling responsible for a certain amount of this persecution.

"I'm sorry," he said to me abruptly.

"What?"

"I'm sorry I bring you here and this all happens. You have enough on your plate without having this added to it. I know you wish you'd stayed home in Bon Temps."

"What I was wishing was that I were more use," I said, trying to smile. "Maybe you should have brought Jannalynn, was what I was thinking."

"She would have broken each of Jim Collins's fingers and laughed while she did it."

Oh. Well, in that case. "But at least she would have accomplished something," I said ruefully. What had I done that morning? Did not killing the neighbor count as a positive?

We were out of the truck and walking into the police department as we had this exchange. After we passed through the scarred door, it seemed like a good time to stop talking about finger breaking.

"Sam," said the middle-aged man behind the desk. "When did you get back?"

He had thin lips, and a square jaw that came to a point, and a pair of eyebrows that were straight and bushy. He was smiling, but he was not happy. I wasn't sure what the cause of his unhappiness was. I suspected it was us.

"Hey, Porter. We got in yesterday. This is my girl friend, Sookie."

"If you're going out with Sam, you've got a high bullshit tolerance," Porter said. He was trying to smile, but it wasn't reaching his eyes.

"I put up with him somehow," I said.

"I guess you aren't here just to say hi?" The name on his tag read "Carpenter." Was his name Porter Carpenter? Almost as challenging as Sister Mendoza.

"I wish," Sam said, and I realized that his speech had slowed down a bit and his body had relaxed. He even looked a little younger. He was home. Funny I hadn't noticed that until now. "I'm afraid we had some trouble this morning."

"I been out to the animal shelter," Porter said. "Your problem related to that?"

I let Sam tell Officer Carpenter all about it, and he did a quick job of it.

"So you think this was at least partly Jim Collins's doing?" Carpenter asked. "Jim wasn't too bad until the vampires came out, but that tipped him over the line because that was about when Della died."

Della had been Jim's wife. I filled that in from Sam's brain.

"Then the weres . . . Well, it just made him nuts. Especially when Don shot your mom. He and Don were big buddies."

"So it was okay for his big buddy to shoot his own wife?" Sam asked bitterly.

"Sam, I'm just saying." Porter shrugged.

"I didn't see any evidence Jim Collins put the sign on Sam's mom's lawn or that he killed the dogs at the animal shelter," I said, trying to get the conversation back on track. "At least, none that you could take to court. Maybe you found something?"

Carpenter shook his head. I knew he hadn't looked. I was getting a whole lot from his head that scared me.

Sam said, "The dogs are dead, and nothing's gonna change that. I'd like whoever did that to go to jail. But right now, I'm more worried that someone's going to disrupt the wedding."

"Do you think they'd do that?" Porter Carpenter asked, genuinely taken aback. "Ruin your brother's wedding day?" He answered his own question. "Yes, I reckon there are a few people who would." He thought for a moment. "Don't worry about it, Sam. I'll be there in my uniform, right outside the church. I'll have another deputy with me, too. We'd have traffic duty anyway. Where's the reception going to be? Church hall?"

Sam nodded.

Good. Close and quick to get to, not much exposure, I thought.

Though Sam and Porter talked a little more, there wasn't much else the cop was willing to do until the anti-two-natured took a more drastic step. He was only being as helpful as he was because he'd known Sam and his mom and dad a long time. If it hadn't been for that bond, he would have given us a much cooler reception. A deputy came in while Sam and Carpenter were talking, and he regarded us with the same reserve.

When we left the police station, I thought Sam was more worried than when he'd gone in. The cops who were on our side were already at the Merlotte home, and they weren't in uniform.

We arrived at Bernie's house to see at least ten cars parked up and down the street and in the driveway. I was filled with dismay, thinking these were people who were showing up to give the family some more grief; but then I saw that the new arrivals were positioning themselves all around the little lot. They were facing outward. They were there to protect the Merlotte family.

Unexpectedly, tears welled up in my eyes. I groped for Sam's hand, felt it grip mine. "Hey, Leonard," Sam said to the nearest man, a gray-haired guy wearing a khaki shirt and khaki pants.

"Sam," Leonard said, bobbing his head.

Sister nodded at us. "We'll get this done," she assured Sam. "Day's half over. Bring Sookie to the next class reunion, you hear?"

Though I knew Sam had a real girlfriend and I was only standing in for the weekend, I had a giddy little tingle of warmth at the welcome I'd received from his family and friends. I had to stop in amazement when we went in the front door. The little house was a beehive of activity inside as well as out.

There were some bouquets of carnations on the occasional tables in the living room. One had balloons attached, which made the atmosphere weirdly cheerful. While we'd been gone, not only had the florist van stopped by, but someone had delivered a platter of cold cuts and cheese, and bread. Sliced tomatoes and everything else that might conceivably go on a sandwich were set out beside the platter, along with some "wedding" paper plates. Sam and I helped ourselves, as everyone else had done. Mindy's children were running around in high excitement.

The house felt very small, very full of life, and all the brains were buzzing with excitement and happiness.

While Sam and I ate in the living room, sitting side by side on the couch, Mason brought me a glass of sweet tea, carrying it very carefully. "Here, Aunt Sookie," he said proudly, and though I opened my mouth to correct the title, I just said, "Thank you, darlin'." Mason grinned, looked instantly bashful, and dashed away.

Sam put his arm around me and kissed me on the cheek.

I took a sip of the tea because I didn't know what else to do. I thought Sam was getting a little *too* into his role-playing.

"After all, you are my girlfriend this weekend," he said close to my ear, and I stifled a laugh because it tickled.

"Uh-huh," I said, infusing the words with a little hint of warning.

He didn't remove his arm until he needed it to pick up his sandwich, and I shook my head at him . . . but I was smiling. I couldn't help it. I was so uplifted at the community rallying around the Merlottes and the Lisles. I hadn't felt this hopeful in . . . forever.

That lasted about five more minutes. The brains outside grew jangled with agitation. It began about the same time that I noticed an increased number of vehicles passing in front of the house. Given the general turmoil, I didn't think much of it. However, I glimpsed movement out the front window, and I half stood to look through Bernie's sheers. There were four cars parked across the street and at least twenty newcomers standing around, blocking the cars of the volunteers, and the family cars, too.

Sister was yelling, poking her finger at the chest of a man three times as big around as she was. He was yelling back. And finally, he shoved her and she went sprawling.

Sam had jumped to his feet to look out the window. When he saw his friend fall, he yelled and shot out of the house, Doke and Craig following him. Bernie zipped through the living room soon after, pelting out the front door like the strong woman she was.

There was lots of shouting, lots of commotion, and I wondered if I should join them, if I could be of any help. Then I thought twice. There was something contrived about the whole incident. Why would a confrontation be staged in front of the house?

So something could happen at the back.

Mindy and her children were standing in the hall, and I understood that Mindy didn't want the kids to see any violence through the front or back windows. I nodded at her, held my finger over my lips, and eased into the kitchen. The small wooden bat the men had been using to lob balls to Mason the day before was by the back door, and I picked it up and hefted it. I was glad it was wood and not plastic. I looked out the window cautiously. Yes, someone was creeping through the backyard. A teenage boy, lean and lanky and angry. He had something in his hand.

My heart was pounding a mile a minute, and I had to make myself calm down so I could read his thoughts. He had some kind of a bomb, and he was planning on opening the back door and tossing it in and running like hell. I had no idea what kind of device it was. It might be a stink bomb or a smoke bomb . . . or a firebomb.

I felt a movement behind me, and I glanced over my shoulder to see Mindy creeping into the room. She'd made the kids lie down on the hall floor, and had come in to provide backup. I felt an unexpected surge of emotion. My resolve got a shot of adrenaline.

So here's where I may have overreacted.

When the teenager opened the back door, so very cautiously, and stuck his hand in, I shoved the door all the way open, took a half step, and swung the bat as hard as I could.

THREE

I BROKE HIS ARM. And here's the thing: Though what he was holding turned out to be a stink bomb, not something that would actually physically harm Sam's family, I never did feel bad about it afterward. In fact, in a savage kind of way I was glad I'd broken a bone.

This was the new me. Though I could regret I'd changed, it was a done deal. I couldn't regenerate the tenderhearted me. I didn't know how much of this alteration in my character was due to the blood bond I shared with a big, unscrupulous Viking and how much of it was due to the torture I'd undergone . . . but I wasn't exactly the same nice person, as this boy had just found out.

He screamed in pain, and people came running from all over, both his buddies and the Merlotte family and their friends, and then the police, both in and out of uniform, and it was all chaos for a good forty minutes.

Since Mindy had been standing there while the boy came in the back door—and when he was blubbering in pain, he himself admitted it—I was in the clear.

In fact, his hastily summoned parents were absolutely horrified, didn't try to dodge the facts or excuse his actions. They were stand-up people, which was a huge relief, because the boy was Nathan Arrowsmith, the only child of the Reverend and Mrs. Bart Arrowsmith. Talk about your touchy situation.

What did Sam's family do? Sam's family had a prayer meeting.

My gran had been a religious woman, and I liked to think of myself as a striving Christian. (Lately, I'd been more striving than Christian.) But we'd never had a family prayer circle. So I felt a little self-conscious about standing in the living room holding hands with Doke and Sam while all of us bowed our heads and prayed out loud, one by one.

Bernie identified herself to God, which I thought was kind of unnecessary, and then asked God to make her enemies see the light of tolerance. Mindy asked that God grant his blessing to the wedding and keep it peaceful. Craig very manfully asked God to forgive Nathan Arrowsmith and those who had conspired with him. Mason asked God to give him back his baseball bat. (I winced at that one.) Doke asked God to cure the hatred growing in the people of Wright. I asked God to restore peace in our hearts, which was something we all needed. Sam put in a request for the safety of everyone involved in the wedding. Bonnie got too self-conscious to say anything and started crying—pretty understandable in a three-year-old.

I felt a little better afterward, and I think the family did, too. It was definitely time to get ready to go over to the church again, and for the second time that day I retreated to the guest/ sewing room to get dressed. I put on the sleeveless blue dress I'd borrowed from Tara. I wore Gran's pearl necklace and earrings and the black heels. I pulled my hair off my face with a pearl comb—also Gran's—and left it loose. All I'd had to buy was a lipstick.

Sam wore a suit, lightweight blue seersucker. When I emerged, we looked at each other speechlessly.

"We clean up pretty good," I said, smiling at him.

He nodded. And I could tell he was thinking that Jannalynn would have worn something really extreme, and his family wouldn't have liked it. I felt a twinge of irritation with Sam. Why was he dating her, again? I was beginning to feel sorry for the girl. All weekend, Sam had been glad he hadn't brought her to meet his family. What kind of relationship was that? Not one founded on mutual respect.

When we came out to go to the church, Jim Collins was standing in his yard holding a sign that read NO ANIMAL MARRIAGES IN HUMAN CHURCHES. Offensive, yes. Illegal, no.

I hadn't forgotten from which direction Nathan Arrowsmith had come with his stink bomb.

I stopped on my way to Sam's truck. I took a step off the driveway. I caught Jim Collins's eyes. He wanted to look away, but he didn't. He thought his pride required that he meet my gaze. He was full of hate and anger. He missed Don, thought Don was right to shoot Bernie since in Jim's view she'd been a faithless liar. He knew Bernie hadn't cheated on her husband, but concealing what she really was counted in his book. The constant pain that nagged at Jim Collins's joints made his mind restless and angry. Advanced arthritis.

I said, "You're alone, and lonely, and miserable, and you'll stay that way until you get rid of all that hate." And I turned, walked away, and met Sam at the truck.

Sam said, "Feel better, Sookie?"

I said, "That wasn't a good thing to do. I know. I'm sorry." A little.

"Too bad you couldn't break his arm," Sam said, and he was smiling. A little.

As we opened the truck doors, we both glanced down the street toward Main, alerted by the buzz of voices. The street that had been so oddly empty that morning was now lined with people.

"What the hell?" Sam said. The whole Merlotte party, including the children, froze in place by their vehicles. While we'd been dressing for the most important day in Craig's and Deidra's lives, people with other plans had been gathering.

There were signs, signs bearing hateful messages. HUMAN BEINGS WALK ON TWO FEET, read the mildest one I saw. The others ranged from biblical quotations to obscenities about Craig and Deidra's wedding night. My hand flew up to cover my mouth as I read some of them, as if I could suppress my horror. Mindy covered her children's eyes. Even though I didn't think they could read the signs—and "abomination" is a pretty long word, even for older kids—I understood exactly how she felt.

"Oh my God," Bernie said. "Has the world gone mad? My husband shoots me, and everyone hates *me*?"

"Maybe we should go back in the house," Doke said. He'd picked up Mason, and Mindy had lifted Bonnie into her arms.

"I'll never go back in the house," Bernie growled. "You got the kids, you do what you think you have to. I'll *never* let them win."

Sam stood by his mother, his arm around her shoulders. "We go forward, then," he said quietly.

"All right," I said, bracing myself. "All right, here we go. Craig?"

"Yeah," said Craig. "I'm going to the church. I hope the Lisles can get there. I'm not making Deidra wait for me on our wedding day."

The excitement in all those brains, the churning emotions

and thoughts, battered at me, and I staggered. Sam jumped over to grasp my arm. "Sookie?" he said. "This doesn't have to be your fight."

I thought of the dead animals at the shelter. "This is my fight." I took a deep breath. "How did all these people get here?"

"The Internet," said Sister. She and Rafe were looking around them, alert to approaching danger. "Everyone just showed up, said they'd heard about it on the Internet. That Twitter thing maybe."

A television news van pulled up at the end of the street.

"That's probably good, I think," Sam said. "Witnesses."

But I thought people would act out worse, so their protest would make the evening news. "We better get going," I said. "Before the assholes build up their courage."

"Do you figure the majority of the crowd is pro or anti?" There were signs for both camps. More for the anti, but haters are always the most vocal.

I scanned the signs. "The signs are mostly anti," I said. "The anti folks are better organized, which isn't a big surprise. People of goodwill don't have to carry signs."

We got welcome reinforcements from an unexpected direction. Togo, Trish, and the Biker Babes, along with the Suburban people, came through the backyards to arrive at our sides.

"Road was blocked farther on," Trish explained. "Pile on in your cars. We have a plan."

Bernie said, "Trish, maybe . . ."

"You-all get in, but drive slow," Trish said. "We're going to walk alongside the cars. Don't want any of them getting close to the kids."

"Doke?" Mindy said. "Are we doing the right thing?"

"I don't know." Doke sounded almost desperate. "But let's

go. If we all stay together, it's better than being divided." The two parents crowded into the backseat of Bernie's car, their kids between them, buckled into the parents' seat belts. Craig got into the driver's seat, and Bernie ducked in the passenger side. Sam and I hugged, and then we got into his truck. We pulled away from the curb slowly and carefully, and Togo got on my side of the truck. He smiled in at me. Trish was on Sam's side. The bikers and the other shifters who'd come from out of town surrounded Bernie's car, which would be behind us.

We started down the street, and the yelling began. The people who were trying to keep the peace pushed to get in front of the protesters, linking arms to provide us clear passage to the corner. The news crew had scrambled out and gotten their equipment set up, and the reporter, a handsome young man in a beautiful suit, was talking earnestly into the camera. Then he stepped out of camera view so the lens could pick up the scene of our approaching vehicles.

Sam was punching in a number on his cell. He held it to his ear. "Porter," he said, "if you're in front of the church, we're headed your way, and in case you have your head up your ass, we're in a lot of trouble."

He listened for a moment. "Okay, we'll be there. If we get through."

He tossed the phone onto the seat. "He says it's worse the closer you get to the church. He's not sure he could get through to help us. He's having trouble just keeping the crowd out of the church. The Lisles have made it, because they came early so Deidra could dress in the bride's room."

"That's something," I said, trying to keep my voice steady. I was scared to death. I was looking out the front windshield, and I saw people's mouths moving, their faces distorted; I heard human beings hating, hating. They didn't know Sam or

Bernie. They didn't care that the engaged couple couldn't turn into anything at all. They were waving signs. They were screaming at us. Again Togo smiled through the window at me, but I couldn't smile back.

"Courage," Sam said to me.

"I'm trying," I told him, and then the rock hit the windshield. I shrieked, which was stupid, but I was so startled and it was so sudden. "Sorry, sorry!" I gasped. There was a crack in the glass.

"Shit," Sam said, and I knew he was as tense as I was.

The next rock hit Togo in the shoulder. Though he didn't bleed, he did react, and I knew it must have hurt. Togo, so big and aggressive, probably seemed a better target than Trish, who was gray-haired and a woman.

"I wish I had my shotgun," I said out loud, though I'd thought it twenty times.

"If you had it, you'd shoot someone, so maybe it's better you don't," Sam said, which amazed me.

"You don't feel like shooting some of these yahoos?"

"I don't feel like going to jail," Sam said grimly. He was staring ahead, concentrating on keeping the truck moving at a slow and steady pace. "I'm only hoping none of them throw themselves in front of the truck." Suddenly, a tall figure appeared directly in our way. He turned his back to us and began walking ahead at the right pace to be point man for our little procession. Quinn. Bald head gleaming, he led us forward, looking from side to side, evaluating the crowd.

Sam's phone rang, and I picked it up. "Sookie here," I said.

"There are more of your people here," Brother Arrowsmith said. "I'm sending them to meet you."

"Thanks," I said, and flipped the phone shut. I relayed the message to Sam.

"So he finally grew a pair," Sam said. "And just in time."

We'd gotten to the corner by then, and we had to turn right on Main and go north a couple of blocks to turn onto St. Francis. While we waited for traffic to pass—amazingly, some people were actually trying to go about their everyday routine—I saw someone running toward us out of the corner of my eye. I twisted to see Togo looking out at the traffic, and he met my eyes briefly before he was broadsided by a short, heavy man swinging his sign at Togo's head. Togo bled and staggered and went down on one knee.

"Quinn!" I yelled, and Quinn turned to see what was happening. He bounded over the hood of the truck with a leap that was truly astounding, and he plucked Togo's attacker off the ground and held him there.

The crowd was shocked, and some of them stared, stunned by Quinn's speed and strength. Then they became enraged because this difference was exactly what they feared. I glimpsed more swift movement, Sam yelled, and I saw a tall woman, brown hair flying behind her like a banner, loping across Main at an inhuman rate. She looked normal in her jeans and sneakers, but she was definitely more than human. She went right to the knot of Togo, Quinn, and the protester. She seized the man from Quinn's grip and carried him over to the side of the street. With elaborate care, she placed him on his feet, and then she did an amazing thing. She patted him on the head with one long brown hand.

There was a scattering of laughter from the crowd. The man literally had his mouth hanging open.

She turned to Quinn and Togo, who'd lurched to his feet, and she grinned.

Togo's shoulders relaxed as he realized the crisis had passed—

for the moment. But Quinn seemed frozen, and then . . . so did she.

He bowed his head slightly to her. I couldn't hear what he said, but she bobbed her head at him in return, and she said one word. And though I couldn't really hear her, somehow I knew what it was: "tigress."

Whoa. I wished like hell I had time to think about that, but the road cleared in both directions and it was time to turn. I rolled down the window to let the people on foot know what we were planning, and then we moved out, the shifters running easily beside our little motorcade. We drove only a short distance before the left turn. Just two more blocks west to the church.

If Bernie's street had been crowded and frightening, St. Francis was even more crowded, and emotions were jacked up accordingly.

Sam was concentrating so hard on driving while watching the crowd for any sudden moves that I didn't dare talk to him. I crouched in my seat, every muscle twanging with tension.

The tigress and Quinn were loping ahead of the truck in tandem, their paces matched as if they were in harness. It was beautiful to watch. A woman darted in front of them with a bucket of paint in her hand, and before she could aim it at them, the tigress bent to hit the bottom of the bucket. The paint splashed upward all over the woman, who had the neat, casual look of a soccer mom . . . one who'd strayed way out of her league. Covered in red paint, the woman staggered back the way she'd come, and half the crowd laughed while the other half shrieked. But tiger and tigress kept on running at their easy pace.

I looked in the rearview mirror to see how Bernie's car was

faring, and watched, horrified, as a group surged forward with pieces of wood and bats in their hands to pound on the roof. The children! Togo, drawn by the noise behind him, turned and then cast a quick, doubtful glance at me.

"Go!" I yelled. "Go!"

Togo didn't hesitate but sprinted back to the crowd and began pulling people away from the car and tossing them to the side of the road as if they were cockleburs he was removing from his pants hem. Sam had stopped, and I glanced over at his agonized face. I realized that he didn't know whether to leap out of the car and go to help, or if that would leave the truck—and me—open to attack. Trish was back at Mindy's car helping Togo.

Then I saw a blur move by the truck and recognized Quinn. I swiveled in my seat and looked through the rear window. Quinn vaulted into the pickup bed, making the truck rock on its shocks.

I thought we were all done for, that this violence would spread and spread, and we'd be attacked and overwhelmed. Instead, the people of the town and the shifters who'd come in to support us began to shout for calm.

For the first time in its existence, most likely, the town of Wright heard a tiger roar. Though the sound came from an apparently human throat, it was unmistakable.

The crowd fell nearly silent. Togo and Trish, both bleeding, covered the windows of Mindy's car with their bodies. I could see Trish heaving for breath, while Togo's shirt was soaked on one side with blood. I peered through the windshield to see if help was coming from the church direction. I saw a thick crowd, and way at the rear I could glimpse the brown of the Wright police uniform. Two uniformed officers were trying to make their way through to come to us, but they'd never be here in time if the crowd decided to rush us. I looked back through the window to see Quinn drawing himself up tall.

"There are children in this car!" Quinn called. "Human children! What example have you set them?"

Some protesters looked ashamed. One woman began crying. But most seemed sullen and resentful, or simply blank, as if they were waking up from a trance.

"This woman has lived here for decades," Quinn said, pointing at Trish, whose hair was soaked with blood. "But you harm her enough to make her bleed while she's protecting children. Let us pass."

He looked around, waiting to see if he'd be challenged, but no one spoke. He leaped down from the truck and jogged back up to resume point position with his new friend. She touched him, her brown hand resting on his arm. He looked directly at her. It lasted a long moment.

I had the feeling that Quinn might not need to have a talk with me anymore.

Then the two weretigers began their run again, and we moved behind them.

Porter Carpenter and another uniform had kept an area in front of the church blocked off for our arrival, and they moved the sawhorses aside so we could park. They looked relieved.

"They didn't come help us," I said, and I found that my lips and mouth had been so tense that I could hardly talk now.

Sam turned the truck off and shuddered, having his own reaction. "They were trying," he said, his voice ragged. "I don't know how hard they were trying, but they were on their way."

"I guess this was a little more than they could handle," I said, making a determined attempt to be less than furious.

"Let's not beat them up," Sam suggested. "What do you say?"

"Right. Contraindicated," I said.

Sam managed to laugh, though it was a sad little snort of amusement.

"Are you okay?" he asked. "Before we get out and the madness starts all over again . . . forgive me for dragging you into this."

"Sam, not necessary!" I said, genuinely surprised. "We're friends. Of course I'm here, and glad to do it. Don't bring it up again, you hear? I'm just glad Mindy's already married!"

My weak joke lightened his mood. He grinned at me and leaned over to give me a kiss on the cheek. "Let's get this over with," he said, and we both opened our doors.

The noise had begun rising again. The car's passengers had emerged, too. Mindy and Doke, carrying their children, hurried up the steps of the church. Bernie, her fists clenched, faced the crowd, her eyes fixing on face after face. Some people had the grace to look ashamed, and some people were cheering for her, but some faces were twisted with loathing for this small, ordinary woman. Sam stood by his mother, his back straight.

I was so proud of him.

Craig moved to flank them, and I seized his hand. "Craig, you need to go on in the church now. We'll be in there in a second," I said, and I felt the anger come through him for a second before he understood that I was right. After giving his mother and brother one more look, he hurried into the church to reassure his bride that he'd arrived intact.

"Sam, you and your mom need to go in," I said. "See, Togo's brought Trish."

All the two-natured who'd flooded into Wright were pressed into service by Quinn and his new friend. Togo carried the stunned and bleeding Trish into the church and laid her on a back pew before he took his place in the shifter barrier that formed around the church. The three Biker Babes and the Suburban Weres were joined by the Wright law enforcement officers, though some were more willing than others to man the barricade. They were joined by a score of others.

I saw a tiny woman I knew. "Luna!" I exclaimed, and gave the twoey a hug. I hadn't seen her since I'd stayed in Dallas; it seemed like years ago, but it wasn't.

"You always in trouble?" she asked, flashing me a grin. "Hey, look down the line."

A few bodies away in the living chain, two Weres grinned and waved. One called out, "Hey, Milkbone," and I realized that they were the ones who had picked us up in Dallas. Amazing.

"It's like playing Whac-A-Mole," Luna yelled, to be heard over the noise of the crowd. "We may have busted up that phony church in Dallas, but I bet some of the same people are still here yelling that we ought to die. In fact, I already saw one of 'em. Sarah's here!"

I gaped at her. "Sarah Newlin?" She was the wife of the founder of the Fellowship of the Sun, and she'd gone underground with her husband after the raid.

Luna nodded. "Ain't that something?"

"I got to get into the church," I said. "I came all this way to go to a wedding, and I better go watch it. I hope I get to talk to you later."

She nodded back and turned to scream in the face of a man twice her size who said he wanted to get into the church to shoot the minister who'd perform such a travesty of a ceremony. That's exactly what he said, though he stumbled over "travesty." (Prompted? I think *so*.) Luna didn't even use words to respond. She just screeched. She scared the hell out of the man, who stumbled backward.

I ran quickly up the steps to the double doors of the church, amazed at Luna's revelation and cursing my high heels. (Today had turned out to be about so much more than looking good.) The FBI had been looking for the Newlins since the night Luna and I had escaped from the Fellowship building. They'd found all kinds of interesting things—guns, a body—concealed in the huge building, a former church. Steve and Sarah Newlin had continued their ministry of hate while on the run. The pair had a huge following. I would love to catch Sarah Newlin and turn her over to the law. It was no thanks to her that I hadn't been raped or murdered at the Fellowship building.

Nothing could drown out all the noise from the street, but the vestibule of the church was calm and relatively quiet. I could see through the open doors into the sanctuary that the candles were burning and the flowers were in place. Deidra's army brother, Jared, had brought a rifle with him, and he was standing by the church door ready to use it. Sam was with him.

I could see that the Lisles were waiting in the aisle, though Deidra's mother was struggling not to cry, and Deidra's father looked very grim. He had come armed, too. I didn't blame him. Craig and Bernie were right by them, along with Brother Arrowsmith's wife. She'd brought their son with her, cast and all. He looked angry and horrified and humiliated, and most of all he looked ashamed, because Bernie stood in front of him and looked him right in the face, not letting the boy dodge her gaze.

A door in the east wall of the vestibule opened, the door to the bride's room, and Deidra's sisters peeked out in their bridesmaid dresses, both pretty and very young. And very frightened. Their older brother nodded at them, trying to look reassuring.

"Where are Denissa and Mary?" the younger sister asked.

"The girls who were supposed to sing? They didn't make it," Jared said. The door closed. I knew Deidra was waiting in the little room in her wedding dress. "Their parents were too scared to let them come," Jared told Sam and me. "Sookie, you want to sing instead?"

Sam snorted.

"That's one thing I can't help with. You hear me singing, you'd run the other way." I wouldn't have thought anything could make me laugh, but I did. I took a deep breath. "I'll stay right here and watch the door. You two are members of the wedding."

Jared hesitated. "You know how to use this?" he asked, handing me the rifle. It was a .30-.30. I looked it over. "I prefer a shotgun," I said. "But I can make this work."

He gave me a straight look and then vanished through the double doors. Sam patted my shoulder and followed Jared.

I heard the music starting up in the sanctuary. The older of Deidra's sisters came out of the side room, her lavender dress rustling around her feet, and her eyes widened at the sight of me standing there with the rifle.

"I'm just insurance," I said, trying to look reassuring.

"I'm going to ring the bell," she told me, as if she had to get my permission. She pointed at the door in the west side of the vestibule, the bell tower door.

"Good idea." I had no idea whether it was or not, but if tradition demanded the bell be rung at the time of the wedding, then the bell would be rung. "You need me to help?"

"If you wouldn't mind. My little sister needs to stay with Deidra. She's real nervous. You'll have to put down the rifle for a second." She sounded almost apologetic. "My name's Angie, by the way."

I introduced myself and followed her through the little door into the bell tower. A long red velvet rope hung down like a big thick snake. I looked up at the bell hanging overhead, wondered how many pounds it weighed. I hoped the builders had known what they were doing. I laid down the rifle, and Angie and I seized the rope, braced ourselves on our heels, and pulled. "Four times," she said jerkily, "For a four o'clock wedding."

This was actually kind of fun. We almost came off our feet when the bell swung up, but we managed the four rings. And I heard the crowd go quiet.

"I wonder if there's a speaker outside," I said.

"They put in one for Mr. Williston's funeral," Angie said. "He was in the state legislature." She opened the door to an electrical panel and flipped a switch.

I could hear a crackle outside, and then "Jesu, Joy of Man's Desiring" poured over the heads of the crowd. I heard a yell or two, but I could tell that people were turning to listen.

Angie went over to open the door to the bride's waiting room, and Deidra and her youngest sister came out. Mr. Lisle joined them, and I could tell he was trying to focus on his daughter instead of on the mob in the street. Deidra was a vision in white, and her hands were holding a happy bouquet of sunflowers and daisies.

"You look beautiful," I said. Who could not smile at a bride?

"That's our cue," Angie told her sister, and she opened the door to the sanctuary. The bridal march began, and I could hear it from in the church and from outside. Deidra turned to me, startled.

"All rise," said Brother Arrowsmith's sonorous church voice, and though there were precious few to rise, I could hear a rustle of movement.

Angie went down the aisle first, then her sister. Finally Deidra, her face glowing, took her father's arm and went slowly down to join her fiancé.

I had retrieved the rifle, and I stood in the vestibule halfway between the outer and the inner doors, glancing from one to the other. I saw Deidra's father step forward to whisper something to Brother Arrowsmith, who said, "Please join me on this holy occasion, as all of us, inside these walls and outside, stand together in God's sight to say the Lord's Prayer."

He really came through in a pinch. I stepped closer to the outer doors, put my ear to one of them. After a moment, I could hear voices outside saying the prayer right along with the wedding party. Not all the people outside were joining in, but some were.

I risked going into the bell tower to look out one of the small windows there, and what I saw amazed me.

Some people had fallen to their knees to pray. The few protesters who felt like keeping up with the yelling were being decisively silenced by means both fair and foul by the devout. I dashed to the inside double doors and gestured to the minister to keep it up. Then I went back to look some more.

And I saw her. Sarah Newlin. She was wearing a hat and dark glasses, but I recognized her. She had a sign, of course: IF YOU BARK AND GROWL, IN HELL YOU WILL HOWL. Nice. She was looking around with baffled resentment, as if she couldn't believe we'd played the God card and it had trumped hatred.

Next we had the Apostles' Creed. "I believe in God, the Father Almighty . . ." chorused voices inside the church and out. Brother Arrowsmith's voice rang with sincerity. There was a long moment of silence when the creed was over.

"Today we gather together to join in holy matrimony . . ." Brother Arrowsmith was off and running with what was probably the most ceremonious, solemn wedding ever held in this church; I was willing to put money on that. The people outside listened as Deidra, her voice shaking, agreed to be the wife of Craig, who sounded both strained and reverent.

It was beautiful.

It was just what we needed to turn the corner.

Gradually, the hostiles began dispersing, until only a few die-hard haters were left. All the two-natured stayed. When Craig and Deidra were pronounced man and wife and the organ music swelled triumphantly, there was actually applause out in the street.

I leaned against the wall by the church doors. I felt like I'd just run a marathon. The little wedding party milled around, hugging and congratulating, and Sam detached himself and hurried down the aisle to join me in the vestibule.

"That was some good thinking," he said.

"Figured it couldn't hurt to remind everyone where they were, and who was watching," I said.

"I'm calling the closest liquor store to get a keg delivered at the house and a lot of snacks from the grocery," Sam said. "We've got to thank everyone that came from so far away."

"Time to go to the reception?" The bride and groom, who looked as happy as two young people can be, were leading the way out of a rear door of the church to go back to the fellowship hall.

"Yeah." Sam was busy on his iPhone for a few minutes, making the arrangements for an impromptu party following the church reception.

I didn't want to distract Sam from this happy family occasion, but there were a few things we had to talk about. "How'd they all know to get here on time?" I asked.

"I don't know," Sam said, startled. "I thought Twitter or the Internet. . . ."

"Yeah, I get that. But some of those people had to travel for hours. And the trouble started just this morning."

Sam was intensely thoughtful. "I hadn't even thought about that," he said.

"Well, you've had other fish to fry."

He gave me a wry grin. "You could say that. Well, do you have a theory?"

"You're not going to like it."

"Of course not. I don't like anything about this. But spill it anyway." We were standing on the covered walkway between the church and the fellowship hall, and I realized the entire property was ringed by the two-natured, and they were all looking out. They hadn't relaxed their vigilance, though perhaps seventy percent of the protesters had left. I was glad of that because I didn't really think this was over. I thought the worst had been staved off, at best.

"I thought about this some when I saw how many people were here. I think that this was all planned. I think the word about the wedding spread, and someone decided this was the chance to see how an organized protest went . . . kind of a testing of the waters. If this went well for the assholes who were out there screaming—If the wedding had been put off, or if the weres had attacked and killed a human—then this would have become a model for other events."

"But the weres showed up, too."

I nodded.

"You mean the twoeys were also alerted early? By the same . . . ?"

"By the same people who alerted the anti-furries."

"To make this a confrontation."

"To make this a confrontation," I agreed.

"My brother's wedding was a *test-drive*?"

I shrugged. "That's what I think."

Sam held open the door for me. "I wish I could say I was sure you're wrong," he said quietly. "What kind of maniac would actually make things worse than they are?"

"The kind of person who is going to make his point no matter how many people have to die in the process," I said. "Luna told me she saw someone in the crowd. And then I saw her, too."

Sam looked at me intently. "Who?"

"Sarah Newlin."

Every supe in America knew that name. He turned that over in his mind for a few seconds. Bernie, resplendent in beige lace, glanced back at us, clearly wanting Sam to rejoin her. The bride was ready to cut the cake, a traditional moment that demanded our attendance. Sam and I drifted over to join the knot of people around the white-draped table. Craig put his hand over Deidra's, and together they sliced the bridal cake, which turned out to be spice cake with white icing, homemade by the bride's mother. This was the most personal wedding I'd attended in some time, and I enjoyed the hominess of it. The little plates for the cake were paper, and so were the napkins, and the forks were plastic, and no one cared. The cake was very good.

Brother Arrowsmith came over to me, and though burdened with a plate and punch, he found a way to free a hand to shake mine. I got a huge gust of his relief, his pride that he had done the right thing, his worry about his son, and his love for his wife who had been by his side all day, both in her prayers and physically.

The minister's chest was burning, and he was having heartburn, which he seemed to have pretty frequently these days, and he thought maybe he'd better not drink the punch, though of course it wasn't alcoholic.

"You need to go to a heart specialist in Dallas or Fort Worth," I said.

Brother Arrowsmith looked as though I'd hit him in the head with an ax handle. His eyes widened, his mouth fell open, and he wondered what I really was, all over again.

Dammit, I knew the signs of possible heart problems. His arm hurt, he had heartburn, and he was way too tired. Let him think I was supernaturally guided if he chose. That might up the chances he'd make an appointment.

"You were really smart to turn on the speaker," Brother Arrowsmith said. "The word of God entered those people's hearts and changed them for the good."

I started to shake my head, but then I had second thoughts.

"You're absolutely right," I said, and I realized I meant it. I felt I was such a bad Christian that I hardly deserved to call myself that anymore, but I understood at that moment that I still believed, no matter how far my actions had strayed from those of the woman my grandmother had raised me to be.

I gave Deidra and Craig a hug apiece, and I automatically told Bernie how beautiful it had been, which was simply weird. I met the Lisles, and it was easy to sense their profound relief that this wedding was done, that Deidra and Craig would not be living here, and that they could maybe regain some semblance of their former life. They liked Craig, it was easy to tell, but the whole trauma of the controversial wedding after the revelation of Craig's mom's heritage had smothered their initial pleasure at his joining their family. Mrs. Lisle was hoping fervently that the other two girls would never, ever give a were or shifter a second look, and Mr. Lisle was thinking he'd greet the next two-natured boy who came to call for one of his daughters with a shotgun.

This was all sad, understandable, and inevitable, I guess.

When it was time to leave the church, the tension ratcheted up again.

Sam stepped outside and explained to the waiting shifters what was about to happen. When Deidra and Craig stepped out of the fellowship hall, they went through the church so they'd be protected by a building for as long as possible. By the time we'd gotten back to the church vestibule, I cracked the doors open to look outside. The two-natured had formed a solid phalanx of bodies between the doors of the church and the parked cars. Trish and Togo had recovered enough to join them, though the dried blood on their clothes looked awful.

Craig and Deidra came out first, and the people still there began clapping. Startled, the couple straightened from their hunched-over postures, and Deidra smiled tentatively. They were able to leave their wedding reception almost normally.

The plan was that we would all go to Bernie's house. Deidra's parents had suggested that maybe Deidra should change into her going-away clothes there, and I didn't want to think too hard about why they'd thought it was such a good idea. They'd also told their two younger girls to get in the car and go home with them, and they hadn't made it an option. I managed to hug Angie, who'd pulled the bell rope with me. I had high hopes for her future. I don't think I ever spoke two words to the younger girl or Deidra's other brother.

I was looking around in the remaining crowd. There were still a few protesters, though they were notably quieter about their opinions. Some signs waved in a hostile way, some glares . . . nothing that didn't seem small after the ordeal of getting to the church. I was looking for a particular face, and I spotted it again. Though she looked older than she should have, and though she was wearing dark glasses and a hat, the woman standing with a camera in her hands—she'd discarded the sign—was Sarah Newlin. I'd seen her husband in a bar in Jackson when he was supporting a follower who'd come prepared to assassinate a vampire. That hadn't worked out for Steve Newlin, and this wasn't working out for Sarah. I was sure she'd taken my picture. If the Newlins tracked me down . . . I glanced around me. Luna caught my eye.

I jerked my head, and she came over. We had a quiet conversation. Luna drifted over to Brenda Sue, one of the Biker Babes, a woman nearly six feet tall who sported a blond crew cut. The two started a lively conversation, all the time moving closer and closer to Sarah, who began to show alarm when they were five feet away. Brenda Sue's hand reached out, twitched the camera from Sarah's grasp, juggled it for a moment, then tossed it to Luna.

Luna, grinning, passed it from her right hand to her left hand behind her back. The blonde made several playful passes for it. All the while, Luna's hands were busy. Finally, the blonde was able to retrieve the camera, and she tossed it back to Sarah.

Minus the memory chip.

By that time, those of us who had ridden to the wedding were back in the vehicles. Luna and Togo and Trish got into the truck's flatbed, and the bikers each gained a passenger. Somehow we all got back to Bernie's house without any bad incidents. There were still a lot more people in the streets of Wright than normal, but the protest had lost its heart, its violence.

We pulled up in front of the house to find that the beer was being unloaded and carried into the backyard, and that even more people were bringing food. The manager of the grocery store was personally unloading more sandwich platters and tubs of slaw and baked beans, plus paper plates and forks. All the people who had been too frightened to come to the wedding were trying to find some way to make themselves feel better about that, was the way I took it. And I'm usually pretty accurate about human nature.

All of a sudden, we were in the party business.

The two-natured who'd flooded into Wright now surged through the house and into the backyard to have a drink and a sandwich or two before they had to take the road home. With a pleasing sense of normality, I realized I had work to do. Sam and I changed from our wedding finery into shorts and T-shirts, and with the ease of people who work together all the time, we set up folding tables and chairs, found cups for the beer, sent the rapidly healing Trish to the store with Togo, and arranged the napkins and forks and plates by the food. I spotted a big garbage can under the carport, found the big garbage bags to line it, and rolled it to the backyard. Sam got the gas grill going. Though Mindy and Doke offered to help, both Sam and I were glad when they went home with the kids. After such a day, they didn't need to hang around. Those kids needed to go back to Mooney.

Few humans remained to party with the twoeys. Most of the regular people had seemed to get a whiff of the otherness of the guests, and they'd drifted away pretty quickly.

Though we were short on folding chairs, everyone made do. They sat on the grass or stood and circulated. When Togo and Trish returned with soft drinks and hamburger patties and buns, the grill was ready to go and Sam took charge. I began putting out the bags of chips. Everything was going very well for an impromptu celebration. I went to pump beers.

"Sookie," said a deep voice, and I looked up from the keg to see Quinn. He had a plate with a sandwich and some chips and some pickles on it, and I handed him a cup of beer.

"There you go," I said, smiling brightly.

"This is Tijgerin," Quinn said. He pronounced it very carefully. It sounded like "Tie" plus a choking noise, and then "ine" as in "tangerine." I practiced it in my head a couple of times (and I looked up the spelling later). "That's 'Tigress' in Dutch. She's of Sumatran and Dutch descent. She calls herself Tij." Pronounced "Tie."

Her eyes were as dark a purple as Quinn's, though perhaps a browner tone, and her face was a lovely high-cheekboned circle. Her hair was a shiny milk-chocolate brown, darker than the deep tan tone of her skin. She smiled at me, all gleaming white teeth and health. I figured she was younger than me, maybe twenty-three.

"Hallo," she said. "I am pleased to meet with you."

"Pleased to meet you, too," I said. "Have you been in America long?"

"No, no," she said, shaking her head. "I am here just now. I am European employee of Special Events, the same company Quinn works for. They send me here to get the American experience."

"You've certainly gotten to see the bad part of the American experience today. Sorry about that."

"No, no," she said again. "The demonstrations in the Netherlands were just as bad." Polite. "I am glad to be here. Glad to meet Quinn. There are not so many tigers left, you know?"

"That's what I've heard," I said. I looked from her to Quinn.

"I know you'll learn a lot while you're here, Tij. I hope the rest of your stay in America is better than today."

"Oh, sure it will be!" she said blithely. "Here we are at a party, and I am meeting many interesting people. And the praying at the church, that was very interesting, too."

I smiled in agreement—"interesting" was one word for it. "So, Quinn," I asked, since we were being very polite in front of Tij, "How's your mom?"

"She's doing all right," he said. "And my sister's gone back to school. I don't know how long it'll last, but she seems a little more serious about it this time."

"That's good to hear," I said.

"How's Eric?" Quinn was really making an effort. Tij looked mildly inquiring.

"Eric is my boyfriend," I explained to her. "He's a vampire." I automatically looked out at the backyard to gauge how much sunlight was left. Eric wouldn't be up for another hour. "He's fine, Quinn."

Tij seemed intrigued, but Quinn took her arm and steered her away. "We'll talk later," he said.

"Sure." They fell into conversation with Togo. The three looked like trees among regular people.

Deidra and Craig had already made a round of handshaking, thanking the people who'd come to save their lives and their wedding. Then the newlyweds changed and slipped away on their honeymoon, which was the most sensible thing in the world for them to do. Quinn and Tijgerin walked them out to Craig's car, and when they came back inside, Quinn tracked me down in the kitchen, where I was mining Bernie's pantry for some more garbage bags.

Quinn looked very serious. We were alone in the kitchen, which was pretty amazing.

"Hey," he said, and leaned against the counter. I pulled a bag from the cardboard box and shook it out. Then I pulled the crammed bag from the kitchen garbage can and cinched it shut.

"It's been a long day, huh? What did you want to talk about?" Might as well get right to it. I stuck the full bag by the back door and inserted the new one.

"The last time I saw you, Bill and I got stupid and you got hurt," Quinn said. "Eric ordered me out of Area Five, and I had to go. I don't know if you realized that E(E)E and Special Events are mostly vampire owned?"

"No." I wasn't surprised, though. The two catering and event companies employed both humans and shifters, but I was sure they'd required lots of capital to start up, and they'd begun their operations in a very luxe way. That's kind of a vampire signature.

"So I can't afford to offend a lot of deaders," Quinn said, looking away as if he were sure this admission would make him look weak. "They're silent partners in the rest home my mother stays in, too." Quinn had already paid off one family debt he owed the vampires.

"They've got you every which way," I said. We looked at each other directly.

"I want you to know," he said. "I want you to know that if you don't want to be with Eric, if he's using any kind of coercion on you, if he's got any leverage on you the way they do on me . . . I'll do anything in my power to get you free."

He'd do it, too. I suddenly saw a whole different life opening up before me, and my imagination painted it rosy, for a moment. I tried to picture living with Quinn, who was warm and generous and a magnificent lover. He really would do everything he could to pry me away from Eric if he thought I had the slightest misgiving about my relationship with the vampire, no matter what the consequences were for him.

I'm not a saint. I thought of how wonderful it would be to be with a man who could go shopping with me in the day-time, a man I could have a baby with, a man who knew how to treat a woman well. But even if I decided I wanted to leave Eric, Eric would always be sure, through his vampire contacts, that Quinn paid and paid and paid.

I looked past his shoulder out the bay window to see Tij-gerin, who was happily devouring her third hamburger. I didn't know much about her, but I did know there were very few weretigers left in the world. If Quinn and Tijgerin mated, they could have a tiger baby. And from the way she'd looked at Quinn, I thought I could assume she was unencumbered by a boyfriend at present. She and Quinn had been smacked in the face with their mutual attraction, and I admired him all the more for sticking to his declared program in making this offer.

I took a deep breath before I spoke, aware that this was a huge honor he'd paid me.

"Quinn, you're a great man, and you're so attractive, and I am so fond of you," I said. I looked him right in the eyes be-cause I wanted him to see how much I meant every word. "But . . . and some days I think, unfortunately for me . . . I love Eric. He comes with a thousand years of baggage . . . but he's it for me now." I took another deep breath. "With regret, I'm going to turn you down, but I am your true friend, and I al-ways will be."

He pulled me close. We hugged each other hard, and I stepped back. "You go have a good time," I said, blinking furi-ously, and then he was gone.

After a few moments of recovery—and feeling definitely

on the noble side—I drifted into the backyard to see if Sam needed anything. The gas grill had been turned off, so he'd cooked everything there was to cook. The outside lights were on, but there was a sharp contrast of light and shadow in Bernie's backyard. Someone had brought out a CD player and turned the volume up. I wondered why Jim Collins hadn't appeared to protest.

I saw a small figure emerge from the shadows at the corner of the house. It was a woman wearing a vest with a bra under it, a tiny skirt, and gladiator sandals. The evening was cooling off rapidly, and I figured the newcomer would be covered in goose pimples soon. Her short dark brown hair was slicked back smoothly.

And then I recognized her.

Jannalynn was dressed to kill. I'd imagined her being here in a moment of craziness, and here she was.

Awkward.

Sam saw her at the same instant I did, and I could read him like a book in that moment. He was happy to see her, but he was also flabbergasted—and that's the best way I can put it.

"Hello, young woman," said Bernie, stepping in the Were's path. "I don't believe I've met you yet. I'm Bernie Merlotte."

Jannalynn took in the cheerful gathering, saw all the two-eys having a good time, and I guess she had her own black moment when she wondered why Sam hadn't invited her when there were so many other two-natured guests. I was glad I wasn't in her line of sight. I stepped back into the kitchen . . . because frankly, I was scared to death of Jannalynn. I'd seen her in action, and it was no fluke that the pack-leader of Shreveport had named her his enforcer.

"Hey, honey," she called, spotting Sam over his mother's shoulder.

FOUR

BERNIE TURNED TO check that this young woman was addressing her son. It was hard to read Sam's face, especially from the kitchen. I was looking out the window, thinking it would be better not to make an appearance until this situation had been smoothed out a little. Though this was a minor problem compared to the terrors we'd faced today, I still wasn't rushing into some kind of touchy greeting with Sam's girlfriend.

I didn't know if I was being a coward or simply being prudent. Either way, I was staying put until I got a cue.

"Jannalynn!" he said, and he embraced her quickly. It wasn't exactly a boyfriend hug, more a "Hi, buddy, good to see you!" thing. "I didn't expect you could come." When he took a step back, I could see that his brows were sort of knit with doubt.

"I know, I know, you brought Sookie to meet your family. And I know why. But I couldn't stay away when I heard the news on the Fur and Feathers website."

None of this was scanning naturally. Jannalynn was smiling too brightly and doing a weird imitation of a brittle socialite. She looked exactly like someone who knew she was making a huge mistake.

Maybe I should just stay in the kitchen? For a long time? Maybe the rest of the night? I was pretty tired, but I also didn't want to feel I was being held hostage by my own social sense.

I heard the toilet flush, and Luna came into the kitchen, making a beeline for the back door. When she saw me, she stopped by my side and took in the scene.

"Okay, who's the fashion-challenged skinny chick?"

"Sam's real girlfriend." Luna raised her eyebrows at me, and I hurried to explain. "He'd already asked me to come to the wedding with him, and he hasn't been dating Jannalynn that long. Plus, she has some social issues that he kind of wanted to prepare his family for, and not while they were trying to deal with a pressure situation like a wedding."

"Hmmm. So he brings home the more presentable date, leaving the skinny . . . and very weirdly dressed . . . one at home. And then she shows up. And you think she's his real girlfriend? You *are* having a hell of a day, Sookie."

"Unfortunately, it's not only me who's having it. It's Sam and his mom, too." I scanned the crowd. "Well, at least I only see one or two more humans." Sam's friend Sister was still partying, and I glimpsed Jared Lisle talking to one of the Biker Babes. They were flirting in a major way.

"So, you know, I just thought I'd tell you," Luna said offhand, "I went through the hedge into the yard next door to make out with that cute guy in the camo pants, the Chinese guy? He's a Were cop from Fort Worth, on the tactical response team." She paused for my reaction.

"A hunk," I said. "Way to go, Luna." Lots of pairing off going on at this after-the-reception reception.

She looked pleased. "Anyway, while we were locking lips right on the other side of the hedge there, I smelled something funky in the house next to this."

I closed my eyes for a long moment. Then I told Luna the history of the past two days with Jim. "Can you get more specific than 'funky'?" I asked.

"Funky, as in dead meat. So someone's killed that guy, maybe." Luna's chirpy voice didn't sound especially dismayed. "He doesn't sound like a great loss, but you know the twoeys are going to get the blame."

"I guess I better go check it out," I said, and I can't tell you how reluctant I was. If Jannalynn hadn't shown up, I would've asked Sam to go with me. But that was out of the question at the moment.

I didn't want to try entering the Collins house through the front door. Who knew who might still be watching Bernie's house, maybe taking pictures? I didn't know if the TV stations had gone home or not. Probably yes, but there might be a few die-hards out there with their own cameras. But if I went out the back door, I'd run into Jannalynn—and although that was going to happen sooner or later, the longer I could postpone it, the better. I was trying not to watch her. She was working the party—shaking hands, laughing, with a beer she took long swallows from every few seconds.

"Fuck," I said.

"She's looking good," Luna admitted. "I bet Sam comes inside to get her a jacket within the next three minutes."

I admitted to myself that I didn't like Jannalynn because I thought Sam deserved someone much better, someone with some impulse control. Here I was, peering out the window like a criminal trying to make my escape, just so this girl wouldn't get her panties in a twist.

"She's hungry," Luna said. "She'll go for the food in a minute."

Sure enough, Jannalynn completely turned her back to the house so she could bend over the table, putting condiments on her hamburger bun. I slid out of the house and across the lawn going west at a smooth, fast clip . . . and Luna was right on my heels as I went through the gap in the overgrown hedge.

"You didn't have to come," I muttered. With a yard full of shifters, I had to take care to keep my voice down.

"I was getting bored anyway," she said. "I mean, I get to make out with gorgeous Chinese guys all the time."

I smiled in the darkness. There weren't any lights on in the Collins backyard or in the Collins house, which was odd because it was getting dark now.

There was a living brain in the house. I told Luna that, and she rolled her eyes at me. "Big whoop," she said. "So what?"

"That's my specialty," I said.

"But I can smell something dead," she told me. "Hasn't been dead long, but it's dead. That's my specialty. I know a dog or a Were would be better at this, but any twoey nose is better than a oney nose."

I shrugged. I'd have to concede that one. To knock or not to knock? As I stood flattened against the wall by the back door, debating furiously with myself, I heard a little whimper from inside. Luna stiffened beside me. I crouched and pulled open the screen door. It made the wheezy noise so common to screen doors, and I sighed.

"Who's here?" I said, keeping my voice hushed.

A sob answered me. I felt Luna come in, and she crouched beside me. Neither of us wanted to present a target against the faint light from the Merlotte backyard.

"I'm turning on the light," I told Luna in a tiny whisper. I patted the wall where the switch should be, and sure enough it was there. There were two. One would control the outside lights, and one the kitchen light. Was there a rule? If so, I didn't know it. I flicked the one on the left.

I couldn't have been more shocked by what I saw.

Jim Collins was absolutely, messily dead. He lay sprawled across the low kitchen counter, gun resting loosely in his right hand. Closer to the doorway into the interior of the house, Sarah Newlin sat on the floor. She was hurt somehow, because there was blood on her arm and more on her stomach. Her legs were extended in front of her. She was crying almost silently. There was a gun lying by her side, though I couldn't see what make.

"Call the police from his phone," I said instantly.

"No," Sarah said. "Don't!"

Luna punched in numbers so fast that I thought the phone was going to break.

With convincing hysteria, Luna said, "Oh my God! Bring an ambulance to Jim Collins's house! Some woman has shot him; he's dead and she's bleeding out!" She hung up and snickered.

Sarah Newlin made a halfhearted attempt to climb to her feet. I went over to her and put my foot on her gun. I didn't think she had enough sand in her to grab it, but better to be sure.

"You're not going to get away," I said dispassionately. "They'll be here in two shakes of a lamb's tail. You're hurt too bad to escape. If you don't go to the hospital, you'll die."

"I might as well," she said drearily. "I've killed a man now."

"You're counting this as the first?" I was shocked. "You've been responsible for so many deaths, but this is the one that matters?" Of course, this one counted to Sarah because Collins had been human and on her side, and the others who'd died had been vampires and weres and humans who didn't believe what the Fellowship of the Sun advocated.

"Why'd you shoot your disciple here?" I asked, since Sarah seemed to be in confession mode.

"Steve and I knew Collins from his website," she said weakly. "He had all the right ideas, and he was full of the fire of God. But the plans we had for today failed. God must have changed his mind, turned his face from us. Collins never came to the church. I came here to ask him why, but he was angry, angry with me, with himself. I think he may have been drinking. He challenged me to go with him, to shoot you-all next door. He said we could kill most of you, just like he killed the dogs."

"You weren't up for that?" Luna asked bitterly. "You sure missed an opportunity to get a bunch of us at once."

"Couldn't risk myself," Sarah whispered. "I'm too important to the cause. He even thrust a gun in my hand. But God didn't want me to sacrifice myself. When I told Collins that, he went nuts."

"He was already nuts," I said, but she wasn't listening.

"Then he said I was a hypocrite, and he shot me."

"Looks like you shot him back."

"Yes," Sarah whispered. "Yes, I shot him back."

A police car pulled up in front of the Collins house, the flickering light visible from the kitchen. Someone called from the front door, "Police! We're coming in!"

"Hurry with the ambulance," I called back. "There are two of us who came and discovered the situation. We're unarmed."

"Stand with your hands against the wall!" the officer's voice called back, and it sure as hell sounded like Porter Carpenter.

"Porter," I said. "It's me, Sookie Stackhouse, Sam's friend. And my buddy Luna Garza is with me."

"Hands!" Porter said. "Anyway."

"Okay," I appreciated his caution. Luna walked over to me, and we turned our backs on the doorway and put our hands on the wall. "We're ready," I yelled.

You'd think I'd be distraught and upset. You'd think I'd be overwhelmed, having seen this horrible scene.

But you know what? I was tickled pink. I'd never been a squeamish person, and I'd seen other and worse scenes of carnage, featuring people I cared about to some extent or other.

As it was, it was hard for me to suppress a smile when I saw

Sarah Newlin hauled off to the hospital under arrest. And since the dead man was Jim Collins, I didn't feel a moment's grief for him, either. He would have loved it if the tables had been turned, if he'd walked in on someone who'd just killed Bernie and Sam. He'd have patted them on the back. And I'm being honest when I say that after the hate I'd seen that day, I couldn't be sorry that if someone had to die, that person was Jim Collins, and if someone had to be a murderer, I was fine with that murderer being Sarah Newlin.

"Sookie," said Luna into my ear, "it doesn't hardly get any better than this."

"I think you're right," I said.

Porter Carpenter himself took our statements. I could tell that Luna—and the fact that she'd smelled the dead body— made him uneasy. But he wrote everything down, made note of our phone numbers, and then sent us on our way. Finally, we got to go back to the Merlotte house, where everyone was waiting anxiously to find out what had happened. I'd heard Sam's voice raised outside several times while I'd been answering questions—or simply waiting to be asked questions—and each time I'd smiled involuntarily. Sam was on the offensive.

Luna and I were glad to enter Bernie's kitchen, still crowded with weres, though the bulk of the party had drifted away— including Tijgerin and Quinn.

Sam grabbed me by the shoulders, looked intently into my face, and said, "You okay?" He was vibrating with anxiety like a tuning fork.

"Yeah, I'm okay," I said. I smiled at him. "Thanks. I could hear you yell."

"I wanted you to hear me."

"We had quite an evening over there," Luna said. "Man, getting questioned by the cops is thirsty work!" Her cute Chinese cop took the hint and got Luna a beer from the refrigerator.

"We still have some food, if you're hungry," Bernie said. I could tell she was exhausted, but she was upright.

"Not me," I told her. Luna shook her head, too. "First, let me be sure you-all know Luna Garza from Dallas. Luna did me a good turn at the Fellowship of the Sun church some time ago, and seeing her here tonight turned out to be lucky for me again. . . ."

When we'd related the whole story, Brenda Sue began laughing. And she was joined by some of the other twoeys. "That's just too good," she said. "It's perfect. I know this is probably wrong of me, but I can't help feeling okay about this." There was a lot of silent agreement in the room.

Gradually, the remaining guests of the unofficial party began to leave. I couldn't avoid talking to Jannalynn anymore. She'd been sitting behind the table within reach of Sam since I'd returned, and she hadn't said a word. I knew this situation was hard for her, and I felt sorry it was, but there was nothing I could do about it. She'd known when she'd come to Wright that it was the wrong thing to do.

What could I see in her brain? I saw grief, resentment, and envy. Jannalynn was wondering why Sam couldn't see that she was just like me. She was brave and pretty and loyal, too.

"I have a boyfriend," I said. "You know I go with Eric Northman."

"Doesn't make any difference," she said stoically, not meeting my eyes.

"Sure it does. I love Eric. You love Sam." Already I could tell that saying anything at all had been the mistake I'd thought it would be, that we were compounding the unhappiness. But I couldn't simply sit there in silence staring at her.

Jannalynn could do that, though, and she did. She stared a hole through me and didn't say a word. I didn't know where she proposed to sleep that night, but it wasn't going to be in the sewing room with me, and I was going to bed.

Luna was ready to depart (by a huge coincidence, so was the cute cop), and I gave her a hug and told her I hoped to see her in Bon Temps someday.

"Girlfriend, just say the word," she murmured, and returned the hug.

I didn't see Sam anywhere, but I told Bernie good night and took my turn in the bathroom.

I don't know what anyone else did after that, but I took the quickest shower on record and slipped into my nightgown and unfolded the couch. I had time to pull the sheet up over me about halfway before I was out like a light. My phone buzzed a couple of times in the night, but all I did was moan and turn over.

The next morning, it was raining like hell when I woke. The clock told me it was after eight o'clock, and I knew I had to get up. I could smell coffee and a trace of a sweet scent that made me suspect someone had gone to a bakery.

In fact, Bernie had gone to the store and gotten some Pillsbury cinnamon rolls. Sam and Bernie were sitting at the table. Sam got up to get me a cup of coffee, and I hunched over it gratefully.

Bernie shoved the paper over to me. It was the Waco paper. There was a short article about the upset at the wedding.

"Was it on the TV?" I asked.

"Yeah, apparently," Sam said. "But Jim's murder is upstaging the wedding."

I nodded. All my glee had faded, leaving me feeling sort of dirty.

"Bernie, you did great yesterday," I said. Bernie looked ten years older than she had the day before, but there was vigor in her step and purpose in her voice.

"I'm glad it's over. I hope I never have to go through anything like that again. I hope Craig and Deidra are happy." Three true things.

I nodded emphatically. I agreed all the way around. "You going to church today?" I asked.

"Oh, yes," she said. "I wouldn't miss it for the world."

Sam said, "Sook, you think you can be ready to leave in an hour or so?"

"Sure. All I have to do is grab up my stuff and put on some makeup." I'd pulled on my shorts and a shirt and packed my nightgown already.

"No hurry," Sam assured me, but I could tell from the way he was sitting that he wanted to get on the road again. I wondered where Jannalynn was. I sort of felt around the house for her mentally, got no other brain signal. Hmmm.

We were actually out the door in forty-five minutes, after I said all the correct things to Bernie. I didn't want her to think I hadn't been brought up right. She smiled at me, and she seemed sincere when she told me she'd enjoyed having me in the house.

Sam and I were silent for a long time after we left Wright. I checked my cell phone for messages, and sure enough, I had two from Eric. He didn't like to text, though he would if he had to. He'd left voice messages. First message—"I've seen you on the evening news. Call me." BEEP. Second message—"Every time you leave town you get into trouble. Do you need me to come?" BEEP.

"Eric all bent out of shape?" Sam asked.

"Yeah. About like Jannalynn, I expect." I had to say something. Better to get it over with.

"Not exactly. You and Eric have been together longer, and you seem to know each other a little better."

"As well as a human and a thousand-year-old vamp can, I guess. You don't think you and Jannalynn know each other?"

"She's a lot younger than me," he said. "And she has some impulse-control issues. But she's really brave, really loyal."

Okay, that was just weird. It was like listening to an echo of Jannalynn's thoughts the night before.

"Yes," I said. "She is."

Sam shrugged. "When she left last night, we agreed we'd talk when I got back to Bon Temps and recovered from the wedding. We have a date for next weekend."

I had a limited menu of responses to choose from. "Good," I said, and left it at that.

We continued our near silence most of the way across Texas. I thought of the hateful crowd the day before, their distorted faces. I thought about the flash of sheer pleasure I'd felt when I'd realized who'd killed Jim Collins. I thought of how much fun the party had been before Jannalynn had shown up and Luna had told me about the smell in the house next door.

"I was surprised that the police didn't come over to ask any questions last night," I said.

"Sister called this morning and told me that they were going to, but—well, it seemed so obvious what had happened—"

"That's great. You're free and clear."

This was good. Now we were talking like we had before. A knot in my stomach eased up.

"She said that even before they knew Jim was dead, the Arrowsmiths prodded their son to come forward and tell Porter that he'd seen the e-mails between Sarah Newlin and Jim about marshaling both sides to clash at the wedding. She'd urged Jim to make trouble, to enlist his like-minded neighbors and friends to take action, and encourage them to disrupt the wedding in any way they could. In turn, Jim had insisted she come to town herself to witness the work he was doing. The theory is that the shooting started when the two of them were arguing because the plan didn't work out."

That was pretty much the truth and should sure clinch the case against Sarah. "Why do you think we didn't hear the shots?" I asked Sam.

"According to Sister, all the windows were shut. Probably because the noise of a yard full of folks he hated enjoying themselves was bothering Jim," Sam said. "And with our CD player turned up loud . . . Sarah Newlin told them that she'd been at Jim's house almost an hour before he got worked up enough to suggest they go over and shoot us all. But then her lawyer arrived, and she clammed up."

"You think there's any way she'll get off?" I asked incredulously.

"She won't go to prison for murder. Maybe manslaughter. Of course, she'll claim self-defense." He shook his head and accelerated to pass a beat-up minivan that was poking along in front of us.

"Just think on it, Sook—if Luna hadn't gone on the Collins side of the hedge to make out in private, maybe Sarah Newlin would have called someone to come get her, or managed somehow to crawl out of the house. She might even have made it into her car. Then I think Mom and I would have had a visit from the police for sure."

But that hadn't happened, and now Sarah Newlin would be in jail for a while anyway. That was something, a big something. "I'm not drawing any big life lesson from yesterday," I said.

"Were you sure you were going to?"

"Well, yes."

"We survived," Sam said. "And my brother got married to the woman he loves. And that's all that's important."

"Sam, do you really think that?" I didn't want to pick at him, but I was genuinely curious.

My boss smiled at me. "Nah. But what would you say the moral of the day was? There was a lot of hate, there was some love. The love won out for Craig, the hate did Jim Collins in. End of story."

Sam was right, as far as his "moral" went.

But I didn't think it was truly the end of the story.

IF I HAD A HAMMER

"If I Had a Hammer" is a retroactive story meant to create the basis for a situation that occurs in one of the novels. I needed to show that Sam is willing to help Tara and JB du Rone with their home-improvement project (creating a better bedroom for their twins). Of course, Sookie has to be present to help . . . and in the process, she becomes closer to Sam. I also wanted to introduce the du Rones' babysitter, who shows up later in "In the Blue Hereafter."

Dead Ever After precedes "If I Had a Hammer."

I F I HAD a hammer," I sang, as I used the measuring tape and a pencil to mark where I needed to drill.

From the next room, Tara called, "I'm going to leave if you're going to sing."

"I'm not that bad," I said with mock indignation.

"Oh yes, you are!" She was changing one of the twins in the next room.

We'd been friends forever. Tara's husband, JB du Rone, was part of that friendship. We'd formed a little group of misfits at our high school in Bon Temps, Louisiana. What had saved us from utter outcast-dom was that we each had a redeeming talent. I could play softball, Tara was a great manager (yearbook, softball team), and JB was incredibly handsome and could play football, given good and patient coaching.

What put us on the fringes, you ask? I was telepathic; Tara's parents were embarrassing, abusive, poor, and public in their drunkenness; and JB was as dumb as a stump.

Yet here we were in our later twenties, reasonably happy human beings. JB and Tara had married and very recently produced twins. I had a good job and a life that was more exciting than I wanted it to be.

JB and Tara had been surprised—amazed—when they had

discovered they were going to be parents, and even more startled to find they were having twins. Many children had grown
up in this little house—it was around eighty years old—but
modern families want more space. Though cozy and comfortable for two, the house began to creak at the seams after Robbie and Sara—Robert Thornton du Rone and Sara Sookie du
Rone—were born, but buying a larger place wasn't a possibility. That they owned this snug bungalow on Magnolia Street
was something of a miracle.

Tara had gotten the house years before when Tara's Togs
started making some money. After careful consideration,
she'd chosen the old Summerlin place, a bungalow built in
the late twenties or early thirties. I'd always loved Magnolia
Street, lined with houses from that same era, shaded by huge
trees and enhanced with bright flower beds.

Tara's one-floor house had two bedrooms (one large and
one tiny), one bathroom, a kitchen, a living room, a dining
room, and a sunroom. The sunroom, which faced the front of
the house and lay through an arch to the right of the living
room, was becoming the babies' room because it was actually
much larger than the second bedroom. And the closet that
served that bedroom backed onto the sunroom.

After a summit meeting the week before, attended by me;
my boss, Sam Merlotte; and Tara's babysitter, Quiana Wong,
Tara and JB had made a plan. With our help, they'd knock out
the wall at the back of the little bedroom's closet, which was
between that room and the sunroom. Then we'd block in the
closet from the bedroom side so the opening would be on the
sunroom side. We'd frame that opening and hang louvered
doors. The sunroom would become the new baby bedroom,
and it would have a closet and shelves on the walls for storage.
We'd paint the sunroom and the little bedroom. And the job

would be done. Just a little home improvement project, but it would make a big difference.

The very next day, Tara had gone to Sew Right in Shreveport to pick out material, and she'd begun making new curtains to cover the bank of windows that flooded the sunroom with light.

Sam had agreed to perform the wall removal, but he was pretty anxious. "I know it can be done," he said, "but I've never tried to do it." JB and Tara had assured him they had the utmost faith in him, and with some tips from all-purpose handyman Terry Bellefleur, Sam had assembled the tools he'd need.

Tara, Quiana, the twins, and I had assembled in the sunroom to watch for the exciting moment when Sam cut through the old wall. We could hear a lot of cutting and sawing and general whamming going on, along with the occasional curse. JB was dragging the bits of drywall outside as Sam removed them.

It was kind of exciting in a low-key way.

Then I heard Sam say, "Huh. Look at that, JB."

"What is that?" JB sounded surprised and taken aback.

"This piece of board has been cut out and replaced."

"[Mumble mumble mumble] . . . electric wires?"

"No, shouldn't be. It's kind of an amateur [mumble mumble] . . . Here, I can open it. Let me slide this screwdriver in . . ."

Even from our side of the wall, I could hear the creak as Sam pried the panel out from between the studs. But then there was silence.

Unable to contain my curiosity, I left the sunroom and zoomed through the living room to round the wall into the current nursery. Sam was all the way in the closet, and JB was standing at his shoulder. Both were looking at whatever Sam had uncovered.

"It's a hammer," Sam said quietly.

"Can I see?" I said, and Sam turned and held the hammer out to me.

I took it automatically, but I was sorry when I understood what I was holding. It was a hammer, all right. And it was covered with dark stains.

Sam said, "It smells like old blood."

"This must be the hammer that killed Isaiah Wechsler," JB said, as if that were the first thing that would pop into anyone's mind.

"Isaiah Wechsler?" Sam said. He hadn't grown up in Bon Temps like the rest of us.

"Let's go sit in the living room, and I'll tell you about it," I said. The little room suddenly felt hostile and confined, and I wanted to leave it.

The living room was pretty crowded with five adults and two babies. Tara was nursing Sara, a shawl thrown discreetly across her shoulder. Quiana was holding baby Robbie, rocking him to keep him content until his turn came.

"Back in the early thirties, Jacob and Sarah Jane Wechsler lived next door," Tara told Sam. "In the house Andy and Halleigh Bellefleur live in now. The Summerlins, Daisy and Hiram, built this house. The Wechslers had a son, Isaiah, who was about fifteen. The Summerlins had two sons, one a little older than Isaiah, and one younger, I think thirteen. You would have thought the boys would be friends, but for some reason Isaiah, a big bull of a boy, got into a fight with the older Summerlin boy, whose name was . . ." She paused, looking doubtful.

"Albert," I said. "Albert was a year older than Isaiah Wechsler, a husky kid with red hair and freckles, Gran told me. Albert's little brother was Carter, and he was thirteen, I think. He was quiet, lots of curly red hair."

"Surely your grandmother didn't remember this," Sam said. He'd been doing math in his head.

"No, she was too young when it all happened. But her mom knew both families. The fight and the estrangement caused a town scandal because the Wechslers and the Summerlins couldn't get Isaiah and Albert to shake hands and make up. The boys wouldn't tell anyone what the fight was about."

Tara reached under the shawl to detach Sara, extricated her, and began burping her. Sara was a champion burper. I could feel the sadness in Tara's thoughts. I figured the old story was rousing memories of her contentious family. "Anyway," I said with energy, "the two Summerlin boys slept in the room in there." I pointed to the wall Sam had just breached. "The parents had the bigger bedroom, and there was a baby; they kept the baby in with them. In the house across the driveway, Isaiah Wechsler slept in a bedroom whose window faced this house." I pointed to the sunroom's north window. "I think Andy and Halleigh use it as a den now. One summer night, two weeks after the big fight between Isaiah and Albert, someone went through Isaiah's open window and killed him in his sleep. Beat him to death."

"Ugh." Sam looked a little sick, and I knew he was thinking of the dark-stained hammer.

Quiana's slanting dark eyes were squinted almost shut with distress, disgust, some unpleasant emotion. She left the room with Sara to change her after handing Robbie to Tara.

I said, "The poor Wechslers found him in the morning in the bed, all bloody, and they sent for the police. There was one policeman in Bon Temps then, and he came right away. Back then, that meant within an hour."

"You won't believe who the policeman was, Sam," Tara said. "It was a man named Fuller Compton, one of Bill's descendants."

I didn't want to start talking about Bill, who was an ex of mine. I hastened on with the sad story. "The Wechslers told Fuller Compton that the Summerlins had killed their son. What could Fuller do but go next door? Of course, the Summerlins denied it, said their son Albert had been sleeping and hadn't left the house. Fuller didn't see anything bloody, and Carter Summerlin told the policeman that his brother had been in the bed the whole night."

"No CSI then," JB said wisely.

"That's just sad," Quiana said, returning with Sara, who was waving her arms in a sleepy way.

"So nothing happened? No one was arrested?" Sam asked.

"Well, I think Fuller arrested a vagrant and held him for a while in the jail, but there wasn't any evidence against him, and Fuller finally let him go. The Summerlins sent Carter out of town the next week to stay with relatives. He was so young. They must have wanted to protect him from the backlash. Albert Summerlin was regarded with lots of suspicion by the whole town, but there wasn't any evidence against him. And afterward, Albert never showed signs of a hot temper. He kept on going to church. People began speaking to Daisy and Hiram and Albert again. Albert never got into another fight." I shook my head. "People were sure the Wechslers would move, but they said they weren't gonna. They were going to stay and be a reminder to the Summerlins every day of their lives."

"Are there Wechslers still here in Bon Temps?" Sam asked.

"Cathy Wechsler is about seventy, and she lives in a little house over close to Clarice," JB said. "She's nice. She's the widow of the last Wechsler."

"What happened to Albert?" Quiana asked. "And the baby?"

"Not much," I said. "The older Summerlins passed away. Carter decided not to come back. The baby died of scarlet fever. Albert married and had kids. Raised them here in this house. Tara bought the house from Bucky Summerlin, right, Tara?"

"Yep," she said. She was patting Robbie on the back now. Robbie was goggling around at everyone with that goofy baby look. Sara was asleep in Quiana's arms, and I checked on the nanny automatically. Her thoughts were all about the baby, and I relaxed. Though I'd checked out Quiana thoroughly when Tara had told me she was thinking of hiring her, I still felt I didn't know her well.

If JB, Tara, and I had been considered odd ducks, Quiana had received a double whammy of misfit mojo. Her mother had been half Chinese, half African-American. Her dad, Coop Woods, had been all redneck. When Quiana was sixteen, they'd both been killed when their car stalled on the train tracks one night. Alcohol had been involved. There'd been rumors that Coop had planned a murder-suicide. Now Quiana was eighteen, staying with whatever relative would have her. I felt sorry for her precarious situation . . . and I knew there was something different about the girl. I'd given Tara the green light to hire her, though, because whatever her quirk was, it was not malignant.

Now Sam said, "You think we ought to call the police? After all, there's a detective right next door."

I noticed none of us hopped in to say, *Yes, that's the ticket.*

Sure, the hammer had stains, and Sam's nose was telling him the stains were old blood.

Sure, the hammer had been concealed in the wall.

Sure, a murder had taken place next door. But there might not be any connection.

Right.

"I don't think we have to," Tara said, and JB nodded, relieved. It was their say as the homeowners, I figured. I looked at the hammer as it lay on an old newspaper on the coffee table. Hammers hadn't changed much over the decades. The handle was worn, and when I picked it up and turned it over, I saw that the writing on it read FIRESTONE SUPREME. With the dark stains on it, the tool looked remarkably ugly in the sunny room. It could never be just a tool again.

Tara picked it up by folding the paper around it, and she carried it out of the room.

Tara's action jogged us all into motion. We split in different directions to go to work: JB to the fitness club, where he cleaned and trained; Sam and I to Merlotte's Bar; and Tara to check on her assistant, McKenna, who was running the store while Tara was on maternity leave. As I called good-bye, Quiana was putting the twins down for their nap on Tara and JB's bed since the babies' room was full of dust.

I FORCED MYSELF to go to Tara's by nine in the morning the next day. I had to fight a deep reluctance. For the first time, the pretty little house with its neat front yard seemed gloomy. Even the sky was overcast. I tapped on the front door, opened it, and called, "Woo-hoo! I'm here!"

Quiana was already at work folding laundry, but her full mouth was turned down in a sullen pout and she only nodded when I spoke to her. JB was nowhere in sight. Of course, he could be at the fitness club already, but normally he worked in the afternoon and evening. Tara, too, didn't show her face.

Sam trailed in right on my heels, and we got mugs of coffee in the kitchen. Quiana didn't respond to our attempts at conversation, and she fixed a bottle for one of the twins in silence. Tara was having to supplement, apparently.

JB emerged from the bedroom looking groggy. My old

friend was usually the most cheerful guy around, but this morning he had circles under his eyes and looked five years older. "Babies cried all night," he said wearily. "I don't know what got into them. They're in the bed with Tara right now." He downed his coffee in record time. Gradually he began to perk up, and when we set our mugs in the sink, we all looked a little brighter.

I began to worry. This was a funny kind of day—in an ominous way.

Sam and JB went back into the little bedroom to finish cutting out the doorway. I climbed a folding stool to mount some brackets for shelving, which would be right above where the changing table would be placed. The tracks for the adjustable brackets were already up. (I had learned how to use an electric drill to mount them, and I was justly proud of myself.) I began counting holes on the tracks so the brackets would be even.

"And there you have it, a solid brace," I said with some satisfaction. They were mounted too high for the twins to be tempted to climb on them, when they got bigger. They were designed to hold things Tara would need when she was changing the babies, and on the higher shelves would be the knick-knacks people had given her: a china baby shoe with a plant in it, a cute picture frame with a photo of the twins, their baby books.

"Good job, Sook," Sam said behind me.

I jumped, and he laughed. "You were thinking too hard to hear me come through the new closet door," he said. "I tried to walk heavy."

"You are evil," I said, climbing down. "I don't think I'll work for you anymore."

"Don't tell me that," he said. "What would I do without you?"

I grinned at him. "I expect you'd find a way to carry on.

This economy, there are plenty of women who need a job, even working for a slave driver like you."

He snorted. "You mean a pushover like me. Besides, you have your own financial interest in the bar now. Where are the shelves? I can hand 'em to you."

"JB cut them yesterday, and he was going to paint them when he got in from work last night."

Sam shrugged. "Haven't seen 'em."

"Tara," I called. "You up yet?"

"Yeah," she called. I followed her voice to the current baby room. Tara was changing Robbie. She was smiling down at the baby, but she looked haggard.

"He wants to know where his sis is," Tara said, freely interpreting Robbie's googly stare. "I think JB's got Sara."

"I'll track 'em down," I offered. I stepped into the kitchen, where Quiana was at the stove cooking . . . spaghetti sauce, from the smell. "You seen JB and Sara?" I asked. She was thinking that she didn't like the idea that someone could read her thoughts. I could hardly blame her for that. I didn't like the fact that I could, either. I sensed more strongly than ever that there was something different about Quiana, something that chimed in with my own peculiarity. It wasn't the time to tax her with it, though.

"They went outside," she murmured, her bony little figure hunched over the stove like a junior witch's. I crossed behind her to go out the back door.

"JB?" At first glance the fenced-in yard with its minute patio and lone water oak looked empty.

The shelf boards were there, and they were painted, which I was glad to see. But where was JB? And more important, where was baby Sara?

"JB!" I called again. "Where are you?" Maybe because of the

high fence, there was not a bit of breeze in the backyard. The lawn furniture sat dusty and baking on the bricks. It was hot enough to make my skin prickle. I closed my eyes and took a deep breath, inhaling the scents of town: asphalt, cooking, vehicles, dogs. I searched for a living brain in the area and had just found two when a subdued voice said, "Here."

I circled the water oak close to the west corner of the yard to find JB sitting on the ground. I closed my eyes in relief when I saw that he was holding Sara, who was making those cute little baby noises and waving her arms.

"What's the matter?" I asked, trying to sound gentle and relaxed.

JB had let his hair grow, and he pulled it back with a pony-tail holder. If you had to compare him to a movie star—yes, he was that handsome—he was pretty much in the fair-haired Jason Lewis mold. Physically. "There's something angry and sad in the house," he said, sounding way more serious and troubled than I'd ever heard him. "When we opened the wall and touched the hammer, it got out."

If I hadn't had such a strange life, I might have laughed. I might have tried to convince JB it was his imagination. But my friend was anything but imaginative, and he'd never shown a taste for the dark side before. JB had always been sunny, optimistic, and generally along for the ride.

"So, when did you . . . notice this?" I said.

Sam had approached us quietly. Now he knelt by JB. With a finger, he stroked the line of Sara's plump little cheek.

"I noticed it last night," JB said. "It was walking around the house."

"Did Tara see it, too?" Sam asked. He didn't look directly at JB. The sun set his strawberry-blond hair on fire as he knelt in the yard.

"No, she didn't." JB shook his head. "But I know it's there. Don't tell me I'm making it up or that I'm dreaming or something. That's bullshit."

"I believe you," I said.

"I believe you, too," Sam said.

"Good," said JB, looking down at his daughter. "Then let's find out how to get rid of it."

"Who'm I gonna call for that?" I wondered out loud.

"Ghostbusters," Sam said automatically. Then he looked embarrassed.

"Me," said a new voice, and we all rotated to look at Quiana. She still had the spoon in her hand, and it was dripping red.

There was what you might call a significant pause.

"I know stuff," she said, sounding pretty unhappy about it. "I get pictures in my head."

The pause extended to an uncomfortable length. I had to say something. She was already full of regret at revealing herself, and I could see that clearly, anyway. "How long have you been psychic?" I asked, which was like saying, Do you come here often? But I was clean out of ideas.

"Since I was little," she said. "But with my parents, you know, I knew not to say anything after the first time . . . they got spooked."

That was probably an understatement, and I could completely sympathize with Quiana. I'd had the same problem. Having a little girl living with you who could read your mind had been tough on both my mother and my father, and consequently tough on me.

"How does it happen?" I said, since Sam and JB were still floundering through their thoughts. "I mean, do you get clear pictures? What triggers them?"

She shrugged, but I could tell she was relieved that I was taking her seriously. "It's touch, mostly. I mean, I don't have visions when I'm driving or anything like that."

"That's so interesting," I said, and I was totally sincere. It was kind of neat to know someone else who was completely human but also wasn't normal.

She felt the same way.

"So when you touch the babies," JB said abruptly, "what do you see?"

"They're little," Quiana said with surprising gentleness. "I ain't going to see nothing with them this little."

Since that wasn't true, I had to applaud her for keeping her mouth shut. And I was grateful that she didn't spell out whatever she had seen in her own head, that I didn't have to see it with her. If anything was worse than reading people's minds, it would be knowing their future—especially when there wasn't anything you could do about it.

"Can you . . . You can't change anything?" I asked. "When you see something that's going to happen?"

"I cannot," she said, with absolute finality. "I don't have a bit of responsibility. But people make decisions, and that can change what I've seen." Quiana's golden skin flushed as we all stared at her.

"Right now," said Sam, getting from the bigger picture to the smaller, "do you think you can help us with the problems in this house?"

Quiana looked down. "I don't know how, but I'm going to try," she said. "When I figure out what to do." She looked at each of us questioningly. None of us had a helpful idea, at least not at the moment.

I said, "I'm hoping that the funny feeling in the house will sort of wear away, myself. Sam opened the wall, we've found the hammer, so we know Albert did kill Isaiah. Surely that should set it all to rest."

JB said, "Is that the way it works?" He didn't seem to have a doubt in the world that I would know the answer.

"Friend, I don't know," I said. "If it doesn't work that way, maybe we should call the Catholic priest." One came to Bon Temps's little church from a nearby town.

"But this isn't a demon that needs to be exorcised," Quiana said, outraged. "It's not a devil. It's just real unhappy."

"It has to go be unhappy somewhere else," JB said. "This is our house. These are our babies. They can't go on crying all the time."

As if he'd pressed a cue button, we could hear Robbie start to wail in the house. We all sighed simultaneously, which would have been funny if we'd had a clue what to do. But further conversation didn't trigger any plan, so we figured we might as well go back to the job that had brought us there.

Sam and I picked up the painted shelves and went inside to put them up. Quiana followed, and she returned to the stove to stir the spaghetti sauce, her face tense with distress, her brain concentrating on fighting the unhappiness that flowed through the house like invisible water.

Sam brought in the paint. While I painted the doorframe, the men put up the drywall to close up where the old closet door had been. Once that was done, Sam very carefully painted the new wall on the old babies' room side while I painted the interior of the closet from the new babies' room side. It was odd to hear his brushstrokes just a few millimeters away from mine. We were working on the same thing, but invisible to each other.

It didn't take long to finish my task. JB planned to put up two hanger rods for the twins' tiny clothes, and shelving above them, but he'd left a few minutes before to run errands before going to work. JB had been moving slowly. When he'd gotten into his car, he'd sat for a moment, his head resting on the steering wheel. But before he'd reached the corner, he was smiling, and I felt my shoulders relax with relief.

After cleaning his brushes and drop cloths, Sam left for Merlotte's. It was my day off and I needed to take care of some bills. I could hardly wait to get out of the house. I offered to take Tara with me while I drove around town, and to my surprise she agreed to go. She sat quietly in the car the whole time, and I couldn't tell if she was depressed or exhausted, or maybe both. She grew more talkative the longer we were away.

"We can't leave our house," she said. "I can't afford to buy another one, and we can't live with JB's folks. Besides, no one would buy it unless we can make it a regular home again."

Since I hadn't been in the house as long as Tara, I recovered my spirits more quickly. "Maybe we're just being silly, Tara. Maybe we're making a mountain out of a molehill."

"Or a haunting out of a hammer," she said, and we both managed to laugh.

We returned to eat Quiana's spaghetti and garlic bread in a much more grounded frame of mind. I can't tell you how cheered I was by our little excursion . . . or how bleak I felt after we'd been back in the house only ten minutes. The exhausted babies slept for a while, and lunch was at least tolerable, but always at the back of our conversation was the feeling that any moment one of us would burst into tears.

There wasn't a mind I could read to get any information on what was happening in this house. There wasn't an action I could take, a deed I could perform, that could help. I had a few friends who were witches, but Amelia Broadway, the only one I trusted, was in Europe for a month. I felt oddly stymied.

LATER THAT EVENING, we met back in the living room, even Sam and JB. No one had arranged it—it was like we were all drawn back to the house by whatever unhappy thing we'd disturbed.

Tara had slipcovered the love seat and couch recently, and she'd hung some pretty pictures of the Thomas Kinkade school: lots of cute cottages with flowers, or lofty trees with the sun grazing the tops. This was the kind of house Tara wanted: peaceful, bright, happy.

The house on Magnolia Street was not like that any longer.

Tara was holding Sara, and JB was holding Robbie. Both babies were fussy—again, still—which upped the tension in the room. Tara, uncharacteristically, had decided to turn away from reality. She was blaming JB for the misery in the house.

"He watches *Ghost Hunters* too often," she said, for maybe the tenth time. "I've lived here for four years and I've never felt a thing wrong!"

"Tara, there's something wrong now," I said, as quietly as I could. "You know there is. Quiana knows there is. We all know there is."

"Oh, for God's sake!" Tara said impatiently, and she jiggled Sara so hard that Sara started crying. Tara looked shocked, and for a moment I read her impulse to hand Sara to someone else, anyone. Instead, she took a deep breath and rocked Sara with exaggerated gentleness. (She was terrified of turning into her mother. I think that says it all about Mama Thornton.)

Quiana stood, and there was something desperately brave about the way she went into the sunroom and approached the closet. Her thick black hair pulled back in a band, her thin shoulders squared, her golden face determined. With great courage, Quiana stepped into the space where the hammer had been stowed for so long.

I rose hastily, covering the few steps without a thought. I stood outside the closet looking in. Quiana turned a muddy white and her eyes rolled up. I sort of expected her to fall to the floor and convulse, but she stayed on her feet. Her small hands shot out in my direction. Without thinking, I grabbed them. They were freezing cold. I felt a charge of stinging electricity passing from her to me, and I made my own little shocked noise.

"Sookie?" Sam was just about to put his hand on my shoulder when I stopped him with a sharp shake of my head. I could just see us forming a chain of shaking, grunting victims of whatever had entered Quiana Wong. I could see a shape in her brain, something that wasn't Quiana. Someone else inhabited her for a few awful seconds.

And then it was over. I had my arms around Quiana and her head on my shoulder. I was patting her a little desperately, saying, "Hey, you okay? You need to go to the hospital?"

Quiana straightened, shaking her head as if she had cobwebs caught in her hair. She said, "Step back so I can get out of this fucking closet."

I did so very promptly.

"What happened?" Sam said. The hairs on his arms were standing on end.

Quiana was understandably freaked, but she was also excited. Her skin glowed with it. I'd never seen her look so lively.

The babies were as quiet and big-eyed as fawns when a predator is near. JB looked scared and Tara looked angry, both pretty typical reactions.

By an exchange of half-finished sentences, we agreed to adjourn to the backyard. Though it was hot, the heat was better than whatever had been in the closet.

Tara brought all of us sweating cans of soda from the refrigerator, and we sat in the darkness, the area lit only by the light coming from the house windows. I wondered what the neighbors would think of our silent, somber party if they could see over Tara's fence.

"So, what was it?" I asked Quiana when she looked a little more collected.

"It was a ghost," she said promptly.

"So it must have been the boy Isaiah," I said. "Since he was the murder victim. But why would his ghost be in this house? He was killed next door, right? Andy and Halleigh haven't had any problems, because Andy would have told me." (On purpose or by accident—Andy was a clear broadcaster.)

"There weren't any bones or anything," Tara objected. "Just the hammer." Quiana leaned over to take one of the twins from Tara, and Tara hesitated before letting Quiana take the baby. I could feel Quiana's sadness, but she didn't blame Tara. "Shouldn't there be remains of a body if there's a ghost here?"

"Ghosts don't have to be where their physical remains are laid," Quiana said, her voice weary. "They're stuck where the emotion . . . grabbed them up."

"Huh?" Tara said.

"It's the strong emotion that imprints them on the place," Quiana told us. "It's the trauma."

Now that she'd decided to tell us she was a psychic, Quiana was just full of information.

"What kind of trauma?" JB said.

"Usually the death trauma," Quiana said, a little impatiently. "If a person dies real scared, real angry, he leaves his imprint on the space where that emotion took over. Or sometimes the person gets fixed on an object that played a part in the traumatic event. Like a bloody hammer? And after he dies, that's where his ghost manifests. In this case, the hammer and the closet are the objects."

"Huh," Sam said. He didn't sound like he was automatically signing up for the Ghost Hunters Club, but he didn't sound skeptical, either. More like he was chewing these new ideas over. That was kind of the way I felt. My world had not included this before now. "So you're saying he—is it a guy?—could be buried anywhere."

"In the movies, when you find the bones, the ghost is laid," JB said unexpectedly.

"The murder victim was Isaiah Wechsler, and his headstone is out in the cemetery by my house," I said.

"But someone's not resting easy," JB said, sounding just as reasonable. "You know that, Sookie."

Suddenly I felt tired and depressed, more depressed than I'd ever been in my life. And that just wasn't me. I'm not saying I'm Pollyanna, but this sudden misery simply wasn't my normal style.

"Sam," I said, "do you think you could change to your bloodhound form? And maybe go over the yard? If there was a burial that had to do with the murder, it would be really old, and hard to scent." I shrugged. "But it's worth a try."

"This is real life," Tara said, not exactly as if she were angry, but simply protesting that none of this should be happening.

Real life? I almost laughed. Experiencing a ghost secondhand and looking for a corpse weren't what I wanted from my real life. On the other hand, worse things had happened to me.

"All right," Sam said grudgingly. "But not tonight. It's nowhere near the full moon, so it won't be as easy to change. I need a full night's sleep first." *I wouldn't do this for anyone but her,* Sam thought, feeling ashamed that he was dragging his feet.

I could only be grateful I had such a friend.

THE NEXT DAY I was at Tara's house by midafternoon. Sam pulled up just as I got out of my car.

I was startled to see JB and Tara on their way out, in workout clothes. "I got called in to substitute for another trainer," JB explained.

I looked at Tara, my eyebrows raised. She said, "I have to get the hell out of this house. Quiana just got here. She's in charge of the twins." In truth, Tara looked awful, and JB not much better. I nodded. "We'll keep on with the plan, then," I said, and they were out the door before I could say good-bye.

When Sam and I went in the kitchen, Quiana was bathing Robbie, while Sara sat in her infant seat. The babysitter looked determined to do her job. Robbie was whimpering, and I picked up Sara from her infant seat and patted her back, hoping she'd stay quiet. But she didn't. She began to cry. It looked as if Quiana needed some help for a while.

Since there wasn't a third baby for Sam to hold, he went to work on the hardware for the new closet doors. I walked Sara around the house, trying to make her happier, and when I went through the sunroom, I helped by handing Sam whatever he needed. Sometimes being a telepath can be handy.

"Do you feel as lousy as I do?" he asked, as both babies escalated to full Defcon Five. I chickened out and put Sara in her infant seat in the kitchen while Quiana dressed Robbie.

"At least that lousy," I said.

"I wonder if hauntings are all like this."

"I hope I never experience another one to find out," I said. "I wonder . . ." I dropped my voice to a whisper. "I wonder if any of this would have happened if Quiana hadn't been here. If a psychic hadn't been around, would we have had the same experience? Would the hammer have been a haunted hammer, or just a bloody hammer?"

Sam shrugged and laid down his tools. "Who knows?" He took a deep breath. "Come on. If I'm going to turn, I want to get it over with. Kennedy is watching the bar, but I want to get back sooner rather than later." The atmosphere of the house was having its way with Sam.

I followed him through the house. Quiana watched us pass through the kitchen, her face dark with unhappiness, her eyes shadowed. The babies had finally gotten quiet in their infant seats, watching their nanny clean up from the bathing ordeal. I looked into her brain to be sure that Quiana was herself and that she was alert; Robbie and Sara were safe.

Though I'd seen Sam change before, I could never get jaded about watching a human turn into an animal. I'd overheard some college kids in the bar talking about the physics of shapeshifting, and they'd seemed to think that the transformation was impossible. So much for their impossibilities. It was happening before me: a full-sized man changed into a bloodhound. Sam liked to turn into dogs, because humans weren't as likely to shoot him by mistake. As a true shapeshifter, he had an advantage over wereanimals, who had to transform to one thing—werewolf, of course, or weretiger, werewombat—whatever their genetic makeup was. Sam enjoyed the variety. Sam, who normally had a smooth and swift transition, was panting on the ground when I got a scare.

"Smooth move," Quiana said from right behind me. I jumped about a mile. "I wish I could do that," she added.

"Hell in a handbasket, Quiana! Why didn't you say something?"

"I was making plenty of noise," she said casually. "You were just too interested in watching."

I opened the back door and threw Sam's clothes on one of the dinette chairs. "Aren't you supposed to be with the twins?"

She unclipped a device from the waistband of her shorts. "I got the monitor right here. They're both asleep in their cribs. Finally."

Sam rolled to his feet and ambled over to me. I never knew exactly how much he understood human speech while he was in animal form, but he was looking at the house and his chest was rumbling. "I'm going to check on them," I said. If that sounded distrustful, I didn't care.

The atmosphere in the house seemed somewhat easier, more peaceful. I wondered if the bad influence was wearing away—or was it because we three were out in the yard? That was a disturbing idea. I made myself put it aside, and I looked at the sleeping Robbie, hardly daring to breathe loud. The baby seemed perfectly all right. So did Sara, in her own crib. I put my hand gently on Sara's back. The inchoate dreams of an infant flowed into my head. I thought of putting both of them in the stroller and taking them with me into the back-yard, but the house was so pleasant and cool, and it was so hot outside. We had the monitor.

I went back to the yard. Sam was scouting around, examining the space with his nose. His floppy ears were hanging forward. I'd read that this pushed the scent up to a blood-hound's nose. Amazing. I personally thought he was very cute as a bloodhound, but that got into kind of queasy territory, so it was a thought I had to banish.

"He's working hard," Quiana remarked. She'd perched on the edge of one of the yard chairs, her hands tucked between her bare knees. Her thick dark hair was twisted and secured on top of her head with a clip or two, because it was too hot for long hair. My own was piled up in much the same way.

"You two have been friends a long time," she said, when I didn't respond to her last comment.

"Yes," I said. "A few years, now."

"You have a lot of friends."

"I have a lot of friendly acquaintances. It's hard to have close friends, when you have a mental thing like mine."

"Tell me about it." Quiana shuddered delicately.

Frankly, I didn't know if I wanted to be Quiana's friend or not. There was something in her that put me off. I realized this was pretty damn ironic, since that was the way people often felt about me, but I didn't think Quiana made me uneasy simply because she had an unusual ability. She made me anxious because for a few minutes the day before she hadn't been alone in her skin. Someone else had been there with her.

I turned my eyes away from the girl. I didn't want her wondering what I was thinking about. I watched Sam instead. He was sniffing the ground with the efficiency of a vacuum cleaner.

The lot was long and narrow, with the house leaving very little room on either side. On the north side of the house, there were maybe five feet between the air conditioner sticking out of the kitchen window and the fence that surrounded the yard from the front wall of the house to the rear property line. Naturally, it was in that narrow strip that Sam found a promising scent. He went over it anxiously, and then he raised his head and bayed.

I hoped all the neighbors really were at work. At least the fence blocked the view.

Sam's doleful bloodhound face swung toward me, and he pawed at the ground at his feet. "Awwwrrrrhr," he said.

I got the shovel from the toolshed. This was not going to

be pretty. I was trickling with sweat after the first few shovel-fuls, and I was maybe a little peeved that Quiana didn't ask to take a turn digging. She looked down into the gradually in-creasing hole with an unnerving and unswerving fascination.

I looked at Sam, who was licking one of his paws. "You better go inside and change back," I said. "Thanks, Sam." He started ambling toward the steps and paused, stymied. I pitched a shovelful of dirt at Quiana's feet. "Quiana," I said sharply, "You need to open the back door for him."

It was like I'd stuck a pin in her, she looked so startled. "Sure," she said. "Sure, I'll do it."

I watched her go over to the door, and it seemed to me she stumbled a little, was a bit shaky on her feet. Her mind was blurry, foggy, with strong impressions coming from God knows where. After Sam was in the house, I resumed digging. The faster I went, the sooner we'd know if Sam had found an old turkey carcass or human remains.

After another five minutes I had to pause. Quiana had re-turned to her place at the edge of the hole. Her stance was rigid and her eyes were fixed on the upturned earth.

I heard a couple of slamming car doors. JB and Tara had returned. I felt a surprising amount of relief.

I was leaning on my shovel when they all came into the backyard—all the adults, that is. The twins were still sleeping. Sam had resumed his human form, and he was in his cutoff jeans again. His Hawaiian shirt looked cool with its loose drape around his torso. I envied him. My tank top felt wet and clingy.

JB and Tara were still wearing their workout clothes, so they were as sweaty as I was, but they both looked more relaxed.

"So, there something in there?" Tara asked, peering down at the hole I'd made.

"Sam thinks so," I replied. "JB, you want to shovel for a while?"

"Sure, Sook," he said amiably, and he grabbed the shovel. I sank to my haunches and watched him work.

Sam squatted by me. He never wavered in his expectant posture.

And with a terrible predictability, the shovel hit something that scraped instead of crunched. Without being told, JB started to scratch at the dirt with the shovel blade instead of sinking it in.

We didn't need the monitor to hear the babies begin to wail.

Quiana tore herself away to go in to them. Tara seemed relieved to leave it to her.

JB uncovered a femur.

We regarded the bone in silence.

"Well, we got us a body," Sam said. "Now we need to know who it belonged to."

"How are we gonna explain what we were doing?" Tara asked.

"We could say you were going to plant some beans," I said. "I know it's late for beans, but a cop would believe that." I left unspoken the fact that Andy would believe that if we said it was JB's idea. "We can say we were digging the holes for the runner poles."

"So they'll come get the bones out, and then what? Will things get better in our house?" Tara's eyes were bright with anger. "Will we stop being miserable? What about the babies? I think we have to find out who this guy was."

"It's not Isaiah Wechsler, and we know Albert lived, and we know Carter was sent away after the murder. So who could this be?" I looked around, hoping someone would look as though he had had a revelation, but everyone looked blank.

JB, shovel in hand, was standing by the crouching Sam. They were silently regarding the hole that was a grave. Sam was scowling.

"Tara, we can't ignore this," I said, as gently as I could. I was fighting a rising wave of irritation.

"I know that," she snapped. "I never said we could, Sookie. But I got to figure out what's best for me and my family."

Quiana had been gone a handful of minutes by now. I could still hear the babies crying. Why hadn't she found out what was wrong and fixed it?

The normally placid JB nudged Sam to make him move away from the grave. Sam's jaw set in a way I knew meant he was barely holding on to his temper.

I didn't trust any emotion I felt.

Tara was angry with me, which wasn't normal. Sam and JB were glaring at each other. The anger in the air was affecting all of us. I made myself run into the house to find out why the babies were weeping. Tara should be doing this! I followed the sobs to their little room.

Quiana was sitting in the rocking chair crammed in beside the cribs, and she was crying, too.

"Oh, for God's sake," I said. "Snap out of it."

Her tear-stained face looked at me with resentment written all over it. "I have a right to grieve for what I've lost. Only my brother knows the real me," she said bitterly.

Uh-oh.

"Quiana," I said, suddenly feeling a lot calmer and a lot more nervous, "you don't have a brother."

"Of course I do." But she looked confused.

"You're being haunted," I said, trying to sound matter-of-fact. I didn't want to say the word *possessed*, but it was definitely hovering in the air.

"Sure, that's right, blame me because I'm the one who's different," she snarled in a complete emotional about-face.

I flinched, but I had to pass her to get to the babies, whose cries had redoubled. I decided to take a chance. "You want to go outside?" I said. Then I made a guess. "You can see your bones." I watched her carefully, since I had no idea what she'd do next.

There was someone else behind Quiana's face, someone both anguished and angry. All I could think about was getting her out of the room.

And then Quiana got up and left the room, her face blank. She wasn't even walking like herself.

I scooped up Sara, who was shrieking like a banshee.

"Sara," I said. "Please stop crying." To my amazement, she did. The baby looked up at me, her face red and tearful, panting with exhaustion. "Let's get your brother," I said, since Robbie's wails continued unabated. "We'll make him happy, too." Robbie also responded to my touch, and in a moment I was walking slowly holding the two babies. It was awkward and terrifying.

What would have happened if Quiana had been utterly overrun by the ghost while she was here alone with the twins?

Now that the bones had been uncovered, the emotional miasma in the house was intensifying, without any doubt. It was a struggle to get out of the house, aside from the difficulty of carrying two children. Though I wanted to leave more than anything, I stopped in the kitchen to put them in their child seats. I opened the back door and passed Sara to JB. I went down the back steps with Robbie, moving very carefully. Sam, Tara, and Quiana were in the corner of the yard farthest from the bones, and JB and I joined them there.

In sharp contrast to the lighthearted meeting we'd had

when we were planning the renovation, our conference in the backyard was grim. The late-afternoon sun slanted across the bricks of the patio, and the heat of them radiated upward. Even the heat was preferable to the haunted house.

We waited. Nothing happened. Finally, Tara sat in a lawn chair and started feeding Sara after JB fetched her nursing shawl. Robbie made squeaky noises until it was his turn. They, at least, were content.

Sam said, "I dug some more, and I think it's a complete skeleton. We don't know whose bones, whose ghost, or why it's angry."

An accurate and depressing summary.

"The only neat stories are the ones made up," Tara said.

Quiana, who seemed to be herself at the moment, sat slumped forward, her elbows on her knees. She said, "There's a reason all this is happening. There's a reason the haunting started when the hammer came out of the wall. There's a reason there's a body buried in the backyard. We just have to figure it out. And I'm the psychic. And it's trying to live through me. So I got to try to take care of this."

I looked at Quiana with some respect. What she was saying made sense.

"It's tied to the hammer," Quiana said.

"So, okay, if we want to know what happened so we can fix it," I said, "and since I can read minds, and since the ghost can get into Quiana's mind . . . I'm wondering if maybe Quiana and I can do something with the bones and find out who the spirit—the ghost—is."

Quiana nodded. "Let's do it," she said. "Let's get this bitch settled." She reached over to the old patio table and took the hammer.

We stood, full of purpose.

JB and Sam shot out of their chairs. Sam said, "You don't need to do this, Sookie."

Wild horses couldn't have held me back from this experience. I stepped away from Sam and took Quiana's left hand, bony and strong and cold. We went over to the excavated skeleton. Its skull gaped up at us from its grave. Quiana was holding the hammer in her free hand. Then she gasped and jerked, and suddenly I was holding the hand of someone completely different.

And I was seeing what Quiana saw, but not through Quiana's eyes. I was seeing . . . faces. A round-faced woman working over a kitchen table. I recognized what she was doing; she was making piecrust. She was looking up, bewildered and sad. *Mama.* A burly man bending over something on a tool bench, with the same air of worry about him. *Father.* And looking at a boy—older than me, but still a boy with an open, honest, freckled face, a face that was serious and full of doubt. *Albert.* I would have done anything to remove the anxiety from their faces, anything to silence the cruel words that had caused that unhappiness.

Words spoken by that devil, Isaiah Wechsler.

Part of me could still be only Sookie, and that part felt the growing resolution, the horrible resolve, as the entity in Quiana played out his plan.

The night, the darkness, only streetlights in the distance where town lay. (That almost threw me out of Quiana's mind. Since when had Magnolia Street been out of town?) *Running silently across the short distance between the windows, from my window to his, and his was open in the warm night . . . through it quietly enough not to wake him, Father's hammer in my hand and . . . then* he raised his hand, oh . . . oh, no. In the moonlight the blood looked black.

Back out the window, breathing hard, and over to the one

in my *house, safe now, back home hide the hammer under the bed* but Albert woke up, *Albert beloved brother,* and Albert said *what did you do?* And I said *I shut his foul mouth.*

And there was more, but it was too much for me, Sookie. I had to pull Quiana out of this, but that was impossible until we saw the end.

Then we did. We saw the end.

I gasped and choked, and Quiana folded silently to the dirt as if her strings had been cut.

Sam caught me, braced me, as JB supported Quiana.

JB said, "What happened? Why were you all holding hands, Sookie?"

Tara said, "They'll tell us, honey. Wait a minute." The twins were silent, and when I could see, I realized they were back in their infant seats, at the base of the tree. The evening was closing in. The shadows had gotten so long they almost covered the yard. I could hear a car door closing next door. Andy had gotten home. Should I call out, get him to come look?

"Do you know who it is?" Sam asked, keeping his voice low, pointing at the open grave.

I went over to it. "This boy killed Isaiah Wechsler. This boy is Carter Summerlin."

"But you said his folks sent him away," Sam said.

"In a way, they did," Quiana said weakly. Tara had propped her up against the fence and was giving her a bottle of water. Quiana looked as if she'd survived a death march. "This boy killed himself because he couldn't stand what he did. He climbed through the window at night—the window of the house next door—with the hammer he took from his dad's toolbox. Came back in his own bedroom window, blood all over."

I shuddered. The others stared at us, their mouths open.

"But his big brother saw? Is that right, Sookie?" Quiana asked.

I nodded. "Albert took Carter's nightshirt and burned it in the backyard in the middle of the night, and hid the hammer in the closet wall. Later on, he closed it in. The fight he'd had with the Wechsler boy, it was because—well, Isaiah had made fun of the, what he thought was the effeminate ways of Albert's little brother. And to Carter it was so terrible, so unthinkable a slur, that he had to wipe out the one who'd voiced it. Albert believed he should have protected Carter better; he thought he should have shown Carter how to behave in a more manly way."

"But I felt terrible about killing Isaiah. And about how people thought Albert was to blame. The next week, I killed myself," Quiana said. She was unaware she was saying anything odd. "I hanged myself in that same closet, from a hook. I figured that would make things better for Albert. When they found me, Albert started crying. He told them what the fight had been about and how he'd helped cover up for me. They had one son dead, so to protect Albert and the family's good name, my folks buried me in the yard in the dead of night and told everyone they'd sent me off to live with relatives."

"And Carter haunted them?" I said, not liking how shaky my voice was.

"He haunted his parents, because they were ashamed of him," Quiana said, and I welcomed her return to perspective with huge relief. "But not Albert. Albert had tried to keep faith with Carter, but he must have felt terribly guilty himself every time he saw the Wechslers."

"So Carter started making his presence known again now because . . ."

"Of the hammer. When you found the hammer, that was

the trigger for his . . . activation." Quiana shrugged. "I don't know much about ghosts, but I got that from him. He was full of anger—well, we all got that. He was confused, and agitated."

"What can we do? To get rid of him? He can't stay here," JB said, his mouth set in an uncharacteristically hard line.

"We can call the police," I said. "They'd come get the bones and take them away for evaluation and burial. They'll take the hammer, too. The closet has been reconfigured, so it's no longer the place where Carter died." I wondered, if we sent the bones and the hammer to the police, would the ghost manifest at the police station? I tried to imagine Detective Andy Bellefleur's face.

"Will that do it? End his presence?" Tara asked.

"Ought to." Quiana looked at me.

I shrugged. "Maybe."

There was a doubtful silence.

I cleared my throat. "Or we could just take everything, bones and hammer, and bury the whole kit 'n' kaboodle in the cemetery. By ourselves. And no one would ever need to know, which was what the whole Summerlin family wanted."

They all thought about my proposition for a few seconds.

"I'm for that," JB said. "I don't want people coming around to see where the body was buried. The babies wouldn't like that. People might not let their kids come over to play with Robbie and Sara."

Tara looked at her husband in surprise. "I didn't think about that, JB. Sookie, since your house is right by the cemetery . . . can you and Sam . . . ?"

"This isn't a usual best-friends job," I said, maybe a little tartly. "But okay, I'll do it. You got an old sheet?"

She vanished into the house and came back with a white

percale double fitted. Quiana laid it out by the grave, and Sam and JB disinterred the bones. Wearing rubber dishwashing gloves, they transferred the remains of poor Carter Summerlin to the sheet. The ground was so shadowed by the side of the house, I needed the help of a flashlight to sift the earth, searching for anything they might have missed. I came up with two teeth and a few little finger bones. After a while, we were reasonably sure the entire skeleton had been harvested from the soil. Tara put the hammer on top of the bones, gathered up the sheet corners, and tied them in knots.

There was a pause when Sam picked up the grotesque bundle.

"Oh, all right, we'll go, too," Tara said angrily, as though I'd accused her of being callous.

There was a little car caravan out to my house: me, Sam in his pickup, JB and Tara and the twins in their car, and Quiana in her old Ford.

We tromped through my woods to the cemetery. The dark was closing in around us when we came to my family plot. I was going to be late for work—but somehow I didn't think Sam would dock my pay for it. The space at the back of my family headstone was unusually large, and since it lay at the edge of the graveyard there wasn't another family plot abutting it from the north. We took turns digging—again—by the light of the lantern-sized flashlights I'd snatched from my toolshed.

JB lowered the bundle of bones and hammer into the makeshift grave. We shoveled the dirt back in, a much quicker job, and the men stamped down the new patch with their boots so it wouldn't look so raw. Maybe I'd come back tomorrow and stick a potted plant in the dirt to kind of explain the digging.

When that was done, there was an odd moment, when the night around us seemed to catch its breath.

Her dark head bowed, Quiana said, "The Lord is my shepherd . . ." and we all joined in.

"God bless this poor soul and send him on his way," I said, when the prayer was finished.

Then the night exhaled, and the air was empty.

We trudged back to my house in silence, Quiana stumbling with exhaustion from time to time.

There was an awkward pause as everyone tried to figure out how to cap off the experience.

Finally, JB said, "Y'all gonna come help finish the closet tomorrow?"

I laughed. I couldn't help it.

"Sure," Sam said. "We'll be there, and we'll finish."

And tomorrow, it would just be us in the house. Us living people.

PLAYING POSSUM

Cousin Hadley had a son before she died. This child, Hunter, who's being raised by his father, has become fond of his "aunt" Sookie. When Hunter needs cupcakes for his class party at school, Sookie is charged with bringing them. In "Playing Possum," Sookie and Hunter's telepathic connection is absolutely essential to their survival when a shooter enters the little rural school. After countless incidents in which Sookie heard negative and damaging secrets, I felt it was time to cite an occasion in which her "gift" worked for the good.

"Playing Possum" is set in the fall after the action in *Dead Ever After*.

COUNTED ONCE. I counted twice. Yes! Twenty-three choco-late cupcakes with chocolate icing, liberally decorated with sprinkles. I put the cupcakes, one by one, into the shallow cardboard box I'd begged from the dollar store clerk. Of course I'd lined it with aluminum foil, and of course each little cake was in its own paper cup. A white sugar sprinkle rolled off, and I dropped it back onto the dark icing and gently pressed it down. I tried to ignore the siren song my bed was singing. I was up, and I had to stay up.

I'd been too tired to bake the night before. I'd gotten off work at midnight and had fallen into bed the minute I'd put on my nightshirt and brushed my teeth. Monday nights at Merlotte's Bar are usually pretty light, and I'd assumed the night before would follow suit. Naturally, since I'd hoped to get off a little early, last night had broken the pattern. Rural northern Louisiana is not a big tourist route, so we didn't get a whole lot of strangers in Merlotte's—but members of a Baton Rouge bikers' club had attended a huge motorcycle jam-boree in Arkansas, and on their way home, about twenty of them had stopped to have supper and a few brews at Mer-lotte's.

And they'd stayed. And stayed.

I should have appreciated their patronage, since I have a partnership in the bar-slash-restaurant. But I hadn't been able to stop thinking about those twenty-three cupcakes I had to make, and calculating how long it would take me to mix, bake, and ice them. Then I'd figured how long it would take me to drive to Red Ditch, where my "nephew," Hunter Savoy, would be celebrating Labor Day with his kindergarten classroom. When I'd finally trudged in my back door, I'd looked at the recipe waiting optimistically on the counter along with the mixing bowl and the dry ingredients. And I'd thought, *No way.*

So I'd gotten up with the larks to bake cupcakes. I'd showered and dressed and brushed my long blond hair into a ponytail. I'd recounted the little goody bags, and boxed them, too. Now I was on my way; the boxes with the cupcakes and the goody bags carefully positioned on the floorboard of the backseat.

It's not that long a drive to Red Ditch, but it's not that easy a drive, either; mostly parish roads through rural areas. Louisiana isn't exactly known for its up-to-date road maintenance, and there were crumbling shoulders and potholes a-plenty. I saw two deer in time to dodge them, and as I drove slowly on a low-lying two-lane through a bayou, there was a big movement in the reeds around its bank . . . big enough to signal "gator." This would be a fairly rare sighting, so I made a mental note to check out the bank on my way home.

By the time I parked in front of Hunter's school, I felt like it was already noon, but when I pulled my cell phone from my purse to check, I discovered the digital numbers read 10:03. I had arrived at the time Hunter's dad, Remy Savoy, had told me the teacher had requested.

The Red Ditch school had once been a combination elementary and middle school. Since parish-wide consolidation, it was only a kindergarten for the children in the immediate area. I parked right in front of the wide sidewalk leading up to the dilapidated double doors. The yard was trimmed, but littered with pinecones and the odd bit of childish debris—a gum wrapper here, a crumpled piece of paper there. The low brown-brick building, clearly built in the sixties and not much changed since then, was quiet in the warm September sun. It was hard to believe the kindergarten was packed full of children.

I stretched, hearing my spine make some little crackling noises. Constantly being on my feet was taking its toll, and I was only in my twenties. Then I shook myself. It was not a day to think about a future of aching knees and feet. It was Hunter's day.

I couldn't gather my purse, the cupcakes in their broad, flat box, and the box of goody bags all at the same time. After a moment's indecision, I decided to take in the cupcakes first, rather than leave them in the warm car. I slung my big purse over one shoulder and lifted the cupcakes with both hands. I'd gotten them this far, and they still looked great. If I could just get them into the school and into the classroom without letting them slide around . . . I made it to the front door and up two shallow steps with no incident. By holding up the box as if I were delivering a pizza, I freed a hand to turn the knob, opening the door enough to use my butt to keep the opening wide enough for me and the box. It was a relief to step inside and lower my burden until I could grasp it with both hands. The door thunked shut behind me, leaving a wide bar of light lancing across the floor. Not exactly tight-fitting.

I'd been in the school before, so I knew the layout. I stood in a sort of lobby, the walls decorated with posters advising kids to wash their hands, to cover their noses with their crooked arms when they sneezed, and to pick up litter. Directly across from the double doors lay the school office. Classroom halls began to the right and to the left of the office, six classrooms on each hall, three to each wall. At the end of these halls were doors going outside to the playground, which was fenced in.

The school office had a big window, waist-high, through which I could see a woman about my age talking on a telephone. The window gave visitors a visual cue that they should check in. This was reinforced by a big sign (ALL VISITORS MUST SIGN THE SHEET IN THE OFFICE!). I knew that the proliferation of messy divorces was responsible for this rule, and though it was a pain, it was at least a half-ass security measure.

I'd had a fantasy that the school secretary would leap up to open the heavy office door, which stood to the left of the window. That didn't happen, and I managed it myself after a little juggling.

Then I had to stand in front of the secretary's desk, waiting for her to acknowledge me, while she continued to listen to her caller.

I had plenty of time to observe the young woman's curly brown hair and sharp features, somehow evened out by her almost freakishly round blue eyes. I was getting more and more impatient as she kept trying to speak into the phone, only to be steamrollered by whoever was on the other end of the line. I rolled my eyes, though I knew no one was watching; certainly not the woman, who was suppressing extreme agitation.

My flash of resentment was abruptly eclipsed when I realized that this conversation was anything but casual. All her thoughts were focused on the person she was arguing with, and she almost certainly didn't even register the live person standing right in front of her, getting more and more impatient. The door to the principal's office, to the left of the secretary's desk, was resolutely shut tight, though from behind it I could hear the light click of a keyboard. Principal Minter was working on something.

Meanwhile, I had time to read her secretary's nameplate. Sherry Javitts was having a very private conversation in a very public place. Not that it was a true conversation—the young woman was mostly listening to the diatribe pouring into her ears. She didn't know that I could hear it as clearly as she could, or at least catch an echo of it in her thoughts.

That's my big problem. I'm telepathic.

Sherry Javitts had a big problem of her own—an overpossessive and maybe deranged former boyfriend. She blinked and looked up at my unhappy face, finally absorbing my presence.

She interrupted the caller. "No, Brady," she said through literally clenched teeth. "It's over! I'm working! You have to stop calling!" And she slammed the phone back into its charger before she took a deep breath and looked up at me, making her lips curve in a ghastly smile.

"Can I help you?" Sherry said steadily enough, though I noticed her hands were shaking.

We were going to be civilized and ignore the incident. Fine by me. "Yes, I'm Hunter Savoy's aunt, Sookie Stackhouse," I said. "I've brought cupcakes for the Pony Room's Labor Day party."

She pushed a clipboard over to me. "Please sign in," she said. "Date, name, and time. Purpose of visit in that space, there."

"Sure." I put the cupcakes on top of a filing cabinet while I filled in the required information.

"I didn't know Hunter had an aunt," Sherry Javitts said. In a little town like Red Ditch, everyone would know the children's histories, even the history of relative newcomers like Remy Savoy and his little boy.

I needed to return to my car and get the box of goody bags, but I made myself give her a reassuring smile. (We were just strewing insincere smiles right and left.) "I'm not his actual aunt," I said. "Calling me 'aunt' is just easier. I was first cousin to his mama."

"Oh," she said, looking appropriately sober. "I'm so sorry for her passing."

"We sure miss her," I said, which was an out-and-out lie. Hadley had been in trouble all her life. Though she'd often tried to do the right thing, somehow that had never worked out. Bless her heart.

I waited for some kind of concluding remark, but Sherry Javitts was lost in her own thoughts, which revolved around a terribly threatening person named Brady, the selfsame man she'd been arguing with. She didn't miss him.

"So," I said, a little more sharply than I'd intended, "I can go back to Hunter's classroom?"

"I'm sorry," she said, shaking her head. "Got lost in a cloud, there. Sure, go ahead."

"I'll have to come in and out at least once," I warned her.

"You go right ahead. Just sign out when the party is over." She was relieved I was leaving. At least this time, she was polite enough to rise and open the office door. Sherry was surprisingly tall, and she was wearing an unremarkable pale green dress that I envied only because it was a size 2.

I sighed as I thought of the chocolate cupcake I'd already had that morning.

I edged out of the small office with the cupcakes in my

hands, glancing back through the big window to see Sherry Javitts, back in her chair, bow her curly head and put her hands over her face. That was sure the only way she was going to get any privacy in that fishbowl. The inner door of the office, the one to the principal's inner sanctum, opened even as I thought that.

I remembered meeting Ms. Minter at the spring open house. She was just as nicely dressed today in a tan pantsuit with a dark green scarf, a nice look with her warm brown skin. The appropriately clad Ms. Minter did not look happy, and I wondered if she'd overheard the furious conversation her secretary had had with Brady, whoever he was; husband, boyfriend, secret lover?

As I began walking down the corridor to the right of the office, I confess I was glad to be walking away from the fraught emotions. One of the most burdensome things about my condition is the constant bombardment of other people's personal woes. I can only block so much out; a lot seeps around the edges of my mental walls. I would much rather not have known about the Drama of Sherry and Brady. I shook the incident off and put a smile on my face, because I'd arrived at the Pony Room, second down on the right-hand side of the hallway. I didn't have a free hand to knock on the door, so it was lucky Ms. Yarnell spotted me through the rectangular window in the classroom door.

When I'd gone with Remy and Hunter to vet the kindergarten, we'd all liked the Pony Room the best, so I'd been relieved when Hunter had called to tell me Mrs. Gristede was going to be his teacher. Though I hardly knew her, both Hunter and I had learned telepathically that she was a nice woman who genuinely liked children. She was definitely a cut above the other teachers we'd encountered that night.

Unfortunately for everyone, two weeks before school opened Mrs. Gristede had been in a car accident, and her recovery was going to take her out for a whole half year. Ms. Yarnell was her replacement and, according to Remy, she was working out pretty well.

While Mrs. Gristede was a short, round woman in her forties, Ms. Yarnell proved to be a short, round woman in her early twenties. Despite Ms. Yarnell's youth, she radiated the same pleasure in teaching, the same fondness for children that had so recommended Mrs. Gristede.

The kids seemed to love her, because there were at least six apples piled on her desk. There were different varieties, and some looked a little more battered than others, but I was impressed that she'd inspired such a traditional gift.

I had time to gather this positive first impression while Ms. Yarnell was holding the door for me. All the children were vibrating with excitement at this break in their routine (which had been so recently learned). I set down the box and my purse on a low worktable right inside the door when I saw Hunter dashing toward me.

"Aunt Sookie!" Hunter yelled, and I squatted so I could catch him in my arms. It was like being wrapped in a skinny, warm boa. Hunter was dark of hair and eyes like his mother—and like her, he was an attractive person, an advantage he would need since he'd gotten the family "gift."

I'm so glad you're here, he said silently.

"Hey, Hunter," I said, careful to speak out loud. I'd been trying to help Hunter learn to control his telepathy, which (sadly) meant teaching him to conceal his true nature. Children's emotions are so much purer, undiluted. I hated having to curb his natural exuberance.

You made the cupcakes, he said happily, right into my head. I gave him a gentle squeeze to remind him. "You brought cup-cakes," he said out loud, grinning at me.

Lest you should think Hunter was a pitiful child with no one to love him—not only could Remy have followed instructions on a box of mix and opened a can of icing, but I was also certain that Remy's girlfriend, Erin, would have been thrilled to be asked to make treats for Hunter's first real school party. Though I didn't know Erin well, I knew she genuinely cared for Hunter. I didn't know why Hunter had picked me instead. Maybe he'd just wanted to see if I'd do it. Maybe, since I had to drive farther, I was the bigger challenge. Maybe he just wanted to be around someone like himself; we hadn't gotten to spend much time together since Hunter had started school. I confess that I'd been both surprised and secretly flattered when Remy had called to tell me, in a very tentative way and not within Hunter's hearing, that his son wanted me to attend the holiday celebration.

"Sure, I brought the cupcakes, silly. And if I can unwind you off me, I'll go back out to the car and get the rest of the stuff," I said. "You think Ms. Yarnell would let you help me? By the way, Ms. Yarnell, I'm Sookie Stackhouse."

Hunter detached himself and I stood up. He looked at Ms. Yarnell, hope all over his face.

She patted him on the head, turning to me with a warm smile. "I'm Sabrina," she said. "I'm filling in this semester for Mrs. Gristede, as I'm sure you know." Then her smile faded as she took me in.

I tried not to look as startled as she did. I was getting a strange vibe from Hunter's teacher, and she was getting the same sort of vibe from me. Well, well. This day was turning out to be extraordinary.

"I have a friend who's a lot like you," I said. "Her name's

Amelia Broadway, she lives in New Orleans. Amelia belongs to a small group of people with the same interests." I didn't think any of the kids would know the word *coven*, but I didn't want to test that belief.

"I've met Amelia," Sabrina Yarnell said. "She's a sister under the skin. What about you?" Her voice was casual, but her eyes were not.

"Afraid not," I said. I truly have no magical ability of my own. (The telepathy had been given to me, by way of being a baby shower present to my grandfather.) But it would be silly not to tell her what she was already guessing. "I'm like Hunter," I said, patting him on the shoulder. His otherness could not have escaped the witch; he was too young to conceal it from a real practitioner.

"Can I go out to the car with Aunt Sookie?" Hunter asked, impatient with grown-up talk.

"Don't interrupt, Hunter," I said gently.

"Sorry!" Hunter squirmed, clearly worried that his bad manners might cost him a privilege.

"All right, Hunter, you go with your aunt, but you two come right back," Sabrina Yarnell said, giving me a level look to make sure I understood I wasn't getting permission to take Hunter to Dairy Queen for an Oreo Blizzard, or on any other unauthorized expedition. She was schoolteacher first, witch second.

"Not off school property," I agreed, smiling. "Mind if I leave my purse in here?"

When she nodded, I moved the cupcakes to the top of a filing cabinet, too high for any depredating little fingers. I stowed my purse on Ms. Yarnell's desk after tucking my car keys in my jeans pocket. "Come on, buddy," I said, holding out my hand to Hunter. He waved at his classmates, delighted to be the man of the hour. Most of the children waved back as if Hunter were leaving on a trip; they were clearly revved up by the prospect of the party. Maybe later, say by January, they'd be more blasé—but kindergartners, this early in the school year? Yeah, they were excited.

Hunter and I walked up the hall together, Hunter so full of the joy of it all that he was practically bouncing off the walls. I could hear the murmur of voices in each room. I caught glimpses of teachers and children through each rectangular window. The smell and sounds of school—did they ever change?

"Are you coming to Daddy's cookout Saturday?" Hunter asked, though he knew the answer. Since we were in a public place, he was taking care to talk out loud, which I appreciated, so I was gentle in my response.

"Hunter, you know already I have to work on Saturday. That's the tough part of being the boss, sort of. I have to fill in when other people can't be there." Because of a family wedding, two of our regular servers were going to be out on Merlotte's busiest day. "That's one reason I'm so glad I can be here now," I said. I wondered if I should stop at the office to explain that I had permission to take Hunter out the front door, but Ms. Minter and Ms. Javitts were having such an earnest conversation that I didn't want to interrupt them.

In fact, they looked so worried that I felt a flash of concern myself. But I didn't want to involve Hunter in my anxiety, and I quickly blocked off my thoughts as I pushed open one of the front doors. "Who's going to be at you-all's cookout? Your daddy and Erin, I know. What about your great-uncle?"

Hunter told me about the few relatives and two distant cousins his own age who'd said they'd come grill hot dogs, too. They'd meet at the little Red Ditch park to play kickball and fly kites and throw Frisbees. He was describing his new dragon kite as I unlocked the car door and lifted out the box full of goody bags.

I'd bought the plastic bags stamped with horses (feeling proud that they fit in with the Pony Room theme!) at Wal-Mart, and I'd filled each one with candy, a tiny top, a harmonica, and a sheet of stickers on the advice of Halleigh Bellefleur, a schoolteacher friend. Maybe the twirl you had to give a top was too much for such little kids? Maybe I should have gotten something else? Oh, well, too late now. Hunter seemed pleased, which had been my goal. I let him carry the box, which he promptly tilted to one side.

"Whoops, we dropped one," I said, bending over to pick it up. "You think you can count them again for me? Make sure we have them all?"

"One, two—" Hunter began, and suddenly our heads snapped to look in the direction of the turn into the parking lot. The screeching tires and the racing motor of an oncoming truck were telling both of us that something was wrong.

The pickup swerved into the parking lot and stopped with a spray of gravel in front of the school. We both squatted down, instinctively concealing ourselves. Luckily, there was a van parked between my car and the pickup, so Hunter and I had extra coverage. In Hunter's mind the van provided an impenetrable wall, and he felt much safer. I was not so optimistic, simply because I was larger and therefore more visible.

Maybe I was also more realistic.

If I canted myself at a strange angle I could see the driver's door of the pickup. It hadn't opened. I could glimpse the man behind the wheel. He appeared to be talking to himself, though maybe he had a cell phone in his farthest hand. He was wearing a Red Ditch Oil & Lube baseball cap and a plaid western-style shirt.

I glanced sideways at my nephew, torn between trying to absorb this new development and wanting to protect him. Hunter's eyes were wide and his face looked much older than a kindergartner's should. I could feel his fear beating against my own mind.

The pickup had parked in the BUSES ONLY area, designated by an unmistakable sign and yellow stripes on the pavement. That was lawless enough to rile any middle-class citizen, but that wasn't what had raised the hair on the back of my neck and made Hunter's face go dead white.

The man in the truck was batshit crazy.

I slapped my pocket, but I knew where my cell phone was—in my purse. In the Pony Room. All I'd brought out with me was my car key.

There were fields all around the school, except here in the front, on the west side. Small houses lined the two-lane street leading from Main to the school, but of the six or so dwellings, three were clearly empty right now, the occupants at work, if the lack of vehicles was a reliable indication. One of the others had a FOR SALE sign in front, and two were too far away for me to assess. If I took off for one of them, I might simply be wasting valuable time.

Damn. I had to go back into the school.

Was Hunter safer out here or inside? I could ease him back into the car, tell him to stay down. I had a mental montage of the sheriff's deputies showing up, bullets flying, Hunter hit by accident.

Okay, he had to come with me.

The people in the school had to be warned, especially Sherry Javitts. This man was surely the enraged Brady.

Sometimes I hated my telepathy. You'd think I could have gotten some talent that was useful for offense. I couldn't stop an armed man by thinking at him. But there was a defensive way it could be helpful.

Hunter, here's what we're going to do, I said silently. *You're going to walk into the school with me like we don't have a care in the world, and once we're inside you're going to run like a rabbit, right to the Pony Room. You're going to tell Ms. Yarnell to lock the door, a silly man is here.* "Silly" seemed inadequate, but "crazy" and "violent" and "probably armed" seemed too heavy for Hunter. I took a deep breath. *You and your friends are going to lie down on the floor, where no one looking through the door window can see you. Lie flat like pancakes, you hear?*

His head jerked once. *You come, too*, he pleaded.

I've got to warn the other people, I said. *I've got to try. You get to the room, you stay down, and you don't move, no matter what. Ms. Yarnell will take care of you all.* Sabrina Yarnell was capable of taking care of a roomful of children with both hands tied behind her back, but she couldn't stop bullets. At least, I didn't think so.

We were still squatting beside the open car door. Now, in the slowest way possible, Hunter and I stood up. I took another deep breath as I shut the car door.

Slow and easy, I reminded Hunter, and I smiled at him. It wasn't a good effort, but he smiled back in a very small way. We began strolling down the sidewalk to the front doors. I hoped, with the box of goody bags under my left arm, we made a convincingly casual scene. I put my free hand on Hunter's shoulder and squeezed gently. He looked up at me, no longer able to sustain even a neutral expression. Fear looked out of his dark eyes, and I had to work hard to force away my mental image of what I'd like to do to the man who'd ruined Hunter's happiness. With the box propped against one hip, I opened one of the old front doors. We stepped inside, and it fell shut behind us. I knelt, handed the box to Hunter. I told him, *Scoot, darlin'. I'll see you in a minute or two. Now, run!*

The minute he started down the hall to the Pony Room, I stood and whirled around to look back through the window in the right front door. The crazy man was getting out of the truck, his mouth moving as he talked to himself. I knew he had a gun. I knew it, right from his head.

I spun back around to see Sherry Javitts blotting her face, the principal standing in the doorway of her own office. They were both staring out the office window at me, alerted by my odd actions and body language to the fact that something was very wrong.

"He's out there with a gun," I said as I pulled open the office door. "Call 911 right now! Can we lock the doors?"

Without a word the principal hit a button and an almighty racket sounded throughout the school. "Lockdown alarm," she explained, grabbing a set of keys from right inside her office and hurrying to the entrance to shoot the deadbolt that secured the double doors. She stooped to push the floor bolt that held the left door in place. Once it was pushed down, she reached for the right one; but it didn't work.

Sherry was still gaping at me.

"Call the police," I said, biting back the word *idiot*. She picked up the phone. As she punched in numbers, her thoughts weren't coherent enough to decipher even if I'd had the time or inclination.

I didn't have to look outside to track Brady's progress. The turmoil in the man's brain got closer and closer until his chaos was beating inside my own head in time with his footsteps. He reached the front doors and began pounding on them.

Though they were bowing in, the doors held under Brady's initial assault. Ms. Minter spun on her heel and began running down the left-wing hall to lock the back doors leading to the playground. Sherry was staring at the way the doors were jumping. The phone was still in her hand. Someone on the other end was yelling.

"You need to hide," I said urgently. "If the doors give in, you have to be out of sight."

"But he might shoot someone else," she said. "He just wants me."

I didn't have time to figure out whether that was an incredibly brave thought or simply shock-induced honesty. "He doesn't have to get anyone," I said. "The cops will be here soon."

"Hardly any cops in Red Ditch," Sherry said, "as he's been reminding me every day for months." I could tell from her thoughts that Sherry was resolving to sacrifice herself. She felt surprisingly good about that; she would regain her pride and finally accomplish something big. A tinge of fatalism and self-righteousness colored this decision. If I've learned anything from years of hearing other people's most personal reflections, it's that we never do anything for only one reason.

I didn't want anyone to die today.

I spied a janitor's closet across from the school office. (I deduced this from the fact that a sign on the outside read JANITOR.) I grabbed the secretary's arm and hustled her over to it, opened the door, and shoved her inside. When Rachelle Minter came running back, presumably having locked the playground doors in both wings, I said, "Sherry's in there. Lock it," and she did it instantly. Then she stood and gasped for breath. The principal was not a runner, but she was a damn quick thinker.

I couldn't think of anything else to do. We'd locked the

doors, we'd called the police, we'd hidden the target of the violence from the dealer of the violence.

It was like waiting for a tornado to touch down.

The principal and I stood side by side, our gazes fixed on the old doors with the ominous gap between them and the missing right-hand floor latch. Each time Brady crashed into the doors they spread a little farther apart before they rebounded into place. Though there was more play between the two doors than there should have been, the broken floor bolt would be the deciding factor.

"Maintenance guy didn't fix it," Ms. Minter gasped. "But who knew someone would try to kick the doors in?"

Abruptly, I wondered what the hell we were doing standing there. We weren't armed, and our mere presence would hardly be enough to deter Brady from whatever plan was in his crazy head. So far, he was absolutely bent on gaining entrance and finding Sherry.

"We better get out of the way!" I was surprised at how calmly I spoke, because my heart was racing like a motor on high. The unknown Brady had a lot of stamina. With every blow the doors bowed in more, rebounded more slowly. I grabbed Ms. Minter's hand and began to urge her back into the office.

I should have been concentrating; or maybe it wouldn't have made any difference, since Brady was moved by nothing more than rage and impulse. He hit the doors as hard as he could. Simultaneously, he fired twice through the gap between them. The boom of the gunfire was magnified in the little lobby. Even as I flinched, I felt a yank on my hand and I staggered.

Ms. Minter folded to the floor, still holding on to me.

Caught off balance, I sprawled to the floor with her, land-ing partly across her legs. I knew she'd been hit. There was shock and pain caroming from corner to corner in her brain. In a second, I could see the blood soaking her pantsuit. Her eyes were terrified.

"Oh, no," she said. "Oh, it hurts." Then she passed out.

I lay as still as though I were paralyzed. Had I been hit, too? I didn't think so, but I was so stunned I couldn't move.

I was facedown on the green linoleum, sprawled across poor Rachelle Minter's legs. She'd landed on her right side. I could feel the wetness as her blood pooled underneath me. Brady had continued his assault on the front doors after he'd fired. I could feel the surge of triumph in the gunman's brain. He was pretty sure we'd gone down, but I didn't think he could see us at the moment, and he didn't know if we were dead or not.

I could feel how wet the front of my T-shirt had become in a few seconds. Taking a big chance, I rolled over onto my side so I wasn't putting any more pressure on Ms. Minter. I lay as close to the wounded woman as I could. She wasn't dead yet. I could feel the life in her brain. Before I began my impersonation of a dead person, I opened my eyes a slit to look at myself. I was bloody enough to look seriously wounded, perhaps even dead, as long as Brady didn't try to locate an actual bullet hole.

I made myself go totally limp. I told myself over and over, as I heard the doors finally spring apart, that he could not tell I was alive as long as I thought "limp and lifeless."

He won't shoot me. He won't shoot me. I begged God that Brady would not think a coup de grâce was necessary.

The school was eerily silent . . . to my ears, anyway. In my head, the panic of more than a hundred adults and children beat like an irregular drum. Clearest of all was the regret and terror of the woman in the closet only seven feet away from where I lay pretending to be dead. Sherry was almost incapable of coherent thought. I could totally understand that. At least I knew what was happening, but she was shut in that windowless tiny room, knowing that the man whose footsteps she could hear was there to kill her.

Then those footsteps were beside me. Brady was breathing harshly, rapidly; I could "hear" that he could not believe what he had done, that he knew that sometime in the future he would regret the deaths of the two women on the floor, that he was wondering where Sherry was, that *bitch*, she should be the one who was *dead*.

He screamed then, the sound ripping from his throat as though he were being tortured. "Sherry," he bellowed. "Where the hell are you? I'm gonna shoot you, you whore! I'm gonna spray your guts all over the walls!"

Behind the wooden door Sherry was holding her breath and praying as hard as I had that he couldn't hear her breathe, couldn't smell her skin, couldn't see through the wall to where she was crouched among the cleaning products and rolls of toilet paper.

I couldn't move so much as a fingertip. I couldn't take a deep breath. Limp, I chanted to myself. Limp, limp, limp.

He kicked the wall about two feet away from my head, and then he cursed because he was wearing sneakers. It took every little sliver of will I could scrape together to keep myself from flinching.

I heard a siren . . . a lone siren. Though it sounded as sweet and welcome as a lover's greeting, I was conscious of a certain amount of disappointment. I'd half expected six sirens, or a dozen. I guess I'd been watching too much television. This wasn't Chicago or Dallas. This was Red Ditch. Some state troopers would be on their way, I was sure, but they wouldn't be able to arrive on the site instantly.

Maybe by the time they got here, this would be all over. But I couldn't imagine what the ending would be.

Brady stopped screaming threats and began trying door-knobs. Of course the one to the school office opened easily. He had a field day at Sherry's desk, tossing papers, throwing the telephone, causing as much chaos as he could. Though I knew he was intent on that destruction, I still didn't dare to move because the window overlooked the area where I lay. He might catch any slight movement of leg or arm.

Rachelle Minter was weaker now. I tried to imagine a plan that would save her; one that wouldn't include me getting killed, as well. I simply couldn't think of one. So I kept on playing possum.

The only thing I could do was worry. I spared a sharp moment of regret for Hunter. His day had been ruined, in the worst possible way. From now on, he'd remember his first-ever school party as an event of horror, and there was no way I could make that up to him.

I even had a second of sheer pique that the damn cupcakes were going to go to waste.

But mostly I worried about the children. If Brady started shooting into the rooms at random, sooner or later a child or a teacher would get killed. I had to think of a way to stop him.

Brady had resumed ranting and screaming, even when the siren abruptly cut off. I was so busy breathing shallowly and lying still that it took me a minute to dip inside his head, which was a virtual snake pit.

Brady had lost all his insulation; that was what I'd always called the civilizing influence that kept us from hitting other people when we were angry with them, stopped us from hawking and spitting on the floor of our grandmother's house, advised us to make an attempt to get along with coworkers. Maybe Brady had never had a lot of this insulation anyway. His mental and emotional entanglement with Sherry had stripped all this insulation away and all the wires in Brady's brain were hopping and sparking without any impulse control.

Brady was entirely human, but if I hadn't known better, I'd have called him a demon.

The demons I'd known had been much better behaved. My sort-of-godfather, Desmond Cataliades, was mostly demon, and he wore civilization like a coat.

With no warning, Brady kicked me. I didn't know if he could sense an intruder in his head because he'd abandoned his semblance to a total human being, or if he simply felt like expressing his aggression. It was a huge effort to roll with the kick as if I weren't in my body.

Then Brady fired the gun into the office, and again I had to hold on to my possum persona with all the determination I could muster. I came this *close* to yelling out loud as the glass of the window shattered and rained down on me and Ms. Minter. Now some of the blood smearing me was my own.

I'd always assumed that to save my own life I could endure just about anything. I was finding that wasn't necessarily so. With Brady proving so completely unpredictable, I was fast approaching the jumping-up-and-screaming point.

If I'd been a genuine possum, my masquerade might have been easier.

He went past me again, screaming incoherently and slamming into every door he saw. I heard a door swing open, and I thought, Oh, no! But the cleaning agent smell that wafted out told me bathroom, and I let out the breath I'd taken very slowly indeed.

The crazed man continued down the hall to the left of the office, and I heard not a sound from the teachers and kids trapped in those rooms. I opened one eye. Though my angle of vision prohibited me from seeing very far down the right corridor, which I was facing, I could see that the teacher in the first room had taped construction paper over the window in her door. That was amazingly smart. In the room across the hall, apparently the kids had hidden out of sight of the window, and Brady said, "Where the hell are they?" He sounded merely puzzled. He sounded like a real person, for just a second.

I could get up and run out before he could catch me or shoot me, I thought. He had his back to me, his attention was definitely elsewhere, and if I scrambled up and leaped to the front doors, I could be down the sidewalk and behind the cover of the cars before he could get to the doors and aim.

At least, I hoped I could.

And then I wondered about the lone police officer out in front of the school. I didn't know what kind of person he (or she) might be. He might be so shaken by the seriousness of the event that he was ready to shoot whoever came out the doors, especially a bloody stranger running directly toward the patrol car.

While I was doing my best impersonation of a dead person and listening as intently as I could to both Brady's physical actions and his mental chaos, I kept cudgeling myself to develop a plan. If I was out of his sight for a few seconds, should I move? Was staying right here the best policy? If I hid, where could that be?

Then I did something I should have done before. I reached out for Hunter.

Hunter? You okay?

There was a long moment of silence. *Aunt Sookie? Did he shoot you? We heard a gun.*

He didn't shoot me. I'm all messed up to look at, but I'm not hurt.
Who got hurt?

Ms. Minter is hurt, but I think she's going to be okay, I told him. I
hoped I wasn't lying. She was still alive, anyway.

My cell phone is in my purse, honey, I told him. If Ms. Yarnell
doesn't have one, make sure she uses mine to call 911. There's a police car
outside, but only one.

Ms. Yarnell's been talking to 'em.

Great! Tell her . . . I began, but then I stopped. There was no
way Hunter could relay messages without revealing his secret
to all his peers.

Crap.

Tell her you need to borrow the phone to talk to your aunt, Hunter.
Hold it to your ear. I'll be talking to you this way, but they'll think it's
coming over the phone.

In a minute, he was back on the line—the telepathy line. I
think she knows, he said, but he didn't sound worried about it.
What do you want me to tell her?

Tell her Ms. Minter is down, but she's alive. I'm lying on the floor
beside her. Ms. Javitts is locked in the janitor's closet. The bad man is
named Brady, he was Ms. Javitts's boyfriend.

Why are you lying on the floor, Aunt Sookie?

I sighed, but I kept it in. This was not the best means of
communication, but at least we were communicating. I'm pre
tending to be hurt, I explained.

You're playing possum.

Yeah, exactly, I said, relieved.

Ms. Yarnell says she needs a straight shot at him.

I puzzled over that. Was Ms. Yarnell telling me she needed a
direct field of vision to our attacker, or that she needed no one
in between because she meant to literally shoot him? (I put off
worrying about an armed kindergarten teacher until later.)

I'd been thinking so hard I'd forgotten to listen for Brady. His feet were right beside me all of a sudden. I closed down everything inside. I was afraid he was going to kick me again, and the anticipation of the pain was almost as bad.

He needed to move three steps back to be in a direct line of sight from the door of the Pony Room. There was no way I could make that happen without moving. I tensed my muscles in preparation.

"No, Aunt Sookie!" screamed a voice down the hall.

Oh, God, no. Brady, shocked, stepped away from my prone form and turned to look down the hall in the direction of Hunter's voice.

Now! I said.

"Now!" Hunter said to Ms. Yarnell.

I heard a commotion in the hall. What the hell was the witch doing? I couldn't let Brady get close to the kids! I rolled from my left side to my stomach. Brady's back was to me, but he was about to start down the hall. I lunged across the intervening distance and grabbed his nearest ankle, the left. The minute my hands wrapped around it, I made up my mind he wasn't going anywhere unless he dragged me behind him.

Several things happened then; the front door eased open behind me. I caught a flicker of movement and a glimpse of khaki. But I had to reserve my attention for the man with the gun.

Brady looked down at me and shook his head, as though flies were buzzing around his face. I finally saw him clearly. He was a mess; he hadn't shaved in days and hadn't bathed, either. The plaid western shirt was torn, his jeans spattered with old paint. His sneakers were very worn. But they were able to cause damage when he kicked me, and he was making up his mind to do that again. He balanced on the foot I had pinned, and brought his right foot back to get some momentum. I yanked at his ankle and he had to put the foot back down to catch his balance.

"Bitch!" he yelled, and raised the free foot again to stomp on one of my arms. I ducked my head down as if that would help avert the blow.

I heard a thud and an exclamation from Brady as something hit him on his shoulder.

It rolled on the floor until it came to rest in front of the janitor's closet.

It was a big Red Delicious apple.

I could see past him. It had been thrown by Sabrina Yarnell, who was now holding out her hand to the open door of the Pony Room. One of the children tossed her another apple, a Fuji this time. That apple, too, came at Brady with deadly intent, and this time Sabrina nailed him in the head.

Brady forgot he wanted to stomp me. Suddenly, he was far more interested in finding out who was attacking him.

"Who are you?" he called to Sabrina. "I ain't here after you! Get back in that room."

But he'd been distracted just long enough. A hoarse voice behind me said, "Brady Carver! Drop the gun!" Brady's head whipped around at this new diversion, and though I was too anxious to keep my eyes on him to peek behind me, I figured the new entrant had to be the police officer.

Brady's face had gone through a startling variety of expressions in the last minute: bewilderment, resentment, anger. But now he settled on hostility, and he began to raise his right hand to shoot.

"I don't want to shoot you, Brady," said the voice, still hoarse with tension, "but you better damn believe I will do it. I will shoot you *dead*."

"Not if I get you first," Brady sneered. I was sure I was going to be spattered with Brady's blood, too, but the moment after, something amazing happened.

His right hand seemed to go numb. The fingers weren't able to retain their grip. The hand relaxed completely, and the gun fell from it to clatter to the floor close to my head. To my immense relief it did not go off, and I instantly released Brady's ankle to shove the gun across the floor in the direction of the police officer. I stayed still and low, though I sure wanted to get out of the middle of the floor and out of the line of fire. Just at the moment it seemed more important to keep the situation simple.

Sabrina was standing with her small plump hand extended in Brady's direction. She didn't look like a young schoolteacher at all. She looked like a ball of power and ferocity. I'd never seen a witch really look "witchy," but I practically expected to see Sabrina's hair stream back in an invisible wind while she kept Brady's arm immobile.

The police officer pushed the gun a little farther away from Brady with her foot—yes, the officer was a woman, a brief glance informed me. And then she was screaming, "Down! DOWN!" with the persistence of a banshee. To my amazement, Brady Carver knelt two feet away from me, and I scrambled backward in an ungraceful sort of reverse crab walk. His arms jerked back behind him, ready for the cuffs. His face was full of astonishment, as if he could not believe he was doing this.

In short order, Brady was cuffed, useless hand and all.

Sabrina was staggering from the effort as she went back into her room in answer to an anxious chorus from the kids.

I tried to stand up. It took two attempts, and I had to lean against the wall.

A lot happened in the next few minutes.

The EMTs rushed in, and brave Principal Minter was loaded into an ambulance. Her keys were on the floor where she'd lain, and I pointed out to the police officer that Sherry needed to be released from the janitor's closet. The secretary was an emotional mess. She was taken to the hospital, too, to get something to calm her down.

By that time the state police had arrived.

The old school had never had so many guns under its roof.

All the people in uniform seemed relieved that the human damage hadn't been worse, though a few newbies were silently a bit disappointed that the situation had been resolved without their assistance. Brady Carver was marched out to a state trooper car to be taken off to the county lockup, one arm still flopping uselessly, and the police officer (Shirley Barr) got a lot of slaps on the back for subduing the shooter. Shirley Barr was an ex-military woman of color, and I figured that in the line of duty here in Red Ditch she didn't get too many chances to show what she was made of. She had to concentrate on not looking happy.

The parking lot began to fill with parents who had heard that something bad was happening at the school. With the principal and her secretary absent, there was no one to take charge until the school guidance counselor stepped up, driving over from the nearby high school to do the right thing.

Once I'd turned down an ambulance ride and I'd explained to the police why I'd been on the spot, no one seemed too interested in me. I went into the principal's bathroom, since there was no one to stop me, and I carefully wiped away all the visible blood—Ms. Minter's, and my own from the glass. My T-shirt was a mess, so I gave it to the policeman, who seemed to want it. I rummaged in the big box labeled DONATIONS until I found a T-shirt that was way too tight but covered everything . . . just barely. It was better than being bloody.

I got a lot more attention from the state guys after I emerged in the tighter T-shirt.

But eventually I was able to walk back to the Pony Room to give Ms. Yarnell a hug. The kids were in surprisingly good spirits, which was a credit to their teacher. Hunter was just as glad to see me as he had been the first time I'd arrived that day, but he was definitely more subdued in expressing his pleasure. Ms. Yarnell had told the children that while they were waiting to find out what would happen the rest of the day, they might as well be celebrating Labor Day by partying.

A couple of the kids were too distressed, but most of them had gone along with the plan of singing the newly learned "America the Beautiful" and eating cupcakes. They'd poured out the contents of their goody bags as children ought to do. Hunter had gotten a thank-you hug from one little girl with about ten pigtails carefully composed in squares, and a big smile from a tousle-headed boy with cowboy boots. Hunter was doing his best to play a tune on his harmonica.

I hadn't spotted Remy out front, but then the police hadn't given me much of a chance to look. They were trying to take pictures of the lobby area and figure out the sequence of events.

They also seemed a little puzzled at some of the odder parts of the story.

They thought Sabrina had been suicidally lucky in throwing things at a shooter, and criminally irresponsible at opening the door of her room to step out into the hall. I didn't know if she'd even keep her job in Red Ditch after this. She was well aware of that possibility. "I couldn't let him keep on going," she said quietly, as we stood alone behind her desk.

"It bothers me that it took a lot of us to stop him," I confessed.

"Did any of us have a gun until the cop showed up?" she demanded. "Did he have any restraint, any of the rules of morality or society, when he broke into the school?"

I eyed her with some curiosity. Sabrina was a much more philosophical witch than my friend Amelia. "No, he was purely the devil," I said. "He wasn't hiding anything. That was the real Brady."

"So we all had to show what we really were, too," she said quietly. "And look, we brought down the bad guy. And they don't suspect, none of them."

The inexplicable weakness in Brady's gun arm had been written down to some kind of heart event or even a stroke, and he would be having tests in the hospital after he'd been searched and booked at the jail. Several of the cops had even wished aloud that Brady *had* had a heart attack, one violent enough to kill him. They were eye-for-eye people . . . in their own, true hearts. And I didn't think anyone who had arrived on the scene, or even the officer who'd actually witnessed the event, knew that Sabrina's attack with the apples had been planned to make him look at her, give her magic a chance to weaken him. The police were convinced that only my grip on Brady's ankle had kept him from charging down to the Pony Room and killing everyone in there. They would never know what Sabrina and I really were. At least Ms. Minter would get credit for her outstanding presence of mind and courage; those were her true attributes.

I looked at Sabrina and smiled. "Well, you're right. We did our best with our own gifts. Now we've got to put them under wraps again. Someday, maybe, we'll get to be what we are."

There was so much we didn't know in this world. But looking at the children, some of them playing at the back of the room, some of them obviously distressed and ready to reunite with their parents, I could see that there was a future, that what kids were learning in classrooms all over America was not going to stop because sometimes kids experienced terrifying or simply unfamiliar stuff. . . .

Hunter's little friend, the boy in the cowboy boots, ran up to grab one of Ms. Yarnell's apples and threw it squarely at another little boy, just as he'd seen her do.

Yells of anger. Tears.

Yeah, some things about school would never change.

IN THE BLUE HEREAFTER

I wrote "In the Blue Hereafter" for a sports-themed anthology edited by Toni L. P. Kelner and myself, and my source of information was my daughter, who had played most sports in high school and who had become a renowned softball player. A couple of previously introduced characters make appearances, and psychic Manfred Bernardo (a character in the Harper Connelly books and the Midnight, Texas, series) makes the acquaintance of a woman with a most uncomfortable gift—our own Sookie Stackhouse.

The final story about my telepathic waitress is set in the spring after "Playing Possum." "In the Blue Hereafter" is told from Manfred Bernardo's point of view, but in it he meets Sookie and a babysitter readers met in "If I Had a Hammer."

DURING THE LONG drive of the day before, Manfred Bernardo had had plenty of time to reflect on the fact that he would stick out like a sore thumb in a small town. In fact, he'd been rather proud of that certainty. He'd argued mentally with Xylda the whole way from Tennessee to Louisiana. Since Xylda had died the previous winter, that was the only way Manfred could talk to her, but Xylda herself was not so limited. She played games with her grandson, in his dreams. Sending him to Bon Temps, Louisiana, seemed to be the opening move in a new one.

On this sunny, cool afternoon in spring, Manfred scanned the locals around him in the crowded stands, confident in his own street cred. To his chagrin, Manfred observed several people decorated with as much ink as he was, and several more who had facial piercings. Maybe none of them had gone to the same lengths as Manfred, but two or three were in the same ballpark.

The comparison made Manfred smile, because he was actually in a ballpark for a fast-pitch softball tournament. According to the schedule a buxom brunette softball mom had sold him when he was paying his entrance fee (and she'd been wearing a T-shirt that read *Softball Mom!*), he was sitting in the stands of Field One to watch the opening game of a two-day tournament.

All around the small complex, uniformed high school girls were dragging or toting bags of equipment to their assigned fields, and coaches and assistant coaches were converging on the officials' table. There were clipboards aplenty, there were baseball caps of many colors, and the concession stand had opened to a brisk business. The stand was the hub in the wheel, and each quarter of the wheel was a different softball field. Each field, of course, had its own set of bleachers, dug-outs, and a rudimentary press box. Huge plastic garbage cans were dotted around the venue.

The softball complex was incredibly noisy. Everyone was yelling. A strange green vehicle labeled *Gator* was leaving Field One, driven by two grinning teenage boys who'd been draw-ing the chalk lines and raking the pitcher's mound. (Why was it called a "mound" when it was flat? Manfred didn't know, but he'd seen the term on the program.) The wheels on the equip-ment bags rumbled across the concrete, adding another level of noise, and the loudspeaker at Field One was playing a mix-ture of music that Manfred could only assume had been se-lected by the girls of the home team; in this case, the Bon Temps Lady Falcons.

This was the most unlikely place in America for Manfred to be. For the past three nights in a row, he had dreamed of his grandmother, Xylda Bernardo. She had insisted he come here on this day, at this hour, and she wouldn't take no for an answer. He didn't have any idea why she'd wanted him to be here. They'd played games like this as soon as Manfred had become old enough to recognize his own talent and to appre-ciate Xylda's. Before that, she hadn't been too interested in her only grandson, but when Xylda had discovered Manfred was a psychic, too, she'd done her best to take him over from his mother. His mother, struggling as a single parent, had followed the path of least resistance, figuring Manfred was safer with his grandmother after school was out than he would be at their house on his own.

What do you and Gran do all afternoon? his mother asked.

We play games, he said.

Like Go Fish? Monopoly?

Like . . . Guess why I asked you to do that, or *Tell me what this vision means. You have three tries.*

After that conversation, his mother had driven over to Xylda's by herself and returned flushed and furious. He hadn't been allowed to go to his grandmother's for two days, during which time he'd looked up some porn on his computer, guessing correctly that his mom would check. He'd also made sure his mom would find "evidence" that he'd had someone in the house before she got home from work. Suddenly, his mom and Xylda reached an accord.

The purpose of most conventional games was winning or losing. The purpose of Grandmother's games was to teach Manfred how to make a regular living with a very erratic talent, and how to recognize when he should heed the true compulsions of his gift.

In her disorganized and colorful life, Xylda had experienced moments of true clarity and brilliance as a psychic. She had found lost things and lost people. She had talked to the dead. But those moments had been interspersed with long stretches of making her living by sheer quackery, made credible by her quick and accurate analysis of her clients' desires and needs. After years of this, Xylda's gift degraded. She still had the occasional genuine vision, but it had become almost impossible to distinguish such an event from the flood of canned chatter and vague predictions that made up the bulk of her repertoire.

Manfred's psychic gift was larger, deeper, and truer, but Xylda had taught him how to resort to a certain amount of chicanery to pay his bills. Luckily for Manfred, he had no moral qualms about this expedience.

As Manfred watched the girls warming up out on the field, he realized he was not much older than some of them, yet he felt a decade older in life experience. He tried not to be angry at his grandmother as he calculated how much he'd spent to get to northern Louisiana, both in loss of earning time and in travel expenses. The total wasn't insignificant, especially since he was still paying off Xylda's credit cards. But she had to challenge him in his dreams. "Go down there to see what you can find out," she'd said. "There's a reason you're going. Next time you see me, you tell me what that reason was." In his dream, he'd said, "What's the prize if I'm right?" Xylda had smiled enigmatically, one of her favorite expressions, and she'd said, "You'll know it when you find it." He grimaced at the memory.

"You all right?" asked the woman sitting next to him. The stands had been steadily filling up. He'd vaguely known there was someone next to him because she smelled good. Now Manfred turned to look at her. She was very pretty; of course, he noticed that first. Blond hair, caught back in a ponytail, at least five years older than him, maybe more, which didn't faze Manfred at all. She had remarkable blue eyes and some bodacious boobs, too. But then Manfred spotted a little diamond ring on Blondie's left hand, which (Manfred was fairly sure) meant she was engaged or even married. Too bad. He would have enjoyed flirting with her . . . until he met her eyes the second time.

Those blue eyes were incredibly knowing.

Suddenly, Manfred felt uneasy. There was something weird and different about this woman, and he couldn't relax until he knew what it was.

"I'm fine," he said, forcing a smile. "Just thinking about a dream I had."

"You a fan of softball?" she said, her expression one of gentle inquiry.

Again, he had that uneasy feeling. Though her face and posture were inviting, even benign, Manfred had a strong conviction that she knew what his reply would be . . . if he spoke the truth.

Strong feelings are what psychics are all about.

"I've never watched a whole softball game, or a baseball game, for that matter," he said. "I was never into sports at school."

"Hung out with the Goth kids?" she said.

He nodded.

"I never fit in too well, either," she said, though she didn't seem particularly upset by the recollection. "But I was able to play softball, thank God. I was pretty good."

"So you come to reminisce?" He would have sworn she wasn't the kind of person who'd live in the past.

"I come to watch the home games when my work schedule at the bar permits." That wasn't a direct answer, but as if in recompense, Blondie smiled. The effect was so dazzling it made part of Manfred's body jump in a pleasant way. "Also, I help out the coach from time to time if the assistant's out. . . . She's pregnant. Today she's fine, but the Softball Moms asked me to help with the tournament."

Was this why his grandmother had urged him to come to Bon Temps, to meet this woman? For some kind of love connection? Whoever she was, she was not an ordinary human.

Manfred was absolutely sure of that, and his conviction didn't have anything to do with her sunny good looks. In fact, he was sure that she was not for him, that she had already formed a bond elsewhere. But he was curious. This woman had to be significant. *Xylda, a little clue here? Send me something from the blue hereafter?*

That was how Xylda had described her location, when he'd dared to ask.

"Did you have a special reason to come today?" he asked. Maybe if he dug a little, he'd find gold. Then he could go back to his life and livelihood.

"Special reason? Like, is a niece of mine on the team? Nope," she said, trying not to sound like that was a dumb question. "When the Moms called, I volunteered to help set up the concession stand, which I came in two hours ago to do. And I'm going to work a shift or two later. You have a special reason to be here, yourself?"

"Yes," he said, making up his mind. "My grandmother Xylda sent me here, on a kind of treasure hunt."

She looked at him thoughtfully, her head cocked a little to one side. "And she's passed on, Miss Xylda?"

He nodded.

She considered that for a moment. "I haven't had much experience dealing with the human dead," she said.

That was a strange way to put it. "You don't believe that's possible." Manfred was resigned to disbelief and scorn, both of which had come his way since he was a little guy and his talent had manifested.

"Course I believe it's possible," she said, surprised. "That's just not where my talents lie. And if you had a tough upbringing, mine was tough, too, buddy."

Feeling ridiculously gratified, Manfred grinned at her. She

gave him a decided nod, as if she'd confirmed something in her own mind. She turned to look at the field, unhooking her dark glasses from her T-shirt and slipping them on. A few fluffy clouds scudded across the blue, blue sky. Despite the radiance of the sunlight, the wind made him shiver in his black shirt. Some of the teams had opted to wear their baseball pants and the long socks with their team jerseys, while some had chosen their shorts instead. The ones who'd chosen the pants were far more comfortable.

The Lady Falcons and their opponents, the Lady Mudbugs, had both chosen long pants. The two teams had finished warming up. Each team now huddled before its dugout in a tight cluster. The girls were holding hands. Their heads were bowed.

"What are they doing?" Manfred asked.

The blonde whipped off her dark glasses and looked at him as if he'd asked her why gravity held them to the earth. "They're praying," she said, in a gently pitying tone. After a moment, all the Falcons flung their heads up in unison, gave a yell ("Win!"), and retreated into their dugout. The Mudbugs repeated the process.

"Good afternoon," the announcer said, her voice distorted by the crackling sound system. "Welcome to the tenth annual Louisiana Slam Softball Tournament! The first game will be our own Lady Falcons versus the Lady Mudbugs from Toussaint." There was a lot of cheering.

Manfred leaned forward and looked to his left so he could see into the little hut that passed for a press booth. Sitting behind the microphone was a woman who was surely a former beauty queen. She was perhaps in her late thirties, with honey-colored hair and a smile like an orthodontist's dream. She wore a *Softball Mom!* T-shirt, and she looked as excited as the players. There were a few sheets of paper on the wooden plank in front of her, and she referred to one before leaning in to the microphone. "Coaching for the Lady Mudbugs, Head Coach Tom Hardesty, Assistant Coach Deke Fleming." There was polite applause. "Here's the starting lineup for the Lady Mudbugs," the announcer said. "Heather Parfit, pitcher!" Heather, a thin girl with a formidable mouth guard protecting her braces, dashed out of the visiting team's dugout. She took her place on the third-base-to-home line.

Eventually, the Mudbug and Falcon players had been celebrated and the seniors recognized.

The girls were all colors and all builds, but Manfred saw they had one thing in common. Their faces were intent, excited, and *ready*.

"And that's our starting lineup for today!" concluded the announcer. "Let's hear it for the home team and their coaches, Bethany Zanelli and her assistant, Martha Clevely." There was a lot more cheering as the Lady Falcon starters dashed to their places on the field. The announcer continued, "At this time the flag will be presented by the Bon Temps High School JROTC. All rise for the national anthem."

Everyone rose, and kids in uniforms marched out with the Louisiana flag and the U.S. flag. Hands went to chests, hats were removed, and for a moment all Manfred could hear was the snap of the flags in the breeze and the distant shrieks of two children playing tag ("You're it!"). After a little crackling from the loudspeaker, a country-and-western star's recording of "The Star-Spangled Banner" floated through the air and up into the vast blue sky. People all over the softball park froze in their tracks. Many of them in the stands sang along. The blonde next to Manfred did not. He wondered why.

"Can't carry a tune in a bucket," she murmured, her eyes

fixed on the rippling Stars and Stripes. Manfred had an eerie prickling on his arms. He was now absolutely sure that the blonde could read his mind.

". . . laaaaand of the *freeeee* . . . and the home of—the brave!" There was hooting and hollering and clapping at the anthem's end. Manfred felt a thrill of patriotism, something that had never made his hair stand on end before. The announcer yelled, "*Play ball!*"

All psychics learn to be sharp observers, because observation helps to fill in when the gift fails. Manfred could see that his companion reacted physically, viscerally, to the announcer's cue. Her eyes widened, her muscles tensed, her eyes went from player to player. . . . He could see the ghost of her former commitment to the game hovering over her head. She wanted to play, even now.

She still looked plenty fit and strong for a woman her age, which he revised upward. He was sure she was in her late twenties.

"Well," she said absently, "I stand up all day, most days, and I do a hell of a lot of gardening . . . but I can see thirty coming up in my headlights." She didn't even bother to look at him; she was scoping out the Mudbugs' first batter, a lanky girl with her hair pulled back in a long braid. The batter put on her batting glove and helmet with a look of determination. She began to swing the bat back and forth to ensure that her muscles were loose. She looked confident and trim in her gold and green.

"You might at least try to pretend you can't hear me," Manfred whispered.

"Oh, sorry." She sighed. "I don't often meet someone who won't have an issue with it. It's a real pleasure to say what I'm thinking."

He considered how difficult it would be to disguise the fact that you knew the private thoughts of everyone around you, every hour of every day. "Hard times," he said.

She shrugged. "I'm used to it. Did you come here to meet me? You think that's why Miss Xylda told you to come? What are we supposed to do?"

She was so guileless that she made Manfred feel old beyond his years.

"I think we're supposed to see what happens," he said, almost at random.

"Easy enough," she said. The top of the inning was clearly a time spent feeling out the other team. The Falcons' pitcher ("She's our number two pitcher," Blondie whispered) got two outs, after a lot of work, and though the third batter hit the ball, the right fielder got it to first in time.

The bottom of the first was nerve-racking, if Blondie's reactions were anything to go by. The Mudbugs' pitcher had gotten one out. The next Lady Falcon had made first base, then made second by the sacrifice of the third batter in the lineup. The Falcon runner turned to look around the field, and Manfred saw that her jersey read *Allen*. She was a skinny girl with curly dark hair, but she was fast and she was alert.

"Georgia Allen, junior," the blonde said.

The next Falcon batter at the plate (*Washington*) was a broad-shouldered girl with her hair gathered at the nape of her neck.

"Hit it out of the park, Candice!" screamed her teammate from the dugout. Three rows down from Manfred and the blonde, a very broad woman said, "You hit that ball, Candice!" in a firm voice that implied this was a reasonable command.

Candice Washington's dark face was set in adamant lines. She stood with her feet planted in the batter's box like a statue. The lanky Mudbug pitcher looked nervous for a moment, but then she pinched her lips together, began her windup, and threw a good pitch right at Candice. Because he was intent on the ball, Manfred spotted the moment when it jinked sideways just a little, just a fraction, so Candice's mighty swing smacked it on the bottom instead of squarely in the middle.

"Heads up!" screamed several voices simultaneously. People looked up to spot the ball, and a few covered their heads with their hands. The foul went flying into the visitor stands, to be caught by a boy who seemed to have brought a mitt just for such an event.

"A foul can crack your skull, it hits you just right," Blondie told him. "Did you see that?" She didn't mean the boy's catch.

"Foul ball," called the umpire, a thin woman with brittle auburn-dyed hair. "Ah . . . foul ball," she added in a puzzled voice. She was clearly reviewing the pitch in her head. The ump looked as startled as Manfred felt.

"There's foul play afoot," Manfred's companion said, so darkly that Manfred had to stifle a laugh.

"You must read a lot of mysteries," he said. "And by the way, good play on words."

"I do read mysteries, and thanks. Now let's hush, here's the next pitch." This time, the blonde wasn't looking at the batter, but at the crowd. Manfred watched the opposing team's players; in fact, he tried to watch everyone in that dugout.

Candice watched the ball with her eyes squinted almost shut in grim resolve. Whether by calculation or intuition, she caught the ball square on the bat. The fluorescent yellow orb soared into the outfield. Georgia Allen took off from second like a scalded cheetah, while Candice Washington made it to first before the ball was retrieved by the left fielder. Allen scored, and made a great effort to look nonchalant as she took off her batting helmet. The Lady Falcon fans did a lot of yelling and stomping, and there was a lot of hugging in the dugout.

The next Bon Temps batter in the lineup, a sophomore named Vivian Vavasour, was not as aggressive. Vavasour struck out; whether that was achieved by fair means or foul, Manfred couldn't discern.

"Do you have any ideas?" he said, as quietly as he could and still be heard in the noisy crowd, while the Lady Falcons took the field.

"Well, I doubt it's anyone from Bon Temps," she said dryly. "I was looking at the moms from Toussaint, but I didn't spot any of them doing something witchy."

"What about the assistant coach, Fleming?" Manfred said. "The man in the purple polo shirt, right inside the dugout."

"Why'd you pick him?"

"His fingers were moving funny," Manfred said.

But the man, who was in his fifties, balding, and heavy, didn't do anything odd during the top of the second inning. If he was jinxing the Lady Falcon batters by altering the pitches, he wasn't helping the Lady Mudbug hitters.

The Lady Falcon pitcher struggled but held the Lady Mudbugs at bay. During the bottom of the inning, Jacqueline Prescott (sixth in the Falcon batting order) did something wholly unexpected. The girl, tall and bony and brunette, was obviously nervous . . . so she swung at a ball she absolutely should not have tried to hit. Hit it she did, leaning forward and sideways to do so, while there was an audible chorus of "Oh, no!" from the Falcon stands. The ball thudded to the ground just behind the shortstop and the second baseman, both of whom scrambled for the ball without calling it. In the resulting collision, Jacqueline made it to first. She looked astonished when she realized she was safe. "Yeah, she ought to be surprised," muttered Blondie. Even the Lady Falcons' Coach Zanelli shook her head in amazement, before clapping.

"He looks pissed," murmured the blonde. Following her gaze, Manfred saw that the Lady Mudbugs' assistant coach did indeed look angry.

"He didn't allow for the wild card," the blonde said with some satisfaction.

"I think he'll try harder now; he's mad," Manfred said.

And sure enough, the coach's fingers moved with every succeeding pitch. Jacqueline stole second base, but the next three batters fell by the wayside, and the Lady Falcons took the field at the top of the third with the score still one–nothing. Manfred kept his eyes on the coach, but Fleming appeared to be doing regular coach stuff. He called the batting lineup and kept the team stats. Apparently, the burly man wasn't going to aid his own team, just hinder the opposing one by making Mudbug pitches do unpredictable things.

"He seems to have a code," Manfred said dryly.

"Yeah," the blonde said. "His code is screwing with the challenger. I got to have a word with that asshole."

Manfred could feel the anger rising from her like steam, especially after the Mudbugs scored four runs in the top of the third. The Lady Falcon pitcher had clearly lost her momentum, and a different pitcher was warming up.

At the coaches' request, the pitcher's circle was leveled out by means of a device dragged by the Gator, which created a short break. The announcer took advantage of the lull to say, "Be sure and visit the refreshment stand! The Softball Moms have fixed popcorn, cold soda, hot chocolate, candy bars, and homemade cupcakes. Hot dogs are going on the grill! Go get yourself a chili dog! All proceeds go to support softball. And now, since we've got an unexpected break, instead of waiting until after the game, we'll take this moment to ask players from the past to take the field."

Manfred's companion rose and clambered down the bleachers, greeting people as she went. She stepped out onto the field with eleven other women ranging in age from sixty-five to nineteen. There was a lot more hugging and back-patting. With a sort of proprietary smugness, Manfred decided his blonde was the prettiest woman on the field, if not the most popular. The other women either embraced her with special vehemence or avoided her.

After all this bonhomie, the women quickly lined up in age order to be introduced. When she came to Manfred's blonde, the announcer said, "And we all remember the *three-years-in-a-row All-Conference, All-State player*, Sookie Stackhouse, one of the best right fielders in the history of Bon Temps!"

Sookie Stackhouse (*What a name*, thought Manfred) smiled and waved like all the others. The people who cheered the loudest were the girls in the dugout.

"She helps coach the team when she can get a few hours off," said the older woman sitting past the spot where Sookie Stackhouse had been.

"Sookie told me something about that," he said agreeably, to prime the pump.

The older woman nodded. She was heavy and plain, but Manfred could see the polished goodness in her. "My son is her brother's best friend," she said, as if her exact connection to Manfred's new buddy were important. "They don't come no better than Sookie. No matter what people say." She gave his eyebrow piercings a cold flick of her eyes, as if to imply he might be one of those gossipers.

Manfred would have been fascinated to know exactly what people had been saying, but he didn't dare to ask.

Sookie did a lot of networking on her way back to her seat, including a brief stop in the booth to have a friendly chat with the announcer, who seemed glad to see her. As the current Lady Falcons took the field, the Gator and its rake having done their job, she clambered back up the risers, giving the woman on her right a cheerful greeting and a half hug. She turned to tell Manfred, "His name is Deke Fleming, in case you didn't hear it at the beginning. He's the assistant coach, and he doesn't usually travel with the girls' team. He's usually with the boys. The Lady Mudbugs' regular assistant was sick, so Fleming came along. The boys' team has won the state championship in its division the past two years."

"Let me guess, he became the assistant coach two years ago."

She nodded. "So he's a witch," she whispered.

"Not a warlock, or sorcerer?" Manfred asked.

She gave him a raised-eyebrow look that said clearly, *Don't you know anything?*

"No, he's a witch," she said flatly. But she kept her voice very low. This was a woman used to telling secrets. "I pure-D can't stand people who use their special powers to gain unfair advantage," she added in the same low voice.

"So you think you have to do something about it," Manfred said, not really asking a question.

"Course I do. You don't feel that way?"

He shrugged. "This is a small softball tournament between small schools in a poor state. You sure it makes a difference?"

She had a visible struggle with her temper. "Of *course* it makes a difference," she said between her teeth. "Using magic always makes a difference. The person it's used on changes. The person who uses it changes. There's always a price to pay."

"You sound like you know what you're talking about," he said.

"I do. You see the Lady Falcon pitcher? The one who just warmed up?" While the Mudbug pitcher finished the third inning—three up, three down—the Falcon girl kept moving, throwing ceaselessly to a member of her team. Olive skinned and raven haired, she had the look of a warrior: tall, broad, sturdy. The announcer had called her Ashley Stark. He nodded.

"Bethany—Coach Zanelli—was trying to save Ashley for the next game. So she put her second pitcher in this game, which was supposed to be easy to win. Ashley is being scouted by LSU and by Louisiana Tech. Her family doesn't have diddly-squat. If she's signed by either one of those schools, she can go to college without having a huge debt to pay off."

"Maybe the other team has someone in the same position," Manfred argued, simply to see how Sookie would respond.

"If there is such a girl, she has to earn it fair and square," Sookie said vehemently. "Everyone's got to stand on her own merits. With this assistant coach, the boys' team will never get that chance. Today, neither do the girls. The Lady Mud-bugs have a reputation for crumpling early. Our girls were sure to win." Sookie glared across the field at Fleming. She said, "There should be no magic in softball."

Xylda, did you make me drive all the way to Louisiana to make sure Ashley Stark goes to college? Have I got the answer right, now?

"How the hell do I know why your gran brought you here? My gran seems to remind me of stuff all the time, and it's always to my good. Maybe Miss Xylda just wants you to do the right thing."

"One girl's scholarship?" Manfred felt doubtful, and he didn't try to conceal it. "That just seems weird. Why would Xylda care?"

She gave him a hard look. "Well, don't do anything if you don't want to," she said crisply. "And if Miss Xylda wouldn't care about Ashley, then sadly I think the worse of her. Excuse me. I got to say something to this jerk of a coach." She rose and began making her way down the bleachers again. But people stopped her to talk to her, and a Softball Mom with a clipboard stopped her to go over a schedule, and the fourth inning raced by while Sookie made her way to the Mudbug dugout.

Manfred watched her progress. He was troubled. Xylda—and even his own, more distant, mother—always had a course of action. Part of Xylda's game was making him guess until he got it correctly. He just couldn't figure out what Xylda could possibly want here. Manfred felt he was losing the game. He didn't know the goal he should be trying to reach. And he didn't know the stakes.

Deke Fleming was standing behind the Mudbug dugout going over papers on a clipboard while the Mudbug head coach watched the field. By now it was the bottom of the fifth, and the Lady Mudbugs were sticking with the same pitcher, though her form was suffering. All the girls on the field were encouraging her, their voices a shrill chorus. "*Way to pitch, Heather.... You can do it, Heather.... Show 'em what you got.... You're doing great....*"

Manfred was amazed all over again at the concept of working in tandem. Being a psychic was an essentially solitary profession.

The assistant coach looked up from his clipboard as Sookie approached; he smiled since he'd seen her on the field in the little recognition ceremony. The smile faded utterly as she leaned close to him and began to talk. The anger in her straight spine was clear to anyone who happened to look their way, and there were some troubled glances exchanged between a few adults.

After a moment, Deke Fleming actually stepped backward, looking both furious and guilty. Then he caught himself. His back stiffened. (Manfred thought, *It's like watching a pantomime.*) Sookie's finger came up and she shook it in Fleming's face before spinning on her heel and stalking back to the Bon Temps stands. One of the Toussaint moms called out, "Sore loser!" as Sookie walked by, which triggered some anxious laughter. But the umpire, naturally busy at her job of watching the game, wasn't looking happy, either.

"What's the matter, Sookie?" asked the older woman who'd talked to Manfred earlier, after Sookie had plopped down on the bleacher with an angry thud. "Why'd you go lay into him?"

"Maxine, I think he's . . ." she began, and then called herself to order. "I was sure he was playing his roster out of order, and his pitcher is crow-hopping. It makes me so mad! He told me that the ump had already given the pitcher a warning, and that he had just turned in the roster changes to the umpire and the announcer."

"Hmmm," said the older woman. "Well . . . did you check?"

"Yes, he just did turn 'em in," she said, as though she were chewing glass. "And I see he's going to switch pitchers, so no more crow-hopping."

Manfred had no idea what that meant, and Sookie didn't look as though she wanted to explain the game, so he kept silent.

But when Deke Fleming looked up at Sookie in the stands, Manfred watched her tap the area by her eye and then point at the coach, very surreptitiously. Fleming got the point, though. He flushed and looked as though he would have enjoyed something painful happening to her.

The inning was three up and three down for both pitchers, but the tide was beginning to turn for the Lady Falcons, at least psychologically. Not only did the Falcons have Ashley Stark, their star, on the mound, but after the Lady Mudbugs changed their pitcher, the Lady Falcon batters began to relax. Without Coach Fleming's making the pitches go wild, the Falcons were able to hit, and in the bottom of the sixth the bases were loaded.

Manfred was literally sitting on the edge of his seat. For the first time, he understood how exciting sports could be. And though he found himself waiting for each pitch with almost breathless suspense, in the back of his mind he couldn't believe this was the point of his presence. *Team sports? Really, Xylda? All this way to appreciate bats and balls and team spirit?*

When Ashley Stark came up to bat, Sookie directed Manfred's attention to a man in a purple and gold polo shirt sitting right behind the plate, and a woman in khakis and a bright blue polo shirt who was one row up and a little to the left of him. "Scouts," she murmured. "Purple and gold is LSU. The blue is Louisiana Tech." Everyone on the Bon Temps bleachers seemed to catch their breath while they directed their will toward helping their girl to do well. It was their own kind of magic, a natural magic. Ashley was oddly beautiful in the batter's box, her shoulders level, her grip on the bat relaxed and firm, her face a mask of calm.

The Lady Mudbug pitcher watched the signals from the catcher and gave a quick nod. The tension was so great that Manfred found himself absolutely absorbed in watching the girl wind up and pitch, for the first time appreciating an incredibly complex sequence of movements.

Manfred spared a side glance at Sookie. She was intent on Coach Fleming. The assistant coach was glaring back at her, his hands against his thighs as he stood in the dugout. His fingers were motionless.

Manfred's gaze cut back to Ashley as she swung the bat. Ashley smacked the ball a mighty blow, and it flew straight and hard . . . directly into the Mudbug pitcher's mitt. For a second it seemed as though the pitcher would fly away, the ball smacked her mitt with such force, but she seemed to dig her feet into the dirt to stand in place.

There was a collective groan from the Bon Temps supporters, and an ecstatic shriek from the Toussaint fans.

Sookie covered her face with her hands for a second, then straightened up, shaking the dismay off.

"Are you okay?" Manfred asked. "You went to so much trouble . . ."

"All I wanted was for her to have a fair chance," Sookie said. "And the rest, well, that was up to her. Maybe the rest of the game will go better."

Manfred did not comment on the fact that Sookie's eyes were brimming with tears.

The top of the sixth did go better, to some extent, though Manfred watched it alone. Sookie had to leave since it was her turn in the concessions booth, and Manfred told her he'd come say good-bye as soon as the game was over. He'd known her for less than two hours, but he felt he couldn't leave Louisiana without speaking to the telepath again.

Ashley Stark kept her composure and pitched beautifully, getting three Lady Mudbugs out in a row. In the bottom of the sixth, to Manfred's pleasure, the Lady Falcons scored three runs. They were now tied with the Lady Mudbugs. The next inning would be the last. In Sookie's absence, Manfred considered himself bound to keep a close eye on Coach Fleming, and he also felt obliged, in Sookie's stead, to add his well-wishing to the swell of support for Ashley Stark.

He wondered what had kept Sookie from getting similar scholarship offers. It wasn't much of a stretch to understand why she was so invested in the success of the Bon Temps pitcher.

In the bottom of the final inning, with the score still tied, Ashley got the hit that won the game. With two outs, and no one on base, she swung the bat with incredible precision and power. The softball flew over the fence. Ashley trotted around the bases with a broad smile, happy on many different levels. The other Lady Falcons jumped up and down and ran to meet her at home plate. The Lady Falcon supporters went nuts, hollering and jumping. But all her happiness condensed to one thing: she'd done well, she'd won the game for her team.

Was this why I came here, Xylda? To see this girl's joy at doing something well, something she could only do with the help of others? If I recognize that, do I win, too? He wondered if Xylda was witnessing this moment from the blue hereafter.

On the field, the girls kept their game faces on as they formed two lines and ran past one another, hands held out to touch, chanting, "Good game, good game." And then the Lady Falcons hugged one another, laughing, while the Lady Mudbugs retreated silently to their dugout to gather up their stuff. Their second pitcher was crying, and the first pitcher put an arm around her.

Manfred had never been as lonely as he was while he watched the celebration among the Lady Falcons. Most of the Mudbugs looked as though they were locked in their own private unhappiness, especially the assistant coach. They filed out of their dugout to go to their bus.

Xylda, did you want me to learn that even clever dishonesty can go wrong? Though that didn't seem like a Xylda message. Normally, when Manfred had been able to guess what game Xylda was playing, he'd feel her approval. But he hadn't felt that today, no matter what he did or guessed. He shrugged. Xylda's wiles were beyond him today. He scrambled down the stands to work his way to the concession booth, a squat cement-block building. He looked back at the field. He figured the booth workers could get a glimpse of the scoreboards but not a good view of the events.

Manfred got in line, since there was simply no other way to speak to his new friend. The woman ahead of him (whose daughter was playing in the next game, from her cell phone conversation) got nachos, and he had to control his disgust as Sookie poured tortilla chips from a bag into a paper dish and ladled liquid "cheese" over them, topping the whole toxic concoction with jalapeño pepper slices.

The very young woman working the concession booth with Sookie looked up at him while she handed the woman her change. "Next?" she said inquiringly. When their eyes met, something in his gut lurched, not in lust but in recognition.

"Manfred," Sookie said, "this is Quiana Wong."

Manfred struggled to absorb many impressions at once. This girl (she couldn't be more than eighteen) was a racial mixture he'd never encountered. Her hair was straight, coarse, and black. Her eyes were slightly slanted and dark brown. Her skin was golden, like the perfect tan. She was short and skinny . . . and she was a psychic. Like him.

Her desperation rolled over him like a blanket of fog.

He glanced around; for the moment, he was the only customer at this window, but that wouldn't last.

"I started thinking about why you might be here," Sookie said, to fill the fraught silence. "So I called Quiana. She's an orphan, so she hasn't got a permanent place to live. She's like you, as I can see you've realized. And she hasn't had any training or 'mentoring,' as they call it now." Sookie beamed at him. She clearly felt she'd solved the mystery of why Xylda had manifested herself in Manfred's dream—so he could rescue Quiana. Manfred spared a moment from his contemplation of the girl to understand that Sookie was a rescuer, and she could not conceive that he might not see himself that way.

"You want to get out of here," he said to Quiana. It was evident in every line of the girl's body. "You want to meet other people like yourself."

"Yes," Quiana Wong said. She had a heavy Southern accent. "I don't fit in anywhere. I do want to meet more people like me. You're the first one."

"Quiana's mom was half Chinese, half African-American," Sookie said quietly. "Her dad was no-account white."

Quiana nodded. "He was that and more."

"They're gone?" Manfred said. "Dead?"

Quiana nodded again. "They fought all the time anyway," she said flatly. "Neither of them could rise to the challenge of being together, but they couldn't let each other go, either."

"What do you do now?" Manfred asked her.

"I'm a nanny," the girl said. "I take care of twins."

"I'm not going to be too popular with Tara," Sookie muttered, turning to put more hot dogs on the rotating grill. "Hey, Quiana, can you load up more popcorn?"

Quiana obliged, and then Manfred had to step aside as she became busy. The concession stand was just as noisy as the spectator area, with the background noises from the popper, the chatter of customers, the hum of the crowds, and the crackling of the sound system. Children too young to sit still to watch a game were running and yelling in the space between the back of the stands and the concession stand. While Manfred waited, Quiana Wong and Sookie served a man wanting two bottles of water and a candy bar, a little girl who wanted a hot dog with mustard and pickles, and a boy with braces who wanted a Coke and some nachos. There were also requests for candy bars, bags of potato chips, and sunflower seeds. Two other volunteers were just as busy at the window on the other side.

To Manfred's relief, two plump middle-aged women popped into the stand to relieve Sookie and Quiana, who stepped outside, looking tired. By silent mutual consent, the trio drifted over to an empty area near the fence surrounding the fields, far enough from the entrance booth and the clusters of players to remain unheard.

"I'm eighteen," Quiana said. "I'm free. I graduated high school."

"And you want me to take you when I leave, to find a psychic you can stay with and learn from." Manfred wanted to be sure he understood what was on the plate.

"That's what I want more than anything in the world. I know it can't be you. That wouldn't be right. I need to learn how to control this power, without the sex thing getting messed up with it."

She meant each disjointed phrase, meant it absolutely. Manfred noticed that Sookie was looking at Quiana almost sadly, and he was sure the blonde was revisiting her own teen years in Bon Temps, when she, too, had been on the fringes of everything.

"I'm thinking," Manfred said, when he realized both Sookie and Quiana were waiting for him to speak. Who would take Quiana? If his grandmother had been among the living, his course of action would have been easy. He considered the possible choices in his small community—small in numbers, but spread all across the United States and Canada. To his surprise, a name popped into his mind.

"I do know someone. Marilyn Finn. She's got a going business, real small, but she has genuine talent. She needs some help." She'd told him so via e-mail, not a week before. She'd hinted around that he himself might like a place to stay and work, now that his grandmother was gone. "What . . . are you?"

"Spirits can get into me," she said. "I don't know what to call it."

"You're a true psychic," he said. "That's what I'd call you, anyway. Quiana, let me step away and give her a quick call."

"Great," Quiana said, but her eyes closed and she swayed for a moment. Then she looked at Manfred with an eerie directness, as if she could see through the backs of his eyes and into his brain. "I see you in the desert," she said, almost in a whisper. "I see you in an old place, with lots of old things, and people who have amazing secrets." Then her eyes were focused on the outside of Manfred again. "Sorry. Sometimes I have the foreseeing, too."

Manfred took a deep breath and waited for a moment. She seemed to be through exhibiting her talents, and he was profoundly glad. "Ah, thanks for the heads-up on that. Back to Marilyn. You'd have to work hard. I'm assuming she'd have you meeting clients and giving them the procedure to follow during the readings, taking the money, answering the e-mails, and so on. But Marilyn has a lot of contacts in our community, and she's more social than I am. You'd meet a lot of people and you'd learn a lot. She's a good woman, too."

"Anything is better than sleeping in a room with my cousin's two little boys," Quiana said earnestly.

Manfred gave her a quick smile, walked away, and made a phone call, his back to the two women, though he knew as far as Sookie was concerned this privacy was only an illusion. He was relieved to hear Marilyn Finn answer the phone herself.

When he snapped his phone shut and walked back to the thin girl and the robust blonde, he was smiling with relief. "She said okay," Manfred told them. He didn't add that he had been bound to promise to do two large favors for Marilyn in return.

"Thank you," Sookie said sincerely. But Manfred could tell she had reservations. Any sane woman would, at the prospect of sending a girl into a completely blind situation on the say-so of a brand-new acquaintance.

Quiana was openly excited.

"I swear to you, it's on the up and up," Manfred told Sookie. She flushed.

"I'm holding you to that," she said. "And Quiana will let me know if it's not." She hesitated, then quietly said, "You're doing a good thing."

In Sookie's eyes, Manfred could see he was cast in the role of rescuer of a fair young maiden. He glanced at Quiana, trying not to smile. He had to admit that he didn't exactly find her fair, and he was pretty sure she was no maiden. But he did have a lot of sympathy for her: that would have to do.

Maybe Sookie is right. Maybe this is why Xylda sent me, Manfred thought. Not to meet Sookie Stackhouse, or thwart the Mudbug coach, but to rescue Quiana. *Have I gotten to the goal, Grandma?*

"So . . . how will this work?" Quiana asked, suddenly getting down to brass tacks. "I've gotta tell the du Rones I'm leaving. The parents of the twins. I owe that to them. Where does this Marilyn Finn live? How do I get there? Am I going to be staying in her house with her?"

"Marilyn lives in Oakmont, Pennsylvania," Manfred said. "It's got a lot of charm. I'll take you to the airport in Shreveport when I leave here, and we'll go in and work out the best route for you. Then we'll call Marilyn, and she'll meet you at the airport when you land. Marilyn and I are splitting your ticket."

"What if I don't like her?"

"Then we'll work out something else," Manfred said. "But I'm hoping you two will get along fine." Manfred tried to keep *You'd better* out of his voice, but Quiana understood. She gave him a sharp nod.

"If it doesn't work out, you call me," Sookie said, and Quiana looked relieved.

The Lady Falcons were clustered under a tree about five yards away, and their coach was giving them a serious lecture, rehashing the things they'd done right and the things they'd done wrong. The lecture ended at that moment, and the girls dispersed, some running to get in line at the concession booth, some meeting with their parents, who'd been waiting a respectful distance away. When Sookie, Manfred, and Quiana walked back to the booth (Quiana had to retrieve her purse), a couple of Lady Falcons approached, obviously wanting to talk to Sookie. One of them was Ashley Stark.

Quiana reached into the little building and grabbed her purse, and told Manfred she was going to her cousin's home to call the du Rones and to pack her things. She pointed down the street from the softball fields to a row of dilapidated houses that had obviously all been built at the same unhappy time by the same inept builder.

With the understanding that he would pick her up in an hour, Manfred tuned in to the conversation Sookie was having with Ashley.

"That was the weirdest thing I ever saw," Ashley was saying, and Manfred thought, *Uh-oh*. Though it was wounding to always be regarded as fraudulent, if not worse, Manfred truly believed that the world was better off in general if fewer people believed in the other world, the hidden world.

Sookie said, "It was a fluke, Ashley. You got a great hit in the last inning, Manfred says." She introduced him briefly, but Ashley hardly spared him a glance. She was too worried. Sookie returned to the previous topic. "I just know someone's going to pay attention," she said, hugging the senior.

"I want it more than anything," Ashley said. "If I'm ever going to get out of here . . ." Manfred could read the intensity in the girl, the iron in her.

Sookie jerked her head to the left and said, "Look, Ashley. I think someone's waiting for you."

Manfred turned to look in the direction Sookie had indicated, and he saw a man and a woman who were clearly Ashley's parents, if resemblance was any indication. They were standing with the scout from Louisiana Tech. They were all smiling.

Ashley took a deep, ragged breath. Her back stiffened. She said, "Talk to you later, Miss Sookie," and walked off to meet her future.

Manfred was almost bursting. "Maybe she's destined for great things, or for some spectacular moment, and *that's* why Xylda sent me here . . . to make sure she got that chance."

Sookie Stackhouse laughed out loud. "You got to have one reason?" She sobered quickly. "Seriously, you lead a simple life if things happen to you for only one reason."

Manfred felt himself flush. He couldn't imagine that a barmaid in a hick town could have that complex a life. "Right," he said, and there was an edge to his voice.

She looked at him with a touch of surprise and a little sorrow. "I didn't mean to insult you," she said.

For one of the few times in his brief life, Manfred was ashamed of himself. "Maybe you're right," he said, trying to keep the reluctance out of his voice. "Maybe Xylda wanted me to come here for five different reasons. She loved her little games. She always challenged me. She never made it easy."

"My gran was real different from the way you describe Miss Xylda," Sookie said. "She never played games. She stepped off the beaten track one time, and she regretted that transgression, in some ways, all her days. She was a little superstitious, though. She always thought bad things came in threes."

"Xylda said it was oversimplification to believe that events happen in threes—three deaths, three good things, three bad things. She said it all depended on your time frame." Manfred smiled, trying to smooth things over.

"If you add things up over a year, or over four months?"

"Or an hour," Manfred said. "She thought if you fixed on three, you limited yourself."

"She was quite the psychologist," Sookie said.

"Yes, in her way," Manfred agreed. He allowed himself to feel the sharpness of the grief he'd experienced when she'd passed, far away from home in the cold mountains. "She knew human nature, that's for sure. She wasn't able to control her own," he added slowly. "But she understood how people would react; at least, most often. I don't think she ever met anyone like you."

Sookie smiled and turned to look between the stands at the scoreboard. It indicated that the next game was into its second inning. The Red Ditch Gators were playing a team from Deux Arbres.

"That Deux Arbres team is supposed to be pretty good,"

Sookie said, her eyes narrowed against the bright sun. There was a chorus of shouts from the bleachers. Manfred knew later they were yelling, "Heads up!" But what he heard in his head was his grandmother's voice, saying, *Look in the blue hereafter.*

His hand shot out above Sookie's head without his conscious decision.

For the first time in his life, Manfred Bernardo caught a softball.

He stood frozen in astonishment and delight and horror for a couple of seconds, time enough for Sookie to jump back, looking up at his hand (which stung like the very devil). She lowered her eyes to his face. Her own were full of astonishment and relief.

"Good catch," called one of the Lady Falcons. It was curly-haired Georgia Allen. "Want me to take it back to the field?"

"Sure," Manfred said. "Thanks." He dropped the ball into her hand.

He had a sudden vision of what could have happened, the kind that did no one any good at all. He saw the ball hitting Sookie on top of her blond head. He saw her crumple to the ground, unconscious. He saw the ambulance ride, the bleed into the brain, the blackness. Then that vision evaporated, because that future was not hers anymore. He had changed it by showing up in Bon Temps, Louisiana, on a brisk bright day in early spring.

"So I reckon you won the game," Sookie said quietly. And he understood that she had seen the vision in his head. "Look what you worked into a few hours. You can sure multitask."

"It was my pleasure," he said, trying for a courtliness he'd never aspired to achieve.

"And mine," she said, nodding thoughtfully. "You call me,

you hear? You're being real good to help Quiana. But she may not suit your friend Marilyn."

"At least she'll be able to get help to understand how to live with this trait, from Marilyn," Manfred said. "There aren't that many of us."

"And Ashley will get her scholarship. I wouldn't have known it was the assistant coach affecting the pitches if you hadn't spotted him."

"We stopped him for this game." Cheaters kept on cheating. They couldn't resist.

"And my skull is in one piece."

"That, most important of all."

"So I owe you one," she said, and Manfred could tell that this was a serious statement from her. If Sookie Stackhouse owed you one, she stood ready to help you anytime, anyplace.

"No," said Manfred, surprising himself. "I learned a lot today. I think we're even."

"Time for me to get back to work," she said, glancing down at her watch. "You taking off?"

"Yeah, I'll pick Quiana up and head out of town. We'll go directly to the airport. She'll call you when she gets to Marilyn's, I'm sure."

"You let me know when you get to your desert place, the one Quiana thought you should find," she said.

"I will," he promised. "It may not be for a while. I never thought of going to the desert before." He laughed, and she laughed with him.

"Who's to say that a prophecy is not just your inner wishes divined and spoken out loud?" she said. "After all, when you talked to your grandmother about the rule of three, the one she considered so silly, maybe she had another rule in mind— that your good deeds should always outnumber the bad."

She gave him a little hug then, before she returned to the concession stand for another shift. He saw her begin to scoop up popcorn to fill the striped bags.

And Manfred, wondering if the good things he had done would ever outnumber the bad—or even the neutral—went to his car to pick up a girl he hardly knew to take her to begin the rest of her life with a stranger.

He figured that was what Xylda would have wanted. *I don't know what you think, Xylda,* he thought. *I figure I won.*

ABOUT GOLLANCZ

Gollancz is the oldest SF publishing imprint in the world. Since being founded in 1927 Gollancz has continued to publish a focused selection of bestselling and award-winning authors. The front-list includes **Ben Aaronovitch**, **Joe Abercrombie**, **Charlaine Harris**, **Joanne Harris**, **Joe Hill**, **Alastair Reynolds**, **Patrick Rothfuss**, **Nalini Singh** and **Brandon Sanderson**.

As one of the largest Science Fiction and Fantasy imprints in the UK it is no surprise we have one of the most extensive backlists in the world. Find high-quality SF on Gateway written by such authors as **Philip K. Dick**, **Ursula Le Guin**, **Connie Willis**, **Sir Arthur C. Clarke**, **Pat Cadigan**, **Michael Moorcock** and **George R.R. Martin**.

We also have a strand of publishing in translation, which includes French, Polish and Russian authors. Gollancz is home to more award-winning authors than any other imprint, with names including **Aliette de Bodard**, **M. John Harrison**, **Paul McAuley**, **Sarah Pinborough**, **Pierre Pevel**, **Justina Robson** and many more.

The SF Gateway
More than 3,000 classic, rare and previously
out-of-print SF novels at your fingertips.
www.sfgateway.com

The Gollancz Blog
Bringing you news from our worlds to yours. Stories,
interviews, articles and exclusive extracts just for you!
www.gollancz.co.uk

GOLLANCZ
LONDON